THE GRINGA

THE GRINGA

A NOVEL

ANDREW ALTSCHUL

MELVILLE HOUSE
BROOKLYN · LONDON

The Gringa

Copyright © Andrew Altschul 2019
All rights reserved
First Melville House Printing: February 2020

Melville House Publishing
46 John Street
Brooklyn, NY 11201

and

Melville House UK
Suite 2000
16/18 Woodford Road
London E7 0HA

mhpbooks.com
@melvillehouse

A portion of this novel was originally published in
Zyzzyva, under the title "They Hate Us for Our Freedom."

ISBN: 978-1-61219-822-4
ISBN: 978-1-61219-823-1 (eBook)

Library of Congress Control Number: 2019956590

Designed by Euan Monaghan

Printed in the United States of America

1 3 5 7 9 10 8 6 4 2

A catalog record for this book is
available from the Library of Congress

For my mother and my father

"Peruvian people! Like enraged thunder, your hardy voice begins to express itself in the vibrant, purifying tongue of revolutionary violence . . . The great journey is begun."

Abimael Guzmán, *Let Us Develop the Guerrilla War!*

"Is history possible? Is anyone serious?"

Don DeLillo, *Mao II*

THE GRINGA

AUTHOR'S NOTE

Leonora Gelb hated America.

She hated its heart and its soul, its sick mind and its flabby, diseased body. She hated its dreams of itself, its fantasies about the rest of the world—paranoid, arrogant, weaponized—and she hated its waking realities: the sprawled, filth-strewn cities and prim, stingy towns, the metastatic freeways and supersized cars, the factory farms and clear-cut hills and amber waves of subsidized grain. She hated its festering landfills and its first-class hotels, its frenzied shopping malls and all-you-can-eat buffets, hated its fast-food abattoirs and five-star, whites-only restaurants, the elegance of its ivory towers and the proud ignorance of its gun-toting, flag-waving patriots—ignorance fostered in crumbling public schools and enforced by corporate media all too happy to dance to the hegemon's tune. She hated America's wage-slaves and its business overlords, its gated subdivisions and wasted ghettos and its shared national pastimes: the gladiatorial sporting events and disgusting beauty pageants and goose-stepping parades, the idiot sitcoms and smug TV news anchors and its movies—god, its *movies*—about intellectual dwarves with superior firepower who heroically, democratically slaughter everything in their path.

Leonora—"Leo" to her family, "Comrade Linda" to her friends in the revolution—hated American culture as much as its gunboat economic policies. And what, really, was the difference? The Dirty Harrys and the Marlboro Men who brandished their big dicks and dared you to read their lips, make their day. The pop sensations, barely pubescent girls taught by men to pantomime a grotesquerie

3

of sex for money. The murderous video games and diabetic soft drinks and breakthrough pharmaceuticals to cure phony ailments the populace had to be taught to suffer. All rammed down the throat of the developing world, safe delivery ensured by nuclear submarine, by armed battalion, underwritten by Chevron and the World Bank and relentlessly promoted by lie after slavering lie— lies for which no one would ever be punished, because in America it's not a lie if it turns a profit; not a lie if it upholds the racial hierarchy; not a lie if it oozes from the mouth of someone we admire: soldier, sexpot, self-made tyrant.

When I look at her photograph, that's the first thing I see: her outrage, her refusal to believe the lies. In the shape of her mouth, stretched in a wet scream, the flared muscles of her neck, I see her fury at a government without integrity, a President who deceived the world with impunity. In her piss-soaked jeans, the broken arm stiff at her side, I see her disgust with a country that would spy on its own people, ignore its own laws, kill its own children.

Certainly you've seen this photograph, taken at the infamous press conference in Lima, Peru on August 25, 1998, three days after her arrest. You've noted, in the way she leans toward the reporters—a Doberman on a leash—her contempt for a press that whistled while thousands were rounded up, held in secret prisons, subjected to all manner of abuse; a press that branded as disloyal any who insisted upon the truth. Who hasn't seen this image, nor wondered at the small figure surrounded by soldiers with impressive weaponry, against the backdrop of a foreign flag? No one who's viewed the footage can forget her gale-force anger, the threat conveyed by her every gesture. No one can ignore her clenched fist.

But her eyes tell a different story. When I look into her eyes— small and gray behind thick glasses, open shockingly wide—I don't see the violent criminal so many have described. I see vulnerability, the pain of betrayal. I see innocence of a kind.

How to explain this incongruity, to bridge the gap between that bedraggled figure and her iron fury? How to sort out the truth from the lies?

It's been ten years since that disastrous press conference. I've been asked to find the real Leonora Gelb—a task for which no one could be less qualified.

"People think they know something about my daughter, but they don't know a damned thing," her mother told *Newsweek*, in September, 2000, on the second anniversary of the military trial. "They think she's some kind of radical, but that's just what the Peruvian government wants them to think. If they could only see the real Leo, they'd know my daughter would never hurt a fly."

But who was the real Leo? The "sweet, brilliant child" her mother described? The diligent student, lover of animals, hard worker, caring neighbor, fitful gardener, champion of the needy, role model for her younger brother, Matthew? Or the hardened revolutionary, a soldier of fortune who came to Peru to foment violence in a country that had known far too much of it? Was she the clueless dupe her lawyer made her out to be? A naïve young woman blinded by love? Or a cold-eyed conspirator, the "Gringa Mastermind" behind a plague of deadly crimes?

Leonora Harriet Gelb was born August 9, 1971, to David and Maxine Gelb (née Green) of Cannondale, NJ, a newly incorporated suburb in the northeast corner of the state. Matthew came twenty months later. She graduated from Alden Regional High School in 1989; she was class salutatorian, National Merit Scholar, and editor of the school newspaper, *The Aldenian*, but her high-school years were otherwise unremarkable. In 1993 she received a B.A. in History from Stanford University, where she studied with the controversial political historian Gabriel Zamir. She minored in Art History. Her GPA was a respectable 3.28.

For a time it was assumed that Zamir first put Leo in contact with the Cuarta Filosofía—one of several militant groups that brought Peru to the brink of collapse in the 1980s and early 1990s. He has always denied it. Over the years he's taken pains to distance himself from the matter. "I knew her only briefly and professionally," he wrote to me recently, "but I found Leo Gelb to be an excellent student, uncommonly perceptive and dedicated, with a deep concern for the plight of workers, minorities, and the poor."

One wishes he had more to say about his notorious former advisee. But like everyone who knew her, he measures his words. "Of course I don't condone her alleged actions," he told me, "but the Peruvian government's treatment of her is a deplorable violation of international law."

He signed off with the old battle cry: *¡Venceremos!*

Her voice was low and gentle, sentences lifting interrogatively, in the California style. Her laughter was rare but light. A spray of pale freckles across the bridge of her nose made her look younger than she was; a smile made rueful by babyfat cheeks. She never found a way to keep her wiry copper hair under control—in college she wore bandannas, in Lima she tied it back with yarn or rubber bands, but it soon sprang out in unruly clumps.

In El Arca, the notorious military prison, her hair would grow loose and wild. Fourteen thousand feet above sea level, the thin air tight with cold even in summer. Over time her face would lose its plumpness, her skin grow scaly with psoriasis, hands chapped and arthritic from the relentless cold. Her nose bled, her teeth ached until she couldn't eat solid food. She walked the length of her cell for hours, hunched over to preserve body heat. The bladder infections to which she'd always been prone kept her feverish for weeks. When they finally let her out she was almost unrecognizable. I would not have known La Leo if not for her eyes.

The 1998 press conference was the first time most Peruvians had seen her: eight hectic minutes in which her fate was all but sealed. Raw-eyed, hoarse, she marched into the room without an introduction, turning upon the reporters her battered, vengeful gaze.

"The real danger to Peruvians is not the Cuarta Filosofía, it's their own government! The worst violence in this country is state violence! Ask the campesinos whose land was stolen, whose children are dying. Ask the people whose brothers and husbands have disappeared. Don't just repeat the government's lies!"

It was a Tuesday morning, the ragged end of a restive, clammy winter. The basement room stank of shoe polish and spilled coffee. Three days earlier, on the evening of August 22, the house she was renting in the leafy Pueblo Libre neighborhood had been sacked by Special Forces, ravaged, its windows blown out, its white walls strafed. They'd dragged the bodies of six Cuarta Filosofía cadres from that house, flaunted them to reporters while the President walked through the wreckage and shook soldiers' hands. A demon, he'd called her, flapping her passport at the TV cameras. A psychopath. For three days she'd been locked away while the press stoked public fury. A military court convened in secret, masked and anonymous, to consider her fate. Now she stood surrounded by nervous soldiers, their rifles at the ready—as if to sell her, to sell the idea of her: Someone who required such precautions must be dangerous indeed.

But the demon was doll-sized, something farcical about her wild, wiry hair, her wet pants. *This* was the menace they'd been told to expect? In her powder-blue sweatshirt and granny glasses she looked more like a third-grade teacher than a murderous subversive. They could not match this figure to the footage the whole country had seen: the burning house, the smashed gate, smoke whirling up into searchlights like a vision of apocalypse. They did not see a monster—until she opened her mouth to speak.

"No one can deny the terrible inequality! No one can deny the racism and exploitation that keep millions in poverty while a tiny group enriches itself." Her Spanish was perfect but her accent still wooden. It gave her statement a mechanical, robotic air. "This country was founded on violence! Built on violence! The wealthy protect their privilege with violence! They sell your resources to foreign corporations and if you protest they send soldiers, tanks, they—"

"Just shut up, already!" someone called out. There was low laughter, a ripple in the crowd. They could see steam on her glasses, the stain creeping down her thighs.

"The people of this country won't tolerate these abuses—"

"Why were there guns in the house, Leo?" another voice called. And then a deluge: "Who stole the military uniforms?" "Leo, why did you have blueprints of Congress?" "Were you working with the Cubans? Leo?"

"Is this justice?" she cried. "Is it democracy—"

"Leo, were you the girlfriend of Augustín Dueñas?"

"Do you work for the C.I.A.?"

"Where is Mateo Peña, Leo?" "Did you know Angélica Ramos was in the Shining Path? Did you know she was a killer?"

"—when thousands of children go to bed hungry—"

"Are you a terrorist, Leo?" At this she pulled up, blinking. The room took a breath. "Leonora, are you a terrorist?"

Her eyes scanned the back wall as though looking for a familiar face. The question came again and she licked her lips, a whole country waiting for her answer.

Years later, in the forsaken silence of her prison cell, she would still lie awake contemplating a word. It was an arbitrary sign, of course, a meaningless abstraction. During the weeks of her civilian retrial, in 2002, while the crowd outside the courtroom hurled insults, clanged pots and pans in protest, she would turn the word over in her mind, try to understand its nature, to find her reflection in its empty depths.

"Leonora, are you a terrorist?"

The present work is, among other things, an attempt to answer that question. It was begun in April, 2008, ten years after her arrest, trial, and conviction. It was begun under circumstances that are somewhat cloudy—even, or especially, to me—but in the most concrete sense it began as an article for *My.World*, the self-styled "online omnivorous media behemoth" launched five years prior by Jackson Durst. (You'll recall the site's ambitious tagline: *All the news*.) From the start it was a poor fit for that outlet, owing to the complexity of the subject matter and the attention span of the target audience—to say nothing of the limitations of its author. Put simply, it should never have been assigned to me. But it was, and I've done what I could. What was it Donald Rumsfeld said about going to war with the army you have?

Subsequent events further hindered my progress. Which is to say, I had neither the experience nor the skills necessary to the undertaking. (*And yet you insisted, Jack!*) Anyone might have predicted this; many in fact did. But poor preparation and a general lack of knowledge rarely dissuade the powerful once they've set their course. Quite the opposite, actually—as our country's recent misadventures once again make plain. Once fate pointed its palsied finger there was no turning back—the story, it would seem, was doomed from the start, destined for this sorry, unsatisfying form.

I suppose it's also true that my background, my obsessions and personal concerns, played a role, whatever my best intentions. Detachment, objectivity, qualities natural to responsible journalists, seem not to be my strengths. If they were, I might never have left the U.S. I might have stayed to enjoy the ongoing calamity of our own dirty war, with its unsavory protagonists and hideous mistakes. But for all that I set out, if reluctantly, to tell Leonora's story, not my own. I set out to understand her, to say something valuable and true. I knew there was more to her than a photo, more than shocking headlines—of course I knew. What I didn't know, what I could not have known, was what her story would come to mean to me, nor how badly I would need to see it through.

What I knew—and I knew it immediately—was this: Leonora Gelb hated America. Long before she landed in Lima, before she'd ever heard of the Cuarta Filosofía or its role in Peru's long and ugly conflict. Had America not imposed its will on the world through economic blackmail and nuclear threats? Had it not propped up dictators, cancelled elections, murdered priests, sent the C.I.A. to protect profits at the expense of those who'd lived on the land for centuries? Was it not the world's largest arms dealer, selling guns and bombs to any street thug willing to lower a tariff or privatize a gold mine? When confronted about its actions, had it not *lied* time after time?

And when all else failed, when the lies did not suffice, America would call up the troops, launch the aircraft carriers, shoot first and answer questions later—confident always in the flag-waving, lapel-pin-wearing, bumper-sticker-sticking support of the American People. A bovine People, oblivious, ready to kill and die for the fictions of their country's goodness. Ready to swear, hand over heart, that America stood for something, believed in something, shone as a beacon unto someone for something—liberty, democracy, equality, peace—that it manifestly did not.

How could she belong to such a People? How could I?

Leo, are you a terrorist?

In another photo, this one from 1991, she stands with the editors of the *Stanford Daily* on a hillside overlooking the campus. Smiling and tan, clowning among themselves, she and her colleagues are the picture of freedom, their bright futures all but visible outside the frame. The managing editor stands behind her, two fingers over her head like rabbit ears, or a peace sign.

Was she, or was she not, a terrorist? Did Leonora Gelb, in the prosecutor's words, "knowingly aid, collaborate with, and provide material support to the Cuarta Filosofía in their plans for violent overthrow of the government"? Was she ready to take hostages, plant bombs? Was she willing to kill, or to die?

In these pages, I've tried to sort through the evidence, to determine what she wanted, what she might have felt. From disparate fragments and glaring absences, I've tried to build a coherent narrative, one that does justice to the history and its many victims. I've tried to keep my own feelings out of it. I've tried to consider all sides.

But it's been more than a decade. The words—*terror, freedom, democracy, war*—don't mean the same things anymore.

"Leo!" the reporters shouted. Her hesitation had made them predatory. "Answer the question!"

A man stood on a chair and yelled, "Fuck you, Leo! And fuck the Philosophers!"

"How many of them did you have sex with, Leo?"

"Leo, why did you come to this country? Why do you want to kill Peruvians?"

"How are they treating you in jail, Leo? Have you been raped?"

The soldiers moved to quiet them. Leo's breath came heavily, a shadow of alarm playing across her face. Everyone waited. Just as it seemed there would be no answer, the prisoner cleared her throat.

"The Cuarta Filosofía is not a terrorist organization," she said.

The sudden crush caught the soldiers off guard. Tape rolling, flashes exploding—"Leo!" they called out. "*Leo!*"

"Is it terrorism to love freedom? Is it terrorism to hate injustice, to feed people who are hungry?"

She lifted her broken arm as far as she could, the hand white and clammy, clenched with effort. When I watch the clip I see her trying to quiet the crowd, to finish what she wanted to say. But the press told a different story, repeated it until it became its own truth: La Leo raised her fist in defiance. She made a gesture of militant solidarity. She dug her own grave.

"There are no terrorists in the Cuarta Filosofía," she said. "It's a revolutionary movement fighting to improve the lives of people who've been forgotten." The objections resumed—what about the wounded students? what about Victor Beale?—and she craned her neck, voice cracking: "If it's terrorism to help poor mothers and sick children, then I am a terrorist. If it's a crime to stand for workers and the oppressed, I accept whatever punishment I'm given!"

There it was: the red meat, the money shot. Every newspaper in Peru ran the photo the next morning—the hysterical savage, the white girl brandishing her fist—and the identical headline:

¡YO SOY TERRORISTA!

It was a disaster, a kind of suicide. Her captors could not believe their ears. At the U.S. embassy, lawyers smacked their desks. In a room at the Lima Sheraton, where they'd waited three days to see their daughter, David hunched on the bed and sobbed; Maxine, standing, swore under her breath. Five days later, Leonora Gelb was sentenced to life in prison for treason and leadership of a terrorist group. The prosecutor stood before the judges in their canvas hoods and shrugged, the matter out of his hands.

"Señores," he said, "the prisoner has already confessed."

Now, all these years later, you want me to make sense of it, to explain the inexplicable: how a person of good intentions becomes an enemy of the people, how a child of privilege ends up in torment and squalor. You want me to explore her inner life, to make the connections, show you someone you can recognize.

You want me to tell a good story.

It starts like this: Leonora Gelb hated America. Not for its belligerence or its greed, not for its garish displays of wealth or callous disregard for those in need, not for the appalling body counts its every undertaking achieved, but for its hypocrisy, its galling insincerity, the unswerving insistence that America is a force for good. She hated America because it would never be what it claimed to be, would always mean something other than what it claimed it meant. It was a tragic sleight-of-hand, a disgrace—to be an American was to participate in the worst kind of metaphor: it meant someone, somewhere else, was dying for you.

— *Lima, October 2008*

I

THE WRETCHED OF THE EARTH

1

Any beginning is an act of violence. A shattering of silence. The past flares up like a rag soaked in kerosene. I've been asked to tell the story of Leonora Gelb. Where else to start but with an act of violence?

Los Muertos. A tiny settlement in the desert south of Lima— shanties and shipping containers, broken stone, plastic cisterns on rickety stilts. From above it must look as though a freight train fell out of the sky, the wreckage scattered over the dunes, scrap wood and metal clinging to the edge of a desiccated plateau. Only a few of the shacks have electricity, tapped illegally from a larger settlement half a mile away. A nearby arroyo serves as garbage dump and communal toilet. No running water. No police or doctors or schools. No one should live like this. But in Los Muertos more than a thousand people do.

Did.

It's almost Christmas, 1997. The bulldozers arrive at first light, grumbling across the desert in a long, hazy line. One moment there's nothing, brown pallor, an ocean of dunes and steep gullies. The sky a colorless sweep paling at the horizon. Then the dust-plume appears: a faint smudge in the distance, a growing blur on the hard-packed road below. Now the faint sound of engines, the curtain of dust, glints of metal—a disruption, an arrow through the stillness. A beginning.

From the rocky scarp at the edge of the cemetery, the best vantage on the road, Leonora Gelb hugs herself and watches the caravan approaching: bulldozers, SUVs, troop carriers, the rear brought up by five gray schoolbuses. An acre of bleached niche walls and half-toppled crosses spreads behind her, sinking into scrub and trash. The air smells of woodsmoke, a thin tang of metal, like adrenaline rising.

She turns to the woman standing next to her. "¿Por qué los buses? What are the buses for?"

"There are still a lot of people to remove," Nancy says, without taking her eyes off the road. "Also, probably, they expect problems. Hija, you shouldn't stay."

"Did someone tell them we would be here?" Leo says, gently emphasizing the plural, *nosotros: we.*

Nancy presses her lips together. She's short, heavy around the middle, but with a cloud of wavy black hair that Leo envies. She's Leo's mother's age, or a bit younger, with the same flat, frank way of speaking easily mistaken for coldness. "Of course someone told them. There are no secrets in this country, only informers." Her walkie-talkie rasps and she coughs into it: "Sí, mi amor. They are coming now."

"But why would anyone inform? We're trying to help these people."

Nancy squints at the demonstrators, some scattered among the wood shacks and roofless blocks of concrete, others clustered around a man standing on a crate in the road. Mange-scarred dogs root in piles of trash, heavy teats dragging in the dust.

"These people are very poor. The government can make promises we can't make." She nods at the still-distant caravan, its rooster-tail of dust falling in sepia air. "You do them a favor, you never have to see this place again."

Los Muertos is the newest sector of Los Arenales, a vast and jumbled patchwork of settlements an hour from the colonial pomp of central Lima. Nancy has lived in Los Arenales most of her life; in the early 1970s, when the military government opened the land to homesteaders, hers was among the first families to build, foraging for scrap wood and thatch, sharing one small generator to run what tools they had. They were llama herders, subsistence farmers, illiterates from the provinces fleeing starvation and infant mortality. A barren plot far from the city was the only chance they'd ever have. They built it from nothing, asked nothing from Lima except to be left alone. Twenty-five years later, Los Arenales has half a million residents, shopping malls, a vocational college; Nancy's house has three floors and a satellite dish.

And it keeps expanding. Each year a new wave of migrants—"invaders," as they are commonly called by limeños of greater means—arrives with cloth bundles, no shoes, desperate to get their children under shelter before the heat sets in, before thieves strip them of clothing, photo albums, even their Bibles. Nancy's NGO, Oportunidad Para Todos, provides some assistance as they struggle to tame their patches of dirt: to find jobs, diapers, medicine; to hang on long enough to demand services from the government. Los Muertos is no different from these earlier settlements, except in one respect: they built too far west. On a clear day you can see out to the ocean, an expansive downhill sweep of virgin dunes and empty beach. Bidding opened over the summer; in October, the government awarded the lease to an international chain of golf resorts.

The bulldozers have turned off the main road and begun the long climb to the cemetery. Again, Nancy counts the demonstrators, troubled by their meager numbers: a few dozen local residents, teachers, shopkeepers, and members of the neighborhood councils, all gathered now at Los Muertos' one tiny bodega—a gray concrete cube that sells cigarettes and powdered milk through a locked grate.

"Okay, Leo," she says. "You have to go now."

Leo turns to her in surprise. "What? Why? I want to help."

"Not with this. Listen to me. It's not safe here."

"I don't care," she says, wincing at the petulance in her voice. "Just give me something to do."

"You want to do something? Take the jeep. You know how to drive? The keys are on the seat. Take it back to the office. Don't argue, okay? You shouldn't be here."

In the three months she's worked for Nancy, Leo has never seen her so anxious. It started with the graffiti—¡La tierra es la vida! and ¡El Perú es de todos!—that appeared in red paint soon after the demolition was announced. Slogans followed by the phrase Viene el Cuatro—or sometimes just the number 4. For weeks now, a terseness among the volunteers and employees of Oportunidad, a sense of waiting. When she got to work yesterday, she found Nancy arguing with a man in his early twenties, someone Leo had seen lingering outside the office, chatting with students in her ESL class. He had high, prominent cheekbones, a beguiling smile. People greeted him warily, kept half a step away and looked at their feet. When Leo asked a student his name, she frowned as if at a mildly sour odor. "Le llaman 'Chaski,'" the student said.

"Not here. Not in Los Arenales," Nancy was saying when Leo came in. She folded her hands on her desk and thrust her chin at him. "Tell your friends to stay away. We don't want that kind of help."

"Compañera, you don't understand!" Chaski said, with a salesman's grin. He was bronze-skinned and lanky, his hands always moving. "No one is trying to take control away from the councils . . . "

Nancy wagged a finger at him. "No soy tu compañera." When she saw Leo, she lowered her voice, pointing with her eyes until Chaski looked up, too. They spoke in Quechua then, and Leo, unnerved, hurried to the back room to prep for class.

Now the first of the bulldozers crests the rise and turns onto the broad dirt thoroughfare. The SUV's follow, red lights twirling. Quickly, the demonstrators spread among the shacks in pairs, each with a length of heavy chain and a set of handcuffs. Sensing that Nancy will soon join them, Leo reaches for her arm.

"I can help. Anything. Really. Just tell me. What can I do?"

All last night, sleepless in her hostel, she'd asked herself the same thing. On the dawn bus from Lima she set her jaw, bolstered her determination. It was their home, she reminded herself. It was all they had. But what could she do? If protest turned to confrontation, how would she react? She'd squeezed into Nancy's jeep with six other arenaleños, then waited at the edge of the cemetery while the few remaining residents dragged trash and tires into the road. No one looked at her. When she hauled a dusty tire onto the pile an older man nodded once and walked away.

Gently but firmly, Nancy pulls her arm away. "Look around you, Leo. Do you see other volunteers? The German girls, that boy from Holland whose name I can't remember, the flaquito—" A teenage girl rushes over, a red-faced infant slung across her back, and speaks rapidly in Quechua. "Okay, mamita, ya voy," Nancy tells her, then turns back to Leo and pulls her into a brisk embrace.

"Your friends have the sense to stay away," she says. "It's better you do the same. Take the car and get out of here, Leo. This is something for arenaleños."

Leo squeezes her fists in mute frustration. Across the road, the last residents have lined up next to the buses. A soldier points a bullhorn at them: *One bag for one person. Control your children. No dogs.* So what if she isn't from Los Arenales? If she isn't Peruvian? She's here, isn't she? Unlike the German girls, she came to help. Didn't she?

"They're not my friends," she manages as Nancy hurries away.

With a blast of sand and grit, the bulldozers come to a stop before the first shanties. Soldiers jump from the troop carriers and fan out along the road and the commander shouts into the bullhorn that demolition will start in five minutes. Demonstrators dart across the road, hurling insults at the soldiers; skinny men stare blankfaced from the doors of their homes. A low, swirling wind has kicked up, making everything look washed out, monochrome—like documentary footage. Through the rising dust Leo spots Ernesto, the youngest of Nancy's three sons, moving between shanties with a camcorder held to his face.

"Neto!" Leo shouts. He looks around in confusion. "Neto, over here!"

"Leo!" he says, then something else drowned out by the bullhorn. "*What?*"

He waves an arm urgently and she takes half a step toward the road, driven back by the piercing signal of a bulldozer in reverse. "Go back!" Neto is shouting. "Get out of here, Leo!" She tries to answer him but then sirens cut through the wind and with a fearsome rasp the bulldozers grind their gears and edge forward. Leo covers her nose against the swirling dust, falls back among the headstones as the first bus turns and pulls past her, stunned faces at every window.

When she next spots Ernesto, he's on the roof of the bodega with two other kids, all wearing bandannas over their faces. Nancy and five other councilmembers have handcuffed themselves to the bodega's grate; two soldiers struggle toward them, dragging a welding rig over the rocky ground. There's a brief lull, not quite silence, and then it begins: with a rumble and boom, a terrible crunching, the crack and rustle of thatch as the first shanty collapses into a matchstick pile, pathetically small.

Crouching next to a plastic cistern, Leo watches the bulldozers square off before the next row of shacks. Mouth open, heart pounding—something in her had not believed it would really happen. Soldiers move along the fences, spraying pepper spray into the eyes of protestors, dragging others through the dust while the dogs snarl and feint at their legs. And what now? What will you do about it? *Go back, Leo. You can't do anything, Leo.* The worst part is, she knows they're right: if she throws herself at a soldier, she'll be overpowered in seconds; if she lies down in the street she'll get shoved onto a bus, deported, or worse. It doesn't matter what she does—by tomorrow there will be nothing left of Los Muertos but splinters, dented pots, heaps of smoldering thatch. The people who lived here will be forgotten. No handcuffs or camcorders can change that.

But impotence is no excuse. It's not good enough, not nearly—has she come all this way to stand and watch while human lives get smashed? "The world's not perfect, Leo," her mother said before she left, a statement so banal and cynical that, recalling it now, she lurches toward the bodega out of spite. Nauseated, choking on sand, she shields her eyes, pushes into the wind at a slant between two SUVs parked nose to nose. She puts a hand on the hood to steady herself—and in that instant something smashes into the windshield, a hot and stinging impact that whips past her face, startling her into a crouch.

When she looks up there are flames sheeting across the glass, dancing across the black metal hood—she stumbles back toward the cemetery, hands and feet propelling her across the dusty street, another crash behind her, another wave of heat—and then she sees them through the haze of smoke and dust, like shadows in a dream: half a dozen figures sprinting through the settlement, faces covered in black ski masks, holding bottles stuffed with lit rags. Soldiers chase them between shanties, weapons drawn. Gasping in the stink of gasoline and burning plastic, Leo's paralyzed, exposed, she can't see Nancy or Ernesto through the hot, warped air—she staggers out of the path of another departing schoolbus, eyes streaming, hurls herself toward the nearest headstones but pulls up at the sight of another body racing toward her, a split-second impression of a black mask, a cocked arm holding flame—and then the jeep skids up behind her and someone is calling her name.

"Leonora, get in!" he says, "Come on, amiga, vámonos."

She swipes at her eyes, retching on oily smoke. He leans across the seat and opens the passenger door, motions urgently—the man from the office, the one Nancy was arguing with, in her panic she can't come up with his name.

"Come on, trust me!" he says. "Let's go."

The smash of another bottle, clatter of old wood collapsing—or is it gunfire?—and then she's running to the jeep, pulling the door shut and ducking low, fumbling for the seatbelt as they swerve precariously downhill. They skirt the cemetery and lurch out into the dunes, Leo still clutching for the seatbelt, rolling her window pointlessly up and down, checking the glove box—*for what?*—wheezing and choking down bile, and forcing herself not to look back.

In retrospect, she'd made a mistake—though there may have been no right way to tell her parents about the decision. She'd already waited months, biding her time at the Mission Outreach Project in San Francisco, distributing clean needles to the same ruined and hopeless clients, explaining in grade-school Spanish to a flood of undocumented mothers how to find services, get their children into school, apply for housing assistance—a job she'd held for three years but that had quickly come to seem pointless once she realized it would never end: for every client she helped, a hundred more were waiting. She lived in a dilapidated house on Bryant Street, six kids in a four-bedroom that got tagged every night. Her housemates were vegans and weed dealers and wanna-be Rastas several of whom were, like Leo, secretly studying for the LSATs. When she learned about Oportunidad Para Todos from Gabriel Zamir, who'd profiled Nancy Rojas in a book about Latin American NGOs, she wrote to them immediately. But then Matthew and Samira set their wedding date, and so she delayed yet again, and then she'd given away most of her belongings and sold her squeaky Volvo to buy a one-way plane ticket and was leaving in less than a week.

"But why?" was her mother's reaction. "I don't understand."

They stood at the edge of the dance floor while the band broke down and the bride and groom said goodbye to their wedding party in the marble foyer. Her father was on the terrace overlooking the vineyard, having a cigar with the bride's father and brothers. It had been a lavish affair, $200 centerpieces and scale models of Venetian bridges, gondoliers roaming the ballroom with accordions. Leo was as appalled by the show of wealth as she was by the behavior of Matt's business-school buddies, who'd had crystal shot glasses engraved for the occasion and who leaned on the bar and licked salt and lemon off the bridesmaids' necks. Gabriel had a name for such people: he called them "the ruling class," and Leo'd had more than enough of them at Stanford.

"What about the LSATs?" her mother was saying. She wore a billowing crêpe de chine dress in rose and ochre that Leo thought made her look like a stuffed mushroom. "There are application deadlines, you wanted to visit Yale. I can't understand this."

"No, *you* wanted me to visit Yale," Leo said, immediately regretting her combative tone. She'd chosen to tell her mother first not only because Maxine had once, long ago, been active in political causes—a college summer in Mississippi registering voters, a month canvassing for Bobby Kennedy—but because Leo suspected her father would be genuinely crushed. Still, she knew her mother was telling the truth: having spent decades swaddled in suburban privilege and cut off from reality, Maxine really *couldn't* understand it. It was as if that idealistic young woman had never existed.

"Mom, please, I need you to listen—"

"Tell it to your father, Leonora. See what he thinks," Maxine said, waving to the wedding planner across the room. Matt and Samira would fly to Italy in the morning for a two-week honeymoon, then take a cruise ship back to New York, where a job at an investment bank awaited him. Her parents planned to stay in Napa another few days. They had reservations at the French Laundry. "This makes no sense at all."

Leo closed her eyes. There was no way to explain. It would sound ridiculous to say that her work, her Stanford degree, her whole life made her feel complicit, ridiculous to say that $200 centerpieces and crêpe de chine were killing her. The whole production: the swing band, the fake Rialto built for the ceremony, the groomsmen's immaculate shaves. The way everyone in this room felt immune to misfortune. It was all killing her. She was choking, as if someone had wadded up satin bunting and rammed it down her throat.

"I can't live with myself, Mom."

Maxine took off her heels and winced. "Don't take that out on the rest of us."

She didn't call them for ten days after arriving in Lima. Let them worry, she thought. Let them indulge their worst fantasies about poor, brown people. The first time she rode the bus to Los Arenales, packed in with drowsing swing-shift workers and old campesinas in wool sweaters, she knew she'd been right. She belonged here—among people who understood that life was an uncompromising struggle, who knew what things were really worth. They jounced south on the Panamericana, through gray slums that stank of truck exhaust, tiers of half-built hovels the color of sand or toothpaste, barely visible against the dry hills. The land emptied and flattened, punctuated now by the occasional lumberyard or unfinished brick wall, by desultory outposts of concrete and rebar. Lima, its belligerence, its traffic and noise and jostle, fell far behind. The bus slowed, easing itself onto the patched dirt thoroughfare that led into Los Arenales. Passengers took out handkerchiefs, pulled shirt collars over mouths and noses as they rocked slowly through a street market that reeked of fish. Pedestrians parted to let the bus pass. Out the window, men in tire-tread sandals bent under canvas sacks, squat women in bowler hats, black skirts hemmed with muck. A boy of five or six urinated on the side of a combi with no tires. A teenage girl in a new white dress chased another through the makeshift stalls.

The bus let them off at the side of a small plaza, where old men sat playing chess and women carried flat boxes holding cigarettes, candy, soap, phone cards, and biscuits slung around their necks. Leo was instantly mobbed by drivers who shouted and fought to pull her to their three-wheeled moto-taxis; she chose the least aggressive, a tall, deeply tanned man in his sixties with close-cropped white hair who offered his arm as she stepped over puddles. They puttered from one sector to another, shuddering into potholes and darting, flylike, across busy avenues with unmarked, unobserved lanes, pedestrians cowering by berms of rubble. Leo's teeth clacked, her backside banged painfully on the metal seat. By the time she arrived at the office, in a half-deserted neighborhood of warehouses, and presented herself to Nancy, she had resolved never to go home.

When she finally spoke to her parents she'd been working at Oportunidad for a week and she was so obviously happy that her mother could only ask, with barely concealed exasperation, if she was taking care of herself. "They give the LSATs in Lima once a year," Maxine said, but Leo could hear in her careful tone the acceptance of defeat. Her father asked about the food. He said he couldn't wait to visit. Leo hung up the payphone and beamed at the shabby lobby of her hostel—antediluvian stuffed furniture, weird statues hiding in gloom under the stairs. She'd done it, she'd really done it—already she had an ESL class of her own and Nancy was training her to teach basic reading skills. She'd met men and women from all over Los Arenales, people who'd helped build their sectors with their bare hands, taught themselves to be bricklayers, nurses, firefighters, teachers—taking care of one another, protecting one another in those first vulnerable years. A well-dressed man in his thirties, the head of a neighborhood council, wept with pride as he showed her an old photo and recalled the square of parched land his family came to when he was nine. "My father," he said, crossing himself, "he never had anything. All he wanted was to work."

On Monday, she'd gone with the German girls to San Sebastian, one of the newer sectors, and helped dig a trench for water mains. The two-room brick houses had no glass in the windows, blue tarps for roofs, but each had a little picket fence protecting a few square feet of dirt. Panting in the dank air, her back cramping, Leo gripped the shovel and heaved until skin peeled from her hands. With every load of dirt, every stone she pried out with her fingers, she felt the years of uselessness, of bitter acceptance, receding. No more studying problems from afar. No more pointless demonstrations in Sacramento. No more grant applications or fundraisers, begging for crumbs to keep other human beings alive. Here in Los Arenales she would finally accomplish something. Side by side with arenaleños, she could build a new reality with her own two hands.

In her third week the government posted an eviction notice on the side of the bodega in Los Muertos. Nancy and two lawyers went to Lima to try to get a court order but the judge, whose wife was the niece of the Vice Minister of Tourism, refused to see them. The graffiti started appearing two weeks before Christmas: *Viene el Cuatro*. "What does it mean," she asked a co-worker, "'Here comes the Four'?" But the woman frowned and waved her off. Her foreman at the trench said, "It's a game. People call themselves Philosophers. It's nothing." But as she walked through Los Arenales—some sectors still muddy clusters of construction materials; others with supermarkets and electronics stores, motorcycle dealers and strip clubs—she had the growing recognition of how little she yet knew. Behind the determination of its older residents, the frantic scrabbling of newcomers, there were histories and allegiances she couldn't make out, codes and gestures, competitions for influence, matrices overlaid like the schematic of a complex machine. It was one thing to teach English, to lay pipe—to *help*. But she would not truly belong here until she understood these invisible networks, until she could read the map behind the map. Back in Lima, stiff and exhausted, she lay awake imagining the long bus ride, the way the land changed slowly, until at last they were somewhere else. She chided herself for her fantasy of having become someone different. She wasn't there yet.

The protest at Los Muertos is a matter of record, of history. Not hard to find in newspaper archives or other chronicles of the time. "Somehow she left, I don't know," is what Nancy Rojas told me. "Maybe with Chaski, or whatever that asshole's name was," she said. "It's possible, yes. Why not?"

From there, the scene goes blank. One of countless gaps to be filled in. But who am I to say what happened?

My friend says, "You're the writer, Andres."

The jeep pitches across the desert in sharp turns, stretches of hard rattle and sudden drops that hammer in Leo's jaw. The driver checks the rearview often, his face slowly relaxing, eyes growing thought-ful. There's no sign of the skirmish behind them, only a faint smell of burning gasoline on the wind. Up ahead, Los Arenales' hap-hazard skyline notches the horizon; soon the dunes start to flatten as they descend toward a semi-paved road marked with lean-to's and brick huts. Leo, her throat raw, teeth faintly chattering, stares straight ahead, gripping her knees in the first bloom of shame.

"You're hurt?" the driver asks, glancing at the side of her face.

"What was that back there?" she says. She still won't look at him. "Chaski—that's your name, right? What the fuck was that?"

Little by little, the roadside fills with civilization: lumber piles, streetlights, an open tent emblazoned with a beer logo. With each flash of shadow, she sees again the masked figure running through the cemetery, arm cocked, the flaming bottle—it was a woman, she realizes, remembering the long braid at her back. Somehow this makes it worse.

"Nancy told you not to come, didn't she? You and those—" she rolls the word around on her tongue—"philosophers."

Amusement lifts his high brow. He has thick black hair sweeping back from his temples, a wide and artless gaze. Over a black T-shirt he wears a tiny gold cross on a thin chain. "Relax, Leonora. It's not so bad."

"How do you know my name?"

"Everybody knows your name. You're the gringa. The one who came to help us."

His mockery only makes the nausea worse. Her head throbs, her stomach clenches. When she swipes at her cheek, blood streaks her fingers. She remembers the smash of glass, the sudden heat. She'd run away so quickly.

"Don't call me 'gringa.'"

"But you are a gringa."

"I'm American."

"Somos todos americanos," Chaski says—*We are all Americans*—gently teasing, trying to soothe her. But his solicitude only stokes the anger that's been building since she got into the jeep.

"Why did you leave?" she says, turning now to look at him. "Why aren't you back there burning things with your friends?"

"My friends?"

"What if someone was in that car? You could have killed them."

Chaski absently fingers the little cross. "Is it better they do nothing? They should lie down while the government takes away everything?"

Leo sits back and peers at the hazy skyline, patches of light blue shifting as the fog burns off. It was she who'd done nothing. Who'd stood like a frightened child and then fled at the first opportunity. Again she hears the crack of breaking thatch. Again sees the burning car, flames skittering across the hood, Ernesto and the others pumping their fists on the roof of the bodega while she cowered below. Shame wells higher in her throat, a taste like polished silver.

"We have to go back," she hears herself saying. "We have to help them." When Chaski doesn't answer, she smacks the seat with her palm, her fury only deepened by the childish gesture. "Did you see them back there? Nancy and the others? Neto was on the roof! What's going to happen to them? And you just drive away like they don't matter? What did you even come for, if you just take off when it gets bad?"

He waits until her breath is spent. "Those people had no chance. Los Muertos had no chance. It was finished the minute the government decided. Nancy knew that."

"Then why—" she sputters, but he stops her with another bright smile.

"I thought you are supposed to be smart, Leonora. What happened at Los Muertos was a victory, you don't understand?"

"A victory?"

"Where were the cameras? Was anyone there from TV? A thousand people lose their homes because of a hotel for rich people. Isn't this a big story? Los Muertos could not be saved," he says. "Nobody thought the bulldozers would stop. We don't want them to stop! Why, so a thousand people can keep living with no light, no water, shitting in a ditch, every time it rains they are dying from cholera? You want to save that?"

He stamps on the brake as a rusty, overcrowded minibus pulls ahead of them, spewing a brown cloud over the windshield. "Now people will know. They'll talk about this on the radio, or the TV, and they'll see the government is lying when it says all the problems were because of the war. They will see how the murderers attack their own people. And they will say that something must be done."

She turns away, her anger evaporating as quickly as it came. *Propaganda by deed.* That's the phrase that comes to her—a phrase she first learned in Gabriel's class, one she heard repeated by Black Power activists, environmental warriors, old Berkeley hippies. Move past the rhetoric. Action is its own explanation. Until now she hadn't grasped the cold calculation. She hadn't known it stank of kerosene.

"But you're the ones who attacked," she says, exhaustion making her voice raspy. "It was a peaceful demonstration until your friends showed up."

"I told you, they're not my friends."

"That's what Nancy said, wasn't it? She didn't want violence. That's why she told you to stay away. She didn't want anyone to get hurt."

"Leonora," he says, "tell me a story where somebody doesn't get hurt."

The jeep noses up an unpaved grade, where a gas pump and concrete hut sit at the side of the highway. Chaski gets out and tosses the keys onto her lap. When he disappears into the bodega she closes her eyes, stamps her feet on the floorboards while the traffic passes hot and roaring a few yards away. People had lost everything. They were herded like animals and they lost everything and she'd run. "The gringa who came to help us"—she flushes, seeing now what they must think of her: so earnest, so insistent, demanding a chance to do *something*. But when the chance came, she'd done nothing—nobody had. ESL hadn't helped the people of Los Muertos. Opportunity hadn't saved their homes. All Nancy and her colleagues had managed was to make noise, maybe get arrested. What was the point?

She could go back—that's why Chaski left her the keys, wasn't it? She could find her way to Los Muertos, tend to whomever was left. They could clean up, maybe even start to rebuild—there would be wood, unburned thatch . . . But that would be just another point-less gesture, pure symbolism. The memory of the woman in the ski mask comes back to her, the blast of heat. The force of what happened crests above her like a giant wave; she hunches under it, puts her face in her hands and lets out a single, shaky sob.

When Chaski slides back into the jeep he hands her a paper napkin, leans over to examine the light hatching of cuts on her cheek. "How did you get these?"

"What does 'Viene el Cuatro' mean?" she says.

"It's a slogan," he says. "You know, like political parties have."

"A political party? When are the elections?"

He smiles, then plucks the keys from her lap and they merge onto the highway, accelerating past combis, moto-taxis, rusted Japanese sedans—arenaleños flocking to jobs and markets in Lima. He offers her a plastic bottle of Coca-Cola, but she waves it away.

"Elections aren't important," he says, honking when a panel truck cuts him off. "The dictator was elected. Elections only decide who will have more money in their pockets."

"What does it mean?"

He raises his chin without looking at her. "It means someone is watching."

"Who? Philosophers?"

Chaski lets out a dry laugh. In the hills to the east, adobe huts cling to the slopes like pieces of a filthy jigsaw puzzle. *A victory.* But nothing had changed today. No one had been helped. She squints at the gray hillside, at a tiny, bent figure climbing an endless stair.

"They were real people," she says, clutching at what's left of her indignation. When she gets no answer she lunges for the steering wheel and shakes it violently, provoking a volley of horns as they swerve across the lane. "You can't just sacrifice them. You can't just say there's nothing you can do."

Chaski lifts his hands from the wheel, leaving her in unsteady control as the jeep speeds ahead. Leaning back, he unscrews the Coke bottle and takes a long drink.

"Amiga, when did I say there is nothing you can do?"

2

Here's what I knew about the war: I knew there'd been one. A dirty one, though like most Americans I didn't yet know what that meant. I'd heard of the Shining Path—maybe in some long-ago history class or cable documentary—but I couldn't have told you the first thing about their beliefs or their tactics. I couldn't have said when the war began (1980) or when it ended (1992), or how close it came to bringing down the Peruvian state. When friends referred to "Sendero Luminoso," I nodded gravely, mirroring their grief. But I didn't ask questions. I didn't want to know details, body counts, who butchered whom. I didn't want to hear the arguments, though I knew they still festered; the fury and righteousness, the fear of one's neighbor, were too familiar, reminders of a life I'd tried to leave behind.

But Sendero was a nightmare—a long, bloodcurdling, wing-flapping horror whose shadow still loomed years after the country awoke. Anyone who would write about Leo Gelb has to understand this. From the moment their leader, Abimael Guzmán, launched his Maoist revolt until his unexpected capture twelve years later, Peruvians lived weightlessly, vulnerable at every moment, trapped between a violent personality cult and the vindictive rage of a lawless state. Between them, Sendero and the Army produced seventy thousand corpses, strewn from the Ayacucho highlands to the ancestral homes of Amazon tribes to Lima's most exclusive enclaves. They lay in mass graves and secret prisons, they lay on busy streetcorners, or they lay nowhere at all—unidentified, unaccounted for, deep wounds that could never close. No one was immune, everyone at every level of society knew someone who was killed, or kidnapped, or disappeared, a generation wiped out as if by meteor or plague.

The Cuarta Filosofía (Fourth Philosophy) was not the Shining Path—this, too, I had to learn. It was a footnote, one of a handful of militant groups whose ambitions were eclipsed by Sendero's mayhem. Unlike Sendero, whose custom was to enter a town en masse, execute the mayor, and demand allegiance to Abimael, the Philosophers worked from within, gaining the trust of village councils and union leaders, the blessings of parish priests. Rough-cut Robin Hoods, they harassed only the wealthy and powerful, hijacking shipments of food and medicine, distributing the plunder in village plazas while bands played and armed cadres grilled chickens for the residents. Unlike Abimael, whose id-driven declarations ran to the grandiose ("The triumph of the revolution will cost a million deaths!"), the Philosophers projected modesty and determination: *Only what is necessary, only what is right*, was a common graffito, the two phrases encircling a large number 4.

According to Gustavo Gorriti, Peru's premier "senderologist," both Sendero and the Cuarta Filosofía originated in the villages and farm communities of central and southeastern Peru—regions long exploited to the benefit of the distant capital, their resources pillaged, their darker-skinned residents treated with contempt. In these stony Andean reaches, Spanish was still a second language, subsistence farming the prevailing trade, and illiteracy the norm. Life expectancy was forty-five years, and a third of babies died before their first birthday. Discoveries of gold and zinc, copper and tin had brought not prosperity but cyanotic streams and poisoned aquifers, dynamited mountainsides, private roads for foreign corporations to move profits out of the country.

"[The Philosophers] resisted Sendero's rigid hierarchy and the bloody rhetoric of Abimael Guzmán," Gorriti wrote in a 1999 postmortem, published in *Caretas*.

They accepted democracy as a theoretical future, but did not believe it could be achieved until the oligarchy was dismantled and the economy reorganized according to socialist principles . . . Although they rejected Abimael's vision of a Maoist peasant war, they had no illusions that change would come peacefully.

Such distinctions mattered little to Peru's military. In 1989 alone, more than four hundred Philosophers were killed in encounters with foot soldiers and helicopter patrols, or by ronderos—local militiamen armed by the government and given a free hand to cleanse their villages as they saw fit. Cadres were often lined up and executed with shots to the back of the head. The threat from Sendero was equally grave: Abimael brooked no competing ideology, his revolutionary fervor made no place for naïve sentiments about democracy and reform. Philosophers and Senderistas clashed in the hamlets of Apurímac and Junín, the deep gorges of the central sierra, and eventually the streets of Lima.

"For a couple of years, you did not walk outside," recalls Damien Cohen, a French journalist who covered the war for *The Washington Post* and has lived in Lima ever since. "This was in '90, '91. If you went somewhere, you called it in, you set a specific time when you'd be back. They were like children playing soldier," he says. "Running around with Kalashnikovs, tin cans full of dynamite. Like it was a game, except the bombs were real."

Sendero and the CF fought for control of working-class barrios and pueblos jovenes—battles that went block to block and lasted for days. Youth groups and neighborhood councils were infiltrated, municipal buildings taken, dissenters driven out. At San Marcos, the public university near central Lima, dormitories were controlled by one group or the other, debates devolved into fistfights, parades erupted in gunfire.

"I went to one of these 'debates,'" says Cohen, frowning over a cloud of cigarette smoke. "It was a conference about AIDS, nothing to do with the war. After two minutes, a boy is standing on a desk, shouting, 'Homosexuality is bourgeois decadence, and blah blah blah Abimael this and blah blah Mao Zedong this.' Then another one, something about Fidel, Mariátegui, this mindless screaming, both of them, while their comrades are bashing each other over the head."

He stubs out his cigarette with a bemused look. "Teenagers. Acne on their faces. You wanted to laugh at them. But if you laugh, someone shoots you in the head."

All of this is relevant, all of it was new to me. But my editor says to cut most of it. He says readers don't need all the background. They won't read it.

"Forget the small print," he says. "Just focus on the girl."

The small print: oligarchy, treason, rivers of blood. Who wants to think about such things?

He may be right. Certainly I've heard it before: *Character is destiny*, my teachers always said. History and politics bog down a story. They're extraneous, a distraction from what really matters: the protagonist's experience, her feelings. *Show, don't tell*—haven't I taught students the same thing?

But how else will readers understand, how can they see it through Leo's eyes? And even this leaves out too much: decades of military dictatorship, the 1980 elections, endemic corruption. It leaves out Tarata and La Cantuta, rumors about the C.I.A . . .

I can't leave out Tarata—the 1992 truck-bomb that killed twenty-five residents of an apartment building in the upscale Miraflores district. I can't forget the footage: the building weeping flames, its facade blown away. It was an awakening, a turning point for middle-class limeños who until now had regarded the war as a vague disturbance happening in a not-quite-real part of the country. It was one thing for thousands of poor Indians to die in distant provinces, but this was *Lima*. There were protests, resolutions; the newspapers howled at the smallest acts of civil disobedience, called out leaders for leftist sympathies. They demanded that the government put an end to the conflict by any means necessary. Sendero Luminoso, MRTA, Red Flag, CF: after Tarata the differences no longer mattered. They were all terrorists, and terrorists must be stamped out.

Two days later, a pre-dawn raid at La Cantuta, a college on the outskirts of Lima. Hundreds of students face-down on the sidewalks, soldiers' rifles pointed at their heads. Nine students and a professor were bound, hooded, and taken away; leaked documents later described their torture, murder, and cremation by a special forces unit that took orders from the President's closest advisor.

All that year, the violence spiraled: banks and government buildings were bombed, state officials and businessmen kidnapped, assassinated in public places. Car bombs became so common that even now, fifteen years later, limeños still cross to the other side of the street when they see an old model illegally parked. The government raided businesses, union halls, public gatherings, and rounded up leftists of any stripe. Journalists and aid workers disappeared; students were arrested for possessing socialist pamphlets, CDs by indigenous musicians; demonstrations were met with live ammunition. The President suspended the Constitution, curtailed due process, brought the courts to heel. Terrorism was redefined in markedly vague terms, brought under jurisdiction of a military with little use for notions of "human rights."

More history. More small print, I suppose.

Then, in September, Abimael Guzmán was captured, dragged from a Lima safe house and hauled to the naval base in Callao, displayed to the media in a striped prison suit, pacing a metal cage. The President vowed to chase any remaining terrorists into the barrios, the mountains, to find and destroy their training camps without mercy "until the children and stepchildren of Abimael have been wiped off the face of the earth."

It was over. After twelve years limeños were desperate to forget the war, though their city was in ruins and thousands were missing. By the time Leo arrived, five years later, denial had taken hold, abetted by triumphant reports of foreign investment and double-digit growth. The media obsessed over the private lives of soccer players and socialites, once again ignoring starvation and disease in the countryside. But in the provinces, the barrios, those who had lost family members or spent time in the dictator's dungeons didn't forget what side their neighbors were on. Even now, you find graffiti in Lima districts, in forgotten villages—¡Viva Abimael! emblazoned on a water tower, or a giant 4 on the side of a Pizza Hut. Once, in Babilonia, I saw an argument erupt at an outdoor concert. Three men held their hands over their hearts, thumbs hidden: the number four. They faced off against a cohort of shorter, darker men in heavy sweaters and llama herders' hats— Senderistas, my date said. We'd been there for hours, dancing ecstatically in cold sunshine, warmed by local beer. She dragged me away from the fight. *Please, Andres, now, please* . . . Anything could happen, she said, her voice pinched with fear. I was indignant. The pointlessness of it, the stupidity! The war was a million years ago, I said. My date pulled me steadily through the crowd. Why hold on to these old allegiances? It was tribal, I said, barbaric. Why would you want to ruin things when everyone was having a good time?

She's only been to Nancy's house once. During her first week at Oportunidad, a small party to welcome Leo and the two German girls, whose names she's already forgotten. They'd found their way through Campo Elíseo, one of Los Arenales' original sectors, to an unpaved street of blocky two- and three-story homes painted coral and toothpaste-green. Inside they slurped pork stew from paper bowls and clinked bottles of Cuzqueña while Nancy's husband—a small man with a neat mustache and V-neck sweater—sat smoking on the front stoop. The Germans babbled in perfect Spanish and Leo, alone on the couch, squinted at her lap and tried to follow.

"California?" Nancy's youngest son handed her a fresh beer and sat warily at the other end of the couch. He was seventeen or eighteen, with a wide face and prominent brow, and long-lashed, watchful eyes.

"Sí."

"When—" he began, then shook his head to correct himself. "Which part?"

"San Francisco. Pero yo nací en Nuevo Jersey."

Ernesto's smile shifted all his features. He pulled his sweater up to reveal a faded concert T-shirt: PEARL JAMMIN' AT THE GREEK, HALLOWEEN 1993, it read, over an image of Eddie Vedder swinging on a cable: gleaming eyes, bared teeth.

"You know this place?" Ernesto asked. "You study in Berkeley University?"

Leo laughed. She didn't remember the concert, but it was likely her roommates had gone. "I went to another school, very close to Berkeley."

Ernesto nodded eagerly, half understanding. There was a knock at the back door and Leo heard Nancy talking to someone in low, impatient tones. Ernesto was taking accounting classes in Lima, he said. His teacher had said that after two years, if he scored well on the TOEFL, he could apply for a scholarship to the U.S.

"Berkeley," he said, pointing to the shirt, "is my dream. I have the most . . . the best English of the class. I gain a prize."

Leo was offering to help him study when the kitchen door slammed, rattling the windows. The German girls raised their eyebrows. "Neto, get upstairs," Nancy said, striding back into the room. "Don't you have a test tomorrow?"

Leo had forgotten about that party in the busy weeks and months that followed. On the morning of the funeral, as she turns onto Nancy's street, she remembers that knock at the kitchen door, Nancy's worried expression, and it comes to her with a jolt that it must have been Chaski.

She finds Nancy's husband smoking on the stoop again, with a group of men arguing in low voices. They watch her suspiciously as she passes through the gate.

"Who are you?" says a man in a black leather jacket.

"I work with Nancy," she says, adding, "Y soy una amiga de Ernesto."

The newspapers called it "Massacre in Los Muertos." Four dead, including two children; three demonstrators not yet accounted for. Oportunidad Para Todos hasn't reopened since that morning; instead of working at a Christmas dinner in a community kitchen, Leo spent the day deciphering the newspapers in her hostel, sharing a plate of noodles from a street cart with another Jewish girl, a backpacker from Ireland who left for Bolivia the next morning. She learned the names of the missing from the lobby TV.

She hears Nancy's voice as soon as she enters the house. "No, papito, don't tell me that," Nancy snaps at the phone, in the wry, exacting tone Leo's heard her use on city officials and delinquent contractors. Through the kitchen door Leo sees her leaning against the refrigerator, smoking with fierce concentration. "Listen to me, Guillermo. Talk to Freddy. *Today*, you understand? Go up to Luri and find that idiot, okay?"

In the front room, three women sit at a card table, studying a pile of folders; Leo recognizes one of them from her ESL class. Newspapers cover the floor and couch; coffee mugs sit on windowsills, the ancient television, the bottom stair. Nancy hangs up and considers her cigarette, takes another long drag before smashing it into an ashtray.

"Leo, hija," she says. The women look up. "Nobody told you? I'm sorry, the office is still closed."

"No, pero . . ." When she's nervous her Spanish regresses to short, tenseless sentences. "I know. I come for the funeral."

Nancy searches for the cigarette pack. "The idiots," she says distractedly. "The cemetery is ruined. The army is still there. If they try to go to Los Muertos, they'll need more coffins. Marisol," she says, "what did they say?"

The woman from Leo's class, hair dyed copper and pulled into a bun, shuffles her notes. "Channel 2 said maybe next week."

"The others?" Marisol shakes her head. "Call again," Nancy says. "Leo, you want something to drink? You want a cigarette? I'm sorry it's so disorganized. There are a lot of people we have to talk to. No one important in this city ever goes to their office. Manuel and Tito are in Lima, but I have to be here—"

"I'm sorry about Ernesto."

Nancy links her arm through Leo's. "Okay, hija. Don't worry, he'll come back soon. Look, it's so hot here today. All the classes are cancelled. Those other girls, the Germans, I don't know—maybe this isn't why they came to Peru, you know?"

"Let me help," Leo says. "Give me something to do."

"Call Bill Clinton," one of the women mutters.

"Shut up, María Luisa," Nancy says, not ungently.

"I can talk to someone. You have a photo of Ernesto?" She trails off, noticing the image on the front page of the morning paper: three children, none older than ten, crying next to a heap of broken wood. "Maybe I go to the embassy—"

"The embassy? Why would they care?"

"I don't know," she says, embarrassed, envious of the women at the table, their shared purpose. "Because I'm American?"

Marisol fixes Leo in a stare. "Somos todas Americanas," she says.

"You're very generous," Nancy says. "The people who can help are lawyers, ministers, judges. Can you write a petition of habeas corpus?" She sits on the arm of the couch and balances the ashtray on her knee. "Don't worry. Neto will come home. This isn't 1990. People don't disappear."

"What about Chaski?" Leo says. "Does he know people like that?"

At this, the women turn to Nancy, talking over one another in Quechua. "Don't talk to me about Chaski," Nancy says, poking her cigarette at Leo. "Those assholes don't care about my Neto. Los Arenales was quiet, you understand? And now you see? Babies. They killed two babies. And where is your friend Chaski?

"Listen to me," she says. "Go back to Lima. The office will open in a few days, then you come back and keep teaching these fat cows how to speak English. Until then, it's better you are invisible. You aren't arenaleña, you aren't peruana. If you start talking to people it only justifies their suspicions." She brushes ashes from her lap and moves toward the stairs. "Don't make a mistake, hija."

When Leo steps outside, the men stare bluntly. The morning heat prickles under her sweater. At the end of the street, the noisy crowd is passing by on its way to the funeral. Ernesto's face floats through the intersection on a placard—outsized, black and white—followed by those of the other two missing protestors.

Nancy's husband sits at the edge of the stoop, hands spread over his knees. "Don't worry, señor," Leo says, squatting next to him. "Neto will come home." He stares blankly at her. A thin scar slants up one side of his nose, ending in a white lump at the corner of his eye, like the head of a tiny worm. "He didn't do anything," she says. "They have to let him go. He's innocent."

"The innocent people were on the buses," says the man in the leather jacket. He has wavy gray hair, a deep, avuncular voice. "The soldiers helped the women up the steps. For Neto and his friends, they pulled hoods over their heads and threw them in the trunk of a car." Leo looks from one face to the next, then back to the man, who slowly takes off his jacket. His right forearm is a gnarled tangle of flesh, his last two fingers missing, the skin sealed so tight it twists the remaining fingers into a claw.

"If they take you like that, it's better you're not innocent," he says. "If they torture you, and they decide you're innocent, it's not possible to release you. You understand, chiquitita? They can't be implicated in torture. So you have to disappear.

"Your boyfriend, Chaski, knows this." He puts his mangled arm around her as the three faces float past the corner again, gray and inert as pages from a history book. "In this country, to be innocent is the worst mistake you can make."

But I'm not sure how well she even knew Ernesto Paucar Rojas. They couldn't have met more than a handful of times. Former employees of Oportunidad Para Todos told me he would sometimes stop by the office, a two-room concrete hut in the Las Brisas sector, before catching the bus to his classes in Lima. Maybe they rode together, Leo and Neto. Maybe they spent the hour practicing his English, practicing her Spanish. Yes, why not? Maybe she asked him about growing up in Los Arenales, about Chaski and the strange graffiti. He asked about California, about the swimming pools and red convertibles, the blond girls in bikinis he'd seen on *Melrose Place* and in Snoop Dogg videos. Most Peruvians I meet want to know about those girls. They want to know about the mansions.

Or maybe they talked about their brothers: Manuel, who drove a taxi but wanted to study law, and Tito, who worked at an elementary school and was jailed when the union went on strike; Matthew, whose greatest challenge in life was the co-op board at the Murray Hill apartment Samira's father bought them as a wedding gift. Leo would have been pleased by these conversations. She would have sought them out. At work she was just one more disposable do-gooder, but she wanted to be something else, to know Peru and its people from the inside. She wanted to make connections, to change herself. And what better proof she'd done so than this: she'd made a friend.

"Why you are here?" Ernesto asked the last time they'd met, a week before Christmas. He avoided her eyes, doodled in the exercise book she held on her lap. She was starting to think he might have a crush on her.

"I love it here," she said. "I love this country." He squinted, frankly skeptical. She'd showed him pictures of Stanford, described the old house in the Mission with its pear tree and unruly wisteria, its sagging back porch. "People like me have an obligation . . ." she began, but broke off, hearing the note of condescension.

Yes, why not?

I have her at the vigil at Nancy's on the day of the funeral. But where did she go from there? I can see her joining the procession, linking arms with arenaleños as they picked their way from sector to sector, holding their banners and blown-up photos. The air full of sirens, bullhorns, chants shouted from the backs of pickup trucks. But Leo had seen plenty of protests—in downtown Lima the previous week alone there were marches by sanitation workers, veterans, municipal clerks, something called Poder de Juventud. Nothing was accomplished. They marched, screamed themselves hoarse, burned the occasional effigy—but no one expected anything to happen. No one thought the President and his ministers could be moved by *shouting*. So I can see her there, with that sad, angry crowd. But not for long.

When she arrives at the office, she finds the front room scattered with picket signs and half-rolled banners. Someone has taped the giant photo of Ernesto to the wall: a handsome teenager in a pressed shirt and collar, his hair neatly combed. She can still hear the noise of the procession, its volume cresting as it winds toward Los Muertos. In the classroom, Chaski sits behind the teacher's desk, hands folded, while an older man stands before him and sobs.

"Mi Juancito," the man says. "No tengo otro hijo, ¿me entiende?" He holds his hat over his heart, bows his head when Chaski slides something across the desk. Everything is as Leo left it: the faded map of Peru, half a dozen student desks, and an old flippable blackboard marked with verb conjugations: *I have, You have, He/She has.* "What will I do?" the man says as he takes the money. "My spouse, she died in the war."

When he leaves, Chaski looks up to meet Leo's stare. "I hope you're happy," she says. "I hope that picture in the newspaper was worth it. How much are you paying the families, anyway?"

His eyes follow her across the room. "Leonora—"

"Did you read the story in *El Comercio*? They said it was a street gang that burned those cars. 'Delincuentes.' They didn't mention 'viene el Cuatro.' You didn't get your free publicity. That man's son died for nothing. For your victory."

"Juancito isn't dead, only missing—"

"Like Ernesto."

Chaski sighs and looks away. "Nobody made the government do these things."

"But you knew they would," Leo says.

Wordless, he stands and clasps his hands behind his neck. He's taller than she realized, his arms thin, almost fragile, one wrist encircled by a loop of red and gold yarn. When he stops at the blackboard, scanning the scrawled vocabulary, the plaintive tilt of his head makes Leo regret her accusation.

"If somebody burns your car, that means you kill their baby?" he says. "If somebody takes your food, you break their arms? Why someone can't defend his house without dying?

"Juancito's father, Eulogio? He had a business, a good business, selling books outside the university. After Tarata the police came and took everything. They beat him until he almost died. So Juancito left school and went to work delivering pizza in San Isidro. Only tips, and he has to buy the gas. He makes twenty dollars a week. Maybe twenty-five. But when someone steals the scooter, the dueño makes him pay the whole thing, six hundred dollars, or he says he'll call his brother in the National Police and denounce Juancito as a terrorist. Nalda, who is also missing? Her cousin was at La Cantuta when the death squad came. They don't kill him, but since he leaves the jail his mother has to feed him with a spoon. Her father works in a copper mine in Cajamarca. He sends one hundred dollars a month and comes home twice a year. The mining company makes a hundred million a year, and all of it leaves the country, because the dictator sold the rights. Nothing for Peruvians. Nothing for his own people."

He delivers this speech in a quiet voice, staring at the floor in disbelief. Out the window, a bus rattles past on the highway, the squeal of a cracked engine belt trailing toward Lima. When he looks up at Leo, she turns away.

"That doesn't make it right," she mutters, hating herself, this useless anger. Chaski had known Ernesto, too. He'd known all of them. The mockery of the man with the maimed arm still rankles. He was right: she didn't understand, not really. She hadn't lived through any of it. Still, part of her wants to retort: *But I'm here!*

"If there's violence, let it be on their conscience," she says. "We're supposed to be better."

With a tired smile, Chaski untwists the chain around his neck. "If you're fighting for your life, how do you worry about keeping your hands clean?"

In silence, they straighten the classroom, moving desks, pushing the blackboard into the corner. As Chaski gathers the placards, folding the smiling faces of Ernesto, Nalda, and Juancito under one arm, Leo's heart swells with sympathy: he's young, smart, good-looking in a puppyish way. Surely he didn't want to be here, she thinks. He must have ambitions, desires, dreams of being someone else. But he's put those things aside. Has she ever been so selfless? Has anything she's done not come back to herself?

"What will you do now?" she asks as they walk outside.

Chaski shrugs. "They don't tell me yet. It's not for me to decide."

"Who? Who decides?" She thinks of the woman in the cemetery, her flaming bottle. Of the graffito that appeared on the steps of the National Cathedral the morning after the massacre: *Solo lo necesario*. And the number 4.

"Why do you want to know this?"

"I want to understand," she says. Then, blushing, "Where are these people? Maybe I want to meet them."

A dust-coated combi pulls to the side of the road and lets off passengers. Beyond it stands an abandoned playground, netless basketball hoops and a solitary picnic table. In three months she's never seen children playing there. When the combi pulls away, two old women in bowler hats pick their way through the trash and dust. Chaski's eyes follow them until they've vanished into the neighborhood.

"They're everywhere."

3

In the first weeks of writing this story, I put together something I called the Leo File: an assortment of news clippings and photos and transcripts, downloaded documents, printouts from microfiche, lists and timelines, notes to myself. At first, as the folder got thicker, I felt reassured, a soldier going into battle with a pack full of gear. I spent hours staring at grainy images, reading page after page of history, politics, waiting for the story to open itself and let me in.

But soon the Leo File came to oppress me—there was just so much, every article or photo led to others, every answer raised a dozen more questions. I bought a second folder, then an accordion file, but it, too, kept growing, expanding in the vacuum of my ignorance. Everything seemed relevant, everything in the last fifty years connected to Leonora somehow. With so much information, how could I ever begin?

Among more familiar images of Leonora—shouting at the press conference, being led in handcuffs to a waiting helicopter—I found one taken at a café in Miraflores. Here she is, relaxing at a sidewalk table, smiling over a bottle of Inca Kola. Her face is flushed and healthy, bare shoulders splashed with sun, a copy of Fanon's *The Wretched of the Earth* lying next to a vase with a fake pink carnation. She could be anyone: a college student on semester abroad, a backpacker taking a day's leisure. The undated photo ran in the *Bergen Record*, her parents' local paper, during the trial. From the decorations in the park behind her, I'd guess it was taken soon after New Year's, 1998.

I'd guess she was there on Chaski's instructions. That it was Chaski who'd told her to order the foul-tasting Inca Kola—*No ice, no glass*—and then to wait. He hadn't said anything more. It seems plausible, this first meeting, even necessary. Or did I read it in a novel by Graham Greene?

She'd imagined a smoke-filled warren, maybe underground, a metal door, a password. But the Café Haiti is bright and loud, crowded with locals in designer sunglasses, European tourists who leave expensive cameras right on the table. Across the street the prim park bustles with pedestrians, sidewalk easels, nannies pushing strollers. Then as now, Miraflores, with its broad avenidas and sweet, peppery ocean air, is worlds away from Los Arenales. The jewelry boutiques and department stores would not seem out of place on Fifth Avenue or in Union Square. If her mother could see her now, Leo thinks, she'd feel much better.

She waits more than an hour, sipping the nasty soda and watching schoolchildren and businessmen walk past. She tries to look confident and casual, trustworthy. More than once she resolves to leave, remembering suddenly the woman in the ski mask racing through Los Muertos—that wasn't what Leo wanted, not someone she could ever be. But Ernesto and the others are still missing, she reminds herself. For all their persistence Nancy and her friends haven't heard anything, not even confirmation of his arrest. To do nothing is impossible, immoral, she reminds herself, staring blankly at her book. To let it be other people's problem, other people's lives. That's not why she came to Peru.

When she looks up, a waiter is standing over her, arms crossed. "¿No viene tu amigo?" he says. Thick and broad-chested, not quite tall, he wears a tiny silver ring in one ear, a thatch of dark hair at his chin. His eyes are a surprising cool blue. "Your friend, he doesn't come?"

"Soon," she says, checking an invisible watch.

"Sorry," he says in English. "You keep this table, you gotta spend more money."

She rolls her eyes, picks up her book. "Where does it say that?"

Then he's sitting across from her, arms folded on the back of a chair. "Perros, son hombres, no? Men are dogs." He's Leo's age, maybe younger, his voice low and swampy, something predatory in his smile. "You meet someone in a discoteca last night, maybe go back to the hotel with him, now he doesn't want to see you. Qué terrible."

"Excuse me? It's none of your business. Déjame en paz," she says. The oversweet drink has begun to sit heavily in her stomach. All afternoon a tingling headache has lurked at the base of her scalp. "Leave me alone. I just want something to drink."

"Inca Kola," he says.

"Is it a problem?"

He shakes his head slowly. "No problem, Soltera. Only you pay now, okay?"

She ignores the insult—soltera, *spinster*—and takes out two filthy bills, worn cottony thin. He gives a mock bow and walks to the back of the café, stands against the bar with one foot on the rail. Over his shoulder, he says something to the bartender, who looks her way and laughs. She tries to ignore them, to focus on her book, but the sourness in her stomach has tightened to a small sharp ache, like a hot pebble. She'd bought lunch at a street market: a bowl of thick soup with a webbed, pimply chicken foot floating in the murk. She'd drunk every drop, gratified by the old cook's approving stare.

When the waiter comes back he lays one of the bills flat on the table. "Lo siento, Soltera. We don't accept these."

"What?"

"It's counterfeit."

"No, it's not," she says. Just that morning she'd changed her last dollars on the street, haggling the rate with a slow-eyed young woman and her calculator. "What about the other one?"

He smooths the bill on the table, scratches at a corner. "Qué pain in the ass," he mutters. "You got a credit card?"

"No." She fumbles in her pocket. "This is crazy." Two well-coiffed women at the next table watch and whisper behind their hands. The heat in her belly gives a sudden stab. She doesn't know if the waiter is flirting or just tormenting her for fun—it wouldn't be the first time she's been the object of what limeños consider their rough charm.

"You kidding? Your father didn't give you a credit card? He lets his little girl walk around this dangerous place with no money?"

"I have money," she says.

"Yeah? How much?" He leans in and speaks quietly, his eyes dark now and unblinking. "Can't do anything without money, Soltera. Maybe you got some back at the hotel? You want to call the Sheraton?"

"I'm not staying at the Sheraton."

"No shit? Where you staying?"

She swipes the bills off the table and closes her book. When she stands, the headache lunges across her eyes, the taste of the greasy soup bubbles into her throat. "Is there a manager I can talk to?"

"This is a good attitude," he says. "Muy princesa. Like a nice American girl."

"Keep those bills," she says. "I'll come back with the money. Te prometo."

"Now throw it at me."

"What?"

"Yes, throw the bills in my face," he says, flashing the sharklike smile. Bells are ringing all over Miraflores, swelling in her skull as though she were underwater. "Treat me like your servant, like a spoiled princess."

"I can't believe—"

"You're not listening," he says. When he touches a fingertip to the back of her hand, she flinches. "Throw the money at me and get out of here and don't ever come back. Tell Chaski no more rich gringas. Now go. But first, tell me I'm an asshole."

"Do it," he says. Her hand closes unconsciously around the wrinkled bills. His finger strokes her knuckles. "Do it in English."

"Asshole," she whispers.

"Louder."

"You're an *asshole*," she shouts, and when he straightens up laughing she flings the money in his face and snatches her book off the table.

"¡Muchas gracias, Soltera!" he calls after her, turning to the other patrons. "These gringos, ¡carajo! Who do they think they are?"

More of the parents, I think. More of what she's pushing against.

"Listen to this," Maxine says. "*A young woman, twenty-three, sexually involved with the love of her life, the President of the*

United States. The young intern wrote long love letters . . . You can't believe this lunacy. Who is this Matt Drudge person?"

"I don't know, Mom," Leo says. "It's politics. Of course it's stupid."

"No shame. 'The love of her life'? It's like a soap opera. Who cares?"

"You do, I guess."

"They'll stop at nothing, these people," Maxine says. "It's despicable."

Eyes squeezed shut, Leo squats below the hostel's payphone in her pajamas, monitoring the weather in her intestines, which is momentarily calm after three days of squalls. She's hardly left her rooftop room except to use the toilet, edging her way down unlit stairs in the middle of the night, praying she'll reach the bottom before her guts squirm and liquefy. Days of squalid lethargy, the tiny cell swelling with heat, perfused with her body's salty, loamy smell. Sirens outside, the pounding of feet on metal, the fire door flung open and laughter of backpackers—French, Australian, Dutch—returning from the clubs late at night. She sleeps in hourlong bouts, twisted in the damp sheet, her fever so high its heat lingers in the pillowcase.

But to miss the weekly phone date would be to invite a German opera of allegation and remorse, building to an aria about trust betrayed, priorities misplaced, and unthinkable parental suffering—or worse, Maxine might call the hostel directly to beg assurance from Ricky, the dueño, that her daughter has not been eaten by cannibals. Leo concentrates on breathing while Maxine's indignation spools out, her mindless allegiance to Bill Clinton puzzling as it's ever been. Hadn't he thrown millions of poor people off the welfare rolls? Didn't he kowtow to the same neoliberals and investment bankers who'd bankrupted half of the developing world? But to raise such trifles with Maxine—the erstwhile campus activist, the Red-Diaper baby—is to provoke a recital of platitudes about the "little people" and "Camelot" and Leo, dysenteric, doesn't have the strength.

"Maybe you should run for office," her mother is saying. "Of course it would be easier if you had a law degree. You sound tired, Leo. Are you alright? You have to be careful, baby, you have no idea what you could catch down there."

Leo clutches the phone and squints into the lobby's gloom, the waxed, checkerboard floors and winding staircase of an old colonial house gone to wreck. Ricky watches from the reception desk, looking up from his heavy, leatherbound ledger.

Now it's David's turn: "We worry about you, sweetheart. Why don't you ask someone you work with to recommend a doctor? I'll pay for it."

"I'll be fine," she groans. "I'm already starting to feel better. Anyway, the office is closed for a while."

In fact, the office is closed indefinitely. Last week an article in *El Comercio* named Oportunidad Para Todos among several groups being investigated for their role in the Los Muertos Massacre, and in the "coordinated lawlessness" of the funeral procession, at which nearly a hundred arrests were made.

"There must be private clinics. Good ones, for people like you."

"People like me?"

"It's your health, Leo," he sighs. "It's no time to stand on principle."

"Who am I, Dad? Am I a celebrity? A visiting dignitary?"

"Go to one of the nice neighborhoods. That's where the best doctors are. Please, Leo," he says. "Do you have any idea what your mother's going to put me through?"

She slumps to the floor, head knocking the wall loudly enough that Ricky looks up. *The nice neighborhoods. The best doctors.* He doesn't have to say the rest of it: *Where the Jews live.* She's been hearing it all her life. Unlike Maxine, Leo's father cares nothing for politics—"They're all crooks," he'd long ago diagnosed, correctly—but his sense of the world comes filtered through an idea of Jewish exceptionalism as unshakable as it is infuriating. At least Maxine goes to synagogue once a year, to say Kaddish for her father. David wouldn't even know how to get there. His Jewishness has no spiritual content, no historical consciousness. But drop the name of a famous actor or sports hero and he's sure to ask, "Did you know he's Jewish?" He considers it a travesty that Philip Roth hasn't won the Nobel Prize. His most urgent criticism of Henry Kissinger is that he renounced his religion.

"Dad, it's a stomach infection, not a national emergency. Nobody cares who I am. I'm nobody."

"You're somebody to me, Leo," he says. "You're my daughter and I love you."

"¿Todo bien?" Ricky asks when she bangs the phone into the cradle.

Leo hauls herself toward the lobby bathroom. "Mis padres," she says, and swirls a finger around her ear—a gesture she knows immediately to be Maxine's. "Locos."

An hour later she forces herself into jeans, girds herself with a dry roll and a banana and sets off into the sad rumble of doves, the wash of January heat. In a farmacia on Abancay, shivering under fluorescent lights, she pantomimes her distress until the bent old pharmacist shakes a dozen pills from a box. Leo's face has thinned, her cheekbones sharpened. Short of breath, a little dizzy, she makes herself walk faster. She doesn't need a doctor or a nice neighborhood; if the fever won't leave her, she'll have to vanquish it, stomp it out on the grim, clogged avenues.

Down constricted cobblestone streets puddled with water and piss, where vendors hawk cheap schoolbooks, wristwatches, contraband blue jeans, plastic bowls of every imaginable size. Moneychangers and pickpockets prowl and swarm, drawing back when she meets their eyes. She walks hours without stopping—no map, no destination—ignoring the stares of shopkeepers, bored cops. Through neighborhoods of silent, unused factories, others of long streets crammed with tiendas, crowded lunch counters, used appliances, crates on the sidewalk filled with lengths of pipe, pirated books, inflatable plastic toys. The hot sun nearly invisible, pale and distant, Leo rests briefly, sitting on benches below statues of winged angels or horsemen, catches herself drowsing, flings herself into motion again. She's determined to understand this city of moldering colonial mansions and concrete eyesores, of sedans with tinted windows and dark-skinned boys who thread into traffic selling newspapers, chewing gum, plastic bags of colored liquid. She's determined to know it from the inside.

"Travelers should be alert to lingering and unpredictable terrorist activity, as well as rampant street crime," read the notice her mother sent: the U.S. State Department's advisory for Peru, a diplomatic translation of Maxine's bourgeois hysteria. Leo knows she's just as guilty. Hasn't she stayed at Ricky's hostel, with its flow of white-faced tourists, rather than take a room in Los Arenales? Hadn't she fled Los Muertos at the first sign of trouble? Her life, she decides, has been a series of gestures, edging ever closer to the line, too afraid to cross. If she's ever to help anyone, she'll have to rid herself of this fear.

That night she sits on the roof of the hostel, her feet swollen and blistered, listening to the news on an old tune box Ricky loaned her. On her lap lies a copy of Mariátegui's *Seven Interpretive Essays on Peruvian Reality*, an English translation she picked up at a stall in Breña. On every side the city is an immensity of orange lights muted by humidity, twinkling to the syncopated noise of car alarms, sacked by the meaty smell of the river a few blocks to the north.

"I've been in this war for a long time," says a twangy voice on the radio, one of Bill Clinton's advisors. "It's a vendetta, that's all it is. The President's political enemies out to get him."

"Who's going to win that war? Who's going to win it and why?"

Leo lays the book on her lap. Three weeks, she thinks. Three weeks since Ernesto was taken, since the people of Los Muertos lost everything. The country is moving on already, distracting itself with trifles. How many limeños remember Ernesto's name?

The first pages of Mariátegui's book say it all: invasion, conquest, centuries of race-based brutality. Having stolen all the arable land, the Spaniards made their own laws, hired their own thugs, brutalized the native residents who stayed on as tenant farmers. They forbade the cultivation of food crops needed in Peru, preferring the sugar and cotton that fetched high prices abroad. They grew ever wealthier, ever more powerful, while the land's rightful owners starved.

If Peru is to progress, Mariátegui wrote in 1928, *it is imperative this feudalism be liquidated.*

Leo stayed at the Hostal Macondo, three blocks from Lima's main plaza, from October 3, 1997 to February 8 of the following year. One wonders why she never took a room in Los Arenales, as most of Oportunidad Para Todos' volunteers did, given the long commute. When I put this question to Manrique "Ricky" Díaz Poma, the Macondo's proprietor from 1996 to 2000, he frowned as if at a nuisance.

"Who knows?" he told me. "She was different, that one. Muy rara."

On the night of her arrival, she'd rung the bell sometime after two AM only to learn the room she'd reserved by fax had been given away hours earlier. "But I have to sleep," she'd said, pressing back panic. The hostel was on a badly lit corner, deep in the maze of the immense city. The taxi was long gone. Shamefaced, she slid a twenty-dollar bill across the ledger. "¿Por favor?"

Ricky rubbed sleep from his face, took a blanket from a pile, and led her up three flights, down halls littered with energy-bar wrappers and beer bottles, through a third-floor fire exit and up a last narrow staircase to the roof. The amber lights of Lima ran into the hills like the arms of a starfish. The room was a windowless storage shed with a flimsy tin door and a padlock. The springs of the narrow cot sang like a swarm of crickets; one bare bulb spun a web of shadows at her feet.

"It's fine," she said. "Muchas gracias." Ricky bowed sardonically and handed her the key. Two days later he offered her a real room, with a window and a closet, but she turned it down. She'd grown attached to her rooftop cell, proud of the modesty of her needs. She never forgave him for having seen her fear.

On the sixth day of her fever, Ricky knocks on the metal door of her room, rousing her from heavy sleep. "Please come now," he says, his face stern, mistrustful. Achy and blurred, she wonders if she forgot to pay him. "Someone waits for you."

In the lobby, she finds Chaski staring bemusedly at the gaudy old furniture. Ricky walks quickly back to the front desk, surveying the lobby as though to make sure nothing was stolen.

"Sick?" Chaski says, as he and Leo make their way upstairs. The air is hot and stale, layers of cigarette smoke hanging in gray sunlight. On the second floor, a woman stands in her underwear, screaming in Italian at someone inside her room.

"Still getting used to the food," Leo says.

"Many tourists have this problem."

"I'm not a tourist."

His laughter is warm and bright, without mockery. "Yes, you are still a tourist."

The air is cooler on the roof. When the enormous bells of the church across the street toll the hour, she can feel the vibrations in her teeth. Chaski stops at the door to her cell and peers into the dark and musty lair.

"This is where you live?"

"What did you expect? The Sheraton?"

He looks almost crestfallen. All at once she remembers a dream—he was standing on a beach at dusk, a Hula-Hoop gyrating at his hips. The screech of seagulls loud and rhythmic, like sirens; when she looked closer the hula-hoop was just an oily old tire. She yanks the sheets from the bed and flaps them to drive out the sweaty air. It's the first she's heard from Chaski since the abortive meeting at the Café Haiti. In lucid moments she's cursed him, cursed his obnoxious friend and wondered what she'll do next—something better, with smarter people. But where would she begin?

"Did you come here to criticize my room?" she says now. "Or do you have another friend you want me to meet? The last one was really nice."

He stifles a smile. "Comrade Julian doesn't know you. You can understand this?"

"Comrade Julian is an asshole. I don't even know why I was there."

He paces her tiny room, stooping to read the spines of the books piled on the chair: the Fanon, Gabriel's *Bicentennial of Blood*, a leather-bound copy of *Moby-Dick* her father randomly gave her as a going-away present. In the back of her mind she can hear her mother warning her about "strange men," but Chaski's crooked smile is disarming. Since the day at Nancy's office she's felt oddly comfortable around him, even protective—as if they'd known each other a long time and, for whatever reason, he looked up to her.

"The chicos are still missing," he says. "There are helicopters over Los Arenales every day."

"What am I supposed do about it?" Leo says, wilting onto the damp sheets.

"This is a good question." He frowns at the flimsy walls, the gummy gray floor. "How much you pay here?"

Something in his tone catches her attention and she sits up, quickly regretting the sudden movement. "I'm not rich. Not all Americans are rich. Is that what you thought?"

"No? How much does Nancy pay you?"

"What does that have to do with anything?"

Carefully, he sits at the far end of the bed, slightly hunched, hands in his lap like a schoolboy. "People help in whatever way they can," he says, shrugging. He stares at the floor, at the twirl of shadows from the bulb overhead. When he looks up, she's reminded again of how young he is—twenty or twenty-one, she guesses. But his eyes, clear and earnest, are much older. "Julian made a mistake. He has to be careful, of course. But he needs you, Leonora. We need someone like you."

"For what?" she says, just as a new torpor makes her head loll. She lays back on the stinking sheets, the fever reaching out for her again.

"Soon," Chaski is saying. He's standing over her now, a worried expression on his face. "First you get healthy, OK? Don't worry about anything. I'll come back soon."

After what seems like several minutes, she realizes she hasn't answered him. She tries to sit up, but her body has become part of the mattress: warm and damp and leaden. The bells are ringing again, shuddering the tin roof, swelling the room with echoes. When he speaks, she can't find him in the dark.

"Don't return to the café, Leo. Stay here, or go to a museum, or the beach. Go shopping. You're a tourist, remember? And don't speak Spanish. Even to the dueño."

"¿Por qué?" she manages, dissolving into the fever. "¿Por qué?"

"Because you're a gringa. This is what they expect of you. So we let them believe."

¡SINVERGÜENZA! reads another clipping in the Leo File: SHAMELESS! In this photo, printed from the archives of a defunct tabloid, an old woman in the sturdy shoes, canvas skirts, and knee-high stockings of a campesina stands on a bench in the Plaza de Armas. Her thick gray braid hangs over one bare shoulder. There's something unhinged in the pits of her eyes, her stretched and toothless mouth. Behind and around her, demonstrators hoist placards, encircled by

cops in white helmets, backdropped by the old, canary-yellow buildings with their ornate wood balconies. The forbidding Presidential
Palace, with its gray stone and high, spiked fence, is just visible at
the photo's edge. With one hand the woman waves her brassiere
overhead; her heavy breasts stare at the camera like an accusation.

My friend Yesenia Francia Durán recognized the image immediately. "The Protesta de Tetas," she said. "I was there!"

In 1998 Francia was teaching chemistry at a private school in San
Borja, participating in political street theater on weekends. "We live
at this time a double life," she told me. "You have to be so careful.
Everyone knows there is a line. You think you know where it is. You
think you know which person you are. But you don't know."

Her theater troupe was called Bufón: the Jester. "We go to the
Plaza San Martín and draw a line, one side is Democracy, with
games and dancing, the other side is Dictatorship, everyone with
blindfold and tape on the mouth. Or we stand across the street
from Congress, holding big mirrors for people to see themselves."
Groups like Bufón were officially tolerated, proof to the outside
world that freedom had returned to Peru. But they knew their existence was provisional. Like everyone in Lima, they knew they were
being watched. One morning, all the students in her class brought
in photographs they'd received in the mail. All the photos were of
Francia: walking on a street near her house, waiting at a dark bus
stop, shopping. In every one, she was alone.

"The government knew everything I did," she said. "They knew
me better than I knew myself."

The "Protesta de Tetas," as it came to be known, was organized
by the Abuelitas de la Ausencia—the Grandmothers of Absence—a
group that had been demonstrating since the end of the war to
demand information about missing family members. A ragged
assortment of other groups, including Bufón, had joined the march,
which Francia remembers indistinctly, as just one of many humiliating failures. When I asked if Leonora, living only blocks away, might
have been there, Francia shrugged and smiled her charming smile.

Yes, why not?

She might well have stumbled upon it, heading back through
the city center after another day of aimless walking. The fever

sputtering out, a calm hardiness reasserting itself in her appetite, a pleasant ache in her calves. From blocks away, she might have heard the swell of voices, the clamor of pots and pans, felt the energy carried on the air. She would have known she shouldn't be there. Chaski had been clear. But it had been a month since Neto was taken—what had Chaski, or Julian, or anyone else, done about it?

By the time she crosses into the Plaza, there are three women standing on benches, bras in hand. Two others balance on the lip of the giant brass fountain, supported by arms from below. They gesture to the crowd, keening imprecations at the cops—*¡Asesinos! Murderers! Liars!*—who stare back uneasily and flick cigarettes into the flowerbeds. Ernesto's face bobs on a handful of placards, along with Nalda's and Juancito's—alien faces, made strange by their familiarity.

You would lie to your own mothers! shouts one of the women.
They would kill their mothers! cries another.
Their mothers are whores! says a man in the crowd.

When a line of mounted police emerges from between two buildings, one of the women raises a mischievous eyebrow and puts her hands on her hips, provoking a ripple of laughter. From somewhere in the crowd rises the first strains of an old song—

> *Vengan todos a ver, ¡Ay, vamos a ver!*
> *En la plazuela de Huanta, amarillito ¡Flor de*
> *Retama!*

—and the onlookers stiffen in response, quickly taking it up. Old men fish scraps of red fabric from their pockets and wave them overhead.

> *The blood of the people perfumes the air,*
> *With jasmine, violets, geraniums, and daisies—*
> *And gunpowder! And dynamite!*
> *And gunpowder! And dynamite!*

It's an old protest song, "Flor de Retama," a lament for student demonstrators massacred by the military regime in the 1960s. Years later, during a week-long lockdown, Leo's cellmate will teach her the words: *Oh come, come all, to see! They've come to kill the students, the proud students of Huanta* . . . But now she understands only that it's a provocation: the line of cops is tightening, their eyes beneath the white helmets growing hard.

She knows she shouldn't be there. *You're a tourist*, Chaski said. *Let them believe.* At first she thrilled to the intrigue, the sense of infiltration: she was undercover in Lima, observing without being seen. But he hasn't been back in a week. Here, now, something is happening—the first tentative surges of the crowd, the seductive smell of adrenaline and sweat and fear. Could he really expect her to do nothing? Who benefitted, other than the government, when good people stood idly by?

A loud whistle, piercing and quick. Another—and then an old man limps into the gap between cops and demonstrators. "Don't look!" he says and whistles twice more. "Don't look at her! Sons of bitches, close your eyes!"

A restless hush slowly takes hold. Bent nearly double, in a gray blazer and a fedora, the old man looks uncertainly back at the crowd. His long face and white whiskers, the dark mole at one temple, remind Leo of her Grandpa Carol.

"Close your eyes," he cries, shaking a finger at the cops. "This is your mother! You want to look at your mother?" One of the half-clothed women turns full circle, giving everyone gathered a proper look. Laughter rattles among the restless crowd. "Shut up, fools," the old man says. "You allow this indecency?"

"Get out of the way, Papi!" a woman shouts.

"Go home, viejito!"

"You let them look at your mother? You want to fuck your mother, you pigs?" One of the demonstrators reaches for his arm but the old man shrugs him aside. Furiously, he searches his pockets and, finding nothing, strips off his wristwatch and flings it at the police line, where it smacks against a plastic shield and falls to the ground.

"Close your eyes! Close your eyes!" he cries, limping past the cops, and when he stoops to retrieve his watch a foot shoots out and kicks him squarely in the ass—he staggers forward, splaying face-down at the edge of a flowerbed, his fedora nudged by the wind just out of reach.

The pause is long enough for Leo to suck in breath—then the crowd swells forward with a howl, a mass of bodies accelerating, expanding in every direction. From somewhere behind her she can still hear singing—*¡Vengan todos a ver! ¡Ay, vamos a ver!*—but now the clang and pop of tear gas canisters hitting the flagstones, screams and moans, the crack of wood on iron. She shouldn't be there—she knows it, she should go back to the hostel, write a postcard, do as she was told. But when she spots three of the old women, small and pale, marching arm in arm toward a line of armored vehicles, a flutter of alarm rises in her chest. *A tourist.* That's what she'd been at Los Muertos. A thoughtless spectator. Why did she always stand aside while others took the risks?

The old man limps through the flowerbed, holding a bloody rag to the side of his head. Next to him, a cop raises his truncheon. With a sudden whoosh, the tanks fire their water cannons, long spraying jets that arc over the old women's heads and splatter to the pavement like a sudden ovation—a warning shot, a threat, and as the tanks retarget, lining those flimsy bodies in their sights, it's as if the decision were made somewhere outside her, some collective mind moving Leo's body toward the place she's needed most. She's running now, not knowing what she'll do only that she'll finally do *something*—the giant fountain ahead of her, its bowl dry and coated with green and white scum, one of the old women still standing, doubled over and retching in the smoke, and just as Leo reaches the concrete platform, reaching for a handhold to climb up next to her someone grabs Leo's elbow, drags her off balance from the fountain, rushes her through a flowerbed footless and blind and shoves her backward to the grass.

"What do you think you're doing?" he says. Gasping, one leg twisted under her, she looks up to find a man with a mop of curly hair standing over her. "Are you crazy?"

"I wanted . . . quería . . . ayudar," she says. "I was trying to help."

"You think this is a party?" he says, looming over her, shifting when she moves, blocking her from the view of the policemen. He's fair and slender, mid-thirties, a strong chin and full, almost feminine lips. "This is no place for you. Get out of here now, before they see you."

"Las mujeres . . ." she stammers, twisting to look for the old women, "ellas están en peligro—"

"English!" he hisses, bending toward her. "He told you only speak English, no?" As she stares, uncomprehending, one of the cops detaches from the line and starts toward them, peering suspiciously. "Are you going to do what you're told?" the man says. "We can't help you if you don't know how to listen."

She nods, heart banging. "Sí—yes, okay."

"Then get back to the hostel. Nobody can see you here. You hear me?" He watches her until he's sure she understands. Then, sensing the cop approaching, he straightens and raises his voice. "Stupid fucking gringa, go back to your hotel. Go hike the Inca Trail!"

Again the roar of the water cannons, the thud of a baton against flesh. She clears her throat, mustering all her confusion. "I just wanted to know what was happening," she says, biting back tears that may even be real. "I just wanted to see."

"You want to see something?" he shouts, grabbing his crotch. "Look at this!"

When he takes off across the plaza, she eases herself to her feet, sodden and ridiculous. Her face burns, her breath comes in nervous half-sobs. She ignores the crude laughter of the cops, who stare at her wet shirt, her mud-smeared jeans. The smoke and gas have begun to lift, tanks clearing the streets with blasts of water, backing off to let the horses prance. No one stops her when she limps out of the plaza. She appears in none of the photographs of that ordinary day.

When she gets back to the hostel, filthy and wet, the lobby is full of Swedes—hale, towering explorers clustered around the couches, their trussed backpacks heaped on the checkerboard floor. She threads her way toward the stairs, but a glance at the television stops her, the sight of a familiar streetscape rooting her in place.

"Be quiet," she says. "Everybody, please. ¡Cállate!"

A reporter stands at the edge of a deserted playground, a small crowd gathered nearby. Police tape runs along the sidewalk and surrounds the concrete bungalow in the background. The sound is too low, the reporter talking too quickly for Leo to make out. Across the bottom of the screen, the caption reads, *Se encuentra tres cuerpos en Los Arenales.*

Three bodies found.

"Please," she says. "Please, shut up." But the Swedes are oblivious, inspecting their maps, lashing ice axes to their packs. Leo sits on the bottom step, transfixed by the familiar image of the playground—its rusty swings and forlorn basketball hoops, the drab office where she'd spent so many days. Early that morning a scavenger had come across a trash heap in a corner of the lot, covered in new-looking cardboard he thought he could sell. He had not thought anything was amiss until he saw the shoe.

"Be quiet," Leo pleads. Ricky remembers wondering if she was sick again. "Please, you have to see this."

Two men and a woman. Late teens or early twenties. They'd probably died the day before. Their skulls had multiple fractures, their half-buried bodies showed signs of torture: burn marks, broken ribs, long welts where they'd smashed against restraints.

Let it be a mistake, she thinks. *Please, let it be someone else.* When the camera scans the small crowd, she examines every face, desperately hoping to recognize his shy grin, his solemn eye. *My Neto,* Nancy had called him. Leo remembers her steely focus, like a lance she held pointed at a thundercloud. *My Neto,* she'd said.

Of course she'd known he wasn't coming back.

4

"You're being obstinate, Leonora," Maxine says. "Will you please go to a doctor? This is exactly what I worried about. I told your father not to let you go, but he had—"

"*Let me* go?"

"Just get yourself checked out, young lady. Take the credit card and find yourself a good doctor. This is your health. I don't care what it costs."

"What credit card? What are you talking about?"

An odd little pause. "You never found the credit card?"

A group of Israelis tromp through the lobby in a blur of harem pants and cigarette smoke. Bill Clinton waggles a finger on the television while Ricky polishes the front desk and pretends not to listen. Everywhere, life persists in its absurdity and self-absorption: soap operas, traffic disputes, her mother's endless prattle. No one stops to see what's happening all around them. No one cares. That's why Ernesto is dead, she thinks, resisting the urge to scream at them all—because no one can be bothered to care.

Four days since they found the bodies. There's been no word from Chaski, no sign anything will be done. The police have already closed the investigation: *Inconclusive*, they said. Possibly the same gangs who caused the Los Muertos disturbance. Possibly a retaliation. Leo can't sleep, the shadows full of movement, the resurgent fever lurking in every dank recess. When she finally nods off she dreams of children running, of bodies broken and lit on fire. She lurches awake with the stink of burnt flesh in her throat.

This is no place for you, the man in the plaza said. She knows he was right. Chaski, her mother—everyone was right. She doesn't belong here, was a fool to think she could change anything. The women of Los Arenales are no better off for their handful of English phrases. The trenches she dug are still empty; no one has the money to lay the pipes. She's accomplished nothing, benefitted no one. She's worse than a tourist: she's not even having a good time.

A new voice comes on the line, jokey and self-assured: "Hey, Leo. How's life in the Third World?"

"Matt?" she says, bracing for a wave of fatigue. "What are you doing there?"

"Just popping in for Sunday brunch, give the parental units a thrill."

She hasn't heard her brother's voice since the wedding and is surprised at how adult he sounds—more solid, somehow, than the people around her. It had been a shock, this grown-up Matthew; when she'd seen him under the chuppah, holding hands with Samira, she'd hardly recognized the man he'd become—as if somehow he'd leapfrogged her and now she was the younger sibling, looking up in resentment and awe.

"Mom says you got malaria," he says. "That sucks."

"I'll live. How was your honeymoon?"

Rome, he says, was "a nonstop party," Venice a disappointment, "too much attitude for me." Then the long, lazy ocean crossing that brought them back to New York. "Sami won like two grand at the roulette table. It practically covered our whole bar tab! Do they have casinos in Peru? Maybe we'll come down there."

Leo eyes the Israelis, who've draped themselves over the lobby furniture and spread playing cards on the table. "I don't think you'd like it here."

"Come on, Leo. I'm not Dad," he says. Then, lowering his voice, "Seriously, though—what's it like?"

The question brings on an unexpected surge of loneliness. How long has it been since she and her brother shared secrets? For a moment she wants to tell him: about naked toddlers wandering amid trash heaps, mute beggars outside government buildings, water cannons and heartbroken old men. But these things would mean as little to Matt as stories about Atlantis: fantastical tales of creatures in another dimension, to be wondered at, even pitied, then forgotten.

"This friend of mine," she says, "he disappeared—"

Just then the Israelis erupt into wild cheers, bottles and ashtrays toppling in the commotion. On the television, a soccer player sprints barechested across the field, waving his shirt over his head, mouth open in a bellicose howl.

When they quiet down, Matt is saying goodbye. He has to get back to the city, to prepare for a Monday presentation. "Send me a postcard, Leo. And be careful, okay?"

She hangs up, defeat welling in her throat. Three and a half months here. What has any of it meant? She imagines her parents and brother sitting down to brunch, talking about the same old things, moving in patterns established a lifetime ago. Does she even exist in that world anymore? Or has she become one of those strange creatures—a story to be told, even marveled at, but not believed?

"¿Todo bien?" Ricky says.

She forces her mouth into a mirthless smile. "No comprendo," she says.

But is it enough? Is any of this enough?

A few photographs, some demonstrations, suggestions in the Leo File—but how does she get from there to the house in Pueblo Libre, from Pueblo Libre to a prison 14,000 feet above the sea? Chaski, her family, even Ernesto, even the death of a friend—such things don't lead to the Cuarta Filosofía any more surely than a butterfly leads to a car bomb. Why did she cross the line?

At her civilian retrial, in 2002, Manrique "Ricky" Díaz Poma described Leonora as friendly, if solitary and high-strung. He remembered her dowdy glasses and how she carried herself: hunched slightly forward, as though to investigate a faint sound. He testified that he hadn't seen anything strange about her work in Los Arenales. What made him suspicious was her decision to live on the roof.

"This was where we sometimes allowed the cleaning woman to sleep," he said. "Why would a gringa from a good family choose to live there?"

I've seen the ledger, Ricky's giant leather journal, traced my fingernail back through months and years until I found her scrawled signature. I was lucky—the Macondo was to be demolished the very next week, to make way for a new Zara. The current dueña regarded me with irritation, as if I were a cross between a building inspector and a mouse. But standing at that high desk, in that dusty old foyer, I felt briefly like a real reporter, doing what I was supposed to do, finding something that could pass for the truth.

Gracias, amigo lindo, she wrote when she checked out. *¡Venceremos!*

Kilroy was here.

So what?

That night she sits up late, sewing buttons on a torn shirt with quick stabs of the needle, folding laundry, sweeping her room with swift, vicious strokes. There are no more sudden tears, only a profound disorientation that intensifies when she looks across the roof at the glimmering city. The radio plays old pop songs, interrupted by flashes of news. Every so often the announcer repeats the three names—*Juan Vargas Quispe, 23 años; Nalda Calderón Flores, 23 años; Ernesto Paucar Rojas, 19 años*—already just words, faceless entries in the record. History.

But he was her friend. Leo remembers the chaste way they would kiss in greeting, how his thigh pressed against hers on the bus. What is the relationship between that person and a corpse? How can a name on the radio replace an entire life?

And what about her life? What does it amount to? For as long as she can remember she's wanted to justify it, to be worthy of it, to do *something* for *someone*. For a month or two she thought she'd found a way. But she was not living in the same world as Ernesto, or the old women in the plaza. She'd never really found the way in.

"Be patient," says a woman's voice. "Take a deep breath, and the truth will come out." Leo glares at the radio, considers hurling it off the roof, but Ricky would probably charge her for it. "There is a vast right-wing conspiracy. I'm very concerned about the tactics that are being used, the intense political agenda at work."

Nothing, that's what it amounts to. Her blistered hands and bleeding heart have changed nothing—just as the old women changed nothing, just as Nancy's years of work for her neighbors, putting her body between them and the abyss, couldn't even save her son's life.

But what was the alternative? Ski masks and Molotov cocktails? Crushing someone else to save yourself? She can understand the impulse, intellectually she can see why, in time, you might come to feel you had no choice. At least the masked woman in Los Muertos had stood up for herself. At least she'd extracted a price. But kill or be killed was not a choice, it was an obscenity, a degradation of Leo's every idea about justice, about humanity. Was there no third option? No better way?

She finishes straightening the room, packs her books, leaves tomorrow's clothes folded on the chair. She'll go wherever the first bus goes. Her desires, her conscience—these things are worthless, the worst kind of gringo narcissism. She'll keep moving, find someone who will put her to work. What other option is there? Just because there's nothing she can do doesn't give her the right to do nothing.

Sometime later, she wakes without knowing why. She lies still and listens: a door closing, footsteps on the stairs, whispers across the roof. Probably drunken backpackers, the Swedes smoking one last joint before their trek. Soon there's a small crowd outside her door. When she pulls on a shirt and flips the light switch, the light doesn't come.

Outside, a dozen people are gathered at the edge of the roof, faces pale against a section of the city gone dark. The sky glows damp mauve, sagging like a satin udder. The church's dark belltowers stand watch over a sea of black that stretches east into the foothills, north to the river and beyond: the anti-city, an absence stamped out of the glittering pattern.

"Fucking Peruvians," one of the Swedes says. "This better not affect my flight."

"I think the hamster running on his little wheel died," someone else says.

Leo spots Ricky and his wife and moves through the congregation of shadows, standing with them at the low wall that looks onto the churchyard.

"I'm leaving tomorrow," she tells Ricky. "Me voy." Her voice sounds too loud, as if the blackout has thrown everything out of scale. "Gracias para todo."

"¿A dónde va?"

Before she can answer, a gasp goes through the crowd, mutters. A reddish glow has sprung up along an eastern hillside, orange sparks snaking skyward. The first low rumbles arrive seconds later, heavy thuds as if from a distant battle. With a loud sizzle, a volley of white fireballs rises toward the thick clouds, the whole hillside starts to sparkle and flash, an endless and intensifying barrage that makes everyone shield their eyes.

"Puta madre," Ricky mutters. Then, to his wife: "You see?"

"What is it? What's happening?" Leo says.

"Your friend, the cholito," he says, his face dull with contempt. "Ask him."

Sirens are ringing across the city; down below, the headlights of emergency vehicles bounce through the dark neighborhood. As the turmoil of light and sound begins to ebb, Leo has the sense of walking in a dream—murmurs, hazy air, faces played in light and shadow. Moment by moment the flames on the hill contract, until they've shrunk to a legible form, surprisingly clear, a silver sign seething in the dark:

4

"Adiós, Leonora," Ricky says. "Cuídese bien." He shakes her hand mechanically, already dismissing her, another name in the ledger he'd just as soon forget.

For a long time after, Leo stands at the wall, overlooking the darkness. She knows she won't sleep tonight. The bright lesion shimmers silently on the distant hillside—a message for someone, or a warning. She waits until the others have gone down—in the sudden stillness she could be floating or falling, she could still be asleep—then brings the chair from her room and sets it at the edge of the roof, the sign seared on her retinas, still there when she closes her eyes, when she rests her head atop the cool slate wall, still there hours later when the fire burns itself out.

5

"To narrativize is to dehumanize."

So begins Gabriel Zamir's monograph *Genocide/Historiography*, published in 1986, three years before Leo Gelb first took his class. The book, a mishmash of theory, documentary research, personal recollection, and fictionalized "re-enactments," earned him tenure at Stanford and suspicion among historians who feared the delegitimization of their field.

> It is not enough to say, à la Zinn, that all stories have a forgotten remainder, usually [people] who have endured too much cruelty to be admitted to the conscious narrative [. . .] Even the apparent protagonists of history have always already been rendered alien and inaccessible. Once translated into an object of history, the subject is lost to history. He ceases to exist.

Zamir's point, as I understand it, is that all stories, whether imagined or based in fact, are by definition fictions, and not only due to the choices every author makes—inclusions and exclusions, emphases and compressions—nor the unconscious biases a rigorous historian knows to guard against. Zamir's thesis is more radical: the demands inherent to storytelling inevitably contaminate the source material, warping it into a form with no claim to historical reality. Readers think they're reading a "true story"—accurate, thorough, sufficient for understanding the world as it was—when in fact what they encounter is pure artifice, engineered to hold their interest, to provide a coherent sense of meaning. A "good story," in other words: with a beginning, middle, and end; with characters whose desires are clear and relatable, whose actions have logical consequences—all that history, in its unbounded chaos, is not.

"Everything is narrative," he wrote. "Thus, history is impossible."

I wonder what Zamir would think of this story, this blind and hobbled attempt at history. My efforts to understand her, to find her humanity somewhere in these grim, yellowed clippings. The longer I try to write it, to shape the muck and muddle into something alive, something true, the more I see his point. "To narrativize is to dehumanize." Who is this person on the page?

My editor is unmoved by such ethical wool-gathering.

"Screw all these ideas," he says. "Two paragraphs: good guys, bad guys, body count. Then get right to the good stuff, the stuff people want to read. Like this demonstration," he says, "the topless ladies? Why not lead with that?"

I tell him "the good stuff" can't be properly understood without context. There's a whole country to be considered, the suffering of millions. There's sociology, economics, language suppression. How disrespectful to make it all about Leonora Gelb.

"Shining Path, Sandinista, Weather Underground, same diff," he says. "Poor people with dynamite. Rich people with tanks. A few spoiled kids pissed off at their parents." Readers don't want ideas, he says. They want conflict, romance, they want to see hopes dashed, obstacles surmounted, sinners redeemed. "Wake up, dude," he says. "You're a writer. You tell stories. So get on with it."

Leo Gelb *is* the story, he says. "Find the college boyfriend who broke her heart. Figure out what her daddy did to make her so angry. 'Portrait of the Terrorist as a Young Woman'—people love that kind of shit."

I remind him that she's not a story, she's a person. That seventy thousand people died in the war. Real people. What did it matter what readers *want*?

"I get that," he says. "I admire your integrity. But I've got a business to run and you've got a deadline. Fix it."

Miraflores is quiet in the milky, failing light. Lovers walk arm in arm through the park, nannies push strollers through clusters of pigeons—everything softened by humidity, blurred like a Monet riverscape. She buys a cup of Jell-O from a vendor and savors the cold, sweet wriggling in her throat, watches the Lima gentry on their evening promenade—as if nothing has happened, no one's grandmothers have been humiliated, no one's children murdered. As if these things hadn't been done in their name.

In a corner of her room, the copy of *Moby-Dick* lies splayed and gathering dust, a shiny new American Express card taped to the inside cover. *To my own little Ahab,* her father had written. *May you never stop chasing your dreams.*

Across the street, the bright café bustles with activity: bowtied waiters glide among sidewalk tables, silver-haired men take their wives' coats. Over the clink of glasses, the sweet voice of Edith Piaf warbles into the night. A waiter opens a bottle of champagne, popping the cork with a flourish; the seated couple smiles up at him, their laughter thickened by the warm air. One more step, Leo tells herself. Take one step, then the next—or spend your life on this bench, enjoying the show.

When the waiter reappears she hurries to cross the street. "Got a light, amigo?" she calls out. She touches her lips with an imaginary cigarette. "¿Fuego?"

She almost laughs at his confusion. When Julian reaches into his apron, she says, "Oh, shit, I forgot my cigarettes! Thanks anyway"—then saunters past the cosmetics store, the frozen-yogurt shop, and into the anonymous night to wait.

For ten minutes she wanders the back streets, admiring Spanish bungalows and prim townhouses, wrought-iron balconies, high walls trussed by bougainvillea. Her vision is sharp, her sense of smell heightened—since the fever passed she's felt honed, whittled down; she moves through her surroundings watchful as a cat. At a corner, she stops before a long gray building surrounded by a wrought-iron fence. She studies the impassive facade, the arched windows and mounted security cameras that lend an air of vigilance, of dignity. When the footsteps come behind her, she doesn't turn around.

"What did I tell you?" he says, his breath hot on her neck. "I said don't go back there. Are you stupid? You don't speak fucking English?"

"What is this place?" she says, nodding at the dark building. "What's with all the cameras?"

"You don't listen to Chaski, either?" His face close to hers, the blue of his eyes surprises her, their lower lids plump with fatigue. "You're gonna get people hurt, Soltera. Maybe you'll get yourself hurt."

She moves down the fence until she can read the plaque affixed to the gate: *Sociedad de Imanuel.* She can just make out the silver mezuzah at the door: a synagogue. She hasn't been to one since they buried Grandpa Carol, two years ago. Of all the places to find herself, she thinks—remembering that morning, her mother's profound loneliness, the way her father kept a hand on Maxine's shoulder to steer her through her grief. Leo stood apart, alone with her sadness—though family friends offered kind words she was unconsoled, their tender communions held out no meaning.

"Who are you?" Julian says. "What are you doing here?"

"I'm here to help you."

He steps back, sneering in disbelief. "I don't need your help."

"Yes, you do," she says, ignoring the trembling in her knees. "Or do you want more kids getting killed like Ernesto? That's why Chaski wanted me to talk to you. Isn't it? Because you need something. So cut the bullshit and tell me." She takes a breath and lowers her voice. "Look, Neto was my friend. I can't leave without doing something."

Julian smiles his shark smile. He lights a cigarette and peers through the smoke. "What do you want, a gun? You want to join the revolution, carry a gun like Jane Fonda? You gonna assassinate the President? Or maybe you just want a boyfriend, some sexy revolutionary in your bed?" He steps closer, until her back is pressed to the fence. "You got money, Soltera? You give me money, I'll find you a boyfriend. I don't care what Chaski told you. We're not babysitters. You don't have anything we need."

Leo looks down, barely containing a smile. At last it was out. "Then why did you agree to meet me in the first place?"

"No sé," he says, taking a thoughtful drag. "I thought maybe you'd be prettier."

He waits, grinning, for her reaction. When she gives none he turns abruptly, walks away down the silent avenue. From the hunch of his shoulders, the practiced way he flicks his cigarette into the gutter, she knows he can feel her watching. He's performing for her—but there's something forced in his delivery, self-conscious, as if he knows he's shown his hand. She lets him go, playing out the line, knowing he won't get far; when he glances back, she steps into the street, keeping her distance for a block or two. There's no hurry now, she thinks. He's not fooling her anymore.

At the far corner a soldier stands guard outside a jewelry store, his shadow moving in and out of the light. "You're not very smart, *comrade*," she says when she catches up to Julian. Before he can retort, she takes his arm, pulls him close when he tries to yank it away. "I know where to find you. I know your name, where you work. How stupid is that? People are dying. People are disappearing while you waste time insulting me. Maybe you don't really want to do anything. Maybe you just want to show everyone how big your dick is. Go stick it in someone else. I came here to help."

"You sound so tough, Soltera," he whispers. "But you were better when you were playing a rich girl in the café. More natural. Who are you pretending to be now?"

Their silence leaves only the faint clocking of the soldier's boots on the pavement. "Give me a cigarette," she says. Bored, he shakes one from the pack and hands it to her. As she approaches, the soldier draws himself up, rifle held to his chest. In the window behind him, a triple-strand diamond necklace glitters on black velvet.

"Light?" she says, flashing her most genuine smile. "¿Fuego?"

He sets the rifle at his feet and pulls a lighter from his pocket. Leo sucks in the smoke and stifles a cough, lets her voice come low and husky.

"How old are you?" she asks. "¿Cuántos años tienes?"

"Veinte y dos."

She arranges her mouth into an alluring smirk. "Qué pena. Too young."

To his astonished face she shrugs vampishly, stands at the window another moment—long enough to break it, or spit in the soldier's face. She can feel Julian watching from the shadows, both of them waiting, learning what she can do. Heart in her throat, she runs a fingertip down the glass, savoring the soldier's confusion.

"Buenas noches, amigo," she finally says, and leans up to kiss his cheek. He doffs his cap, still smiling, as she saunters away, every nerve ending sparkling.

"You see?" she tells Julian. "I can be anyone you want."

The boy was nine when the Shining Path came to his village in Vilcashuamán. It was a cold spring morning; early rains had loosened the soil and left the stones of the plaza dark and slick. Most of the men were in their fields, so there was no one to greet the fighters, teenagers mostly, who arrived wearing heavy ponchos and wool hats, the men all unshaved and the women with their hair cut short. They carried knives and slingshots and one rifle between them, taken from a police station near Huambalpa.

"We claim this town as a strategic base, in the name of the glorious revolution," their leader said. They took the mayor and police captain to a field and shot them, and three of the girls dragged the schoolteacher into the square and beat him unconscious.

The boy watched with his schoolmates from their classroom window. The Senderistas came inside and told them the revolution needed their help. They could protect their parents, said one of the girls who'd attacked the teacher, by doing chores for the cumpas: collecting food from every family in the town, patrolling the fields and footpaths, reporting what the adults said and who they said it to. She drew a picture on the chalkboard of a hammer crossed with a scythe and said, "You are Red Pioneers. Your bravery will help us defeat the Yankee imperialists and their genocidal puppets. The strength of the revolution is forged in the furnace of armed struggle."

The boy was the first to volunteer. His mother and father owned the town bodega, where the mayor had his office in a back room, and the boy worried that the fighters would come back for them. The Senderista hugged him and asked if he was a fast runner. He would carry messages between the cumpas, she said. She taught him a song about Abimael called "The Sword" and said the students should stand at the window each morning and sing loud enough for the town to hear. If the teacher objected, the boy was to tell her immediately.

"Sí, señorita," he said.

"Don't call me señorita. That's the language of the colonialist oppressor. Now we are equal," she said, clenching his hand. "Compañeros."

A week later she asked the boy if all his classmates were singing the song. "Who sings the loudest?" she asked. They took the worst singers outside and forced them to strip naked and sing while another cumpa pointed the rifle at them. The whole town witnessed this humiliation. Later, the father of one of the bad singers found out who had informed on them, and the messenger boy's parents were dragged out of their bodega and into the square. The Senderistas stripped them from the waist down and told them to kneel with their backsides facing the church. The bad singer's father had denounced them as government collaborators. The town's only phone was in the bodega, and he had told the Senderistas that the boy's parents called the militares and asked for help.

"This is how we deal with snitches," said the leader. Another cumpa yanked back the boy's father's hair and the leader cut out his tongue, and then the mother's, and tossed them in the dust where stray dogs fought over them.

The boy saw all of it. He stood in the door of the school, held back by the girl who'd recruited him. She wrapped her arms around him and sang softly in his ear while his parents were dragged away moaning and spitting blood. "It's okay," she told him. "It's okay, little errand boy." She used the Quechua word for "runner": *Chasq'i.* She said his parents would get better when the revolution was over. Everyone would get their tongues back, so they could sing about the victory.

"So, Soltera, are you sure you want to be a revolutionary?"

Leo shakes herself out of reverie, the image of the young boy and his parents lingering though it's Julian's face that hovers close to hers. They're sitting on a bench in a roundabout a few blocks from the ocean. The townhouses and apartments have given way to stately manors that rise above whitewashed walls set with jagged glass. Behind them, a statue of a man on horseback sits on a pedestal, sword raised. The sky is bruised, roiled with clouds; scraps of fog twist in the treetops, the mist coating her face.

"What happened to his parents?"

"They died. Of course. The army came in and killed all the Senderistas. Then they killed a lot of villagers they said were loyal to Sendero."

"So they weren't the collaborators?"

"No, they were," he says, turning his cruel smile on her. She can feel herself shivering, a shaking beneath the skin. "But these people," he says, nodding at the nearest house, "they don't know anything about it. To them, it's a bunch of crazy cholos. This is the problem, not the President or the army. These people, who choose to know nothing."

She peers at the house, a three-story monument of oversize white bricks and broad verandas under a steep, red-tiled roof. "Who lives there?"

"Ricos," he says with a wave. "Foreigners. Killers. You see, Soltera? There's nothing you can do here. Go back to the United States. The revolution thanks you for your service."

"I've got money."

He watches her for a long moment, nodding steadily. Now that she's said it, she's sure it's what he was waiting for. "You can have it," she says. "Whatever you need."

Julian stands again, beckons her into the street, which ends at the long, curving malecón, at the top of high cliffs overlooking the ocean. She keeps two paces behind, face lowered against the stinging wind; the gusts rise as they move south, fisting into her mouth, drawing water to the corners of her eyes. After a few minutes he stops at the edge of a construction site, several acres of the malecón scraped flat and sectioned off by chain-link fence. Through torn plastic sheeting, she sees scattered trailers, backhoes and pickup trucks, piles of steel beams—and beyond it all the edge of the cliff, jagged and convex as though something reared up from the sea and took a bite out of the land. The clouds have broken apart, the sky brilliant with moonlight, the ocean a sheet of corrugated pewter. The plastic snaps and smatters in the wind.

Julian shakes the fence and whistles, until two low, gray shapes dart across the site, snarling. "Hola, perritos," he says, in a surprisingly tender voice. He takes something from his pocket and feeds it through the fence. "Oh, sí, sí, amores." The dogs snuffle in the dirt and snap at each other and gobble up the treats. Julian pulls hard on a section of fence, opening a gap, and gestures for Leo to go first. When she hesitates, he laughs.

"Mira," he tells the dogs. "She wants to make a revolution without trespassing."

He moves through the construction site, skirting piles of timber and rebar, spools of cable, a pyramid of cinder blocks taller than she is. Behind them, the empty windows of apartment buildings stare darkly at the ocean. At the end of the path, where the earth is marked by rain channels and sudden drops, Julian holds out his hand. "Ven," he says.

She permits herself only a brief hesitation. He takes her arm, almost tenderly, and then twists, thrusting her down to her knees, one hand clamped to the back of her neck.

"Viva la revolución. What do you think, Soltera? Was it worth the struggle?"

When she opens her eyes, the long drop leaps up at her. Spotlights dazzle her eyes. She can't breathe for the swirling wind, the dirt and grit flinging against her cheeks. Directly below, a labyrinth has been carved out of the cliff, a lattice of tiers and terraces stretching a hundred feet down, rough stone dynamited and jackhammered into wide platforms and long, curving passages—an Escher-like warren framed by stairways and concrete pillars, all struck in cold moonlight like a black-and-white photo, vivid and unreal.

Julian turns her head to one side. "This is where the parking will be. Over here," he says, "Pizza Hut. Tony Roma ribs. And Pollo Perú, chicken in the Andino style, owned by KFC. Down here, J. Crew and The North Face, alpaca sweaters sold by Mexicanos, Nike sneakers made in Vietnam, movie theaters owned by Argentinos, and the largest Tiffany store in South America, with gold from mines right here in Peru.

He bends lower until his voice rasps in her ear. "But over here," he says, turning her again, "this is the best, the highest achievement in the development of our country. For this we had twelve years of war, seventy thousand people dead. Yes, it's been terrible, but now finally Lima will have the Hard Rock Café."

The contempt in his voice is so coiled that she closes her eyes and waits for him to let go, let her fall to an ironic death in the concrete shell of a Pizza Hut. A moment later he yanks her back to land and releases her, staring down as she gasps in the dirt.

"Vía América. That's what they call this atrocity. The American Way. No, Soltera, we don't want your father's money. This country has all the dollars it needs."

The wind drops, and in the sudden silence she hears the guard dogs hacking and coughing, a car alarm wailing pointlessly in the distance. "You're lying," she says, still sucking the air. She grits her teeth and says, "What are they going to say when you tell them you turned down money? Just because I'm a girl? Because your ego is too big to admit you need help?" It's all been a test, she's sure of that now. *Nobody can see you here*, the man in the plaza said. But he'd seen her. He'd been watching.

Again the sound of the dogs retching, whimpering somewhere in the stockpiles. She climbs to her feet, dirt smeared on her clothes, her face. "When are you going to drop it, *compañero*?" she says. "There isn't time for this game."

"Estúpida," he says, his control fraying. "Why don't you ask Chaski about the revolution? Ask him about Abimael, the great savior. Sendero was the best thing that ever happened to this government. Now they can do whatever they want. They can take over your neighborhood, your university, they can take you off the street, put you in a bag and break your ribs, put a gun in your mouth, a broom in your asshole. They can erase you, ¿entiendes? What's your fucking money going to do about that?"

"It's already been decided," Leo says. "Enough with the act. Just tell me what you need me to do."

He stares at her in mute fury. Again the pathetic growling, the high, breathy wheezing of an animal in pain. When he turns away she follows him—back toward the malecón, skirting pallets piled with bags of concrete, heaps of rock and scree. He snatches a cinder block from the high stack and steps into the light of the clearing, where a small gray shape lies squirming in the dust, darkness pooled around its head.

"What did you do?" Leo says. She tries to squat next to the dog but Julian hauls her standing. "What did you do to him?"

The dog jerks pitifully, its eyes rolled up, back legs pumping without rhythm, as though it were caught in a terrifying dream of pursuit. Its muzzle matted with a foam of blood and mucus, its eyes wide and bright and uncomprehending, chest rising and falling rapidly. With each exhale the whining grows fainter and more strained.

Julian, still holding the cinder block, looks down at the dog, jaw set with pity. "I'm telling you one more time, Soltera," he says. "Go home. This isn't a place for you."

Leo's voice belongs to someone else: "I can't."

With a sigh, the door creaks open. "Ay, pobrecita," he tells the dog. "I know, mi amor. You've suffered enough." Hearing something in his voice, the dog turns its frightened eyes to them, and before Leo can stop him Julian raises both arms and hurls the cinder block down on the dog's skull.

"You want to help us, Leonora?" he says. He lifts the concrete block and smashes it down once more. The dog's body straightens and quivers violently and then is still. She can feel herself falling, the dust of the construction site tilting, but her body doesn't move, anchored once again by Julian's grip. A rivulet of milky blood winds through the dirt toward her shoes, Leo stuck in a half-crouch, one hand petting at the air above the dog's body. When he speaks again a shard of terror burrows into her throat's tender pit.

"You want to know what we need?" She nods through tears, as he lights a cigarette and hands it to her. "We need a house."

ANDRES

The first time I heard the name Leonora Gelb, I was at a soccer match with a pair of Dutchmen, a Brit, and three Peruvian girls. Late March or early April—the rainy season had sputtered out, the mountain air begun to dry. We sat on the home team's side of the stadium, a little hungover, floating woozy in a blast of Andean sun. The noise of the crowd came through a layer of soft, warm cotton and I leaned against the concrete and spread my arms behind my friends' backs. Life was pretty good.

"You must be so proud of your countrywoman," said Oswaldo, a ridiculously tall Aryan who led groups of European tourists around South America. He spoke flawless English, but his heavy accent sounded like Peter Sellers playing a Nazi. "Someone for you to look up to, I think."

I leaned over Lucrecia, whom I'd been dating, if that's the right word, and tried to flag one of the little kids selling bottled water. Lucrecia ignored me and whispered something to her friends in Quechua. It was Lima's best team, Universitario—or "La U"—against Babilonia, as we called the provincial town we lived in. Nobody expected Babilonia to win. Babilonia never won.

"It was an unusual strategy," said Jeroen. "Brilliant, if you think about it." He was broad and dark, with the hooked nose and heavy stubble of a football hooligan—which is exactly what he was. He'd been in Babilonia the longest and owned a full wardrobe of the team's uniforms. He worked for some kind of nonprofit, something to do with AIDS. He was always trying to get me to volunteer. He also claimed to write poetry. "Instead of sending the military to make trouble, you send a girl. Who would suspect?"

"Because of budget cuts," Oswaldo said. "Slick Willie had to find cheaper ways to overthrow foreign governments."

Jeroen waved a dismissive hand. "Don't be stupid. The American President has nothing to do with the military budget. He's a spokesman, only for television. He has no power at all. Don't you remember Reagan and that idiot colonel—"

"Ah, bullshit. You think *George Dubya Bush*"—his Texas twang sounded more like a constipated squirrel—"has no power? Tell that to the good people of Baghdad."

"Exactly my point! Even the Americans wouldn't re elect such an imbecile if they thought he actually—"

They went on like that. I closed my eyes and let the sun seep into my brain. I'd been listening to their arguments for years, since soon after I arrived in Peru. I'd quickly come to understand the Dutch penchant for certitude. They had no use for doubt. Sometimes I envied them.

Mark leaned over from the other side of the girls. "You lot are forgetting one thing." The smoothest of us all, Mark, a Londoner, had tousled blond hair and reddish stubble, a movie star's jaw and a slow grin. He was co-founder of a local English-language newspaper, *The Navel,* that came out every few weeks. You saw copies of it in café bathrooms, or trampled on the floor of the Irish pub. I'd lined my one shelf with it.

Oswaldo pushed his glasses up the bridge of his nose. "Please, señor. Educate us."

"Why would the U.S. want to overthrow the government? Fujimori was very right-wing. He opened the country to foreign investment, slashed public spending, destroyed the unions. From the Americans' perspective, he was ideal."

Jeroen stuck a finger in the air. "But he was a dictator! And Americans hate tyranny. They believe in democracy and freedom. It's why they start all their wars."

The other two laughed. I put a hand on Lucrecia's knee, but she just watched the field, twenty-two men scrambling in unpredictable discord. Her friend Rosa glared at me.

Mark sipped his beer and put an arm around Flor. I'd introduced them at La Luna the night before. I had a vague memory of watching them make out on the dance floor. "Still, they must have known of her activities," he allowed. "The U.S. does like to know what its people are doing."

Mark had studied political science at Cambridge. He'd been in Peru almost ten years, including two in Lima, married to an heiress. He'd come back to Babilonia with an amethyst stud in one ear and a tattoo on his arm and started his newspaper, which combined current affairs with reviews of expat clubs and restaurants, and tongue-in-cheek items like "Ten Easy Ways to Avoid Being Choke-Robbed at a Discoteca."

Oswaldo stood and stretched, provoking grumbles from behind. He peered down from his great height. "The U.S. likes to know what everyone is doing. Sí, Andres?"

"Careful, Ossie," Jeroen said in a stage whisper. "They'll hear you."

It was a favorite pastime among my friends—"slagging off" the U.S., as Mark called it. They insisted on saying "you" when they talked to me about the government or the military, any of a thousand sins: Iraq, Israel, Britney Spears. When the conversation turned to Guantánamo Bay, or Predator drones, or "la CIA," the ribbing took on a sharper edge. I tried to stay out of these conversations. I didn't care about any of it, I told them. That's why I'd come to Babilonia: so I didn't have to care.

"But it is outrageous," Jeroen said, that peculiarly Dutch look of scorn on his sunburned face. "You learn it from your government, sticking your nose in other people's business. There is no respect. You talk about democracy and freedom but wherever you go you have nothing but guns and bombs. Let's look at Iraq—"

"Let's not," I said.

"It's a classic example. Classic! This is where she learned this arrogance. Peru should keep her in prison forever. If this were the U.S. you would execute her."

He kept staring at me, but I refused to meet his gaze. Just then a defender snuck the ball away from a Lima midfielder and started streaking downfield. The crowd shrugged to its feet and cheered him on. Rosa and Flor screamed, pumped their fists, but Lucrecia sat quietly, hands in her lap. She turned her sad eyes to me. It was a Saturday afternoon, warm for the first time in months, the beer smoothing the edges and softening the light. The player with the ball seemed very small, surrounded by emptiness, advancing with silent grace toward the waiting goalie. Everything was lovely.

Everything was lovely. If there's a description of that time, this would be it. Lovely and light, ultimately meaningless. And that's how I wanted it. It's how everyone wanted it, or at least that's what I told myself. I suppose I knew it couldn't last.

We stopped off at Paddy's, the Irish pub on the main plaza, to pass the hours before heading out to dance. Paddy's was a landmark, a starred favorite in *Lonely Planet*. Its booths and barstools were always full of tourists, from college kids who'd come to hike the Inca Trail to European retirees grateful for an English-speaking bartender and a pint of Guinness. Trust-funders from Lima came to trawl for dates. From the balcony you could watch Peruvian teenagers congregating in the main plaza, hippies and shamans twirling sticks, gringos haggling with campesinas who sold handicrafts on the sidewalks, drunk locals pissing on the side of the cathedral, crossing themselves as they staggered away. If you stood there long enough, Mark said, you'd learn everything there was to know about Peru.

On the way upstairs, someone slapped me on the back. "Good fucking game, no?" It was the owner of La Luna, one of the many limeños whose names I never remembered.

"We almost beat you," I said.

"We!" He turned to someone behind him. "Mira este caballero. He thinks he's from here." He had a rough, swampy voice, blue eyes with an arrogant twinkle. "Okay, so the cholos score one goal. Maybe it's the altitude. We gotta give them something or they all become terrorists." A few heads turned at the top of the stairs, but he slid right past. "See you at the club tonight," he said.

"Maybe."

He reached out and tousled my hair. "I know you, cumpa. I'll see you later."

We commandeered a table and bought hamburgers for the girls, big bottles of beer for ourselves. Mark was the mayor of Paddy's, working the room, hugging the bartender, introducing himself to anyone he didn't know. The walls were covered with Irish street signs, beer posters, a pink neon clock in the shape of a giant bottlecap. A toy train chugged overhead along a track bracketed to the walls—the Shamrock Express, Paddy's pride and joy. The Eagles were on the stereo and a table of students raised their mugs and sang along. It was all pointless and perfect. The TV showed silent highlights from the soccer match and the limeños howled in victory and then a clip of a white girl in frumpy eyeglasses, with a nimbus of wild, wiry hair, screaming herself red in the face.

"Andres, you also studied at Stanford University." Oswaldo towered like a lit candle over everyone's heads. "Maybe you had a class with her."

I'd already forgotten the earlier conversation. "With who?"

"La Leo. Andres, are you already drunk?"

I held Lucrecia's hand, though she seemed not to notice. Rosa was shouting into her cell phone while Flor eyed Mark as he chatted with two blond women—limeñas, by the looks of them: glossy hair, designer jeans, expressions of absolute entitlement.

"Please, Oswaldo, you must be realistic," Jeroen said. "Can you imagine these two in the same class? Andres, tell me: Who is the president of Peru? What is the capital? You see? He is not a political person."

"Yes, he is a lover of peace."

"You make it sound like a bad thing," I said.

The clip ran in slow motion, again and again, the woman shouting at the camera, head tilted like a snarling dog. Shouts arose in the bar: "¡Puta! ¡Maldita!" "Go fuck yourself!" someone said. A string of curses too fast for me to catch: lesbian, witch, cunt.

"Who is that?" I said.

Oswaldo rested a long arm across my shoulders. "That is your countrywoman."

She couldn't have been taller than 5'2", a round face, freckly skin and a doughy, pointed chin. Everything about her was unlikely: the nerdy glasses that magnified her eyes, the intensity of her screaming, neck muscles strained. And the caption, which read, "LEONORA GELB CONFIESA QUE ES TERRORISTA."

"What did she do?" I said.

"Don't you read newspapers?" Oswaldo said. "They were planning to attack the Congress and take hostages. It was '97 or '98, I think. The army shot up a whole house of them." They showed it on the television: a big, three-story house, a high stucco wall scorched and pocked with bullet holes, broken glass, a battered wooden gate and one spindly tree snapped at its base. Inside, a stairwell spattered with blood, then some kind of arms cache: rifles, dynamite, a heap of what looked like military uniforms. The caption read, "LA CASA DE C.F. EN PUEBLO LIBRE." Apparently, she was up for parole.

The story had begun to sound familiar—even her name, as if I'd once been aware of it and forgotten. But so many things were like that now, every time I looked at a U.S. newspaper online, or someone sent me a magazine from back home, I thought I'd read it before, or someone had told me about it, or they'd already made a movie from the novel based on the true story. I couldn't keep track of it all, and I didn't want to. War, poverty, torture, people blowing each other up in the name of some ideology or other—all those things I couldn't do anything about. Why think about them at all?

Besides, it didn't affect our lives up here. Nothing did. The sun went down and the party started. Whatever you wanted from life— girls, drugs, a certain forgetfulness—Babilonia offered it cheaply and in abundance; what you didn't want could be left at lower altitudes, in other countries. No matter what was happening elsewhere, at midnight we'd load up on Cuba libres, head to La Luna and dance for hours, then stumble out into an icy dawn, glaciers glowing pink at the horizon: one more blissful, vanishing day in this city twelve thousand feet above sea level, twelve million miles from home.

"What do they teach you at Stanford University, Andres?" Oswaldo's arm was still heavy on my shoulders. "This was very big news. Amnesty International, the Red Cross, even your Slick Willie got involved."

They showed her on the TV again, screaming—and then a picture of the former president of Peru waving something over his head, a passport. Mark came over with the limeñas, who stood whispering with their backs to the rest of us. "Don't you remember, Ossie?" he said. "Andres majored in dancing."

"Ah yes, he's the King of Salsa." It was a standing joke: I couldn't dance to save my life.

"I studied creative writing," I said, stressing the words as if they didn't embarrass me. "I was there on a fellowship. I've told you a hundred times."

"Yes, don't you listen, Os?" Jeroen said. "He is a writer."

"Writers don't follow the news?" Oswaldo said.

"Not in America. They live the life of the mind."

They both watched me, clearly enjoying their little Teutonic tag-team. "Are we going to La Luna or what?" I said. Lucrecia was eyeing me levelly. "What?" I said.

Flor leaned over. "My brother was there. He . . . living in Lima, same block with this house. DINCOTE go up his roof, the"—she asked Rosa for a word—"the snipers. They make he and his girl-friend to hide in one room with the baby."

"DINCOTE?" I asked.

Mark patted my arm. "Counterterrorism."

Rosa took a cigarette from the pack on the table. "These estúpi-dos." She was big-boned, with wide nostrils and streaks of crim-son in her hair. She had a rough, jokey manner and spoke better English than her friends. "Why they no stay in the jungle and shoot their mothers? Always they say they want help poor people, so why always is poor people who die?"

Flor looked at her lap. "Yes, but Cuarta Filosofía no is Sendero." In Spanish, she said her uncle had been the head of a sanitation workers' local, in Abancay. After a group of Philosophers marched with them in a demonstration, the army stormed their union hall. Her uncle had been missing now for nineteen years. There was a framed picture of him on her parents' table, surrounded by flower petals and votives. Flor stared blankly at each of us in turn. She picked up a french fry and frowned at it.

That's when one of the blondes turned to the table. "¿Qué pien-sas?" she asked Flor, impatience coloring her cheeks. "¿Tenemos que aguantar bombas, matanzas, por tu tío?" She waved a finger in the air. The Philosophers declared war on the government, she said. If your uncle the garbage man hadn't joined them, nothing would have happened to him.

Flor looked stricken, as if she couldn't decide whether to hide her eyes or flip her plate in the blonde's face. "Well, it's complicated—" Mark said, but Rosa cut him off.

"Shut your mouth, hija de perra," she told the blonde. "Only a fat, rich girl could say something like that."

The limeña's face twisted with indignation. "Escuchame, cholita—"

"Only a stupid girl whose daddy buys a Mercedes for her quinceañera could be so ignorant—" Rosa said, pushing away from the table. Quickly, Mark and the Dutchmen stepped between the girls.

"Who wants another?" I said, and headed for the bar.

As I waited for Paddy to notice me, I could still hear them arguing. I could sense that face on the TV overhead. The night was being ruined, it seemed—and for what?

In truth, none of it seemed real to me. It had happened in another world, one that didn't exist in the same way ours did. The images on the TV—a pit full of decomposing bodies, a burning apartment building—these things were just *footage*. The screen contained them and made them luminous. All I knew about the war was what I'd gleaned from late-night conversations, from the way my Peruvian friends hurried past police officers, or flinched at sudden noises. But I did know what could happen when a government feels vulnerable, when it feels it has no choice but to stamp out the threat. I knew, too well, how quickly self-defense turns into something instinctive and vicious. I'd learned all that back home.

But here, at least, the war was over. There was no more Shining Path, no soldiers in the street. Why not leave it on the other side of the screen, where it couldn't touch us anymore?

When I got back to the table, Rosa and Flor were putting on their coats. "Why we are dance with these pitucas?" Rosa said, sniffing at the limeñas, who'd turned to flirt with the American students. "You go with them, Andres. Be careful your money!"

Lucrecia was watching me, her mouth pressed into a line. She had stick-straight black hair that she tucked behind small ears, a narrow face with a faint scar on her forehead that I liked to trace with a fingertip. She was soft-spoken and agreeable; until that morning we'd never argued about anything. I couldn't imagine her hating anyone, shrieking like that face on the TV. It was what I liked most about her.

I raised her hand to my lips. "Are you ready to dance with the King of Salsa?"

She snatched her hand away. "This no United States," she said. She poked me in the chest and said I should go with the limeñas. "Is better! Is better!" she kept saying, tears in her eyes.

"Good work, Andres!" said Oswaldo, as Rosa and Flor led her away. "Another peruana is not talking to you. Soon you have to go to La Paz to find a girlfriend."

Jeroen tried to stifle his laughter. Mark poured a beer and pushed it toward me.

"She is your girlfriend?" said one of the limeñas, as if something smelled terrible.

Over our heads, the toy train chugged around the room, ducking into little tunnels, letting out puffs of steam. "No, no, no." Jeroen raised a bottle to the television, where Leonora Gelb was still screaming, jaw snapping open and shut. "Andres's heart belongs to his countrywoman."

Everyone found this hilarious. "Stop calling her my country-woman," I said. "I'm not responsible for everything some stupid fucking American does. None of it has anything to do with me, okay? Leave me out of it."

They all stared at me until the train came around again, whistling idiotically. "Well, I think it's time for someone to go dancing," Oswaldo said.

The limeña put down her glass. "Somos todos Americanos," she explained, then flounced back to the bar. Mark watched her go, then shrugged and drained his beer. Now there were soldiers on the TV, a bombed-out mosque, President Bush grinning in the Rose Garden.

"Yes, Andres," said Oswaldo. "We are all Americans. You must not forget."

I'd come to Babilonia when I was thirty-three—Jesus's age, people often told me—and I hoped I'd never leave. From the minute I stepped off the plane, I felt an easing of the heart, a relief that was almost dizziness. The thin air, the bursting browns and greens of the Andes: almost hyperreal. A cloudless sky the color of blueberries, everything struck in cold sunlight. It felt like a secret paradise, surrounded by icy mountains that promised to keep the rest of the world out.

Sitting in a café that first afternoon I was overcome by a cold sweat, vertigo. Next thing I knew, a waitress was fussing over me, stroking my hair. She brought sugar and coca tea and rubbed my back as I shook off the altitude sickness. The next night, she took me dancing. I remember looking up, drink in hand, to find myself surrounded by Peruvian women, all teeth and shiny black hair, a sweaty club full of Israelis, French, Germans, Australians, everyone untethered and ecstatic. I remember smiling and smiling. I remember thinking, *I am someone else now.*

I found a room in a hillside neighborhood of whitewashed stucco, blue shutters, and wrought-iron balconies. There was a low, rickety bed and a desk by a window, with a view of a little garden. I set up my laptop, unpacked a few books, then stood on the balcony looking out over Spanish tile roofs, steep streets paved with stones worn smooth over centuries. I felt so happy I laughed aloud. When I walked down to the café each day I felt an unfamiliar solidity where my feet touched the ground. When I sat reading in the plaza in the chill afternoon light, the altitude buzzed at my temples and shone a faint penumbra around objects in my peripheral vision. I felt larger somehow, substantial, already a part of this place. It was *real*, I thought, in a way I'd never been real before.

What I'd been was an aspirant, all purpose and energy, trying to attach to my name some lasting significance, to make myself, in some way, *more*. More than what, I couldn't have said. I'd fancied myself a writer, built an identity on little more than that fancy, then shouldered the stone hard and long enough that it began to be true. I went to graduate school, published a few stories, won a couple of minor prizes. At thirty, I sold a novel, *The Light Inside*, about shiftless post-grads and Silicon Valley washouts who start a commune in rural Oregon. As publication approached I felt myself accelerating, gliding on a runway, ready to lift off into a bright future. Alone in my apartment, I couldn't stop touching my book. I pressed it to my face and smelled the paper. I'd done something of consequence, made a mark on this world that never before had cause to know me.

None of it mattered. Two days before the novel was released, the invasion of Iraq began. The newspapers were full of stories about yellowcake uranium and Tomahawk missiles, diagrams of F-14 jets; on television we watched night-vision bombing runs and billowing oil clouds, we heard experts describe the effects of nerve gas and anthrax. Our days shuddered with passionate intensity: we argued, we accused, we marched. "I feel just horrible," my editor told me. "What awful luck." Bookstores were canceling orders; readings and interviews were postponed indefinitely. "You'll write another one," she said cheerily. I felt vaguely mistreated, like a pedestrian who gets doused by a car speeding through a puddle. Something had been promised and not delivered, some inner worth gone unrecognized. I couldn't imagine going through all that again.

And it was just beginning: the war, the long and bloody occupation with its daily updates and mesmerizing graphics and escalating body counts. A procession of deadly mistakes, of unknown unknowns, lies upon lies denied and finally dismissed as the trivial whimperings of a "reality-based community." We wandered amid this cacophony of lies, arid statistics, *footage*, and told ourselves this was not our country. But we had no other—most people couldn't find a way out, or couldn't imagine it.

I could.

After a year, I hardly remembered life back in the States. After two, I was an honorary resident: "medio-peruano" they called me. I knew most of the waitresses in most of the cafés by name. I knew bouncers and bartenders all over town. Never much of a dancer, in Babilonia I was first out on the floor, flaunting my fake salsa with the prettiest woman in the room. My laptop sat unopened month after month, but I'd let it slip that I'd published a novel, and now I was something of a local poet laureate; people were more impressed than they should have been. It was as if, in this Andean Neverland, I was allowed to be the person I'd always wanted to be: easygoing, accomplished, admired. The locals had a name for that person: They called him Andres.

For a while I'd taken Spanish lessons in a school run by a Dutchwoman—Oswaldo's ex, which was how I'd met him and

Jeroen. Browsing in the English-language bookstore, I fell into conversation with Mark, whose office was down the block. Others came and went—Toni, the Aussie, who fell in love with a peruano, opened a restaurant, failed, and went home; Kate, a bawdy Irishwoman who worked with illiterate mothers; Geert, a thuggish Rotterdammer who dated our friend Luz, beat her up once, and told us all to fuck off on his last night in town. We were a kind of royalty, to use Fitzgerald's phrase: the expats who lounged in the cafés and at Paddy's, who always picked up the tab. It was a life almost unbelievable in its pleasantness, its absence of real demands. I could write or not write, I could forget about the war, about Americans, for weeks on end. And if sometimes I spent whole mornings staring at the ceiling, wondering what this new life meant, by noon the sharp sunlight had returned to me that peculiar presence, absolute, the sense that there was nothing at stake. And the nights always ended at La Luna.

But recently the horizon had begun to creep closer: The money from my book advance had dwindled, the small investments I'd hoped would keep me in Peru forever were looking shaky as the stock market teetered. I resolved to spend less, to live more modestly, but each month my budget grew gloomier. If something didn't change, if some rabbit didn't leap from my hat, I would not be able to stay. The idea of going back to the States filled me with such dread I could only look away, laugh it off, buy another round. I could not be that person again.

My third year in Babilonia, I'd finally started a new book. I had a bunch of scenes, a notebook full of ideas. It was about all of us— our adventures, our conquests, the hilarious things that happened here. I was thinking of calling it *The Moon Also Rises*. I knew I'd never finish it.

Düd, are you still in Peru? read the email I received the next morning. It was from my old San Francisco roommate, and sometime friend, Jackson Durst. I was unsettled as soon as I saw his name. *Give me a shout, k? Have I got a job for you!*

It was past ten o'clock, clean morning sun sheeting across the window. My room was an unheated cube, with adobe walls and wood floors slick with wax polish. The bathroom sink ran only cold water, the shower equipped with what they called a "ducha electrica"—basically a heating coil screwed to the end of the pipe. On a good day, you'd get about five minutes of tepid drizzle before the contraption shorted out; on a bad day, if you weren't wearing rubber flip-flops, you could find yourself lying in a puddle in the dark with the worst headache of your life.

I went out to the balcony for a smoke. My clothes from the night before hung on the rail, to air out the cigarette stench. I'd lived with Jack Durst for two years, in a run-down Craigslist apartment with a spectacular view of Market Street and the Bay Bridge. We didn't see much of each other—I was working on my novel, and he was doing something for a website called *HookupLookup*, where he'd been the fifth employee. When *HookupLookup* was acquired by *Match*, he made a small fortune; he bought a four-bedroom Beaux-Arts cottage on Liberty Hill and launched *The Durst Report*, a news aggregator spiced with opinion pieces by artists and celebrities. Jack's ambition and flamboyance were catnip to investors—soon he'd swallowed up several competitors and renovated an old machine shop in the Dogpatch, adding three stories, a bowling alley, and a rooftop tiki bar. Naturally, he christened it "Durst Castle." To better reflect these expanding horizons, the website was relaunched with a new design and a new name: *My.World*.

For a time I was a semi-regular contributor. Whether from generosity or an overestimation of my literary fame, Jack let me post at will—at last count, I'd written sixteen pieces, all essentially saying the same thing: the war was a travesty, our leaders were evil, etc. They weren't very original, but they made me feel better. And he paid very well. But there came a day when I couldn't write them anymore, when the world let me see just how irrelevant they were, how risible my indignation. When I left for Peru I stopped returning Jack's emails. That part of my life was over, I told myself.

It was another bracing, searingly bright day. After coffee and the daily gamble with electrocution, I headed downhill. In the warming air all the smells of Babilonia rose from the stones: bread baking in the pastelería, animal blood from the butcher's stalls, decades of excrement from the toilet built into the side of a church. I got a shave and took out cash—careful not to look at my account balance—all the while trying not to think about Jack's email. Somehow, I already knew what he wanted.

"You gotta write it, dude," he said, when I called him from the Telefónica office on the main plaza. "The story's got your name all over it!"

"The story?"

"A terrorist," he went on, as if he hadn't heard me. "A real-life American terrorist. And a girl! Do you have any idea how many clicks this shit'll get?"

Already I regretted calling him. I still don't know why I did. Maybe I'd convinced myself he wanted something else, something easier. I needed the money, that was certainly true. Or maybe I just wanted to hear a voice from back home, a reminder that I'd once existed. I had days like that sometimes, when I couldn't remember how long I'd been gone. A night at La Luna was the usual cure.

"Says here she's getting parole pretty soon," he was saying. "She's got an apartment in Lima. Is that anywhere near you?"

"No."

"Whatever. I'll fly you there. First class. Just let me know how many puka shells or whatever it costs, a'ight? Think you can put something together by the end of the month?"

"Forget it, Jack." I said, "No way."

There was a clatter and a hum as he took me off the speaker-phone. "Listen, dude. Who better than you? Think about it: you're the same age, you both went to Stanford—"

"I was on a fellowship," I said, as if this exonerated me.

"—you live there, you know Peru. Remember those columns you wrote? It's right up your alley. Holy *shit*, it's like fate!" he said. "You're exactly where I need you to be."

"I don't know anything about this," I said, loud enough that the cashier looked up. My head was pounding. I reached for a ciga-rette but remembered I'd left them at the barber shop. "Listen, Jack, thanks for thinking of me. But it just isn't me."

"I don't believe you," he said. There was more clatter, and then he muffled the phone, said something to someone. "Look, think it over. Call me mañana. You know me—I'm not taking 'no' for an answer."

. . .

I had plans to meet Mark for lunch—ceviche and beer, a Saturday ritual—and as I walked down the Avenida Sol, I argued with Jack in my head. I was bothered by the call, offended, even—why in the world did he have to ask *me*?

Mark's office was near the post office, two rooms with a view of the mountains, upstairs from a shoe store. "What, already?" he said. "I thought you'd still be in bed." There were two desks surrounded by file cabinets, shelves full of binders, a drafting table strewn with photographs, magazines, derelict power adapters. "Steph, you remember Andres, Babilonia's resident scribe?"

Stephanie was his editor and business partner, a Canadian journalist who wrote stories about local politics. She was tall and rangy, with a pinched nose and a cloud of blond curls. The first time I'd met her, the Dutchmen and I had been drinking for days. She didn't hold me in the highest regard.

"Hola, Andres," she said. She wore a coarse wool sweater, motheaten at the wrists, a long peasant skirt, huaraches. "¿Cómo has estado?"

"Andres is writing the great Babilonian novel," Mark said. "It starts with a memory of the smell of roast guinea pig. It's called *In Search of Lost Mind*."

She smiled dutifully. "Actually," I said, "a weird thing just happened."

I told them about my conversation, playing up the absurdity of Jack's coming to me, of all people. This was my usual approach to matters of any seriousness: I'd emphasize my incompetence, cop to it, lest anyone expect too much of me.

Mark and Stephanie were looking at each other strangely. "It's funny you say that. We were just talking about La Leo."

"Mark, no," Stephanie said.

"But we can help our friend, can't we? Our fellow journalist?"

"I'm not a journalist," I said. I felt nervous suddenly, as if I'd wandered into an audition. "I told him to find someone else."

Mark went into the other room and rummaged, while Stephanie

smoothed her skirt and avoided my eyes. He came back with a pile of old newspapers, which he sifted until he found what he wanted. "Look. Volume one, issue eight. See that dateline?"

I squinted at the yellowed tabloid: *22 agosto, 1998.*

"It's the day after she was arrested," he said.

The front page was dominated by two photographs, one of a mass grave in a town in central Peru, the other of a guerrilla fighter in a ski mask, rifle at the ready. The layout was amateurish, the images badly cropped. But it was the banner that struck me: a woman's eyes, wide open. Her irises reflected what she was looking at: soldiers on the march. "LOS OJOS DEL MUNDO," it read. THE EYES OF THE WORLD.

"It never came out. By that morning, everyone in the house was dead. They pulled her off a city bus, mate. They made her watch."

"Who?" I said, turning the page. There was a story about a protest at an American-owned gold mine, a poem by Neruda, a photo of peasants with rifles slung across their backs. On the back page, an editorial flowed around a large, blank square.

"It's a fascinating story," Mark said wistfully. Stephanie was typing on her clunky desktop, but I knew she was listening intently. "Someone should write it."

"Not me," I said. "It has nothing to do with me."

"Aren't you a writer?"

"Not like this."

Mark cocked his head. "Like what, then?"

It was a good question, one I'd asked myself a lot. The handful of reviews of my novel had been decidedly mixed: some called it "hip" and "knowing," others "mannered" or "smug." One writer dubbed it "Gen X's *The Big Chill.*" But one line had stuck with me, kept me up at night: "In times such as these," the reviewer asked, "why should we care about the narcissistic crises of the privileged class, however competently written?"

For days I brooded over this, railing silently against the reviewer. When, at the one reading I gave, in Berkeley, a breathless older woman asked if I thought my novel was still relevant, "given everything that's happened," I was ready for her.

"Empathy is always relevant," I said. I gave a spiel about how a writer's duty is to see beyond himself, how imagining the lives of others was an inherently political act. "If more people practiced empathy, maybe this war would never have happened," I said.

This elicited thoughtful nods from the eight people in the audience. But inwardly I felt sick with shame. Why *should* readers care about characters like mine? Well-off, well-educated, mostly white, their ambitions and resentments played out over three hundred pages as their utopia slowly unraveled. Meanwhile there were American cluster bombs flattening whole Iraqi villages, soldiers getting their legs torn off. Meanwhile our leaders had lied to us, lied to the whole world. People—real people—were dying by the thousands, and here I was, a cheese plate and bottles of wine set out before me, talking about *empathy*. It came to me that I was a terrible fraud.

"Listen," Mark said, as though he'd read my thoughts. "This woman—American, smart, privileged. How does she end up a terrorist? Don't you want to figure her out?"

"Not really," I said. I was still holding the newspaper, the empty square on the back page gaping up at me. A pull-quote read, *We are the ones you want to forget. But we have not forgotten you.* Leonora had been in my dream, I suddenly remembered. Tangled and trapped under heavy blankets, I couldn't escape.

"If he's not interested, he's not interested," Stephanie said sharply, startling both of us. "Can't you see he's busy? We don't want to keep him from La Luna."

I put my hands up. "Hey, it wasn't my idea."

"Of course not," she smirked. "No one would accuse you of that."

Mark squinted at her, then took a pack of cigarettes from his drawer and offered it to each of us. "Someone will write it, Steph," he said quietly. "If not you, then someone else. Why not help him? He's never written something—"

"He's completely ignorant!" She gestured at me as if I were a runway model. "Look at him—he knows nothing. *Nothing.* He's a perfect American. He has no idea how little he knows."

That was enough for me. I put down the paper and said, "Look, it's not going to happen. So everyone relax. I've got a new project I'm working on. Anyway, it really has nothing to do with me."

"It has everything to do with you," Stephanie said.

She snatched her sunglasses from the desk and disappeared down the hall, the soles of her sandals flapping flatly on the stairs. When I heard the street door bang shut, I turned back to Mark, who was straightening papers on the desk. He picked up *Los Ojos del Mundo* and stared into those unblinking eyes. Then he looked at me and smiled.

"She'll come around."

I'd met Lucrecia in the plaza on the first day the rains broke. I'd noticed her from a few benches away—her girlish hair, graceful neck, and widely spaced, regal eyes. A month later, I knew how she danced, how many Cuba libres it took to make her drunk, what she liked for breakfast, and not much else. She'd been engaged, she told me, but had recently broken it off. He was "un bruto," she said, which could mean he was violent or just that he was rough, ignorant, beneath her. She carried herself with the tentative poise of a fugitive—when we walked into a bar or restaurant, I felt her eyes scan the corners. She didn't tell me anything more about their relationship and I didn't ask.

Babilonians had a name for local women who dated gringos: "brichera," a word that implied a certain canniness, promiscuity with an ulterior motive. Peruvian men used it as a synonym for prostitute. You saw some enterprising women at the clubs every night, with a new gringo for each season—a scandal in Babilonia, where people's Catholicism was even more resolute than in the capital, if no more devout.

But Lucrecia was no brichera. She'd never dated a gringo, and always seemed embarrassed when a group of us took over a table or a dance floor. I didn't worry she was after my money or thought we were getting married or anything like that. We had a nice time together, that was all.

The morning of the soccer match, she'd stayed in the bathroom a long time, then sat quietly on the edge of the bed until I jolted upright.

"A week," she said, when I asked how long. She was always exactly on time, always two days after the full moon.

"A week," I repeated. "That's not much." Out the window, I

watched a hummingbird hovering, lunging at the goldenrod with its needle beak. Lucrecia made a sound of despair and started tugging on her clothes.

"Cariña," I said, "¿qué te pasa?"

She wheeled around, her sweater pulled halfway down, one bare, delicate arm pointed at me. "What you think?" she said in English. "What you think of me?" She yanked down her sweater and started looking for her shoes. I stopped her at the door, put my hands on her shoulders and summoned my most reassuring voice.

"Lulu, it's okay."

"Qué estúpida soy," she cried, her features puckered in misery. "Qué estúpida."

"You're not stupid. Calm down and we'll talk about it." Somewhere up the hill, a brick of firecrackers hissed and spattered, followed by the deep-throated boom of an M-80. "Everything will be okay," I said. For no reason at all, I added, "I'm your friend."

She sniffled, drew her sleeve across her nose. "My friend," she said.

Now it had been nearly a week since I'd seen her. The Dutchmen and I had been out a few times, but I'd avoided La Luna. Lucrecia knew where to find me, I reasoned. For now, the kindest thing to do was give her space. We'd talk about things once she'd calmed down. We'd figure out what was best for everyone.

But late on a Thursday night, Oswaldo and I tramped through the plaza, ducking into the arcades where the Quechua women were wrapping their bundles. "Only an hour or two," he'd insisted—which was how things usually began. He was leaving in the morning for a five-week tour: he'd drag twenty Germans through Argentina and Chile and come home with enough in tips to hold him for six months or more. Earlier in the week, he'd met a woman from Pucallpa, in the jungle—a "charapa," as they were called, "so, so hot," Oswaldo said. If he didn't show up tonight, he'd lose his chance.

"You owe me, Andres," he pointed out, which was true.

La Luna was an enormous, sunken ballroom—part Studio 54, part last-days-of-Rome—a warren of stone with thick, cracked columns blazing in and out of strobe. Balconies and catwalks hugged the walls, which were covered in DayGlo petroglyphs; at the far end, a DJ booth shaped like a UFO jutted over the dance floor. But the glitz and flash couldn't hide the club's essential squalor: the wobbly chairs, the dangerously overloaded outlets, the slick and filthy bathrooms. Every so often the circuit breakers blew, plunging the whole carnival into darkness. The bartenders moved an astonishing amount of beer, using cigarette lighters to flip the caps off the bottles.

"I see Jeroen!" Oswaldo shouted, pointing to a table across the floor. Lucrecia and her cohort were there, with two Peruvian men I didn't know. I vaguely remembered Flor saying her brother was coming to visit from Lima. Madonna's "Music" crashed and bleeped through the club; on a catwalk, half a dozen girls danced out of sync, eyes shut, reveling in the attention gusting up from below.

I volunteered to get beer and plunged into the frantic crowd. "Cumpa, where you been?" shouted the owner, when he spotted me at the bar.

"Busy!"

"Make sure your friends are drinking, okay? Oye," he slid two bottles toward me and flashed his wolfish smile, "you like the local girls, no?"

"Thanks for the beer," I said. Lucrecia was waiting. I was suddenly sure she'd come to tell me everything was fine, it was a false alarm. We'd dance and get drunk and go home in sweaty, blissful relief. I was eager to get that process started.

"You gotta be careful, OK? This brichera you're with," he said. "Who's this guy she's bringing here?"

"Don't call her that," I said. I peered through the crowd, trying to make out my group through the anarchy of bodies. "That guy's not with her. It's her friend's brother."

He squinted at me and shrugged. "I just don't want any fighting."

I shoved my way out, threading between whirling couples. The smell of cigarettes and body odor was overwhelming. "Andres, how wonderful he is here!" cried Rosa, embracing me with exaggerated pleasure while the Dutchmen laughed. When I bent to kiss Lucrecia's cheek she looked up with pleading eyes. Flor's brother and his friend eyed me blankly.

"Soy Andres," I said, extending a hand.

"Ronaldo," said the one next to Lucrecia. The other crossed his arms.

"¿Cerveza?" I pushed a bottle toward them. Jeroen plucked the other from my hand. When I asked Lucrecia to dance, she looked appalled. "¿Rosita? Vamos," I said.

Rosa clasped her hands. "You mean I am dance with the King of Salsa? Oh, gracias señor, gracias!"

The thicker the crowd, the better a dancer I was—and the crowd at La Luna was always thick. The DJ played "Roadhouse Blues" and we reeled and stumbled to the center of the floor. Rosa stared over my shoulder while we danced, lights glinting off the ruby stud in her nose.

"Where is your friend Marco?" she shouted into my ear. "Flor is very sad!"

I hadn't seen Mark since our lunch the previous weekend. But Jack was emailing me every day. *Don't leave me hanging, amigo!* He could give me until the middle of May, he said. And he'd pay three dollars a word—a fortune, even by U.S. standards. *Five thousand words sound doable? 15 Grovers buy you lot of wampum.*

Once or twice that week I'd gone online to read about Leo Gelb and the furor her parole hearing had stirred. There had been threats against her lawyers and the judge; family members of soldiers who died in the war were going on television to vent their disgust. Next to each article, the same image appeared: the red-faced, screaming gringa. If I looked at it for too long, I felt myself grow uneasy, then inexplicably angry.

A slow song came on and I put a hand on Rosa's waist, swaying and dipping. Over her shoulder I watched our friends sitting glumly at the tables—all but Oswaldo, who was talking to an older, heavily made-up woman: his charapa, I decided, a brichera if I'd ever seen one. After this song, we'd go back to the table. I'd apologize to Lucrecia for my insensitivity and she'd hold my arm. Then the happy reconciliation could begin.

"How long is Flor's brother staying?" I asked Rosa.

She squinted and drew back, and then an open-mouthed smile of surprise and delight spread across her face. "No es su hermano," she shouted. "Is not Flor's brother!"

It was past midnight, the club a near-solid mass of undulating bodies, a vast undulation of heads swept by colored beams of light. Next time I looked, Ronaldo had an arm across the back of Lucrecia's chair, talking to the side of her head. Her eyes searched the dance floor. Jeroen and the other Peruvian stood talking animatedly, the Dutchman pointing an index finger which the other man batted away.

"Voy al baño," I told Rosa, nodding toward the stairs.

She kept dancing, arms overhead, bangles shimmying down her wrists. She closed her eyes and wriggled her fingers sardonically. "Ciao, Andres," she said.

From the balcony's cooler climes, I watched the dance floor convulsing, a thousand faces flashing in and out of existence. There was a shiver near the bar as bouncers tried to break up a fight, the flailing, frantic activity of a struggling animal inching toward the door. As I caught my breath, I felt as if I were looking back not only through distance but through time, at something already freezing into memory: the dancers on their catwalks, all those bodies spasming. I watched a waitress moving against the tide, carrying a tray of bottles to a table—our table, I realized, though Oswaldo and his charapa were no longer there, only Jeroen and Ronaldo and three other Peruvian men, Lucrecia hunched over, face hidden in her hands.

"Hola, Andres. What a surprise to see you here."

Startled, I nearly stuck my nose into the cloud of blonde hair at my shoulder. Stephanie stood with her elbows on the balustrade, staring over the crowd. Her cheeks were flushed, hair damp at the temples. She wore a sleeveless black T-shirt and the same peasant skirt; instead of sandals, she had on a pair of stylish, high-heeled boots.

"I'm speechless," I said. "I'd never think to see you here."

She set her lips in a hard line. "Why not?"

"Don't know, La Luna seems too . . ."

"Fun?"

"I was going to say 'seedy.' I figured you for the classier places. Actually, I figured you didn't come to discotecas at all."

"I like to dance," she said. She smiled to herself, a sweet and private smile. "Actually, I'm on a date."

I tried not to seem surprised. "I thought I was, too."

I didn't find her attractive, not exactly. There was something too austere in her bony shoulders and small breasts, the slight upturn of her nose, something stingy. But in the crucible of La Luna we were off our guard—though we might dislike each other, there was a kind of recognition, the reflexive comfort we expats always felt with one another. I felt this as a calming of my heart, what one might feel when reunited with a long-estranged sibling. We were strangers with too much in common.

"Stephanie, I'm not going to do it," I said. "Don't worry. I don't want to write the story." She pursed her lips and considered this, long fingers clasped at her waist. I wanted her to look at me, to acknowledge that, whatever my deficits, at least I knew this story was beyond me. I had turned it down on principle. I wanted her to respect me for that.

She turned back to the dance floor. "I always feel so disoriented here," she said quietly. "There's something so . . . enclosed. Do you feel that? It's like a dream. The outside world could end in fire, but we'd all keep dancing in our little amusement park."

As if on cue, a burst of techno music crashed through the club. Colored spotlights gave way to pure, white strobe. "I think that's why I like it here," I said.

"Because it's not real?"

"Because you feel like it will go on forever."

She nodded, gathered her hair and twisted it into a knot. We watched dancers with pale, pixilated faces, suddenly frozen when searchlights swept the crowd. Across the club, I saw Lucrecia stand up from the table in slow motion, holding Ronaldo's arm with both hands. Rosa stood next to them, pointing at the dance floor, her movements insect-like and ominous, the whole scene caught and dismantled by the merciless strobe.

"My brother is in Afghanistan," Stephanie said. She turned to me, and I was taken aback by something in her eyes, something frightened. "That's why I can't write it."

"I don't understand," I said.

"He's twenty years old."

"He's in the army?"

"The Marines. He's with a reconstruction team working in Kandahar." A bead of sweat blinked green, red, blue at her temple. Behind her, a Peruvian I recognized came out of the men's room and made his way toward us.

"That must be hard," I said. "But why—"

"Because he could die," she said. "He could get killed because of you."

"Me?"

"All of you. George Bush, Rumsfeld, Leonora Gelb—"

"Now hang on a second . . ."

"You have no idea how to write that story. Not because you don't know anything about Leonora—because you don't know anything about yourself."

Her date came up behind her and nodded at me. He was tall and lean, with rimless glasses, mid-forties or older. He owned a small hotel not far from where I lived.

"You're a smart person, Andres," Stephanie said. "Maybe you're a good person. But you live in a fantasy world. You and the rest of America. You have no clue what's been done to build that fantasy for you, how many people have been slaughtered and starved. And still you go around lecturing about freedom, barging in where you're not wanted. You think the whole world is just waiting for you to save us."

She took her date's arm and the strobe stopped, all of us blinking in a sudden, bright silence. Just before the pounding returned, I saw something strange: across the club, Ronaldo and his friends were hurrying up another stairway; down below, Jeroen was sitting on the filthy floor, a group of strangers trying to help him up.

"Go ahead and write it, Andres. It doesn't matter. I'm sure you'll come up with something very entertaining that misses the point entirely. If there's money to be made, someone's going to do it, aren't they?"

"Stephanie, you've got me all wrong," I tried to say.

"I don't think so," she said. "You're a fiction writer, aren't you?"

She turned away, her date shooting me a puzzled, sympathetic look. I stood a moment longer, silently arguing my case, as if the whole, exhausted crowd were waiting to hear my explanation.

But then, at the far end of the balcony, Ronaldo and his friends emerged, stamping up the last step and squinting down the hall. Rosa was right behind them, shouting something that sounded like encouragement, and though the scene felt distantly humorous it occurred to me that I should find the nearest exit, that maybe I should get out of there before somebody got hurt.

II

A CONSPIRACY OF HOPE

1

Once upon a time and a very good time it was there were moppy little dogs chasing cars down the lane and a racket of sparrows out the kitchen window. The schoolbus stopped on the corner and when she rode in the mornings to the brick schoolhouse on a hill she leaned her cheek against the cold glass and watched the trees curve up into a milk-shot sky and the power lines drooped and rose and drooped and rose and disappeared into green glare spangle.

The gardener came once a week. Out the bay window she watched the truck pull to the curb and the short, gray-faced man went back and forth on the lawn making noise and when he left she went outside and flung fistfuls of cut grass and sneezed. He had a funny mustache and was called Pablo. Sometimes he left a coffee can with newcut flowers on the doorstep. In summer it was hot and the air rang with insects; her mother made lemonade and brought Pablo a glass, which he drank at the bottom of the porch and handed back. She left an envelope in place of the flower can. Pablo never came inside.

In kindergarten you pressed your hand into wet cement—blue for the boys, pink for the girls—and brought home the hard, heavy plate. You built buildings with plastic logs and drew your mother and father in sixty-four colors and each morning you stood proudly with hand on heart and pledged allegiance to the flag. Miss Daniels gave her a cup of chocolate ice cream with a tiny wooden paddle and sent a note to her parents: "Leonora has a sunny disposition and a love of learning, but she is quiet shy [sic]."

There was a stream behind the house and neighbor children roamed the woods playing military games. Ash and maple and dogwood, tall ferns and the stink of skunk cabbage. When you rolled a stone the damp dirt wriggled with salamanders. In summer they picked strawberries at Bryce Farm and in winter they sledded down Sam's Hill until Sam's Hill was sold to developers and then there were big houses where rich people lived.

"We're not rich," her mother said. "Just lucky."

Cannondale, New Jersey, sprung from farmland twenty-four miles from the Lincoln Tunnel. The garage door rumbled under the house each night and then her father was home. When they drove into the city she wore a dress and buckled shoes and looked like a real lady. Her brother combed his hair. The car went down through the long tunnel and her father pretended to hold his breath the whole time. Her mother stared straight ahead when the men with dirty faces rubbed newspapers on the windshield.

"Just go."

"The light's red, Maxi—"

"Just drive."

When it snowed, Pablo shoveled the driveway. But then, in spring, a different man mowed the lawn and she asked her mother where Pablo was and her mother fixed her barrette and said Pablo had to go home. Matthew got sick and went to the hospital and she had to stay at Grandpa Carol's for a week. In first grade they rode the bus to see Betsy Ross's house and the Liberty Bell. Danny Goldstein threw up going home and it crept down the aisle and then two more kids threw up.

"Leonora has excellent penmanship," Mrs. Brill wrote. "She always says please."

David had a favorite chair and he sat in it each night. Ice made a sudden snapping in his glass. The swim club was down the road and in summer wet feet slapped on the deck and Matthew learned to jackknife; orange soda and Marathon bars gave you a stomachache. That winter they took a family vacation on a big ship. Her mother wore a floppy hat. When they came to an island everyone stood at the rail and waved. They threw coins in the water and black boys leapt from the pier, thrashing in the water and showing their teeth. She pleaded with her father for a coin and as she pulled back her arm a boy on the pier smiled at her. She wanted him to get the coin.

Then there was shouting, many heads frothing in the water and men running down the pier with a cloth stretcher. She would never know if the boy they pulled from the water was the same boy. She would never know if he died.

Miss Gallo had to have her appendix out and the substitute played a guitar and sang a song about answers blowing in the wind. She lost the spelling bee when she misspelled *tortoise* and she cried in her room and her face was burning. When she came downstairs the tall man was on the television again, the same one every night, with the long, white beard and the black turban. There was a crowd of younger men with black beards kneeling in the street, or waving guns over their heads. Her father looked into his glass, his tie undone, and said, "Jesus, Jesus."

Outside the town library, there was a black cannon on a pedestal overlooking Charlie's general store and the police station. Miss Gallo said not to climb on it. The cannon had been there since before there was a town, since before anyone could remember, glimpsed each morning by fathers on their way to work, saluted at the Fourth of July picnic as they reflected on the blessings of liberty, on the country that had given them circular driveways and summer crickets, Little League and revolving credit, blessings secured by hard work and sacrifice and defended, when necessary, by heavy artillery, by satellite surveillance and incursions on foreign soil and when all else failed by the threat of Armageddon—like the fourth-grade boy who said *You have to play my way!* and then punched Maria Salierno in the stomach and got sent home. It was hard to understand, Miss Gallo said, but sometimes when people are lucky it makes other people mad. It makes them want to take what those people have.

"Sometimes we have to protect what belongs to us," she said. "We have to stand up for what's right."

Here is your portrait, your well-rounded character. I've been asked to tell Leo's story, a story of terror and bloodshed, of a country convulsed by war. But readers will only "invest" in that story if they care about her, my editor says, if they get to know her as a person: where she came from, what forces shaped her. *She liked chocolate and strawberry, but never vanilla. She had a habit of plucking the eyes from rag dolls and for a brief period was fascinated by frogs.* My job is to locate the offending pea under the plush mattresses—the one that so tormented her she chose to take up arms against a foreign government, to stockpile explosives, liquidate legislators. *She was the first in her class to master long division. She was inexplicably terrified by her grandfather's show poodle, Audrey.* The better I can dramatize those early provocations, explain her later actions as *reactions*, the more integrity the story will have. Or so the theory goes. The better average readers can relate to her, see themselves in her, the higher the return on their investment.

Or so the theory goes.

So let us not leave out Miss Moore, the third-grade teacher whose obsession with American Indians caused concern at the PTA. Let's not forget Leonora's love of Choose Your Adventure books, or her early struggles with ballet. Can we fail to mention her fourth-grade presentation on Martin Luther King, or overlook the implications of the undated report, "Madame Defarge: A Role Model for Women"? My editor wants me to find trauma, some primordial harm against her person—but there's only the child's clear eyes, doubled in the windows of the schoolbus, following the power lines as they droop and rise, droop and rise, carrying light into peaceable American homes.

> O, the wild rose blossoms
> On the little green place.

I'm hardly the first to go looking for trouble. "Nothing," is what Maxine told Oprah Winfrey in 1999, in the first flush of Leo's martyrdom, when asked what in her daughter's upbringing might have led to "this."

"She was a normal kid. Smart, fun-loving. She would never hurt a fly."

"But there must be something, some memory. Was she ever in trouble, did she complain about—"

"She abhorred violence. She was not interested in politics. I don't think the word 'revolution' ever crossed her lips." Maxine was unswerving in her exculpations, not offended so much as practiced.

"She was a model student, a model sister. David and I used to say how lucky we were."

"Perfect," Oprah offered.

"Yes. As much as any parent can say it—"

"A good girl."

"Everyone wants to find something. Everyone wants to explain it." She smoothed her skirt and looked straight into the camera. "There's nothing to explain."

She remembers piles of leaves, orange and brown and wet underneath. She remembers the thick, soily smell. Snow days when the lane disappeared and a sea of white becalmed every house. She remembers soccer practice and the Statue of Liberty, chicken pox and sore throats and "Casey at the Bat." She remembers voting for Jimmy Carter, her mother holding her up in the voting booth to pull the lever that made all the buttons pop back out with a heavy *ka-chunk*. She remembers times tables and the pyramids of Egypt, dodgeball and monkey bars, a special room full of puzzles and microscopes that gifted students could visit once a week. She remembers Lisa Kim, the Korean girl, her straight, oil-black hair in the front row of the class. Every other student at Clarence E. Singer Elementary School was white—she remembers that now, sees their faces in class photos. But it didn't occur to her, or to anyone else, at the time.

She remembers the hostages. Every night on TV they told you how many days it had been. Carter tried to save them but it didn't work. The old man with the beard always frightened her, the sound of the word "ayatollah." She remembers asking her father why the old man wanted hostages and her father stirring his drink with his index finger. "It's hard to explain," he said. Her mother turned off the TV and said, "No, it's not."

She remembers Carter losing, after a long day when her mother called every name on a sheet of paper and reminded them to vote. Her father smiled reassuringly and said nothing would change, and it didn't. She remembers the Miracle on Ice, her father and Matt whooping for joy in the family room. She remembers the morning she found her mother crying in her bathrobe, listening to the kitchen radio. She remembers the name Mark David Chapman. She remembers when the hostages went free.

She remembers these things during her first year in El Arca, during the solitary confinement mandated for terrorists. She walks a butterfly pattern in her cell, two blankets around her shoulders, draped shawl-like over her thinning hair: six steps lengthwise, seven diagonal. She's decided a hundred circuits equals one mile; she walks ten miles a day. She's let outside for thirty minutes each morning. Stale bread and cloudy soup comes on a tin tray, if the guards don't steal it first. She eats slowly, despite the foul taste. She's allowed no visitors, no phone calls, no contact with her lawyer or the embassy, no books. She spends hours at her cell's small window, assembling home movies in her mind, shoring up sepiatone fragments, looking for patterns. She's trying to make sense of it—like my editor, like me, she's trying to understand.

She remembers Morning in America. She remembers the Son of Sam. *The Love Boat* and *What's Happenin'?*, *The Electric Company* and The Captain & Tennille. She remembers John Hinckley, Jr., the scuffle by the limousine. She remembers Live Aid and Abscam. Have It Your Way. Be All That You Can Be.

And she remembers the Burned Man: his too-white eyes staring from a blackened face. How the shadows scurried all around him but no one came to help. She remembers how she recoiled in the backseat, pressing up to her brother until he shoved her away. She must have been six or seven—the hot, scratchy feel of tights, her scalp still stinging from her mother's vigorous brushing. They'd gone to see *A Chorus Line,* and on the way back to the tunnel they took a wrong turn and found themselves on a dark, empty street, girders and overpasses criss-crossing overhead. Her mother's agitation: "David, David," she breathed. They saw a bright light at the corner, flames flickering out of a trash can, shadows running away. Her father made a high, choked gasp and took off his seatbelt but her mother gripped his arm and said, "Do not get out of this car."

The man was slumped against the building. His hands were black. His clothes and his shoes were black. Tiny tongues of flame still skittered along his pants. The hood of a heavy parka framed his blackened face, but his shocking white eyes stared at Leo as the car slid past.

"Drive away," she remembers her mother said.

"Maxine, someone has to help—"

"Get out of here, David. Just drive."

She remembers this as clearly as she remembers waxy little boxes of chocolate milk and the home phone number her mother drilled into her, as clearly as she remembers who shot J.R. For years at a time she would not think of the Burned Man, but then for no reason he'd come back. Once, in college, she'd told the story to a lover, someone she met in Gabriel's class. She described his eyes, glassy and surprised, his swollen black hands. Maybe there was a smell. Yes, if she tries hard enough she can remember a terrible smell.

But it never happened—or not the way she remembers it.

"There was something," her mother says when she asks about the Burned Man. "Something in the newspaper, some kids from Long Island did it, I think. It was right after we moved to Cannondale— Matt was a baby." She shuts her eyes and shakes her head to dislodge the memory. "I think it happened in the Bronx. They poured gasoline on him while he was sleeping. Mayor Koch went on TV. I'm surprised you remember that."

But they were there, Leo insists. She remembers the pained sound her father made, the look on her brother's face, the long glow of the tunnel when they finally found their way home.

"What do you think, Leo? That I wouldn't remember?" Maxine tilts her head as if she can't recognize her daughter. David slumps against the wall of El Arca, his face sallow with altitude sickness. Leo closes her eyes and the man is still there: propped against the wall as if to be carted off, his shocked and accusing gaze.

"What kind of people do you think we are?" Maxine says. "You think we'd just drive right by something like that?"

She remembers the first time she heard the term "death squad." Sixth grade, maybe seventh, flopped on the couch with homework. David in his armchair, muttering over the newspaper, Matthew sprawled on the carpet, mashing buttons on a hand-held football game. Her fingers smelled of formaldehyde from the morning's frog dissection. She remembers the map on the television, the slick, foreign names: Nicaragua, El Salvador. A red-faced Congressman slapping the lectern. The U.S. did not belong there, he said. We had no business funding death squads.

"What does that mean? 'Death squads,'" Leo said. She had a picture in her mind of undercover cops: leather jackets, fake mustaches. Like *The A-Team*.

"Nothing," her father said behind his paper. "Don't worry about it, Leo."

"It means we're killing people," Maxine said from the kitchen door. "It means we help the people we like kill the people we don't like."

"Maxi," her father said.

"Why shouldn't they hear it?" Maxine said. "It's on the television."

Leo turned back to the TV: men in camouflage, dark faces sweaty and unshaven, lying in the dirt; others in neat uniforms, standing at attention on an airport runway.

"Why don't we like them?"

"Because they're poor," Maxine said. "Here, Leo, have a banana."

What you could not do in Cannondale: You could not make connections. Between Thomas Jefferson and Pablo the gardener, between the weaponry on the library lawn and the price of fruit. There was no big picture, no throughline: the squeegee men, the swim club, the hostages home from Iran; the varsity football player who pumped cheap gas on summer break, the ROTC pamphlets in the guidance office. The giant malls along the highway and the boarded-up houses you saw on visits to your father's parents in Paterson, how your mother checked all the locks whenever you stopped at a light.

There were no businesses in Cannondale, no commerce to mar the lush hills and leaf-scattered lawns. This was called "zoning," your mother explained, an obscure, inoffensive word like *aglet* or *photosynthesis*. A kind of natural law. Across the highway, the town of Millbrook didn't have zoning. It had a diner, where your father and brother went after Little League games. It had a liquor store, a pawn shop with golf clubs in the window, a bowling alley and a dilapidated motel and, according to Maxine, no Jews. When your friend's older sister was caught in that motel with a boy from Millbrook, the gossip in the school cafeteria, at the nail salon, was laced with disgust: she had crossed the barrier, this girl, contaminated Cannondale, made a connection. She was never seen again.

She remembers *Fantasy Island*, where rich people got anything they wanted: the beautiful woman, the dead come back to life. She remembers *Sanford & Son*. Peter Jennings and Ted Koppel told you each night what you needed to know: three black kids shot point blank on the subway. Twenty-one Hispanics shot point blank in McDonald's. Three hundred thousand dead of famine in Africa. A billion people in China. The numbers were interchangeable, make-believe: a thousand, a million, who understood the difference? Two hundred fifty-one Marines killed in Beirut ("Why were they there?" asks Leo), and the same month seven thousand U.S. troops invade an island you've never heard of. (Population: Who cares?) No one can explain why.

"I don't think anyone knows," your father says.

"But that's not fair," says the twelve-year-old terrorist. She remembers helicopters over fallow fields, soldiers with rifles jogging down a beach. "They can't just do it because they want to."

Your mother makes a sound like strangling. "Kiddo, you've got a lot to learn."

She remembers when Matt voted for Reagan in the mock election. "Mondale wants to take our money away," he coolly explained. She remembers Grandpa Carol's garden, where tomatoes hung like plump jewels and the carrots pulled long and smooth from the soil. Grandma Bess made sticky rugelach and Leo slept in a room with a canopy bed and tall windows and watched fireflies glistering over the reservoir.

In El Arca, where mice long ago relieved her mattress of its stuffing, she recalls the exact scent of that garden in summer, the thick, particular splash of sunfish jumping in the reservoir. "Hard work, Petunia," Grandpa Carol said, surveying his Westchester estate while she hung upside down from the crabapple tree. "Hard work."

She remembers when they watched *Gandhi* in freshman history: boys in the back snickering at the men in loincloths, whistling at the women with baskets on their heads, the tense, sulky mood that took her when Gandhi was shot.

"It's just a movie," her friend Rachel snorted. "God, Leo!"

She came home that night to India on the television: ambulances, dead cows, mothers lying next to their children in the street. Men with bandaged faces, blinded by the chemicals in the air. This happened before she saw *Gandhi*, but in her memory, in my memory, the two are fused.

"Mom, look," Matt said. Palm trees, soldiers, smoke from a hundred bonfires drifting past the factories of Bhopal. It was people, her brother said. He turned up the volume and wailing filled the room. "Look, Leo. They're burning people."

The colonel was a handsome man, square-jawed, salt and pepper at his temples. His slow, boyish smile left you with an impression of ease, as if he were slouching, though he sat ramrod straight. He reminded Leo of those senior boys, athletes mostly, whose popularity was so vast they could afford to be nice to everyone. The colonel, proud in his uniform, raised his arm and swore to God and Leo put down her geometry proofs to listen. He spoke thoughtfully, brow creased with sincerity—he wanted to understand the question, to give an honest answer. Leo almost sympathized.

"I do not recall," he said. Maxine squeezed her gin and tonic, chewing on the ice. "I do not recall," the colonel said to another question. He whispered something to the man next to him; they laughed and then the colonel turned back to the questioners, a touch of insolence in his posture, and said it again: "I really don't recall."

No one believed him. Leo turned up the volume. No one believed him, but the strange thing was he didn't seem to care. This man, Oliver North, didn't expect anyone to believe him. He didn't want them to. He pursed his lips, nodded with great seriousness, and suddenly she understood: he was humiliating them, daring them to call him a liar, knowing that nobody would. He was demonstrating the depth of their powerlessness, rubbing their noses in it, then offering a sympathetic smile they were also not to believe.

"I believe he's already answered that question, Senator," said the man next to the colonel. Snickers from the gallery, from reporters crosslegged on the floor. Leo clutched a pillow to her stomach. The colonel folded his hands. He was really enjoying himself.

"I don't recall! I don't recall!" Maxine said. "You asshole."

The facts of the affair didn't interest Leo. They seemed too small, like some pathetic sixth-grade cabal. She couldn't take her eyes off the colonel—his easy confidence, the glimmer of his medals. By now she knew what a death squad was. The whole country knew: they'd seen the bodies on television, they'd read about the murdered nuns. Something had happened to separate Cannondale from Millbrook, from Managua and Beirut, from *Gandhi* (*It's just a movie!*). Something tectonic. And in the gloom of that chasm slithered men like Oliver North. It hadn't happened by accident. She listened more closely to the words: *freedom fighter, constitution, help me God*. She watched his slow, taunting smile and she started to make connections.

"Have you signed your postcard yet?" The voice called through the hot crush of the crowd. "You, with the hair! Sign a postcard, Curly. Let the dictator hear your voice."

Leo stopped to look for the source of this directive. Rachel and Megan bumped into her from behind, the three girls forming a snag in the human current, the swarming heat of Giants Stadium in June, seventy thousand people smashing their way from hot-dog stand to bathroom to the blazing exposure of seats in the upper tier. She kept one eye on Matt's blue jersey as it winked through the swirl of bodies. Music thudded in the girders and concrete, snatches of melody escaping from the entrances to the stands.

An arm waved at her from behind a table. "C'mere, Curly, help free political prisoners!" Now she saw the speaker: a man in his twenties, feathered hair, a perfect tan.

"Whatever," Rachel said. "Hey, you think that guy in the Zeppelin T-shirt will buy us beer?"

"Is her mom cool?" Megan said. "Leo, does your mom care if we drink?"

She angled toward the table and the man tilted his head sardonically. He held up a white card. "Augusto Pinochet?" He had an

Australian accent and a chipped front tooth that gave his smile a leering edge. His shirt bore the same logo that was on her ticket and on banners all over the stadium: a lit candle wrapped in barbed wire. Above the candle it read: *A Conspiracy of Hope*. "Want to write to him?"

"No," she said, trying to sound flirtatious. She wanted him to call her Curly again.

"Do you even know who Augusto Pinochet is?"

"No."

"Course you don't." He regarded her sadly. "Chile, '73? Kissinger's best friend? He's your man in South America. Totally psychotic." There were brochures spread on the table, binders full of photographs. Two women stood next to him in tight T-shirts with the same logo, waving at the men walking by. "Alrighty, don't like Pinochet? We've got Deng, Mubarak, Gorbachev. Pick a card, any card. Here—" he flapped a postcard under her nose. "P. W. Botha. Fantastic! Help smash apartheid."

A muffled roar crested around them as Joni Mitchell played her finale, "Big Yellow Taxi." Leo pictured her mother back at the seats, dancing by herself. It was supposed to be Leo's birthday present—a daylong concert including U2, her favorite as well as Rachel's and Megan's. For months they'd swapped pictures of Bono, the most beautiful boy they'd ever seen; in the parking lot, she'd spent a whopping $15 on a *War* T-shirt. But so far the day had been boring—and *hot*—her mother singing along with people they'd never head of: Peter, Paul, and Mary? Jackson Browne? When a salsa band took the stage and Maxine started moving her hips, hands in the air, Leo's embarrassment was so profound it felt like vertigo.

"You do know what apartheid is?" the man was saying. "They teach you that?"

Leo rolled her eyes. "I know what it is."

"Good! Puts you ahead of most of this lot." He slid an open binder toward her. "Did you know today's the tenth anniversary of the Soweto Uprising?"

At first she couldn't tell what she was looking at, the jumbled images, a collage of faces and limbs. Slowly she began to make out bodies heaped on concrete or face-down in the dust, sniffed by dogs, children sprawled on bloody mattresses, strewn like garbage. He turned the pages slowly, as though revealing secret delights. "Happens all over the world. People tortured, raped, buried alive. People like you, your brother, born in the wrong country, under the wrong regime. You know about Steve Biko?"

Leo slid the binder closer. This photograph was different: a single body on a gurney, covered by a sheet. Only his battered face was visible. The gurney sat in an empty hallway, squalid but clinical, somehow official.

"What happened to him?"

"Torture. Twenty-two hours straight. He was a youth activist, very popular. Until you lot killed him. How do you like the music, by the way? Y'having a good time?"

Behind her, Rachel and Megan were asking for their ticket stubs. Matthew was waiting for his hot dog. But Leo felt space opening around her.

"I didn't kill him."

He crooked a finger and leaned across the table. "The U.S. is South Africa's number-one friend. Didn't know that? Most of their guns, their tanks, you sold to them. It's good business for your arms dealers. Who d'you think makes the decisions, anyway?

"These people wouldn't be in power if it weren't for you," he said. "Pinochet, Saddam Hussein, Shimon Peres. You ought to be ashamed of yourselves. But you're not, are you?"

"I'm fifteen."

"Your mum and dad, then. Didn't know they were killers, did you?"

Leo could not look up, her eyes drawn to the dead body, its solitude. She suddenly hated the man behind the table, wanted to shove some insult at his smug face.

"What's a card going to do?"

Another cheer went up inside the stadium and the man leaned closer. "Sorry?"

Her face grew hot. "What good is a postcard going to do?"

He pondered this, then shoved a stack of cards at her. "Just send them. Give them to your friends. Maybe they'll let some of these prisoners go free."

"Why would they set them free?" she said. He straightened with a familiar, reluctant insolence, but she would not relent. "It's just a stupid postcard. My grandmother sends me postcards every month."

The man sucked his teeth while the women glared. "Look, Curly. Are you planning to start a revolution?" He peered at her T-shirt. "You and Bono? Who are you? Nobody. This is the only thing someone like you can do." He squeezed her hand closed on the stack of cards. "Write the bloody postcard, alright? Tell your father to donate to Amnesty International. Now run on back inside. You don't want to miss Bryan Adams."

As she pushed through the concourse, Leo felt she'd won a small victory. She was pleased with her sarcasm, the anger she'd brought to the man's face. But climbing to the seats, late sun stabbing over the stadium rim, that sense of triumph leached away, leaving in its place the image of the gurney, the dead man's face so small and alone. They'd just left him there, an unclaimed body, a nobody. Already, she'd forgotten his name.

For the rest of the concert she felt dazed, a little out of breath. The air around her felt still and dead. The sky thickened with indigo and the stage glowed far below, across a sea of writhing bodies. Matthew fell asleep with his head in their mother's lap. Megan and Rachel moved down three rows to talk to some older boys. They tossed their hair and laughed while the boys punched each other and passed a joint down the line.

"Are you OK?" Maxine asked. "You got a little sunburn. Put your sweatshirt on."

Her face was tight, her skin tingled. "I'm fine."

In the sky above the stadium, helicopters hovered and banked, spotlights sweeping the crowd. For some time a drum had been tapping out a slow metronome, insistent and ominous. The stage was dark; all the stadium lights were dark. Over and over, the halting drum struck; one by one people lit matches, held up cigarette lighters, until the stands glimmered with thousands of tiny flames.

"You're freezing," Maxine said. The thudding drum grew more urgent, and then a low guitar note stabbed into the darkness. It came again, a cruel, droning sound, and then the singer, Peter

Gabriel, was alone in the spotlight, his voice nasal, clutched in the back of the throat like a man singing through pain:

Oh, Biko . . . Biko . . . Biko.

Leo's teeth started to chatter. She thought she must have heard it wrong. From the massive speakers the name came again, ghostly and unmistakable, thousands of voices singing along.

The man is dead, he sang. *The man is dead.*

She couldn't sit still. She felt a kind of desperation, a shrinking from that voice and from the galaxy of lights. When she stood she nearly lost her balance. One helicopter sat high in the sky, its silver beam steady and watchful. *Biko . . . Biko . . .* The drum held its unbearable rhythm, the guitar rang out relentlessly. The sound of bagpipes rose like whirring crickets, fluttering and crackling in the summer air. There were women on stage now, black women in colorful dresses and head-wraps; their languorous deathwail washed across the sky.

The man is dead, he sang—crouched at the edge of the stage, beckoning—*And the eyes of the world are watching now.*

She hugged herself, shivering, shook off the arm her mother put around her. The women on stage swayed together, crying their wordless chant over and over. It was grief—pure, liquid grief that crashed in waves all around them. The body on the gurney, abandoned and worthless, a body no one would ever take home—it was this body they cried for, not just his death but his aloneness. Everyone swayed and chanted, when she looked down she saw Megan, the arm of one of the boys around her waist, waving a lighter over her head, and without warning Leo burst into tears.

She knew she was ridiculous. Hunched over in her seat, she knew she was exhausted, sunburned. It was all ridiculous: the song, the phony African women, even the photograph—puny and ridiculous and beside the point. She could feel her mother fussing over her. She knew her friends would look at her with scorn and she hated them. She wanted to take Megan's cigarette lighter and burn her with it so she would stop singing—she had no *right.* None of them did. She shivered and sniffled but she couldn't stop picturing the dead body in the hallway, still there, still alone. And these people singing.

The stage was empty, the women returned to darkness though their chant echoed through the stadium. Only the tap-tap-tap of the heavy drum, receding into the tide of applause. The crowd released itself, returned to plastic seats, rows strewn with cardboard, sticky with spilled beer. She could hear herself sobbing but she didn't try to stop, not when her mother draped the sweatshirt over her, not when the lights came up and Rachel cried "Leo!" in astonishment and disgust, when Matt roused himself and howled with laughter and announced to their section, "My sister's on the rag!"

What else shall I write about the terrorist's origins, her influences and early indoctrinations? What more would you like to know?

"She was a little more serious than the rest of us, a little moody sometimes," writes Rachel Schraft, now an admissions officer at Yale, "but otherwise she was just a normal teenager. I don't remember ever talking about politics. It wasn't our foremost concern in tenth grade, as you can imagine. She was just *Leo*."

A normal teenager. A perfect child. An excellent student. These are the terms people use to describe her—nothing that stands out, no damaging revelations or early glimpses of the avenging angel. One struggles to locate the real person, to bring La Leo to life. For a time she was a vegetarian—though this may have been prompted by health concerns. For two years she donated her allowance to a UNICEF-backed charity—but when the letters arrived from children in Zaire she couldn't bring herself to read them. One notes the two thousand dollars she raised in a Walk-a-Thon for AIDS research. One notes the caption she chose for her yearbook photo: *I have a dream*. One finds, in other words, scattered markers of a dawning awareness that might loosely be called "political" but that prefigures the fury of the Lima press conference only when they are held up, deliberately, side by side.

And yet, the dots must be connected, a route, however serpentine, established from Point A to Point B. This, I know, is the writer's job: to dive into time's landfill and emerge, gasping and shit-smeared, the lost wedding ring clutched triumphantly in his fist.

"Nice American girls don't wake up and decide to be terrorists," my editor insists. By which he means to keep swimming. "You'll figure it out," he says, by which he means there are gaps in any story. If we can't learn the facts we make educated guesses. If we don't find the gold ring—if there's none to be found—a scrap of scorched foil will do.

But her childhood, by all accounts, was Arcadian, her family history an ordinary picture of middle-class striving and satisfaction. The house in Cannondale, sold in 2002, has been photographed many times, its suburban blandness remarked upon as if it were a shrewd disguise. That the Gelbs were unassuming, friendly, that they gave to the Sierra Club and the March of Dimes; that David coached the Millbrook Dodge Yankees, Matt's Little League team, from 1982-1985; that Maxine volunteered at a nursing home in Paramus and led a petition drive to have a stoplight installed outside the Cannondale Library—such things have been noted, written about, picked over, have acquired in their triviality an air of sinister relevance. One learns of Maxine's father, the radio and TV actor Carol Green (né Abramsky), blacklisted in the 1950s after writing an essay for *The Daily Worker*; and of David's grandfather, Sam Rubin, a prominent labor organizer in the Paterson textile mills. One notes Maxine's summer in Mississippi; one notes David received two draft deferments, that he worked pro bono for Newark community leaders after the '67 riots. One learns of the family's employment of a Dominican housekeeper. One notes Leonora's rejection from Brown.

In other words, they were liberals, the Gelbs. Good, modest, community-minded, garden-variety Jewish liberals. Like most Jews in Cannondale they considered themselves enlightened and lucky. They knew it was money that got them there, gave them lives their grandparents couldn't have recognized. But they knew money was not enough, good fortune can be revoked without warning or explanation, replaced with slavery, extermination. And so they volunteered, they donated, they walked and ran and baked to benefit causes. They taught their children kindness and charity and above all *reasonableness*. Reason, the theory goes, is the bulwark against butchery. Reasonable people, the theory goes, can disagree, but in the end those who prevail do so through the soundness of their arguments, the humility of their convictions, the ability to see more than one side. To prevail through force or deception is no victory; to stoop to invective or violence is to be defeated in some transcendent, shameful way.

I know these people, Jack. I know their concerns and aspirations, the particular smell of their self-regard. Their liberalism is a kind of insurance policy: having entered the land of privilege, one need only remember the less fortunate and one will be permitted to stay. It's a doctrine of weakness, of vulnerability, a tragic misunderstanding of what it means to be American.

Leo was no liberal. She made that clear one morning in Lima, showed the world how unreasonable she could be. Reasonableness, she knew, never stopped a bomb from falling; enlightenment never stays the torturer's hand. But to make the leap from these unre-markable roots to El Arca requires more than persistence, more than art. I'm asked to tell Leo's story—with fragments, decryptions, the muck of others' faulty recollections. To define her, fix her in a reader's mind, though I myself see only blurs and blanks. It's a crime, this empathy, a violation: from the safety of my desk chair, I'm to reach across the divide, touch her life, make the connection.

The station wagon sped smoothly over the highway, the interior gloomy and sedate as the lights of commerce played over weary passengers. Leo leaned her cheek to the steamed window and watched car dealerships and carpet stores and office parks flash past. When they stopped at White Castle, she stayed in the car; the smell of what Matt and the others brought back in their grease-thinned paper sacks turned her stomach. She ground her teeth to hold back another inexplicable bout of tears.

"I'm so pissed they didn't play 'New Year's Day!'" Megan said, again and again. "But they played the other one," Maxine said, raising her eyes to the rearview. "'Bloody Sunday,' you like that one, right Leo?" Leo barely heard. When they dropped the other girls at their houses, she grunted in sullen farewell. She would see them soon enough, at the swim club or the movies, at high-school dances and basement parties and secret forays into Greenwich Village and Herald Square. But she would never lose the image of Megan danc-ing at her seat, waving the cigarette lighter idiotically, singing a name that meant nothing to her: *Biko! Be-caw! Beeeeeeeak-O!*

If stoned teenagers could sing that name without knowing, if they could join the mindless chorus and claim to care about something to which they would not give another thought until the moment, much later, when it flattered their sense of themselves to say, "I was there!"—then nothing that happened in South Africa, or Chile, or any of those other places could be said to mean anything here, inside the bubble. No one was watching. The man was really dead. Here in Cannondale, he had never lived.

"Quite a day," her mother said, when they pulled into the garage. Matt ran inside, leaving behind a cool silence, only the ticking of the engine and the scent of gasoline through the open window. "Are you feeling any better?"

"I'm feeling fine."

Her mother reached back to smooth Leo's hair and Leo jerked away, felt the tears coming up again. She was furious with herself, she wished she could wrinkle her nose and transport herself to her room without seeing her father or answering his kind and point-less questions, throw herself under the blankets and howl until her throat bled.

"What's going on with you?" Maxine said. "What happened with Megan and Rachel?"

"Have you ever heard of Pinochet?" she asked. This was not the point, and Leo knew it, but she had to find a way to give voice to her wretchedness.

Her mother drew back. "In Chile? Of course."

Something on her mother's face pushed Leo over the edge. She rocked forward and blubbered helplessly, "Then why didn't you *tell* me?"

For a minute or more she sniffled and hiccupped; she could feel her mother looking at her, feel her gaze go from concerned to per-plexed to annoyed. She could hear her brother's careless footsteps overhead, the murmur of her father's voice.

"Leonora, there are a lot of bad people in the world," Maxine said finally. "A lot of ugly things happen."

Leo looked up in anguish. "But why?"

The killer's smile was fond and unbearable. "That's just how it is."

Leo closed her eyes. She felt flattened, her jaw and joints ached. "Nobody does anything. That's why."

"Didn't you see a million people at the concert? Of course people do something."

"Do you?" she said. "What do you and Dad do?"

Maxine pressed her lips together and stepped out of the car. The pinging of the door chime filled the garage.

"Huh?" Leo shouted after her. "What do you do?"

Out of sight, her mother said, "We live our lives. We try to be good people, raise good children. That's all anyone can do."

"That's not enough!"

After a pause, her mother said, "I know."

The garage door rattled back into motion, thicker gloom descending. She thought her mother had gone inside. But a moment later her voice came through the dark. "Time for bed, Leo. It's been a long day. You can't take things so personally." Then the door closed, leaving Leo in the restless, cooling car, listening to a creaking house, the receding footsteps and imperceptible mutters of a family on its way to a good night's sleep.

2

"Oh, it was such a happy house. Always full of food and laughter. And music. Even when we were small children. My father was a great lover of jazz. Duke Ellington. Louis Armstrong. Chet Baker. Every Sunday we walked home from the church and my father played those records until the whole house felt brighter, like there was more sun. Which is good, in this city with its ugly weather."

Señora Zavallos is a tall woman in her forties, pale and nervous, with graying hair pulled back in a severe bun. There's something lonely in her green eyes—and behind it something offended by this loneliness. "My father used to say a life without music is like a marriage without sex," she says, running her fingertips along the banister as they climb to the third floor. "He would invite his students to the house and play records all night. They loved him, those students. They taught him about Charlie Parker, Miles Davis—"

"What did your father teach?" Leo says.

"Economics. He was head of the department at Católica. Students would fight for seats in his class. That was before the trouble." At the top of the stairs, the señora opens a door, sniffing mistrustfully. "Of course you know about that."

Leo peers into the cavernous, empty room—windows along one long wall, the other marked and discolored where mirrors and a barre had once been anchored. A short hallway leads to a changing room with a toilet. The mention of a third-floor dance studio with its own entrance was what had drawn her attention to the ad, which declared WE SPEAK ENGLISH in bold type.

"Not really," Leo says now. "I mean, we didn't hear a lot about it in the U.S."

"I'm not surprised," the señora says.

"But it's over, right? I mean," she says, putting on her best frightened gringa—"it's *safe* here?"

"Lima's a different city now." The señora crosses the floor, her steps echoing on scuffed parquet, and shoves at a stuck window until it flies open. She frowns at something on the street below. "You'll learn which areas to avoid."

They'd arranged to meet at a bus stop on the Plaza de la Bandera, then strolled through orderly Pueblo Libre, past dignified homes and small, well-kept parks that gave off tropical warmth and the smells of dying plant life. Fog simmered low in the sky, flattening all sound. The señora talked ceaselessly, pointing out the elementary school, the dry cleaners, the pasteleria that specialized in banana-cream cakes for quinceañeras. Leo spotted the house from a block away—three boxy, whitewashed floors behind a high wall, bigger and uglier than the houses surrounding it. The señora tried several keys before she was able to open the gate. When Leo saw the flagstone courtyard, a jaunty lime tree in the center, bare rosebushes at the base of the wall, her heart prickled with satisfaction.

"You plan to have art classes?" the señora says, inspecting a long crack in the wall of the second-floor hallway. "What a nice idea. There are very talented students at Católica, if you're looking for teachers. Don't take anyone from San Marcos. You can't trust them. Are you a painter? When I was an adolescent I used to paint watercolors."

"I'm not really an artist," Leo says. The señora looks at her queerly. "My friends have the talent," she explains. "I'll run the business, design ads, make schedules, things like that. I'm not so creative. I'm more . . . motivated."

"The administradora," Señora Zevallos says, pleased by the explanation.

"Exactly!"

Downstairs, light floods through the living room's tall windows. Despite the morning's humidity, the house feels dry and dusty, chilly from disuse. The señora leads her down a narrow hallway into a kitchen tiled white with tiny blue cornflowers; she rises on her toes, turning a slow pirouette to point out the cabinets and the pantry, the ancient stove scored by vigorous scrubbing. A back window looks out on a decrepit toolshed, a dry birdbath, an unplastered brick wall trussed with bougainvillea.

Leo counts out hundred-dollar bills on the counter—"I will accept only American money," the señora said over the phone—and asks about Arequipa, where the señora now lives with one of her sisters. The weather is better, the señora says, but the people are closed and haughty. She doesn't know her neighbors; she spends her days caring for her sister's two children, walking to the market without being greeted by a single person.

"And your mother and father?"

The señora tucks the cash into her purse. "My father lives in Chicago with my oldest sister and her husband. My mother . . ."

"I'm sorry."

"When they took my father away, when he was gone. She couldn't bear it. Three months, they would not tell us where he was. They would not even tell us if he had been arrested. But of course we knew."

Leo keeps her voice low. "Because he taught economics?"

"Of course not. He wasn't a Marxist! His department didn't tolerate the garbage they taught at San Marcos."

"Then why?"

She takes a last look at the kitchen, smiling sadly. "It was the music. All those students coming over at night. Someone had to notice." She turns to Leo, her voice sharp with accusation. "All they did was listen to records and drink pisco. They never even talked about the war."

Outside, the señora locks the gate behind her and hands Leo the keys. She points to the bodega at the corner. "If you wait there, you'll get a taxi quickly enough."

"I'll walk. I like to find my way around the city."

The señora's expression is bemused, disapproving. "It was a beautiful city at one time. But now the people are animals. It was better during the dictatorship, even with the long lines for bread and coffee. It's terrible that I would wish for that time. Isn't it?"

"Things always seem better when they're over."

The señora buttons her sweater and peers into the haze, as if testing the wind. "No. Things seem precisely as they were. But what comes next is always worse. Good luck, Leonora. I hope the school succeeds. I'd like to visit one day."

Knowing she'll never see the señora again, Leo chances an awkward hug. "Please come anytime."

Four years later, at the civilian retrial, Leo was astonished to see Señora Zavallos enter the courtroom as a government witness, previously unnamed—as were nearly all the witnesses, to protect them from "terrorist reprisals." She had aged visibly, her skin stretched against her skull, one hand trembling in her lap. After confirming that she owned the devastated house in the photographs, she held her chin high and identified the defendant as the young woman who came to see her on that February morning.

"She was a fool. You could see that right away. Going around with so much money. So arrogant. I tried to tell her about the neighborhood and its history but she wasn't interested. She thought she knew everything. Immediately, she acted as if the house belonged to her, as if she could do whatever she pleased."

Gently, the prosecutor asked why, if the señora had such a poor opinion of the defendant, she had agreed to rent the house to her. "I needed the money," she said quietly. She scanned the faces in the galley. "It's a terrible thing, to be so desperate."

She takes a corner room on the second floor, with large windows that squeal horribly when she cranks them out. The room is bright and breezy, with a high ceiling and ornate crown molding. Years of dust and flaked paint have accumulated in the corners. She spreads her dirty laundry on the floor, uses *Moby-Dick* for a pillow, wakes at dawn to the crow of a neighbor's rooster and the acute sense that she's alone in the enormous city. At the corner bodega she buys sponges and a broom, floor polish, bread and a wheel of rubbery cheese for her breakfast, Nescafé and condensed milk, a flimsy saucepan scorched on the bottom. The old dueño nods affably as he counts her change.

"¿De dónde es?" he says, squinting through thick glasses. "Where from?"

"United States, señor."

"¡Americana!" He points to an old Dallas Cowboys calendar on the wall: buxom, silver-skinned cheerleaders.

She can't stop herself: "Somos todos Americanos, señor."

By midday she's acquired two scratchy blankets, a sleeping pad, a Bugs Bunny beach towel. She mops the floor of her bedroom with old rags while the radio she liberated from Ricky's stammers the latest absurdities from Washington: "*I would never walk away from the people of this country and the trust they've placed in me . . .*" For a week she keeps herself busy, scouring grime from windowsills, pulling cobwebs from the corners, scrubbing grout until it gleams. Her eyes sting from mingled fumes, her arms and shoulders burn. No word yet from Julian. In the late afternoons she strolls the neighborhood in widening circles—from sleepy blocks lined with shade trees, flowerbeds in the medians, to boulevards frantic with construction: pert row houses, a new supermarket the size of an airport hangar. Waiting. Learning her surroundings. She smiles at the passersby—her neighbors—carrying her secret like a candy under her tongue, the knowledge that at last she's doing *something.* That soon she'll do more.

But when? As one day melts into the next she grows restless, finds herself standing at a third-floor window, watching the street, wondering at every passing car. It's a different city now, yes: a manic city, drunk on peace and awash in capital. But what of the hillside barrios teeming with refugees, the makeshift dwellings washing off in the first rains? What of ruined villages all over the countryside—wrecked schools, salted fields, no able-bodied men left to rebuild? What of Los Muertos? Were these the areas Señora Zavallos thought she should avoid? Were these the animals she had in mind?

At night she lays awake watching lights slide across cracked plaster, remembering the open wound of Vía América, the long and gusty drop. She listens to the creaks of the empty house. When she closes her eyes, she can't quite conjure Ernesto's face.

"We need *space,*" Julian said, when he left her at a bus stop on a dark stretch of the malecón. He wanted a big house, two entrances. "I don't want my face in someone's ass every time I turn around."

Space for what, she'd asked? And who else would be there? And what then?

"Questions don't help us," he said. "You want to ask questions, stay in your fucking hostel."

The first time she uses the oven, the kitchen fills with a sweet, gamey smell, greasy smoke gusting from the door. She pulls out the broiler tray to discover the corpses of four mice, blackened and petrified, among charred scraps of paper, dead leaves, burned matchsticks. She lets out a cry and the tray clatters to the floor, scattering the tableau of rodent tragedy across the tiles. When her heart stops pounding, she sweeps the dead mice and ashes into a paper bag and dumps it all in the backyard's overgrowth. She opens a package of steel wool, attacks the oven's filthy insides until her hands chafe and bleed. Under the rangetop, decades of grease have fused to a stinking black glue; she chisels soot with a butter knife, gasping at the smell, and reminds herself of a formulation she once read about what it means to be a revolutionary:

"Honor is to be useful without vanity."

And then, one morning, Marta is there. A week later, two weeks—there's no record or testimony, no way for me to know. "Before the first of March, she was joined by a second Philosopher," is all the government documents state. How many hours have I wasted trying to nail down the exact date? As if it could possibly matter—a Monday? a Thursday? As if someone's life depended on it.

"Up!" says the woman, her voice cutting through the dawn silence. "Get up now."

Leo startles on her bedroll, gropes for her glasses. The voice comes again—"You! You-self . . . Up, now!"—a brusque contralto emanating from the blurred form in the doorway. Her first muddled thought is that it's Señora Zavallos, come to avenge some insult to her father's memory.

"What's happening?" Leo groans—but the stranger has already scooped the bedding and marched out to the hall, the whole mass before her like a pregnant belly.

At the bottom of the stairs, she shoves the blanket into Leo's arms. "These room," she says, pointing at the ceiling, waggling a forbidding finger. Her face is narrow and stern, her gaze unblinking. "No for you."

Out the living room windows, day is just breaking, fleet shadows flittering musically around the lime tree. There's a duffel by the front door, two black cases with chrome latches. "Who are you?" Leo says, still shaking off sleep. "¿Quien eres?"

"English!" the woman says. She points to the ground-floor bedrooms. "You . . . I . . . Sleeping."

"You're moving in?" The woman's face darkens with incomprehension. Leo sets her bundle on the new-swept floor and carefully touches her shoulder. "You live *here?*"

All that is known about Angélica Ramos Urpay—Comrade Marta—was recounted in Gustavo Gorriti's *Caretas* article: born 1966 in San Martín de Porres, a working-class barrio west of central Lima; her mother a migrant from Puno who cleaned houses for the wealthy, never married; attended the prestigious Pontificia Universidad Católica del Perú, just down the road from San Marcos, her tuition paid by one of her mother's clients (Gorriti surmises it was the girl's father), where she later taught photography from 1994 to 1997.

I can add nothing to this bio. Ramos's mother, Luz María, died in 2006; her school records (as if a grade in freshman biology might bear on this mess) vanished long ago. I keep a copy of her faculty photo in the Leo File, clipped from an article about the raid—a photo recognizable to most Peruvians, one of the images most closely associated with the Cuarta Filosofía. There's something vulnerable in the bow of Marta's lips, the scattering of freckles on her thin neck, but it is not a conventionally pretty face, not soft or symmetrical. There's a severity in her gaze, something both intimidating and guarded. One can imagine her smiling patiently, but never with delight. It's a face that inspires fascination, pity even, but not empathy—viewed side by side with photographs of Augustín Dueñas and Mateo Peña, Comrade Marta's face is most convincingly that of a terrorist. I can't look away.

After taking the rest of her belongings to one of the downstairs bedrooms, Leo finds her in the kitchen, sipping from a mug and examining the spotless oven. She's long and elfin, with narrow hips, an almost flat chest. She wears cargo pants and a plain black tank top; her lean biceps flex as she washes out the pot. Leo feels shy and careful around this stranger, keenly aware the space no longer belongs to her.

"Tenemos que amoblar este sitio," the woman says. "We need beds, and pots to cook with, plates. It must look like a house where somebody lives."

Leo answers her Spanish with English. "We do live here."

"No. Don't accustom yourself to this. You understand? It doesn't belong to you."

"I only meant—"

"Maybe we stay here one week, maybe one month. Then somewhere else. It is not our role to decide." She gestures at the tile floor, the bright window. The sun has crept over the backyard wall, shining on the tall grass. "This is a story we are telling for this moment. But you must not believe it."

Seeing Leo's shrinking expression, the woman holds out the other mug. Leo accepts it cautiously, happy to find it full of hot coffee.

"Chaski comes tomorrow. You go to the market so we can get the house ready."

Ready for what? Leo stops herself from asking. Chancing Spanish, she says quietly, "Is it permitted to ask for your name?"

The woman blows into her mug. "You will call me Marta."

On a hunch, Leo says, "But this is also a story?"

Marta looks up in surprise, a smile curling her mouth's corners. The waiting has come to an end, the weeks of solitude—soon, Leo thinks, the house will be filled with people, conversations, plans. And she and this Marta will be at the center: roommates, comrades. Maybe they will be friends.

"Soy Leonora," she says, holding out her hand. "I don't have another name."

"You will."

3

It was a glamorous case, L'Affaire Gelb, a cause célèbre in international circles and among the hand-wringers of the intellectual class. Grim as it was her story had sex appeal, an air of adventure, Leo as American archetype: the swashbuckler who got in over her head. First came the rumors, garbled dispatches barely audible beneath the clamor of Bill and Monica: *American citizen . . . political prisoner . . . guerrillas.* Then news of the military trial—*life sentence . . . hooded judges . . . inhumane conditions*—and photos of the press conference: the tiny white woman surrounded by swarthy men in body armor. We were not shown the weapons, the guns and grenades taken from Pueblo Libre. We did not see car bombs or corpses, carnage from the war Peruvians were trying to forget. For us there was no war. There was no context or history—only a burned-out house, a President strutting among bodies: outrageous. Only the wounded girl raising her fist: unbowed. And despite being the world's most inveterate bully, or maybe because of it, America does love an underdog.

First the left-wing press, then NPR and the nightly news, a segment on MacNeill-Lehrer, a four-page spread in *Time*. Peru's actions were "excessive," "unacceptable," "counter to the norms of civilized nations"; its government was "authoritarian," its anti-terrorism laws "brutal" and "unbefitting of a democracy." Suspension of habeas corpus, domestic spying, indefinite detention, torture—such practices were hateful to Americans, they offended our most cherished ideals. We were reminded of Latin America's penchant for dictators, its overactive militaries and secret police. *There but for the grace,* we thought. It was 1998, 1999. Such things could never happen here.

They called her a freedom fighter, a revolutionary, the folk hero who stood up to a brutal regime—like David with his slingshot or Nelson Mandela, like Luke Skywalker or that kid in Tiananmen Square. There were T-shirts and fundraisers, a letter-writing campaign, a benefit concert in Golden Gate Park. The cities of Berkeley and Madison passed resolutions. Eddie Vedder was photographed wearing a *Free Leo!* pin. The story felt familiar, its pulse beat to a rhythm we knew: the outcry would build, the petitions and editorials, an off-the-cuff comment by Madeleine Albright, a presidential finger poked into the camera. And in the end, we assumed, the U.S. would get its way, as the U.S. usually does. We waited for the news flash: footage of diplomats spiriting her across the tarmac, the press conference at Dulles or JFK. She would appear on *Good Morning America*, she would accept an award from the ACLU—then she'd vanish forever from the vast, churning kaleidoscope of America's attention.

But it didn't happen that way.

"There are reminders to all Americans that they need to watch what they say, watch what they do," Ari Fleischer informed us from the White House three years later, at the dawn of a new era. In this era, one does not defend political violence. One does not speak of uneven playing fields or collateral damage, of cancelled elections or stolen oil or the snapped necks and empty stomachs of realpolitik. In 1998 one might still talk of "rebels" and "revolution" with a certain romance. One might applaud "the megaton detonation of self-respect," as Gabriel Zamir did in *Bicentennial of Blood*, to describe the topplings of Batista and Somoza, uprisings in Chiapas and East Timor, to admire the Afghan mujahideen.

But in 2001, one no longer spoke of such things. One watched what one said and what one did. There were no more rallies in Bryant Park, no more screeds in *Mother Jones* or portraits of La Leo on the grassy quads of the Ivy League. In the ruins of Lower Manhattan, the smolder of a Pennsylvania field, her name was forgotten, her face too blurry to recognize. Since 2001 we've learned to distrust fine distinctions. We've reconsidered the dictator's point of view and found it somewhat more reasonable. *Tyranny, torture, patriot, self-defense*—in the accelerating mayhem there was no time for semantics, for the splitting of hairs. There was only one word for her now, a meaningless word, an unspeakable word:

Leo, are you a terrorist?

But all this, too, is irrelevant, my editor says, all beside the point. Afghanistan and Dick Cheney, the Geneva Conventions. Blackwater. Halliburton. Guantánamo Bay.

"Who the hell is Subcomandante Marcos? You think our readers know what's in the PATRIOT Act? Stick to the story, dude," he says. "Let someone else explain how the world works."

But what is the story? What does it really mean? I stare at her picture and see an anger too deep for easy explanation, for the reassuring clichés of the *bildungsroman*. How to get past the headlines and stock images, to scrape away encrusted myth until the real Leo gleams in my palm?

I don't want to explain how the world works. I just want to tell the truth. But all I have are stories: incomplete, self-serving, warped by time and grief and fear. Like peering through frosted glass, Leonora's just a shadow, dim and receding—until, in the end, there's no one there.

"Remember the Rule of Three," Maxine says. "You have to wait three years, or plant new rosebushes three feet away. Do you know how long they've been dead?"

"They're not dead."

"Well, Leo, it's summer there, right? Have they flowered? You're not a magician, you know."

Leo closes her eyes and leans against the doorway of the bodega, letting sunshine bake into her scalp. "They're not dead, mom," she says. "It just takes a little work. You don't just throw things out."

It's an old argument, familiar roles, but her own words sound strange to her, as if she's playing a part in some amateur production written in a foreign language. When she tries to picture her mother sitting at the kitchen table in Cannondale, the day's crossword puzzle and a mug of tea before her, what comes to mind is Nancy, how she'd smoked her cigarettes down to the nub, barking into the phone after her son disappeared.

She's spent the last few days working in the courtyard, ripping out weeds, turning hard, dry soil, trimming and staking the anemic lime tree. She spread compost around the bare, twiggy rosebushes, vowing to coax new buds before summer's end. There's dirt under her fingernails, long, itchy welts on her arms. Chaski hasn't come; Leo's vowed to be patient, to stay focused on immediate tasks, however unglamorous. One afternoon she took a bus to Breña to browse at an art-supply store. She brought back sketchpads, boxes of charcoal, thumbtacks, half a dozen painter's smocks—but when she dumped her booty on the floor of the upstairs studio, the pile it made looked improbably small.

She's seen little of her new housemate, who's gone each morning by the time Leo wakes, leaving a yoga mat under the living room window, a coffee mug set to dry on the kitchen counter. Once, Leo cracked open the door to Marta's bedroom and found it empty but for a bedroll and the locked black cases. To one wall were taped a dozen black-and-white photographs: street children in tattered clothes; empty, trash-strewn lots; an old Indian woman bent under a basket. The images were urgent, disquieting, the focus so sharp they seemed hyperreal. Leo stared for a long time, mesmerized— like Marta herself the photos contained secrets, their surfaces hiding things she can't yet understand.

After hanging up with her mother, she heads home, mentally ticking off the day's remaining chores: bathmats, a mop and floor polish, oil the window cranks, do something with the overgrown backyard. She hears the banging from a block away; when she rounds the corner, Chaski is standing outside the gate, peering up at the house. A battered pickup truck idles in the street behind him.

"Where have you been?" she says, trying to sound playful. "It's already Friday!"

"Please, we go now?" he says. "Miguel needs his truck by three."

He drives offhandedly through the city's snarled center, one wrist slung over the wheel, the other flipping channels on the AM radio. The cloying smell of gasoline seeps through the floorboards; Leo keeps her window down as they cross the river, taking in the slums on the other side, the windowless huts of dusty pink, toothpaste blue. She bites her tongue to keep from asking questions: about

Julian, about Marta, who else is coming, what is the plan? She steals glances at Chaski's freshly shaved jaw and remembers the day he came to the hostel, how he'd sat on her bed while she swooned with fever. It's hard to think of him as a fighter, a revolutionary. But then she remembers Julian's story about a boy whose parents were mutilated right in front of him, and a surge of anger and compassion hardens her stare. Of course he's a fighter, she thinks. What choice did he ever have?

In San Juan de Lurigancho, the sidewalks are frantic with activity, storefronts and cafeterias spilling bodies into the current. On the grassless median old women sell bowls of stew from battered pots to shirtless men carrying slings full of firewood or pushing mud-caked wheelbarrows. Chaski honks at a passing moto-taxi, waves to someone down a street heaped with broken asphalt. Two teenagers in the door of a bodega call his name.

"Is this where you live?" Leo says.

"Not anymore," Chaski says. "During the war, too many problems here. Soldiers, helicopters . . . for someone who looks like me, not so safe. Also," he laughs, "everyone here looks like me."

He'd bounced from district to district, sleeping in rooms with a dozen strangers, or with others who'd fled their villages for the relative safety of Lima's multitudes. Eventually he wound up at San Marcos, taken in by militant students who controlled two floors of a dorm with bars on the windows and sentries in the stair, the electricity long since having been cut.

"Is that where you met Julian?" Leo says.

"No. I met Julian because of Enrique."

"Enrique?"

Chaski gives her a strange look as he pulls a U-turn in front of a fenced lot stacked with furniture. "His brother."

A burly, red-faced man with thick gray hair greets them at the gate. He gives Leo a quick nod, but then grips Chaski by the shoulders and hugs him hard. Not until the two men disappear into a small office at the back of the lot does Leo recognize him: the man from Nancy's house, with the mangled arm.

A few minutes later, three kids start hauling furniture out to the sidewalk: bed frames, crude wooden chairs, mattresses thin as seat cushions. Soon the truck is stacked and cluttered as an attic. For another hour, Chaski hurries her through the cramped stores and dark, constricted bazaars of Lurigancho. At every turn people greet him with kisses on both cheeks, rumpling his hair, hardly acknowledging the gringa standing next to him, her pockets full of cash.

"Oye, gordita, ¡no seas mala!" Chaski says, teasing a pregnant girl of seventeen or eighteen, who sits between towers of aluminum pots. "Give me a better price. The boys are hungry. How will they eat?"

"They can eat their fathers' balls, amigo."

Chaski feigns shock. "Yes, okay, but they still need something to cook them in!" They both laugh, and the girl kicks him flirtatiously in the shin.

Leo waits in silence, furtively peeling bills when Chaski nods to her. Armful by armful, she lugs their purchases to the truck—bundles of towels thin as paper napkins, plastic plates, curtains—ignoring the stares of children who trail her at a distance. So Julian has a brother, she thinks. First Marta, now Enrique—her sense of the group, the house and its purpose, is shifting daily, the hazy equations by which she tries to ascertain her own function. She wonders when she'll meet this Enrique, if he'll be pleased with what she's done. She wonders if Enrique will be the one to tell her what comes next.

She's pulled from this reverie by the sound of raised voices, a heavyset woman snatching an electric kettle out of Chaski's hand.

"Get out of here, joven. Where are we, in the campo? I gave you a fair price."

"But mamá," Chaski says, "a few soles, it's not so much—"

"Tengo seis hijos con hambre, amigo," she says. "¡Eres como un judío!"

"Okay, mamita, okay!" Chaski says, laughing. He holds out his hand for the money, but Leo, startled, doesn't notice.

Como un judío, she'd said: *Just like a Jew.*

Leo stares at the older woman, who swats the dust off the kettle with a filthy rag. She's never heard it firsthand before, so casual, so unnoticed. She can't quite place it—as if some comic-book villain, laughably familiar, had walked up to shake her hand.

"Amiga?" Chaski says.

Leo blinks at him, sees the confusion on his face. He has no idea. She counts out the coins, slaps them into his oblivious palm. The woman, still muttering in Quechua, takes the money without looking up.

There's long been a minor preoccupation with Leonora Gelb's Jewishness—her family's "self-professed" or "alleged" Jewishness— as though it were, depending on the context, either the source or the disproof of her guilt. Though the Gelbs belonged to the Temple Beth Shalom, in Alden, NJ, from 1975 to 2002, they rarely attended. Neither Leo nor her brother was bar mitzvahed; they did not attend Sunday school; the entirety of their religious education seems to have been yearly Seders at the Greens' home in Armonk and a Broadway outing to see *Fiddler on the Roof*. Early articles referred to the family as "lapsed" or suggested David had "renounced" his faith. In 2000, when the Central Conference of American Rabbis sent a delegation to Lima, some reporters wondered whether the Gelbs' "rediscovery" of Judaism was a cynical stratagem. An editorial in *El Comercio* called them "judíos manqués."

As a child Leo never thought of herself as Jewish. In Cannondale, Jews were as unremarkable as station wagons; she was more surprised to learn that a friend had gone to Mass. Only at Stanford, surrounded by skateboarding Californians and fleeced Colorado nature-kids, did she start to feel a difference in herself—her "East Coastness," as one suitemate put it. She saw herself through their eyes—darker, more solitary and intense—saw these same qualities in some of her colleagues at the *Daily*, in speakers at rallies whose anger was honed with irony. Among campus activists, being Jewish was a complicated matter—one took pains to disapprove of Zionism, to express solidarity with the oppressed Palestinians and admiration for Arafat, the freedom fighter. "To be Jewish has nothing to do with Israel," Gabriel, who came from an Orthodox French family, often said. Yet she couldn't deny her involuntary affinity for the Jews she knew, the protectiveness she felt for these people (she would not say "her people"). She would not call it kinship, but she couldn't deny a sense of recognition. She tried not to talk about it.

"We don't concern ourselves with technicalities, bloodlines and things like this," Rabbi Arturo Eisen Villaran, head of the conservative Sociedad de Imanuel, in Miraflores, told me. "If a person comes to us in trouble, we do what we can to help."

A bearish man of sixty-five, with a powerful grip and a large, bloodstone ring on the pinky of his right hand, Rabbi Eisen has led the temple since 1987. Educated at Brandeis, he speaks excellent English, his accent threaded with humor. On his office walls are photos of the rabbi embracing Peruvian politicians and businessmen, and one of him praying at the Western Wall. During Leonora's solitary confinement he made several trips to El Arca on the family's behalf. There were rumors he intervened with Interior Minister Rudolfo Gallegos de Silva, whose wife belongs to the temple; but such an intervention, if it happened, had no obvious effect.

"This is a family that has been through a terrible time," Eisen said with a shrug. "The trouble is not because they are Jewish or not Jewish, so I respond to them not as a Jew or a rabbi but as a human being." When I asked if he thought Leo's heritage influenced her politics, if the much-noted Jewish concern for social justice might have led her to the Cuarta Filosofía, he laughed dismissively.

"I can tell you absolutely there is nothing in Jewish teaching that says this. Help the suffering, yes. Heal the world—tikkun olam—fine, of course. But we draw the line at violence." He gazed out the window and into the temple's courtyard, where a reinforced security post stood below loops of razor wire. "There were no Jews in the Shining Path. There were no Jews in Cuarta Filosofía. Peruvian Jews are not associated with the left. We're a small community, quiet people. We don't get involved like this."

"But she's not Peruvian," I reminded the rabbi.

He folded his heavy hands on the desk. I could see him wondering something about me, and then deciding. "She should thank God," he said.

When she and Chaski get back to the house, the gate is open, the courtyard and flowerbeds littered with scrap wood. A man stands over a sawhorse, running a table saw from a cord that leads into the house. The sound of hammering drifts from the upstairs windows, along with a horrible metal rasping Leo feels in her molars.

"Chaski, oye negrito, you got everything? Where you been?" Julian sits in a second-floor window, shirtless, smoking and peering at the street. "What do you think of this place? Like Club Med, right?"

The house is full of workers, men in worn jeans and T-shirts who hurry to take the planks and blankets off Leo's hands. Broken slats and loose screws litter the living room floor, a paint-spattered tarp lies heaped at the base of the stairs. Chaski greets the workers in Quechua; most answer with a grunt or a curt nod.

"I didn't know you were a millionaria, Soltera," Julian says when he comes downstairs, brushing sawdust from his work pants. His gut is pudgy, but his shoulders are strong, his nipples large and dark red, enswirled by hair. "Did you hire a maid and a cook, too? Look at this place. *Pueblo Libre*? Is that a joke?"

"You said big and inconspicuous," Leo says. "It's hard to do both."

He takes out a cigarette. "I shouldn't have listened to Chaski. Of course you find a house like this. Just like home, no?"

Leo stares at her hands. She's sulky and overheated, still unsettled by the exchange over the tea kettle. "What's wrong with Pueblo Libre?"

"You see all the mamis on the street gossiping? This is a *family* barrio—" he spits the word as if it were a food-borne illness. "Police are everywhere. They arrest you for lying on a park bench. We should be somewhere like Lurigancho—con el pueblo, with the people we're fighting for."

"Don't be stupid," she says. "They don't need revolutionaries in Lurigancho. That's exactly where they expect us to be."

Amused, Julian drops his cigarette in a coffee can. "You think you're a revolutionary?"

For the rest of the afternoon she stays out of sight, busying herself in the kitchen, muttering to herself as she cleans and stacks new plates and cookware. *He said he would do everything he could to help* . . . says a woman on the radio, the latest Clinton accuser. *He touched me. He put his hand on my breast.* Fuming, she flips to another station. She can't shake the look on Chaski's face when she'd told him she was Jewish—as if she'd just claimed the sky was made of water, and she could breathe it. Why can't anyone stay focused on what really matters?

"You got enough food for these guys?" Julian says when she ventures back to the living room. He buttons his crisp, white shirt and fixes her with his stare. "Chaski's gotta take the truck back to Miguel, but maybe you want to go to the store first?"

"That's very thoughtful," she says. She reaches for the broom, sweeps screws and splinters toward the door. "What are they doing upstairs?"

"Fixing things. Getting ready."

There's that word again. "Don't you think we should have asked the señora?"

He picks up one of the blocky new chairs and examines it. "Why?"

"Out of respect? If you want me to take care of the house, I have to think about what the señora will say."

"Fuck the señora."

"She's been good to us."

"Good?" he says. "What's good? Taking our money, that's good?" He lights another cigarette and pointedly tosses the match to the floor. "The señora is a bourgeois criolla who ran out of money. Now she has our money. She better be good to us."

"You don't know anything about her."

"No, *you* don't know anything about her. You think your friend the señora would rent this house to Chaski?" He nods at one of the workers, a short, dark man with a low brow and a widow's peak. "Or Artemio? You don't see what people in this country are like. They treat you different. It doesn't matter what we do to the house. If the señora sees Artemio she's going to call the militares to bury him in a fucking hole."

Artemio stares, clearly having no idea what Julian is saying. Chaski examines a curtain rod and avoids her eyes. She wishes Marta were home—she's tired of being surrounded by men, lectured by men, their certainties and their careless gestures.

"Sometimes you need to trust people," she says.

"A revolutionary doesn't trust anyone."

"I wonder if Enrique agrees with you."

Julian freezes, the cigarette held halfway to his mouth. "What did you say?"

"Amiga—" Chaski warns.

"Your brother. Enrique. Maybe you should check with him first."

Pleased to have silenced him for once, Leo goes back to sweeping, pushing dust and stray chunks of foam into a pile. Someone calls down that the work is finished, but gets no answer. When she next looks up, Julian is standing too close. He takes the broom from her hands and leans it, very gently, against the wall.

"Go into your room, Soltera. Stay there until we leave."

"What?" she laughs. "Come on, Julian. All I'm saying—"

"Shut your mouth. This is my house now."

"I signed the lease," Leo says. "It was my money."

He rubs the back of his neck and closes his eyes. Then he seizes her arm and drags her toward the front door. Chaski looks up in helpless alarm, but before he can speak Julian has whisked her outside, hustling her through the courtyard where she trips over the extension cord, dragging her in halting half-steps toward the gate and throwing her against the wall so her breath flies out in a silent cough.

"Are you living here?" Julian's eyes are dull and hard. She gasps for breath and he shakes her. "You said you wanted to help, remember?"

She nods, eyes watering. "Yes."

"You'll do anything. You remember? Now I'm telling you what to do: shut your fucking mouth. If someone wants your opinion they'll ask. But no one's going to ask."

Helplessly she scans the upstairs windows but finds only reflections of warped sky. "That's not—how you inspire loyalty—"

The blow is unexpected, twirling her and stealing her balance so she crouches with her cheek pressed to the wall. For a second she can't hear anything, and then her head fills with roaring, a hot throb that spreads down her throat and behind her eyes. Her glasses have fallen, but before she can retrieve them he pulls her to her feet, propels her through the gate and past the empty truck. Without a word he shoves her into the street and releases her—she takes two wild steps and stumbles, only a split second to brace herself, to hope there are no cars coming, before she hits the pavement hands first and curls up to protect her head.

"You want loyalty, find the Three Musketeers," he says. "I told you you were in the wrong place, Soltera. But you don't listen."

She fights to calm her breathing, to hold back tears, until she hears the wood gate slam shut. A sob builds in her chest but she strangles it. The street is silent. She knows she has to get up before someone sees her. Her palms are burning, seeping blood and asphalt grit. She should get up, limp to the bodega, wait for a taxi. Who would blame her for leaving now?

All her belongings are inside, her passport, the credit card. Her head is ringing, blood oozing over her wrists. If she goes back inside, she knows, she'll have to obey him, submit to his authority, his casual cruelty. But to leave now, just as something is starting to happen, would be to admit that she doesn't belong here, to prove he was right. She pictures herself knocking at the door of Ricky's hostel, bleeding and pitiful, or slinking through the lobby of the Sheridan, riding the elevator with nervous tourists, and her throat grips with misery: to come this far only to admit she's not cut out for it, to pass up a chance to help because someone is *mean* to her. Aren't people's lives more important than that? Isn't Neto's?

Honor is to be useful without vanity, she thinks, pushing herself off the pavement.

Then, with a wave of disgust: *Eres como un judío.*

The street is empty, even the sparrows have stopped chittering. She can still feel the handprint hot on her face. A great fatigue settles in her bones as she steps onto the sidewalk. The gate is locked. She knocks—lightly, and then louder, and when she hears a voice on the other side she says quietly that she's sorry, that she'll keep quiet from now on, that she'd thought she was being helpful but she understands this was arrogance, a product of her privilege. She won't question or argue anymore. She's sorry, she says again. Please, let me come inside. When the gate opens she walks straight across the flagstones. She doesn't stop to pick up her glasses or look at the men in the living room. She goes to the back of the house, but the room where she's been sleeping is crowded with furniture; her bedding has been moved across the hall. Leaving the door open she curls up on the soft pile, clutches a corner of a blanket and pushes it, dry and fuzzy, into her mouth, sucking on the sour, dampening cloth, and refusing to choke.

Marta wakes her with hot tea, a towel bundled with ice that she presses to Leo's cheek. "Hold this," she says. She opens a bottle of peroxide and cleans the cuts on her hands and forearms; the torn flesh burns and throbs and Leo clenches her sore jaw until her body shakes. Marta works quickly to pick out the dirt and gravel, making gentle sounds of disapproval when Leo tries to pull away.

The windows are dark, the house quiet. Someone has left her glasses by the bed, the arms bent so badly they sit lopsided on her face.

"Does he do that to you?" Leo says, her voice hardly more than a whisper.

Marta frowns into her tea. "No," she says, which only makes Leo feel smaller. She remembers Chaski's face when Julian dragged her outside, the workers standing around like spectators. She climbs to her feet, the room briefly tilting. In the bathroom, she brushes her hair with fierce, stinging strokes. The house is empty, the living room cleared of trash, the rickety new chairs pushed against one wall. There are beds in the second-floor bedrooms, new shutters locked across the windows, thin mattresses piled in the hallway. The stairs to the dance studio are blocked by a steel mesh door. She shakes the knob with all her strength, but the door barely shivers. She stares at the door a long time. Julian was right: it's not her house anymore.

Back in their room, Marta sits cross-legged on her sleeping pad, a toothbrush in her mouth. One black case lies open at her side, a camera nestled in protective gray foam. Marta hums to herself, cleaning a lens with a cloth.

"Is he afraid of you?" Leo says.

"I'm older than he is." Seeing she's not satisfied, Marta lays the lens in her lap. "In the war, the people I was with"—she pauses to choose her words—"there were many women in command. It's different now. Here. But Julian knows to respect me."

"Were you a commander?"

Marta stares at her lap, as if thinking back upon a puzzle. "No."

"That's too bad."

This brings a thin smile to Marta's face. She screws the lens into a camera, scans the room, and finally points it at Leo.

"Pose."

"What?"

"Pose. For the camera."

Leo holds still until the shutter clicks. "You've known him since the war?"

Marta looks at her over the viewfinder. "You look like a passport photo. Pose."

Impatiently, she throws back her head and approximates a saucy smile. "Good," Marta says. "Again." Leo cocks her hip, runs a hand through her hair. She bats her eyelashes, attempts a smoldering gaze.

"I know him since I was a student," Marta says. "More I know his brother."

"Enrique."

"How do you know this name?"

Leo takes off her glasses and stares out the window, at shifting shadows, faint light from a streetlamp creeping over the property wall. Such a huge city, she thinks, remembering Lurigancho, the man with the mangled arm, the man at the protest who'd dragged her from the fountain. All just hints, glimpses of something too large for her to see. She wonders if there are others like Marta and Julian and Chaski—in other houses like this one, waiting, getting ready. Maybe, somewhere, there's even someone like her.

"Where is Enrique?" she whispers.

"Pose."

"Is there film in that camera?"

"Just pose."

She moves around the room, flattening herself to the wall, throws herself seductively across her bedroll. "Is he going to live here?"

"No."

"Why not?"

"Get up," Marta barks. "Are you a fighter? Are you a revolutionary?"

"I don't know."

"Show me."

She bares her teeth and lunges in Marta's direction. "More," Marta says. "Are you angry?" Leo cocks a fist, kicks one leg as high as she can. She clasps her hands and points an imaginary gun at her roommate, growls deep in her throat and rushes at Marta until she slips and stumbles onto the blankets, knocking over the camera case as she falls.

Marta lowers the camera, satisfied. "Soon I take you to meet someone. A printer, someone I know from a long time ago. He will help us."

"Help with what?"

"El futuro," Marta says.

Leo holds excruciatingly still, but Marta says nothing more, only slides into her sleeping bag and reaches up to shut off the light. Far off in the neighborhood, a string of firecrackers goes off, echoing for several seconds, a welter of howls and barks arising in its wake. Leo lies in silence, staring at Marta's dark shape and listening to the empty house. *El futuro . . . el futuro . . .* Wide awake, she picks up the camera and stands by the window, pulls back the curtain until moonlight floods the room, casting Marta in pewter. She holds her breath, squeezes the shutter.

"Go to sleep," Marta says.

Leo lets the curtain fall. She remembers the burning silver sign, the locked door at the top of the stairs. Neto's face on a placard, carried off into the distance.

"Why isn't Enrique going to live here?"

She waits for Marta to scold her. But after a long silence, Marta's voice comes disembodied through the dark.

"Because he is dead."

4

According to the civilian prosecutor, Leo first met Josea Torres Medina at Taberna Tambo, on the tenth of March. Torres is mentioned in the Truth & Reconciliation Commission's report as a "reformed" subversive: detained twice, in 1989 and 1991 (the report states that he was "subjected to aggressive interrogation"), after the war he married an accountant, bought a flat in Surco, and opened a print shop specializing in brochures and manuals for government agencies. This respectability, the report says, was a useful front for the Pueblo Libre group, "but it is probable he was not told of their true plans."

Tambo, one of Lima's oldest public houses, is tucked into the labyrinth of the old city, at the corner of two unlit alleys. It was once known as the "Cradle of the Revolution," Damien Cohen told me—since the days of Simón Bolívar the bar has served as a gathering place for intellectuals, communists, anarchists, malcontents. Mariátegui was said to have launched his political party from a corner table. During the war you could find rival groups sharing tables, debating Stalin vs. Trotsky, the Chinese vs. the Cuban model; on particularly bloody days the tavern served as a field hospital where volunteer doctors tended to wounded demonstrators. But like everything in Lima, Tambo seems to have shed an old skin. When Damien took me there, the tavern was full of middle-aged men in suits and towering blond backpackers. A golf tournament was showing on the TV. When a group of teenagers wearing Che Guevara T-shirts and cartoon scowls peeked inside, the bartender promptly waved them back to the street.

"You see? Nothing can happen here anymore," Damien said, bemused. "Only reenactments of things."

The room is like something out of a Hemingway novel: a long zinc counter, marble café tables, cigarette smoke twisting under a lazy ceiling fan. Leo sips a foamy beer—her first drink in weeks—and shifts in the wobbly, cane-back chair. The walls are crammed with old photos of vintage cars, ladies in high-necked dresses, proud officers with handlebar mustaches—but the music is pure '80s MTV: "One Night in Bangkok," "Lucky Star," "Everybody Wants to Rule the World."

The man who approaches the table is in his late thirties, lean and handsome, with a beaked nose and wavy hair tucked behind his ears, eyeglasses hanging from a thin chain around his neck.

"So this is the gringa?" he says.

"Es nuestra compañera," Marta says, standing to kiss his cheek. "Give her respect."

"Of course," he says, with a mock bow. "I beg your pardon."

"This is Comrade Michel—" Marta says, her hand lingering at his elbow.

"Enough of that shit," he says in English. "My name is Josea. You can tell me your name or not, I don't care. Mucho gusto conocerte."

"Mucho gusto," Leo says, as pleased by his disarming manner as by having been called "compañera." He bends to kiss both her cheeks, bestowing upon her a smile both playful and fatherly—as if they'd met before, as if he knows her secrets—before turning the full wattage of his attention back to Marta.

"You look good, cariña," he says, and though she doesn't reply, Leo spots a faint gleam in Marta's eye, the subtlest of smiles drifting across her lips.

Leo sits quietly while they catch up on old comrades, mutual acquaintances, trying to keep up with their inside jokes and indecipherable, rapid-fire slang. There's an unfamiliar lightness in Marta's voice; she laughs freely, touches the back of Josea's hand. On the TV a man in a trenchcoat, a morose duck of a man, speaks into a bank of microphones. *Starr to subpoena bookstore purchases*, the caption reads. *Lewinsky reportedly gave "phone-sex novel" to President Clinton.*

It's been a trying week, her days full of busy work and a churn of optimism and impatience that's made her feel almost manic. She

beetled back and forth to the markets, bringing home hallway run-
ners and ceramic teacups, blinds for the kitchen windows, colorful handwoven cloths to hang on the walls. At the art-supply store
she bought a dozen easels, standing lamps, rolls of heavy paper,
boxes of brushes and colored pencils, then piled it all outside the
new metal door until the upstairs hallway was impassable. She
dusted and redusted windowsills, sang along to the transistor radio,
attempted Marta's yoga poses until her legs gave out. She spent
hours on her knees in the garden, turning the soil and kneading in
rose food with bare, grubby fingers.

She's seen Marta only in flashes—gray glimpses at dawn, hazy
shufflings late at night. At some point new photos appeared on the
wall: a one-armed man selling magazines from a median; a pair of
Indian girls, no older than thirteen, standing on a streetcorner in
halter tops and makeup. Like the earlier photos, the images were
stunningly sharp, almost hallucinatory, cropped uncomfortably
tight; the subjects look straight into the camera but seem, at the
same time, unaware of it—an intrusion, a violation, their innocent gazes made Leo feel uncomfortable, somehow accused. As the
days passed her resentment grew: What was Marta doing when she
wasn't in the house? Where were Julian and Chaski? *El futuro . . .*
When would she be told of the plans?

After half an hour, Josea leans back, scans the room, picks at
something on the tablecloth. "And tell me, cariña," he says, "how
is Casimiro?"

Instantly the easy mood changes. Marta sets down her drink
and folds her hands. "You were an hour late, compañero. Let's not
waste any more time."

Josea sits straighter and sucks his teeth. Leo watches his face,
watches Marta, fascinated by the shifting dynamic. "Bueno, comandante," he says. "If you're determined to do this, then here's what
I require."

In the early years of the war, Peru's many leftist groups published a multitude of newspapers—some polished and professional,
distributed as far away as European capitals; others no more
than photocopies handed out at demonstrations and union halls.
Sendero sympathizers knew where to find their paper, *El Diario,*

just as followers of PUM or Red Flag knew which newsstands carried theirs. Like most, *El Futuro*, the Cuarta Filosofía's paper, was shut down after the Tarata bombing, in accordance with the new anti-terrorism laws; the editor fled the country; the printing press was destroyed. Marta had explained all this on their way to the bar. Offhandedly, as if remembering a minor home repair, she'd said it was time someone brought *El Futuro* back to life.

"From now on I talk only to the gringa," Josea tells Marta. "After tonight, I won't see you. I'm sure this upsets you terribly."

In a quiet voice he lays out the procedure: a café to be chosen beforehand, at a prearranged time Leo will drop off a SyQuest cartridge with the files. "Fonts, style sheets, everything has to be there," he says. "If I don't understand something, you'll have to accept what I decide. You know how to use PageMaker?"

Two days later, the newspapers will arrive at Álvaro's furniture store. If the papers don't come, they'll meet here, at Tambo, exactly one week later. "No one comes to my shop under any circumstances," he says. "Remember: I don't know you people."

"Muy amable," Marta mutters.

"You're lucky it's a small job," he says. He cleans the glasses hanging from his neck and scans the café. "I don't do this anymore, cariña. My clients are respectable people, you understand?"

"Politicos," Marta says drily.

"And others. I had a meeting today with Orient Express. They pay very well."

"'Only what is necessary,' ¿no?"

He leans back in irritation, gestures to the bruise under Leo's eye. "And what made it necessary to give her that?" Leo turns away, blushing furiously. "Now let's talk about money," he says. "This is a business, okay? We aren't running around anymore painting slogans and throwing sticks at the army—"

"Some of us were doing more than this, *cariño* . . ."

Leo stands without excusing herself, pushes through the swollen crowd as another forgotten hit blares over the speakers—*I wanna be . . . your sledgehammer* . . . In the bathroom she holds the sides of the sink and studies the fading bruise in the mirror. Since that afternoon she's felt like a grounded teenager, rebuked in some bid for adulthood. Over and over she's replayed her decision to stay. But now everything is changing: no more whiling away days among flowers, no more playing Cinderella in an empty old house. She has a job to do, something important to the group. What will go into *El Futuro*, who will write it, what it should look like—all of this remains unclear. But already she feels more solid, enlarged by this new purpose. Ready to prove how useful she can be.

Back at the table, Josea is winding a scarf around his neck. "Send my greetings to Comrade Julian," he says. "Tell him the job will be taken care of, out of respect for his brother."

"Gracias, tío," Marta says. "And my greetings to your wife."

Josea laughs. "I'm not your tío. Also, this craziness in Los Arenales . . . Don't get ahead of yourselves, okay? I'm telling you as your friend."

"Don't worry. You don't know us, remember?"

"But do you know yourselves?" He frowns and looks around the crowded room. "*El Futuro*. What happened to that, anyway? It turned out to be shit. Ciao, compañera," he says, turning to kiss Leo's cheek. "Enjoy the wax museum."

The moon hangs high in a cellophane sky when they leave Tambo, casting glimmers over the old buildings, the traffic circles and featureless apartment blocks. The scent of jasmine wafts like rotting food. Leo doesn't speak or ask questions, concentrates on keeping up with Marta, mirroring her long, confident strides—as if one wrong move, one unwelcome comment, might undo the night's giddy progress. Marta checks her watch frequently, takes unexpected turns, stopping on corners to peer anxiously in both directions until Leo wonders if she might be lost, or drunk. They walk for over an hour, Leo's cheeks damp, the tip of her nose cold—through the silent Campo de Marte, dark trees standing sentinel, blocking out the lights of the surrounding city; down the Avenida Salaverry, still loud with traffic, with the chatter of families huddled around food carts and the lit windows of cheap comedores. It's late, tomorrow's chores massing in the back of Leo's mind—but she doesn't complain about the roundabout route or the growing chill because her terse, inscrutable companion has uncharacteristically begun to talk.

"In San Martín de Porres, the district where I grew up, everyone was a leftist," Marta says. People identified with the villages their families came from—one group loyal to Sendero, another to MRTA or Patria Roja. "These are your neighbors, your cousins—you know who is their girlfriend, who in the family is sick, you borrow bread or blankets from them if you don't have money. So when the army comes and asks questions, no one says anything. You don't inform on your neighbors."

At Católica, she says, allegiances were more fluid. The children of Lima's business and military elite strolled the well-tended grounds speaking of cultural hierarchies, economic slavery, linguistic genocide. Though outright protest was rare, student groups claiming loyalty to political parties both legal and illegal organized symposia and art exhibits, demonstrations of traditional dances, film screenings about the bloodletting in the provinces. She met Josea at a debate about Cuba. He was a graduate student in psychology and the leader of a group that called itself 14 de Junio.

"He was very popular. A good speaker." With a glance at Leo, the flicker of a smile, she adds, "And very attractive."

Josea took her to meetings in other parts of the city—the back room of a bookstore, the basement of a half-empty office building. "You go to a streetcorner, and there is an old woman selling candy, if you tell her the password she unlocks a door. All of this is so exciting when you are young. Like in a James Bond movie." Eventually, Josea was asked to recruit a small group for an "orientation" at a farm an hour from Lima. That's where they met Casimiro.

He was tall and fair-skinned, his blue eyes finely alert, crimped at the corners with private humor. The son of a retired general, he spoke little, but projected a calm competence that reassured anyone near him, man or woman. He was also a student at Católica, and though he was among the youngest at the meeting it was obvious to everyone that he would one day be the group's leader.

Over the next few months, the three of them went to meetings several times a week, often staying out late for beer and french fries, arguing over the readings of Hegel and Marx, Lenin and Mao, debating whether post-capitalist Peru should follow the precepts of Plato's *Republic* or be organized like the communal *ayllus* of the

Inca empire. In time, they could sense they were being groomed, singled out for their dedication. They were interrogated by handlers, probed for ideological inconsistency. They were sent into the slums to speak to neighborhood councils and youth leaders. After a year, Marta and Casimiro were sent to a training camp on the edge of the jungle. Josea was not invited.

"They wanted to split us apart," she says. "Monogamy is a threat to the group. It means you are loyal to one of your cumpas more than all the others."

They spent a month in a tiny outpost with no electricity, miles from any roads, no radio or phone contact with the outside world. They never learned the names of the other recruits. They ran for hours, lungs burning from the altitude, received instruction in how to handle rifles and handguns, how to rig dynamite with a timer, to pack a car with TNT for maximum explosive force. This was where she first took Marta as her nom de guerre. At the end of the month, Casi was put in charge of a cadre of students from Católica and San Marcos. By the time they returned to Lima, with instructions to go about their normal lives, they had become lovers.

"Josea was so sad. I don't know if he was jealous for me or for Casi. But you see how he is: such a Romeo! Soon he had ten new girlfriends. Then he has no energy left for the Movement."

The Tarata bombing happened a few months later, the government moved quickly to militarize the city and gain control of the universities. Hundreds of students and faculty were arrested. At San Marcos, radicals barricaded themselves inside dorms and classrooms, emerging in spasms of gunfire. Marta and Casi woke one morning to the sound of helicopters flying low over the neighborhood. Already a crowd had formed outside Católica's gates and they hurried to join the march. There were chants and raised fists, students thrown up against walls, bursts of tear gas that sent people running into side streets. They didn't hear the troop carrier roll up behind them until it came to a stop, trapping a dozen protestors beneath an overpass.

"I want six!" shouted the commander, as soldiers spilled out, throwing students to the pavement, pointing rifles at their heads. They tore open bookbags and ripped back pockets, forced their fingers into men's mouths and under women's belts. "Give me six! Give me six! ¡Vámonos!" When Marta looked back she saw Casi being dragged away, his legs limp, a soldier smashing his head with the butt of a rifle.

"He had in his pocket a red bandanna," she says. "That was all. No weapon or propaganda. Just a red bandanna. It was enough."

Over the next several days, most of the students were released. But no one heard from Casi. She went first to the local police station, then the army garrison, but no one would tell her anything. She tried to contact his father, the general, but he would not speak to her. After two weeks, she and a group of friends went to the university president to demand he make a formal inquiry to the military. For eight hours, they refused to leave the administration building. Finally, the president's secretary brought them a reply.

"She said there is no student with that name. She said no one with that name ever studied at Católica."

The streets are familiar now, the damp air has cooled in Leo's bones. It's long after midnight, her feet ache; but she's held by Marta's voice, awed by this sudden intimacy. It's dizzying, the change—in a day she's gone from housekeeper to confidante, traipsing home from the ball with glass slippers in hand. But still, something in the story nags at her—something insistent in Marta's quick glances. Marta's trying to tell her something, but she can't yet take it all in.

At the corner of Almagro, Marta stops in front of the bodega, closed up for the night, and peers down the dark street. "After the war," she says, quieter now, "his name was on a list from Amnesty International. But the government says they can't find him. They say he was at the headquarters of DINCOTE only a few days and then released. This is what they say when they have tortured someone to death. One day maybe they will find his bones in a garbage dump, or an arroyo. Or maybe never. It doesn't matter."

Leo watches her, waits for something more. For the first time in days she thinks about Ernesto. She remembers Nancy's husband, the stunned look in his eyes. With a shudder of intuition, she says, "Enrique. Casimiro—that's Comrade Enrique. That's Julian's brother." Marta stares at the street, a slight purse to her lips the only indication she's heard. "Oh, god, I'm so sorry . . ."

"I didn't tell you this so you can be sorry. I don't want your condolences."

Leo follows her gaze, and in that instant becomes aware of unfamiliar sounds—the distant tick of music, a mutter of muffled voices. There are lights burning in the third-floor windows of a house halfway down the street.

"Then why did you tell me?"

"People don't remember these things," Marta says. "They forget the war, like it was only a bad dream. Now they are buying televisions and cars, pretending it never happened. They pretend the people who are gone never existed. Everyone wants to believe this new dream. They will fight or kill to defend it. You understand?

"You don't have to stay," Marta says, leaning closer. She touches Leo's chin, examines the bruise along her cheekbone. "No one will follow you or ask where you've gone. I make that promise. You can say you were never here."

Leo can hardly get words out. "Like it was my own dream?"

Marta's eyes move across her face. A car passes, taking a speed bump too fast, striking sparks on the pavement. After a long silence, Leo says, "Who's in our house?"

When there's still no answer Leo pulls the key from her pocket. Her cheekbone stings hot at the bruise, with embarrassment at how easily Marta deceived her. The meeting with Josea, the long walk, even Marta's story—all a diversion, a sleight of hand to keep her away from whatever was happening at the house. After all she's done, they still don't trust her. They don't think she belongs.

Marta catches up to her at the gate. "Stop, Leonora," she whispers.

Fumbling, Leo drives the key into the old lock. "I have a right to know who's here."

"Don't talk about rights," Marta says, reaching for her wrist. In the failing moonlight, they stare at each other and at the open gate, the dim light leaking out at their feet. Up above, the once dead house is aglow with life, restless with shadows in the upstairs windows. Marta's grip is unshakable, her gaze flat as a stranger's.

"No one is here, compañera," she says. "You have made a mistake."

5

At her civilian retrial, in October, 2002, Leo insisted she'd had no idea who was living on the third floor of the house in Pueblo Libre. There were four or five of them, she said. She'd never seen them, didn't know their names. They came and went as they wished, using the back stairway. What they did with their days was not her concern. She'd needed tenants—opening the art school was taking longer than anticipated—and so she'd put up fliers at the universities. When a man came to the door with cash in hand, she gave him a key, no questions asked.

"This man you saw. Do you see his face now?" the prosecutor asked, pointing to the board where photographs of six corpses hung side by side.

"No," she said, her face showing no reaction. "The man who came to the door didn't live there. He just wanted a place for his friends."

"I see." The prosecutor was a short, fastidious man of Japanese origin. He wore a cheap tan suit and shoes that had been polished too many times. "So you lived in this house full of terrorists for six months and you didn't know what they were doing. You didn't know they had acquired"—he checked his notes—"eight hundred and twenty sticks of dynamite, timers and blasting caps, sixty-four hand grenades, eight Zastava assault rifles and ten FAL rifles with more than five thousand rounds of ammunition. You never saw the stolen uniforms or the blueprints. The terrorists held meetings with superiors and conducted training exercises, all while you were downstairs knowing nothing. Can you tell me, are all Americans so stupid?"

Leo took grim satisfaction in the insult. "Señor, there were no terrorists living in the house. And I think only some Americans are stupid."

She was rewarded by low laughter from the gallery, a momentary lessening of tension. Even her red-eyed, desperate lawyer looked up with something like hope.

The prosecutor sat on the edge of the judges' table. He removed his glasses and rubbed the bridge of his nose. "Señorita," he said, mildly astonished, "if you had no contact with these people, how can you know they were not terrorists?"

According to Gustavo Gorriti, the original cohort of eight Philosophers arrived in Lima between March 8 and March 13, escorted by Julian and Chaski, who had met them in Abancay with a rented van and taken a circuitous route back via Nazca and the coastal highway. All but two were from the Huambalpa region of Ayacucho; the others came from farther north, in the mountainous La Mar province. The youngest, Faustino "Macho" Risco, was seventeen; the oldest, Freddy "César" Huatay, thirty or thirty-one.

"We thought it was students, leaving and returning each day, fooling around in the yard," a neighbor, who asked to remain anonymous, told *La Republica* after the raid. Others added that Pueblo Libre was rapidly changing, as the revived economy brought an influx of residents with neither the family names nor the fair skin of older inhabitants. Juan Carlos Castille, a third-generation libreño, told *Expreso*: "Once you have this element living among you, it is inevitable there will be problems."

Today Pueblo Libre feels like just another upper-middle-class neighborhood, Lima's equivalent of Noe Valley or the Marais: cafés, gelato, the tourist draw of the Museo Larco. Rents are rising. Traffic is a problem. Air quality, high tuition, finding good help—these are all problems. Everybody's got problems. Once I saw a group of thirty-somethings outside a restaurant, waving frantically at passing cars: *S.O.S.*, their signs read—handwritten, in English. *Save Our Sushi.*

I have a different problem. A narrative problem: What was she doing all that time? From the cumpas' arrival until the date of the first newspaper, a month later, there's no concrete record, surprisingly little speculation. There are no secret tapes, no photos from the inside. The Leo File is silent. If one discards the outré theories—sex parties, Satanic rituals—one is left with a giant blank, a high white wall. What was happening behind it? What are the quotidian habits of a "terrorist mastermind"?

I'm overthinking it, Jack says, getting hung up on things no one can know. He's tiring of these conversations, starting to wonder if he made a mistake. He tells me to draw on my own experience, to use my imagination.

"Jesus H. Christ," he says. "Just try to have a little fun."

She wakes at five each morning, drags herself to the kitchen to make coffee, which Marta takes to the third-floor. The metal door clangs shut and shivers overhead. She leaves baskets of bread and cheese, a bowl of oranges, boiled eggs, oatmeal, at the bottom of the stairs, lingering at the muffled sound of voices from above: Marta's low drone, the restless shuffles of invisible men. On warm days the voices resonate through the bathroom pipes; Leo stands dripping in the shower, straining to make out the words.

The rest of the morning is taken up by shopping, lugging home ten-kilo bags of potatoes, a backpack laden with bread, fruit, sacks of rice, meat if it's cheap; the afternoon by cleaning, washing towels, hanging them to dry. Her arms grow ropy and taut, her hands white and chapped by bleach, soil-brown under the nails. On good days she finds an hour to work in the garden—*her* garden, as she's come to think of it. By late March she's brought daisies and violets into bloom, coaxed a spray of goldenrod in the sunniest corner. But the rosebushes are still barren, twisted like prisoners at the base of the wall. Marta's voice drifts from a third-floor window. The metal door clangs and shivers.

"What do you talk about all morning?" she asks Marta.

"Don't worry."

"I'm not *worried*," she says, chafed by the condescension. There's been no talk of what happens next, no mention of *El Futuro*. "But maybe there's something else I can do?"

"When there's something for you to do you'll be told."

The house reminds her of a dormitory, full of music at all hours, thunder on the back stairs, the dislocated rumblings of unseen bodies. She's not to see those bodies—Marta has made that clear. She's not to mount the stairs, or raise the kitchen blinds when the cumpas are in the backyard. This is to protect her, Marta says. It's to protect all of them. The men upstairs—she assumes they're men—are a rumor, a theory: like mice, or ghosts, their noise is everywhere and nowhere. The metal door clangs. When, in rare moments, the house is silent, she can almost believe she'd dreamed up the whole affair, so unlikely is it that she, Leo Gelb, would find herself living there. (Ironically, this is also how some commentators have seen her—Gorriti: "the American who rented the house and who was tried and *mistakenly* convicted for her role in the plot" [italics mine].) By dark, the noise has ebbed, the men have settled, and Leo remembers how the house once felt, in that first week when she was alone. Marta leaves without a word after dinner, camera bag slung over her shoulder, and rarely returns before midnight. Leo knows better than to ask where she goes.

One night she wakes to voices, low mutters through the floor. Cracking the bedroom door, she sees light down the hall, pads carefully toward the kitchen. At the sound of Julian's voice, she presses her back to the living room wall like a child.

"And how long? Enough of the fucking talking. Sitting here like a bunch of women, doing nothing. What are we waiting for, the next election?"

"Calm yourself," Marta says. "Going too fast is how you end up with a disaster like Los Arenales."

"Sí, Profesora. And too slow is how you have a disaster like this country."

She hasn't heard his voice in weeks, had not expected the heat of humiliation with which it fills her. The bruise under her eye has shrunk to an ocher smudge, a prickle of fury. She's practiced how she'll speak to him—careful but dignified, her loyalty intact. But when the anger ebbs she finds it leaves not fear but anticipation, a feeling of tentative hope: something would soon happen, a larger purpose would be revealed. Julian's done his worst, she thinks. He taught her the lesson he wanted her to learn. To both of their surprise, she's still here.

"There are many things to discuss," Marta is saying. "We need to establish a political line, lay out our principles. There can be no action without consideration—"

"You want a line? No more killing and torture. Close El Arca, let the prisoners go. That's the line."

"And what then? Who will guide the cumpas' ideology? You have to think like a scientist, hermano, not an adventurist."

"Don't call me hermano," Julian growls. "And fuck your science, okay?

When a chair scrapes over the tiles Leo slips back to her room, more restless than ever. She sleeps badly, wakes late and has to rush to make breakfast. All morning she fights a feeling of confinement, of tense expectation. She's exhausted by solitude, shaking like a top wound too tight. When her chores are done she takes the bus to Miraflores, but even the warm ocean air can't quell this resentment: Will she never see the bigger picture?

At a tourist shop she finds something truly hideous: a framed needlepoint of a llama, with long, flirtatious eyelashes, its fur a nauseous orange against a purple background. The llama sports a bowler hat, the kind worn by married Quechua women. Beneath this revolting figure, white, cursive letters read *¡Yo Soy Peruana!* She carries the monstrosity to the cash register in exultation, imagining Julian's annoyance. There's a spot at the bottom of the stairs where the llama will fit perfectly. It will be the first thing anyone sees when they come through the door.

El Futuro was an anachronism, as Josea pointed out, a reminder of the war's heady promise and its ultimate failure. Moreover, it was known to the government. "So unless you want a reunion in El Arca," he'd said, "you'll need a new name."

With no further instruction, Leo takes the task upon herself—a way to put her stamp on things, to demonstrate her value. For days she makes lists on scraps of paper, tries names out loud while hanging wet sheets. *El Tiempo? New Dawn? The Messenger?* She tests them out on the computer—a clunky black Dell she bought at a mall in San Isidro, along with a flatbed scanner and SyQuest drive, set up on two card tables in the dining room—and tries to fashion a convincing front page.

But what sounds impressive in the raw autumn air of the garden looks flimsy and old-fashioned on screen. They need an inspiring name, something that speaks to the *now*, to this generation's seething discontent, that tears away the cynical lies about progress and reconciliation and wakes people up again. *¡Despierta!*, she decides, convinced of it for a day or two. *Wake Up!* But it sounds like a publication for children, or evangelical Christians. *Ojos Abiertos* reminds her of an optometrist's newsletter. She collects stories from newspapers and magazines, scribbles thoughts in the margins; she looks through a stack of Marta's photographs and mentally notes which to include. Whatever their plans for the paper, they'll need a name, and soon, but everything—*The Spark, The Argument, El Militante*—sounds forced, artificial, nothing speaks to the strength of purpose, the moral urgency she wants to convey.

Then, one morning at the bodega, an old Bryan Adams song comes on the radio. She has a quick, vivid memory of her high-school friends Rachel and Megan dancing to "Summer of '69" at Giants Stadium a decade ago. Walking home, she remembers the fight with her mother, the unbearable pressure of sadness and anger—it probably *was* PMS, she decides—and in a jumble recalls Peter Gabriel and his African backup singers, a paper she'd written on youth movements in South Africa, the morning Winnie Mandela visited Gabriel's class, striding into the lecture hall as if she'd stepped out of the pages of the Iliad or the Mahabharata. She can feel something coming to her, asserting itself through the white noise of memory—Chaski in the jeep as they fled Los Muertos: *Where were the cameras?*—runs awkwardly the rest of the way home, humming to herself: *the man is dead . . . the man is dead.* The photos she saw that day, the body on the gurney, Ernesto's gentle smile. Has it been three months already?

She picks a stately font, positions her title across the top of the page and stretches it to fill the margins. One by one she tries Marta's photos, scanning and cropping, but none is exactly right. The banner should reach out for readers, freeze them where they stand: a bolt of awareness, an epiphany. At the bottom of the stack she finds what she needs; her hands shake as she lays it on the scanner and waits for the image to unfurl, one line at a time, on the monitor. Her blood starts to tingle: *There*, she thinks, *there it is*, staring awestruck into the monochrome glow of her own eyes, bright with rage on the night Marta told her to pose.

THE EYES OF THE WORLD. It's *perfect*, she thinks, laughing as she swipes a tear from her cheek. It says all there is to say about responsibility and historical necessity, about the power of collective action. You can't read those words, see that image, and turn away. If the world had been watching in Los Arenales, Ernesto would still be alive. They'll run his picture on the front page, she decides, with a description of what had been done to him. Volume one, issue one. Such things won't happen once people are made to *see*.

April 5 marked the anniversary of the President's *auto-golpe*, the 1992 "self-coup" in which he'd dissolved Congress, slashed civil liberties, and put in place the machinery of what many Peruvians describe as a police state. As in previous years, demonstrators gathered outside the Palace of Justice that morning—pensioners and students, a contingent of nuns leading prayers. The Abuelitas de la Ausencia lined the steps of the high court, leveling their gaze at passersby, while in the park across the Paseo de la República, Bufón mounted a production of *Julius Caesar* for picnicking families, with the actors dressed as characters from *Sesame Street*.

Shortly after one p.m., a band of masked vigilantes descended on the crowd—some on foot, others on motorcycles—wielding heavy chains and spray paint. Eleven people were hospitalized for concussions, fractured ribs, second-degree burns. Several actors were beaten and doused with orange paint. The abuelitas were bound, stripped to the waist, and shoved face-down on the Palace stairs, the word PUTA scrawled on their backs. Police officers made no attempt to intervene. Though a spokesman for the President condemned the violence, no arrests were ever made.

The image of the violated women ran on page five of *El Comercio* the next day. (I also came across it in an obscure academic text, *Por Amor de la Madre: Las Guerras Sucias desde una Perspectiva Freudiana*, and, somewhat bizarrely, a coffee table photo-book, *Mujeres Poderosas de Las Américas*.) While the incident had little effect on the national discourse, it may have galvanized the Pueblo Libre group—the same photo appears on the back page of the first issue of *The Eyes of the World*, with an accompanying editorial titled "We Must Resume the Struggle!"

"You're happy, Profesora? You see what we get for all your fucking theory? Grandmothers! Lying there with their tits out. Little kids in the fucking hospital."

Julian looms over the kitchen table, red-faced, out of breath. He smacks a rolled copy of *El Comercio* on the edge of the table so Marta's coffee sloshes over her cup. "Fucking fascists. You know why they do this? Because they can. Who's going to stop them? You're so busy with your political line, your pedagogy—"

"Cálmate, hermano," Marta says, face mild, as if confronting a lunatic. Chaski stands uncomfortably in the doorway, lowering his eyes when Leo looks his way. "We can't react with emotions. Lenin said, 'Without revolutionary theory there can be no revolutionary movement—'"

"Don't quote Lenin to me," Julian says, tossing the paper on the table. It unrolls to reveal front-page photos of President Clinton and Paula Jones. "And don't call me hermano. I'm tired of your principles. I'm tired of talking. It's time to act."

Leo opens the paper to the protest, impotence gnawing her gut as she reads. All the waiting has begun to dull her thoughts, shrink the revolution to something drab, academic—like the image before her, outrage reduced to a well-composed photo.

"You don't speak for everyone," Julian says. "Chaski, oye—what do you think? We sit here and talk about shit, study Mariátegui?"

Chaski looks up warily, like a lab animal whose cage has been suddenly thrown open. "Nothing can be accomplished if we're always fighting with ourselves . . ."

"Nothing's being accomplished anyway," Julian says. "You want more nothing? What about Neto and Juancito, man? You forgot about Los Muertos?"

"We're only a small group, compañero . . ."

"Fidel had twelve men."

"We have eight."

Marta sets down her cup. "You see? Even your pet thinks you're wrong. We talk to Miguel before taking any action," Marta says. "That's what was agreed. I will not let your ego put us all in danger—"

"*My* ego? Who compares herself to Lenin—"

With a sigh, Leo takes her cup to the sink and starts on the breakfast dishes. It's too much, this sniping and glowering, this jockeying for control. After what was done to the Abuelitas, to Neto—it's too *small.* Out the window, the gloom is drawing back, giving way to a rare, bright autumn day. What if she were to leave these dishes, this house, walk out into Pueblo Libre and keep walking? Would it change anything at all?

"So what about you?"

It takes a second for Leo to understand she's been spoken to. She turns to find Julian close behind her, as close as the day he threw her into the street. Panic snatches at her thoughts but she forces herself not to shrink away.

"What about me?"

"I'm asking what you think, Soltera."

She sets her jaw, wills her voice to be steady—like Marta's. "I think Soltera's not my name. I think you should stop calling me that."

Julian lets out a laugh. "Okay, good, what else? You've got so many ideas. You're always opening your mouth. So what now?"

She stares into his eyes, their cold blue spiced with something restive. He needs her, she realizes, he's asking for her help. The thought sends a subtle jolt up her spine. The others are watching, waiting for her answer. Upstairs, the metal door shivers. Someone calls for Marta in a low, impatient voice. Bill Clinton stares from the table, one stubby finger poking at the camera.

"I think it's an outrage," she says, a little breathless with new power. She stands a bit straighter, holds Julian's gaze. "I think something has to be done."

The first issue appeared on April 9, five hundred copies that found their way to newsstands in Lurigancho and Callao, to the San Marcos campus, and as far south as Los Arenales. Alvaro's nephews handed them out at busy intersections. A twelve-page jumble of domestic and foreign news, old speeches by Castro and Haya de la Torre, a handful of photos, a semi-accurate timeline of the war. It was an amateurish production: dry and polemical, with dropped text, numerous typos, and the haphazard aesthetic of something thrown together in a rush. The front page bore the images of the Los Muertos Three and an interview with an anonymous eyewitness to the massacre; the back page offered the inciting editorial, quoted at Leo's trial and in countless articles since:

"The Cuarta Filosofía calls on all revolutionary forces, on workers everywhere, all people who love Peru: Rise up!"

The editorial—a manifesto, really—was written by Comrade Julian and delivered to Leo, handwritten, on cocktail napkins from the Café Haiti. "Make it look good," he told her. "And don't change a single fucking word." She'd put the issue together over two sleepless nights—it was urgent they respond quickly to the obscenity at the Palace of Justice, equally urgent that she finish before Julian reconsidered this new confidence in her. As she rode the bus to meet Josea, she turned the bulky computer disks over in her hands and tried to stifle a sense of pride. At last she'd done something tangible, something only she could have done. It was a group effort, she reminded herself—they were Marta's photos; Chaski took care of the shopping while Leo worked—but as she stepped onto the sidewalk, avoiding eye contact with passers-by, she couldn't help but feel larger, in some way more real.

The satisfaction lasts only a day—long enough to hold the first copy in her hands, to accept the thanks of her comrades and collapse on her bedroll, already planning the next issue as she drifts off. Late that night, she wakes to the sound of Julian's voice, disorientingly close in the dark:

Open your eyes, he says. *I'm trying to tell you something.*

She startles, drags herself sitting and feels for her glasses. The window is open, a night breeze rippling in the curtains. The air is moist and cool. It feels like a dream, the goosebumps tingling her arms, the echo of his voice too private, almost arousing.

The dead are alive, he says. *Los muertos viven. The blind can see . . .*

At last she finds her glasses, flings the blankets off and starts to reach for the light. That's when she sees Marta sitting against the wall, knees pulled up, the transistor radio at her side.

"What's happening?" Leo whispers.

It's time to wake from these dreams, compañeros. It's time to cast out the specter haunting Peru . . .

Marta's voice is clear and steady. "Your brave compañero is starting a war."

I was never able to locate a transcript of the speech Julian gave on Radio 2000, a few minutes before two a.m. on April 10. I can't even be sure it was him. There was no recording, only a brief story in *El Comercio* two days later, referring to three "delinquents" who forced their way into the studio and "recited incoherent slogans." But I find the coincidence of dates encouraging. Who else would it have been?

I've imagined the speech here as a version of the manifesto. I've imagined Julian reading it straight off the page: the statistics on poverty, infant mortality, illiteracy, on the dead and missing of the unresolved war. Above all the indictment of the middle class, well-fed in their Lima enclaves while the rest of the country starved. It was *their* war, he insisted, an extermination of those whose humanity they couldn't acknowledge, whose suffering they preferred not to see.

I imagine Leo listening closely, knowing every word by heart, maybe mouthing along in admiration: How many thousands are listening? How many complacent people at last hearing the truth?

A disgrace that has never ended. Nothing has changed, it has only been made invisible . . .

History, politics. Someone had to make them see.

He speaks of the Fatherland. But what kind of father tortures his children? What father throws his sons in dungeons and leaves them to die? Only when we rid ourselves of this cruel dictator will all Peruvians be free.

There's a shuffling of paper and a familiar voice starts translating in Quechua: Chaski. Marta breathes a low curse and turns on Leo an expression of resignation and displeasure—in a breath the implications come to her: They've declared themselves, there's no turning back now, no way to know what comes next. Her first impulse is to protest, to apologize: she'd had nothing to do with it! She'd only done what she was told.

But then she remembers: the gleam of triumph in Julian's eye, the conspiratorial hand on her shoulder that morning in the kitchen. *Something has to be done!* She'd said it more than once. She'd blazed with indignation. The memory brings on a slight dizziness, a shiver of euphoria—a connection.

Rise up, compañeros! Resume the struggle! It's time for a new story. It is time to open your eyes!

"Get back inside!" Julian says. "*Now*, goddammit." He's a shadow in the courtyard, moving with difficulty, half dragging another body toward the house. The moon is a nick in the corner of the sky, lights coming on in houses across the street. "Inside, Marta. And get her the fuck out of here."

At first Leo can't see the other man's face. Only when they cross the threshold does she recognize Chaski. His drawn cheeks and fevered eyes, the shine of vomit on his chin snatch her breath; the smell of sweat and adrenaline, the bloodstained rags trussed around one leg send her sprinting to the bedroom, chased by a string of Julian's curses.

She shuts the door and scans the sparse room—her books, some strewn clothing—tries to ignore the moans in the living room, the heavy thumps as they haul Chaski upstairs. She forces herself to focus: Where is her wallet? Her passport? The Sheraton, she thinks. She'll go to the Sheraton. No one would look for her there. Marta can come, too. But what about the others? What about Chaski? What about all that blood?

Something has to be done! It wasn't what she'd meant. How was she to have known what he would do? But that makes no difference now, she thinks as she shoves clothes in a pillowcase, the American Express card in her pocket. She's as responsible as he is. And what about the computer, shouldn't she do something with the computer? There's no way she can show up at the Sheraton like this. Rattled, her mind blank, she takes up the folder of photos, sits hard on her bedroll and lets it all scatter across the floor.

There was a guard, Marta explains when she comes in a few minutes later. They'd tied him up, but somehow he escaped. The police got there just as Julian and the others were leaving. The bullet hit Chaski below the knee, she says. He'd lost blood, but it appears to have gone clean through. "There's a doctor, a friend of Julian's. One of the cumpas went to call him."

"Doesn't he need a hospital?" But she already knows: he can't be taken to a hospital. No one can see him, no one can leave the house.

Marta is alert, energized, her voice tightly controlled. Staring at her comrade, Leo's own actions come into shameful relief: just like in Los Muertos, her first instinct had been to run.

Half an hour passes before Julian comes down. His eyes are still wild, his face shining with sweat. "Okay, I think it's going to be okay," he says, squeezing his forehead until his hand trembles. "Albert will be here soon. He'll take care of it."

"No names," Marta says.

"The fucking guard!" He paces the room, pulls back the curtain. "I told Macho to knock him out. I *told* that asshole. Why the *fuck* . . . Jesus Christ, Chaski!"

"You should have done it yourself," Marta says.

"I told Macho to do it—"

"Macho was not the leader. You are the leader, compañero."

Abruptly, he stops pacing and looks up. For the first time Leo sees something vulnerable behind all that brashness and swagger—a child, she thinks, he's a child who's taken something too far. He wanted to see what would happen but now someone's gotten hurt and he's terrified of getting caught.

"Where is Miguel's truck?" Marta says.

"On the next street."

"Get it out of here."

"But we need it—"

"Take it to the airport. Or to the beach. Take the license plate. Listen to me: they're looking for you now. They're looking for all of us. And what was gained? A hundred drunks and taxi drivers? People who know nothing about socialism or armed struggle. All for the glory of Comrade Julian. I warned you about your ego," she says, "but you didn't listen."

Throughout this lecture, Julian stares at the floor, shaking his head as if to expel water from his ears. "Are you the leader?" Marta says now. When he doesn't answer, she reaches for his arm. "Julian, asshole," she says quietly, "are you the leader of this group?"

With great effort, he raises his eyes. Slowly, he straightens, nodding. "Yeah, okay." He takes a heavy breath. "Okay."

Leo, transfixed, watches from a great distance, as if they were actors on a stage. There's sand in her throat, a buzzing in her ears, like a powerful drug wearing off. For a long moment no one speaks. It's she who breaks the silence.

"Where's Macho?"

She'd never heard the name before tonight, never laid eyes on the man who answered to it. Speaking it now, the name has a strange power, like an incantation from old parchment, a presence she's conjured into the room.

"Comrade Macho," she says. "Where is he?"

Julian's answer is sober, tinged with disbelief. "Macho knew the risk."

For a long time she turns the words over in her mind, waiting for them to click into place. Her feet feel enormous, her legs iron bolted to the floor. But her head is light as helium, just a pair of eyes blinking at the bright room. A knock comes at the front door and Marta hurries to answer it, leaving Leo alone with Julian, who regards her without mockery, a little sadly, as if seeing her for the first time.

"You said you wanted to be a part of this," he says.

Leo's eyes slide across the photos on the wall, the old and young, the men and women and children caught forever in poses of abjection and endurance. Though their faces are familiar, she can't recognize any of them, or guess where the photos were taken. She can't quite remember what she's doing here.

"Yes," she says, though she's forgotten the question. She doesn't know this person watching her, what he wants, what happens next. She knows nothing—the thought rings in her mind with the clarity of a glass bell. Somebody once told her she didn't belong here. They said it had nothing to do with her, it wasn't her story to tell. She should have listened to them. But she's gone too far to turn back now.

"Yes," she says again, ignoring his puzzled look, shaking off the hand that reaches for her. She knows nothing, understands nothing. Except that she's a long way—lifetimes away—from Cannondale. How had she gotten so far?

"Yes, why not?"

ANDRES

I was a nomad, a stateless actor, a refugee from George W. Bush's America. *Amurka*, he called it, flinty-eyed, squinting—a primitive place, *Amurka*, where trespasses are never forgiven, where arguments are always settled with fisticuffs, a lost eye avenged at the blade of a knife, a lost tooth repaid with your whole fucking head.

Amurka: a place without history or memory, where it's always morning, and to dwell on what you might have done last night— drunk and staggering, smashing bottles, molesting the wenches, pissing on the floor—would be a show of weakness, an impediment to your doing it again. And so when the bartender comes looking for you, or the wench's father, what you do in *Amurka*, what you do if you're a real *Amurkan*, is stand tall, double down, put up your dukes and spit right in the bastard's eye.

"We are all American," my friends in Babilonia used to say. But *Amurkan?* That title is reserved for the kingdom's rightful heirs: they who fear God and love Britney, who never met an assault rifle they didn't like; who hacked their way across a continent, murdering, cheating, infecting, and torturing the natives into submission; who imposed dominion upon a hemisphere, sucked its oil and gouged its gold, poisoned its aquifers, mined its harbors, assassinated its leaders and redrew its maps. It was *Amurkans* who named the animals, *Amurkans* who split the atom, who won the Cold War by threatening to extinguish us all. Don't give me that nonsense about *equality* and *fair play*—*Amurkans* know cooperation is a sucker's game. It interferes with profits. We have no truck with treaties, no time for old-world politesse: we take what we want by force or deception and woe unto your children's children if you dare ask for it back.

What I'd once been: a novelist, a skeptic, a conscientious objector—hardly an American to begin with, that is, subject to constant suspicion, to bafflement and revulsion at my lack of a mortgage and a jumbo TV. Barely tolerated, banished to the margins, I stood outside the fence and watched the unending carnival, the bright pink neon, the clown-grins and the whirl of heavy machinery. I listened to the shrieks of children, the haunting calliopes, smelled the treacle and the burning meat, ever torn between horror and longing, disapproval and loneliness and a clawing sense of failure.

But one bright Tuesday morning I became something else: a naysayer, an outlier, one more obstacle for my country to roll over and pulverize on its way to war. Moments after the first tower fell you could feel it: the rough beast stirring under the ash cloud, itching to rip the sky asunder. Born ready, spoiling for a fight, he burst into the September light, shook off rubble, cast a blue eye far and wide in search of a target for his wrath. Someone would pay, someone would rue the day they'd fucked with *Amurka*—*What are you lookin' at, asshole?*—stand back and watch what happens when you crash our party, when you make the connection.

They hated us for our freedom—that's the story we were told. For being American: successful, peace-loving, the varsity quarterback envied and loathed by the hoodlums in the smokers' lounge. They were savages, psychos—what else could explain it? Not that we'd wrecked their homelands and desecrated their holy sites. Not that we'd raped the planet, colluded in butchery, sold weapons to every sick thug with a medal on his chest and a crucifix above his bed. Forget our military bases ringing the globe, our nuclear subs prowling the oceans, forget every bomb we've ever dropped on poor, brown people. When *Amurka* does these things, you can bet we've got a damned good reason.

When you do it, you're a terrorist.

Yes, I was a castaway, lost in *Amurka*: a country I didn't recognize, or didn't want to recognize. Every time I turned on the radio I heard something else I couldn't understand: yellowcake uranium and smoking guns, flowers and chocolates, the unknown unknowns. None of it made sense, this new language laden with omens, illustrated with PowerPoint slides—but sense was not what we wanted. We wanted blood, we needed a story that justified our bloodthirst, something that walked like a duck, swam and quacked like a duck—so who the fuck cared if it was, in fact, a duck? The only logic that mattered now was narrative logic: it was not necessary that we believe the story, only that we admire its craftsmanship, the elegant arc of its action, its inevitable climax and satisfying denouement. And in fact nobody believed it, even those who swore by it, who brandished their fists at any profession of doubt. Doubt was the new enemy—as much as those monsters, those raghead cocksuckers who attacked us for no reason. Real *Amurkans* have no use for it.

How thrilling it all was, how real! An endless procession of amazements and delights: whole villages leveled, museums ransacked, bombs dropped on places of worship, peasants and shopkeepers buried alive under the stones and timbers of the *Amurkan* rampage. Bounties offered in exchange for names, teenagers tossed into shipping containers, flown to third countries to be tortured while the neighbors counted their cash rewards. Napalm and white phosphorus, private corporations set loose in the wreckage to take what profits they could find. Drone strikes on weddings. Massacres in the dead of night.

We waited for the weekly installment of this new hit series about villains and spies, dashing diplomats and backroom intrigue, bombs hidden in lingerie, a timer counting down in the trunk of a limousine, the handsome CIA agent who clips the wire in the nick of time. We could no longer say if we'd heard it on CNN or seen it on the silver screen. Abductions, secret prisons, citizens whisked off European streets, out of schools and train stations and mosques. Men hung upside down and beaten. Boys with tubes shoved up their noses. *This is not my country*, I said. I pinched myself, clicked my heels, but the wonders kept coming. Like a black mass or a sorcerer's spell: they said the words, made furtive gestures, and one by one the laws stopped working—the Geneva Conventions, the Bill of Rights, the FISA statutes, anything inconvenient to the machinery of vengeance and control. Warrantless wiretaps, indefinite detentions, *habeas corpus* denied because no judge had the proper security clearance to hear the case. They granted themselves access to our business records, our phone records, our library books, the massive eye of foreign surveillance turning to the enemy within. *If you see something, say something.* We were struck mute and blind.

This is not my country. I said it over and over again. We all did. We signed petitions, scrawled on placards, joined the great, screaming mob in its pointless regurgitations: *Imperialism! Occupation! Police state!* We marched up and down and around and back, clenched our fists and decried the monstrous things our government was doing, and when we opened our eyes our government was still doing them and—most terrifying—*it was still our government.* A representation of the country, a distillation of who we really are, what we really wanted. And what we really wanted was to kill people, a lot of people, to crush their homes, turn their hospitals into heaps of broken concrete. To lock children in cages in the Caribbean heat and leave them to die like animals. We wanted to inject people with poisons that would leave them shaking for the rest of their lives. To dislocate their shoulders, fracture their skulls, to hold power drills to their heads and tell them to pray. We wanted to piss on their holy books, show them our asses and fart at them, we wanted to slam them into walls, cram them into crawlspaces, drown them in buckets and bring them back to life. We wanted to show them—we wanted to make damn sure they understood—that the United States of *Amurka* is the most powerful nation in history, blessed by a god stronger and nastier than theirs, that the world belongs to us and if they dared challenge us we would *fuck their shit up.*

No, it was not my country. But what other country did I have?

So I argued, shook my fist, wrote my polemics for *My.World* and read them at open mics. I bought a bumper sticker that read REGIME CHANGE STARTS AT HOME. The body count skyrocketed—ten thousand, a hundred thousand, millions driven from their homes—but back in *Amurka*, I still went to work each day, teaching young writers to *show don't tell.* Diagramming plotlines. Expounding on empathy. Empathy, I told them, was what separated us from the animals. Art, I insisted, could still save the world.

It was a lie, a convenient fantasy. No one knew that better than I. And one morning I woke to the image of a bland young *Amurkan* leading a naked Arab by a leash, grinning and flashing a thumbs-up, as if he were something she'd won on a game show.

Not long after that, I boarded a plane—my apartment abandoned, my belongings all sold. I had no illusions about the value of this gesture, or any gesture. I only knew that if I stayed in *Amurka* I would lose something I needed, some ability to divide the world into true and false. The war, of course, would continue, but I would not be a part of it. I would wash my hands, sever the connection. From that moment on I was not an American: I was a phantom, an absence. I was nowhere to be found.

Mark arranged for me to stay with a friend in Lima, a journalist Stephanie had worked with in the '90s. I arrived on a windy morning, fog shrouding the corrugated tin Pacific and the Callao shipyards as the plane descended. It had been years since I'd seen Lima. The airport was unrecognizable—what had been a filthy terminal swarming with pickpockets had been transformed into a gleaming emporium of jewelry and leather stores, cell-phone kiosks, a crowded Starbucks playing Amy Winehouse songs. The touts and taxi drivers and overflowing ashtrays were gone, replaced by security guards and LCD screens, the stench of broken toilets disinfected by the cool wash of money.

The city, too, was bright and clean—nothing like the dreary, dangerous place I remembered. In the taxi, I gaped at giant supermarkets and manicured parks, upscale bakeries where ladies in sunglasses chatted at patio tables. After years in Babilonia, I felt like a caveman who'd just thawed from a block of ice.

"So you want to write about the Bride of Satan," Damien Cohen said.

"'Want' might not be the right word," I said.

Damien was a tall, reedy Frenchman with a salt-and-pepper crewcut and deep-set blue eyes that narrowed in secret amusement. He was a serious journalist—he'd spent years in Africa, writing about conflicts in Chad and the Sudan, first for *Le Monde* and then *The Washington Post*, before coming to Lima in 1992. Eight years later, he won a Pulitzer for his series on the implosion of the Fujimori government. He lived with his boyfriend, Carlito, in the Magdalena del Mar district, in a cozy flat with brushed-steel appliances and Georgia O'Keeffe on the walls.

"My first advice to you is not to tell anyone your real subject," he said, reclining on a white couch and offering me a Gaulois. "You'll see, Andres. The Peruvians, it's shocking. They all want to stab her in the throat."

"After all this time?"

"She is the most hated person in Peru. More even than Abimael Guzmán."

Three days earlier, Leonora's parole had been approved. The press went berserk, running front-page photographs of dead soldiers and bombing sites, headlines like HIGH COURT LEGALIZES TERROR-ISM and VIENE EL CUATRO. There were demonstrations as far away as Piura, former ronderos brandishing weapons in the streets. Leo's lawyer received hundreds of death threats and the presiding judge's car was stoned. The next day the attorney general stayed the ruling, citing "irregularities" in the handling of the case. Leo would remain in prison, pending a full review.

"Why you care so much about this person?" Lucrecia had asked that morning, as I hefted my backpack in the freezing gray silence. "Is so long ago."

"It's just a job," I said. "You won't even know I'm gone. When I come back I'll take you to a fancy dinner."

"When?"

"Two weeks."

She turned away and pulled the blankets tight. "You won't come back."

"Lulu," I said.

"You will go dancing and meet a rich limeña and she will say, 'Why you want to go back to those rough, stupid cholos?'"

"And I'll say, 'Because I am a rough, stupid cholo.'" I stooped to kiss her forehead. "Try not to think about it. It's two weeks. Maybe three."

Damien showed me the small guest room off the kitchen and handed me a spare key. "Mi casa es tu casa. Help yourself to anything you need. I'm sure you already have many sources to speak to," he said, "but let me know if I can be of help."

My head was abuzz from being at sea level after years at high altitude. I was nervous: it was opening night and I still hadn't read the script.

"The truth is," I said, laughing, "I don't really know where to start."

It was simple: I needed the money. Fifteen thousand dollars: enough to keep me in Babilonia for two or three years. After that, who knew? The news from the U.S. was all bad—the market had slid another ten percent, Bear Stearns collapsed—but there was an election coming up, the end of the Bush nightmare in sight at last. "Hope and change, dude!" Jack said when I spoke to him last. Who was to say a new President couldn't fix everything, put all the murderous genies back in their bottles?

It was also true that I needed an exit—temporary, a little breathing space, time for everyone to think things over. After the night at La Luna, Lucrecia had begged me to forgive her: she'd seen Ronaldo, her ex, in church and confided in him in a moment of confusion, she said. She'd had no idea he would show up at the club. She wanted to be with me, she said. If I still wanted her, she wanted to be with me.

"Of course I want you," I told her. But neither of us knew exactly what that meant, not now, and it seemed best to spend some time apart until we did.

In the meantime, I had to figure out a way into the story. Stephanie was right: I knew nothing, had none of the requisite background, had never been around any of the people—passionate activists, jailbirds, table-bangers—Leonora must have known. What I knew of Peru's history could have fit in a shot glass. The war, the military dictatorships, the centuries of oppression and neglect—I was as innocent of these things as I was of Japanese cinema or string theory. I hadn't come to Peru to study history, after all. I'd come to escape it.

But to write this story I'd need a crash course, enough to keep from embarrassing myself. I'd brought a few books with me—Gorriti, Fanon, Mariátegui—and soon I'd acquired many more: revolutionary theory, memoirs of activists and political prisoners. At a café near Damien's apartment, I spent hours downloading transcripts and communiqués, white papers, human-rights reports, highlighting and underlining until long after midnight. I read all eight thousand pages of the Truth & Reconciliation Commission's 2003 report. My notebook quickly filled with timelines, genealogies, lists of villages with unpronounceable Quechua names. None of it made sense to me: the flood of words, of terminology. By the end of the day I'd forgotten everything I'd read.

When I'd written my novel I'd done very little research: I read a book about communes, another on the dot-com crash, spent two weeks in Oregon on Stanford's dime. For plot, I pored over *The Great Gatsby*, my not-so-secret model—my narrator was a modern-day Nick Carraway, a scholarship kid thrust among people of outrageous privilege. For the characters and their discontents, I drew shamelessly on my own circle of artists and strivers, on people like Jack Durst—the young millionaires who proliferated in San Francisco and disappeared just as quickly. I did no interviews. What need? I had no obligation to real people or events, only to the story. The details were less important than how it was told, the music of the sentences; context mattered less than a vivid description or a startling insight.

Leo's story was different. I'd known that since the night I'd watched the crowd at Paddy's rouse itself to fury. She was a symbol of so many things, the tip of an iceberg that rammed the hull of Peru and nearly took the whole ship down. No one was unaffected; nearly everyone had lost family members, or fled their home, or kept their children inside for fear of car bombs. Their daily lives were shredded, their streets blown up—and here I was, years later, hoping to make a buck off catastrophe.

"It always feels like this, at first," Damien said. "You are always the outsider, the dilettante. You have to move ahead anyway. Part of it is bluffing."

"What's the other part?"

He laughed and poured more wine. After a week I had not started writing. There was too much to learn, the war was a labyrinth that expanded endlessly. Before sleep each night, I took out *The Eyes of the World*, gently handling its yellowed pages. I looked into the eyes on the banner, studied the photos. The blank square on the back page taunted me. What belonged in that empty space? If I stared at it for long enough, what image would emerge?

"Don't talk to me about this one. She is of no interest to me," said
Raúl Quintana, a doughy, forty-one-year-old mestizo, as we sat in his
mother's living room, on the tenth floor of a building in the Residencial
San Felipe apartment complex, and sipped tea. "Yet another tool of
this genocidal puppet government: the fetish of an irrelevant child.
Every day they follow her with their cameras a hundred children die
like flies in the campo. Why don't you write about those children?"

"I'd like to write about all of it," I said.

He went on as if he hadn't heard me. "Why don't you write about
the farmers whose land was stolen by the army? Poor campesinos,
like my father. If they resisted, the government killed them. Like
insects. Is this not more important than a gringa whore?"

It was my first attempt at an interview, and I'd already broken
Damien's rule. Quintana, who'd gone by the nom de guerre
Comrade Rayos, had been captured in Junín near the end of the
war and spent three years in El Arca. Damien had met him years
ago, while writing about Shining Path cadres trying to transition
back to normal life. As I'd waited outside the building, I'd braced to
meet an actual revolutionary—I imagined him tall and command-
ing, with an aura of controlled violence. But Quintana looked more
like an accountant than a terrorist. He wore thick eyeglasses, black
trousers, a red sweater with pictographs of llamas across the chest.
The only thing about him that suggested his former life was a fur-
tiveness to his eyes and movements. Before he let me in, he called
Damien, then put me on the phone for "voice confirmation."

"May I ask about the first time you participated in an action?"
I said now. I slid my new voice recorder across the coffee table,
hoping to convey confidence. "What was that experience like?"

Quintana reached out and turned the recorder off. "Why don't
you write about the American mining corporation, Tuttweiler,
Incorporated, that is killing Peruvians in Cajamarca?" He stood and
paced before the picture windows, the gray city framed behind him.
On one wall of the apartment, a pewter Jesus hung twisted from
his cross. A stack of canvasses leaned against another wall: watercolors of soaring condors and Inca chieftains that Quintana sold at

the weekend markets. "People who are removed from the land they have lived on for centuries, the mountains they worship blown up with dynamite, their water filled with cyanide. Because they don't have *title*," he said, spitting the last word like an obscenity.

"You have heard of the priest, Father Antonio? He tries to organize the people, and one night four men on motorcycles come, private security of Tuttweiler, Incorporated. They beat him with chains. He is in the hospital for a week and when he goes to his house someone has broken all the windows and shit on the floor. Why don't you write about this? When a complaint was made to the U.S. embassy, they said the men who attacked Father Antonio were employed by a Peruvian subcontractor, so it is not the responsibility of Tuttweiler, Incorporated."

"It's outrageous."

"Why don't you write about the ministers who line their pockets with bribes? Why don't you write that the people who live on this land will not receive one centavo from the gold that is found there? Why don't you write that since conquest the Peruvian has been enslaved and murdered by one foreigner after another?

"I will tell you why you don't write this," he said, holding a finger in the air. "You don't write this because of the presence of the American corporation. Without this, you can write about the barbaric Peruvian who brutalizes his own people, so the people of the United States can feel lucky not to live with such a violent regime. But because of Tuttweiler, it is impossible to say this is not a story about Americans. Impossible to declare your innocence. And Americans do nothing in which they cannot declare their innocence."

He turned to watch the city, hands clasped behind his back. I didn't know what to ask next. It was my first conversation with someone who'd actually been in the war, who might see things the way Leonora saw them, and already it was a failure.

"I'm not really a journalist," I said.

He sighed, then pushed up a sleeve and thrust his arm at me. I felt his gaze on my head as I examined what looked, at first, like musical notation—lines and dots, thick swirls of scar tissue twining their way up the skin.

"Do you think La Leo has scars like this? Do you?" he shouted. There was something insincere in his anger; like the speech that preceded it, the outburst was a kind of performed intimidation, an impression of a militant, maybe of Abimael himself.

"I'm sorry," I said. And I was. But I was desperate to change the subject, to extract myself from this unpleasant encounter. Sensing this, Quintana pulled down his sleeve. His eyes blinked slowly behind the thick lenses.

"How is Damien Cohen, the faggot?" he said, dropping heavily to the couch and picking up his mug of tea. "Still writing lies for the imperialist dogs?"

A biology professor whose lab had burned when members of Sendero and Cuarta Filosofía argued over the revolutionary significance of cell mutation. A laundress whose husband and son were killed in a government raid. A left-wing congressman who'd gone into hiding in Bolivia for seven years. A retired Bayer executive who'd been kidnapped and ransomed by the MRTA. A librarian who was kicked out of his "study group" because the leader wanted to sleep with his girlfriend—a week before the group was wiped out by the army. A British journalist whose Peruvian husband was pulled from their car one night on the road to Huancayo and never seen again.

Once I got started, there was no shortage of people to interview, each with their own version of the war. By the end of two weeks I'd recorded more than twenty hours' worth, a catalog of outrage and loss that I couldn't bring myself to transcribe. Everyone wanted to teach me the same history, to relitigate the war by recitation of uncontestable facts—but one man's facts were another's paranoid fantasy, one woman's convulsions of grief another's "collateral damage."

I met them in city parks, in Papa John's pizzeria, in marble foyers and windowless offices that stank of tobacco. I went to neighborhoods of flower-lined boulevards and clothing boutiques; others where toothless women sat on crates and boys kicked plastic bottles down unpaved streets. I did not belong in these places—I felt this so acutely I could hardly speak. I sat and listened and arranged my face in the proper expressions and then I went home and tried to fit what I'd heard into five thousand words. I wrote dozens of first paragraphs. I tried to make an outline, to channel the flood into something straightforward and discrete—but the thought of choosing between horrors, highlighting the most gruesome or redemptive or instructive, seemed ridiculous, a sacrilege. Was one person's tragedy worth less than another's? How could I write any of it without writing all of it?

"For Christ's sake just get started," Jack said. "Don't give me the history of Peru. Nobody's gonna click on that!"

"But they want to know why. They want to understand her."

"Yeah, as a person, dude. A terrorist. Not some history class. Not a piece of a huge puzzle. Who's got time for that?"

But a tiny piece of a puzzle is exactly what she was. You couldn't tell where she fit until you saw the whole picture, but once you did you had to squint to see her. Like Icarus in Breugel's painting: just a pair of pale, drowning knees. Jack wanted a cover girl, a protagonist. I didn't know how to make her so large without making everything else too small.

"It must seem incredible to you. Like savages. Telling this to you I feel I must apologize for my country." I sat in a high-backed leather chair in the Sheraton bar with Aníbal Rausch, a courtly physician in his early sixties. "One must think of it as a kind of infection, a fever. Any small incident serves as the pathogen. It enters the bloodstream and provokes a massive response from the immune system."

He crossed his legs and bounced a tasseled loafer up and down, hands flat on the arms of the chair. He had long, hollow cheeks and a too-prominent jaw. A cane with a gold horse's head for a handle lay by his chair. "This is why, afterward, it is difficult to remember," he said. "As with a fever. The body does what it must to heal itself."

Rausch had been arrested in Huánuco, in 1989, after being named by a convicted terrorist whose sentence was reduced for identifying others. He was taken to the military barracks at Los Cabitos, where he was interrogated for three weeks, hung naked by the wrists from a water pipe, electrodes attached to his scrotum and nipples, and beaten. Though there was no other evidence against him, he was convicted of aiding Sendero and spent two years in prison. Now he ran a private women's clinic in San Isidro. He recounted his ordeal in the low, deliberate voice of one who has told the same story many times, refining it over the years to its most effective form.

"Did you ever think of leaving Peru?" I asked.

His hands rose briefly and settled again. "This is my country. What one man or a hundred men did cannot change that."

"But it wasn't just those men. It was the whole system."

His foot stopped its nervous bouncing and he turned his gaunt face to me. Not for the first time, I felt a steep disorientation, the surreal disconnect between Rausch's creaky dignity and the savagery he described. It was everywhere in these stories, from Abimael, the learned professor who goaded his followers to "cross the river of blood," to the generals and cabinet ministers, educated in Europe and the U.S., who shed tears at Mass before giving the order to wipe their enemies from the earth.

"There is no such thing as a system," Rausch said. He pressed a large, spotted hand on my leg. "Even in the body, what we perceive as a system is in fact separate cells or organs with no awareness of one another."

I looked around the bar at the boisterous professionals and pale tourists. I stirred my drink. He was trying to tell me something. "Were you . . . um, *associated*? In any way?"

He raised an eyebrow. "With the Shining Path?"

"I'm sorry. I have to ask."

He considered this. With a graceful gesture, he pointed to the television above the bar, where a Pentagon official was giving a briefing, something about a village in Pakistan that had been blown to bits. "Tell me, Andres, are you associated with this?

"Associations are never so clear," he said. "The truth is there are only people, each acting according to his desires and according to his conscience. Perhaps others act similarly. Still others benefit from these actions in one way or another. One might call this an association, or a community. But the community is only the expression of those acts, as the sea is turned red by the presence of certain organisms. It does not create those organisms."

He reached for his cane and levered himself out of the chair. When he was standing before me, he offered his hand.

"You didn't answer my question," I said, trying to hide my

frustration. I was tired of performances, gnomic pronouncements. I'd been there for three weeks.

The doctor smiled and patted me on the shoulder. Then he made his way through the crowd, nodding to the other patrons as though they were there at his sufferance. I lost him a moment later, drawn again to the news flashing above the bar: bandaged children, charred corpses hanging out of jeeps. Over the years I'd grown numb to such images, but Rausch's question had renewed their urgency. I couldn't turn away. In the background, a huddle of men argued and glared straight at the camera, as if they could see us all on the other side. The Pentagon spokesman denied there were civilian casualties.

Lucrecia called almost every day, hanging up after one ring so I knew to call back. On the phone her voice was deeper, more intimate, as if we'd somehow grown closer, though in fact everything was tangled and uncertain between us.

"Amor, I miss you," she'd say.

"It's okay," I'd tell her. "Everything's fine."

She'd finally gone to a clinic, an hour's bus ride from her barrio, where a doctor examined her for less than a minute, then scowled and handed her a box of vitamins.

"I am so bad. A bad woman. I am a disgrace," she said. Her mother always told her never to date a gringo but she'd been too stupid to listen. "She will never forgive me," she moaned. "God will never forgive me. Why I don't listen to everybody?"

"These things happen. You're not stupid. We'll figure it out."

I shoved aside a stack of case studies from Human Rights Watch and lay back on the bed. Part of me wanted to comfort her, for her to know she could count on me. But we hardly knew each other. I couldn't forget Ronaldo's face as he stormed up the stairs of La Luna—the hard anger in his eyes, the arms flexed for violence. It bothered me to think she'd been with someone like that. It made me wonder which was the real Lucrecia and which was an act.

"You love me, Andres, ¿sí o no?"

"Of course."

"¿Sí o no?" she said with sudden force.

"Lulu, calm down," I said. "I'll be back soon, and we'll take care of everything."

Her vehemence depleted, she sniffled, "Only one more week? You promise?"

"One more week," I said. I grabbed the voice recorder and cigarettes. I had an appointment at noon, another at one-thirty. I was going to be late. "Maybe two."

On a Friday night, nearly a month after I arrived in Lima, Damien insisted I go dancing with him and Carlito. "Mark says you are the King of Salsa," he said, peering into the guest room, "but all we've seen is smoking and writing. Even the Muse needs diversion, Andres."

This seemed an excellent idea, a reprieve. The endless research had done little to bolster my confidence; the deeper I got, the longer and harder it seemed I'd need to dig. That morning I'd resolved to start writing. I'd cancelled my appointments, spent an hour reviewing my notes. But when I finally opened the computer I got lost in the news: the disintegrating economy, those children in Pakistan, bodies burned beyond recognition.

El Castillo perched above the bright Paseo de la República, the city's main north-south artery. A line of taxis and black sedans crawled up the drive. Damien paid my cover, and as the bouncers frisked us I felt acutely aware of my hiking boots and frayed jeans. With its roped-off booths and uplit shelves, an enormous Inca sun suspended over the dance floor, the club belonged to a different world than the one I'd been living in. The martinis Damien ordered came in sleek goblets, with skins of ice that glowed pale blue.

Until then I'd had little conversation with Carlito, an attorney for an investment bank whom Damien, ten years his elder, described affectionately as "a rich snob from a fallen family." Carlito was slim and handsome, with well-coiffed hair and a hawk's watchfulness. His attitude toward me had been one of polite tolerance, as if I were a repairman whose job was taking much longer than expected. He and Damien had not spoken in the taxi. They seemed at pains to avoid each other's eyes.

"So, Andres," he said now, with forced enthusiasm, "your work is going well?"

I tried to sound nonchalant. "I wouldn't say that."

He blinked at me, then at Damien. Behind him, early dancers chased one another around the floor. "It seems very difficult to be a writer," he said, smiling into his martini. Damien gave a long sigh, the sound of an indulgent parent well familiar with such behavior.

"I hope I'm not in your way," I told Carlito. "I didn't expect to stay this long. The story's more complicated than I expected."

He lit a cigarette and looked me over, like a tailor deciding where to stick the pins. "But Peru is not a complicated country. I'll explain it to you," he said. "In this country, you must consider everything to be an accident or a mistake. Everything is ruined by the stupidity of Peruvians."

"Amor . . ." Damien groaned.

"In this country only the worst ideas survive. Everything else is too difficult for the people to understand." Over the years I'd heard many limeños talk this way: Peruvians were dishonest, incompetent, they were all drunkards and thieves. It went without saying which Peruvians they meant. "But you already knew this, Andres," he said. "You are medio-peruano, no?"

I laughed warily, caught in a too-bright spotlight. "Maybe un cuarto."

Carlito showed his perfect teeth. "Which cuarto?"

"Shall we dance, minino?" Damien said, standing abruptly.

"But we're talking, amorcito," Carlito said, never taking his eyes off me. "I'm getting to know our friend, as you asked. So, which cuarto, Andres? True, your Spanish is passable. And I'm told you are the King of Salsa. But surely there's more? Surely you've learned something about Peru other than bricheras and war?"

He fished his olive from his glass and popped it into his mouth. "You are a writer," he went on. "Have you read the great Peruvian writers? Vargas Llosa? Bryce Echenique? Do you know the poems of César Vallejo? And what about younger writers? I assume you take an interest in our literary culture. Perhaps I can make some introductions for you.

"And of course you've travelled widely—Trujillo, Arequipa, Amazonas? Have you gone to Madre de Dios, or the Festival de

Qollur Rit'i? Have you seen the Nazca Lines? Someone so interested in our country must want to see these places. Don't tell me you've only stayed with the other gringos of Babilonia?"

His smile was thin, one eyebrow raised to the level of maximum torment. I took a gulp of the martini and grimaced at the gin's cold burn. "I'm not a tourist," I managed.

"Then what are you?"

I opened my hands, surprised by the heat in my throat. Damien, too, was paralyzed, unable to come to my rescue. "I just like it here," I said lamely. "I'm just tired of living in a country that embarrasses me."

Carlito watched me a long moment. His smile softened. I almost saw a glimmer of pity. "So instead you write what embarrasses us."

Before I could think of a response, a woman in black pants and a silky copper top strode up to our table, beaming. Damien's relief was extravagant. "Ah!" he cried, nearly tripping over his chair. "Here she is!"

They embraced and traded half a dozen air kisses. She had long, straight hair and high cheekbones, round eyes with fine lines at the corners. For a heart-skipping instant, I thought it was Lucrecia.

"Andres, I want you to meet Yesenia, a dear old friend," Damien said. "Yesenia, here is the new friend I told you about."

"He is the King of Salsa," Carlito added.

Yesenia looked between them with a puzzled smile, then held out a slender hand to me. "Mucho gusto," she said, her voice dubious but willing to be proven wrong.

We danced for a few songs—long enough for me to step on Yesenia's feet half a dozen times, to nearly drop her when I tried a dip. She was kind enough not to show annoyance. She lifted my hands to her shoulders and took the lead, counting to herself as we drifted to the edge of the floor. After a farcical collision with another couple, she asked if I'd like to go up to the roof.

"I haven't been dancing in a while," I said when we were leaning on the rail, the city laid out before us. "I'm usually a little smoother."

Yesenia crinkled her eyes and sipped her drink. "You are the king."

"Standards are lower in Babilonia."

"Ah, Babilonia . . ." she said, with a knowing, devious smile. "This is where you live?"

Lima twinkled all around us, its brightness contained by the ring of dark mountains, the ocean to the south and west. I was mildly drunk but wide awake, determined to shake off my mood. Yesenia was pretty and high-spirited, with an easy sophistication. Her nearness, her slight shiver, brought an immediacy to everything, a crystal sense of *now*. It felt good to be standing on that roof, my sweat cooling, music vibrating from below. Here, at least, was something I knew how to do.

"Damien says you are a writer?" she said.

"A novelist," I said, feigning reluctance. "Nothing like the great Damien Cohen." She asked what I was working on, and I started to tell her about *The Moon Also Rises*, about the nonstop revelry of expatriate life. I stopped when I saw her confusion.

"He told me you are writing about the war."

In a breath my euphoria deflated, as if I'd been accused of some perversion. The argument with Carlito hadn't worn off, the feeling of having been undressed before strangers. He was right, of course—in three years I'd seen very little of the country. Someone—I couldn't remember who—had given me a copy of Vargas Llosa's *Conversations in the Cathedral*, but I didn't like to read in Spanish so it sat on my windowsill year after year, its cover blanching in the sharp light.

"I'm trying to write about Leonora Gelb," I admitted. "It's not going very well."

As she watched me over her drink, I felt the night slipping away. I'd thought to spend an hour talking about something other than politics and slaughter, but politics and slaughter wouldn't leave me alone. It was a setup, but not the kind I'd first assumed: Damien hadn't wanted me to meet an eligible female, he'd wanted to give me a source.

Yesenia had grown up in San Borja, in a middle-class family of teachers and government functionaries. Like most limeños, they'd paid little attention to the war. They read stories, or saw things on

TV, but there seemed to be no reason for the carnage, and no relevance to their own lives.

"The blackouts and the curfew, only things like this bother us. Some girls have to cancel their quinceañeras," she said, rolling her eyes. "What a tragedy!"

In college she'd accompanied a psychology professor on a trip to Huancapí, in the Emergency Zone, to spend a month at a home for children who'd lost their parents in the war. The driver who picked them up at the bus station kept a rifle on his lap. The stories the children told, in words and in crude drawings, made her physically sick, she said. She couldn't eat, she stayed awake at night watching the hills from her window, seeing movement behind every stone and shrub. All she wanted was to leave, to take the first bus back to Lima. "While we worried about parties, these children were watching their parents tortured and killed," she said. "In this country. In my country. I didn't know."

Soon after that, she'd switched to chemistry, relieved to be working with inanimate substances and immutable laws. Her former professor disappeared a few months later; her body, and those of two nuns, were found in a cave not far from the orphanage. They'd been raped, doused in red paint, and shot at close range. With a stab of nausea I realized I knew this case. I'd been reading it the day before. The Human Rights Watch report said it was impossible to determine whether they'd been killed by Sendero or the military. "Both sides committed atrocities," it helpfully noted.

On the night La Leo was arrested, Yesenia and her family had watched the news in horror and confusion. "What kind of person is this, Andres? Does she ever go to the campo? Does she know these children?"

She spoke quietly, staring out at the city's vast sparkle, the looming mountains. There was a huge country beyond those mountains: places I'd never seen, people I didn't understand, things I'd believed had nothing to do with me. But one day soon, if all went as planned, there would be a story with my name on it. When Yesenia squeezed my elbow I felt nearly lightheaded with shame.

"Everything in this country is ruined," she said. "Everyone has suffered. Why does she want them to suffer more? Who is this person, Andres? Can you explain to me?"

Later, I accompanied Yesenia back to San Borja, and we stood kissing inside the gate to her sister's house, amid flowering vines and scattered plastic toys. I could taste the rum on her breath, and I thought how nice it would be to share her bed, sleep late, go out for a fancy breakfast—anything that didn't involve Leonora Gelb. When I whispered in her ear, she gave a groan of regret and pushed me gently away.

"I like meeting you, Andres. But I'm not like those girls from Babilonia, okay?"

It took me close to an hour to find a taxi, wandering the streets until I came to a traffic circle where old women sold roasted potatoes and cars stopped to talk to girls in short dresses. Men talked in low voices. One girl chased another into the shadows. I waited a long time, smoking at the edge of this Dantean scene. I thought maybe I should talk to some of those people—but what would I say? I'd accomplished nothing since coming to Lima. The war had taken over my dreams, hijacked every conversation. I'd heard so many terrible stories. But they were just stories.

The lights were still on at Damien's. When I opened the door I heard voices and I stopped, not wanting to intrude on an argument. Damien stood outside the kitchen. There was a backpack propped against the wall, a mane of blond hair peering into the fridge.

"You see, Andres?" he said. "Our party is getting bigger."

She straightened, beer bottle in hand, and my heart beat quickly, as if I'd been caught in some juvenile disobedience. My breath caught when I saw the bruise under her right eye, splotchy and tender, curving along her temple, fraying at the hairline.

"Hola, Andres," Stephanie said. She sounded tired beyond endurance, resigned to the unpleasantness of seeing me.

I said, "Are you okay?"

She sipped from the bottle and stared dead at me.

"My friends, you are both welcome here," Damien said. "But I regret to inform you I'll be using the couch tonight. Andres, you won't mind sharing the guest room?"

The next morning, I woke early and showered quickly, anxious to escape the apartment before the inevitable conversation. I'd slept poorly, drifting in and out of threatening dreams, minutely aware of every movement from the body next to me. Near dawn, I propped myself on an elbow and, breath held, studied her face, the mottled bruise garish against her pale skin. In my insomniac fog I had the sense that this, too, was somehow my fault.

I spent the morning at the National Museum, where an exhibit of photographs from the war had recently been mounted—to howls of protest from conservative politicians and supporters of the former president. The images were ghastly: a woman covered in blood, weeping over a child's body next to a bombed-out minivan; militants in balaclavas patrolling the San Marcos cafeteria; campesinos gathered at an open grave; three teenagers with bandannas over their faces, pumping their fists on the roof of a concrete bodega. I couldn't say which ones I'd seen before. When I found myself in a blind alcove surrounded by portraits of Comrades Julian, Marta, and Chaski, I felt the same dislocation as I'd felt the night before. Here were the people I was trying to write about. So why did it feel as though *they* were examining *me*?

As I made my way to the elevators, my phone started to buzz. Lucrecia burst into the day's lamentation: she was throwing up all night, in the morning she was too sluggish to get up and she'd been late for work. "I am scared my father will know," she said. "You think is better I stay with Rosa until you come back?"

The long wall opposite the elevators was taken up by the final photograph in the exhibit: a group of Quechua women sat on a bench holding up pictures of young men and women; behind their heads, a banner declared them to be the Abuelitas de la Ausencia, and pleaded for "a world in which our children don't disappear."

"That's a good idea," I said. "Why don't you stay with Rosa."

"But how long? Her room is very small and far from my work."

But I was only half listening, transfixed by the image of the abuelitas, the poignant resignation in their eyes. Someone had chosen them, I thought. Of all the relatives of the disappeared, they picked this exact group, told them to sit just this way.

"Soon," I managed. "Maybe a week?"

"Always you say this," she said bitterly. "Is too long. Please come back, Andres."

When I got back to Damien's, Stephanie was at the kitchen table, scrawling in a notebook, a half-empty bottle of white wine sweating by her elbow. She wore sweatpants and a faded, flimsy T-shirt. The bruise around her eye had darkened to a sour yellow; again, she looked straight at me, as if daring me to notice.

"Working on an article?" I said.

"Writing to my brother." A moment later, she closed the notebook and pushed the bottle toward me. "Wine?"

We made small talk, exchanged observations of Lima—the worsening weather, the ubiquitous construction, the new airport with its fast food and high-end stores. The government had spent more than two hundred million dollars to renovate the airport, she said, though most Peruvians would never use it.

"That's what winning a war will get you," she said.

"So," I said, anxious to steer clear of politics, "how are things in Babilonia?"

She lifted her chin, the garish bruise unignorable. "How do they seem?"

"I only meant—" I stopped, offended by her tone. But when she dropped her gaze and brought the glass to her lips, I saw how much effort it took to project this bravado.

"Listen," I said, not knowing what would come next. "I'm glad you're here."

She laughed. "Oh?"

"I'm sure Mark told you it's not going very well. You're probably not surprised. But I'm going to buckle down, start focusing. I've been trying to learn too much, pack too much into this thing, and it's gotten me kind of paralyzed. You see? But now that I've done that, maybe I can start sifting through it. Definitely I can. You know that thing Michelangelo said about the sculpture?" I hesitated, put off by her flat gaze, then forged ahead. "I've got to start cutting out the stuff that isn't the sculpture. I think I'm ready, but that's where maybe I don't have enough experience, where I could use some help.

"I want to do a good job," I said. "You probably don't believe me, but it's true. So, yeah, I'm glad you're here. I really think you can help me."

I made myself stop talking. Stephanie took a long sip, considering how to respond. "Andres, you think I came here to help you? Are you joking?" She shook her head and stood to wash her glass. "Do you really think—" she said, then wheeled back at me. "Do you think it matters, this silly article? This *website?* Stuck between stories about Brad Pitt and Angelina Jolie, or some baseball player taking steroids. Who cares?

"You want something that matters? Read a real newspaper. Read *Der Spiegel* or the AFP. For God's sake, if *My.World* were a serious news outlet, do you honestly think they would have given the story to you?"

She stood over me while I took this in. One of her hands held the back of the chair and I watched the flutter of her pulse in a vein at her wrist. Her fingers were long and bony, ringless, bitten at the cuticles. A child's hand.

"Please help me," I said.

That's how, early the next morning, I found myself walking through the streets of Magdalena, heading away from an ocean hidden by heavy fog. Stephanie was a step ahead, her outline slightly blurred by mist, though the blocks to the north glowed with clean sunshine. We soon entered a neighborhood of well-tended parks and corner cafés; a few women pushed strollers and talked into cell phones but otherwise the streets were quiet, the houses shuttered and immaculately maintained. On a narrow side street she stopped across from a large house painted forest green, the windows framed with black shutters. Wrought-iron spikes fenced off a circular cobblestone driveway and a stone fountain; a black Toyota was parked at the front door. Inside the fence, rosebushes climbed furiously, pink and yellow and blood-red flowers open to the unquiet sky.

"Who lives here?" I said.

"I have no idea."

I looked at Stephanie, then back at the house. A Frisbee lay on the driveway, and behind it an overturned Big Wheel. I could smell the luxuriant roses from across the street. I felt her watching me as I took in the neighboring rooftops, the puddles of recent rain, the soft clatter of branches in the breeze. When I crossed the street and stood before the fence I began to grow anxious. I had the sense of standing at an invisible threshold. I resisted the urge to turn back and make sure she was still there.

The house was silent, no movement behind the windows. It was impossible to imagine anything but the most generic domesticity taking place here. From this close I could see the imperfections in the facade: pockmarks here and there, especially on the third floor, where layers of paint couldn't entirely conceal the clusters, like needlepoint, around the windows. The shutters couldn't hide the old scorch marks.

I hugged myself against the chill and looked for any sign of the people who lived there. Even a shadow, or the sound of laughter, would have broken the spell. It was an actual house—not a description in a newspaper, not footage. And if the place was real then what had happened here was real, too. At some level I hadn't grasped that until now.

The wind dropped, the rustle of branches fell still. A neighbor's dog started to bark. I crossed back to Stephanie, who watched me with eyes narrowed in something like compassion. When I stepped onto the curb, she hooked her arm through mine.

"Why don't you start here?"

III

THE BEGINNING OF ARMED STRUGGLE

1

"Two miles," the professor said. "*Two miles.*" He stomped to the edge of the stage and crouched, as if to impart a secret. "You could walk there. You could ride your bicycle in ten minutes. But you wouldn't. Would you?"

He was young, maybe forty, thick black curls and mischievous eyes behind plastic frames. He spoke in a lilting, unplaceable accent, but his delivery—wry, purposely overblown—cut through the morning haze and made two hundred students fidget in their seats.

In the front row, Leo pushed into her seat and studied the gum-stained floor. It was her first college class—History 10: Introduction to Your Country. Though the day was hot, she wore dark slacks and the new sweater Maxine had given her when—finally—they left the dorm. Already Leo felt sweat beading at her hairline and behind her ears.

"East Palo Alto, just across the freeway, is the murder capital of the United States. The average family of four earns less than your tuition." He walked back to the lectern and rapped out figures with a knuckle. "The high-school graduation rate—*high school*—is less than thirty percent. Sixty-five percent of men over fifteen have been in prison. Drug addiction, life expectancy, home ownership, health outcomes—every conceivable statistic puts East Palo Alto closer to San Salvador than to Stanford. And yet most students at this fine university will never see it. Do you think that's an accident?"

Again, the discomfort of low coughs, a clock ticking, mutters from the back row where the lanky athletes lounged. The student next to Leo—a heavyset Hispanic girl with a heart-shaped face and lips lined in black—scribbled furiously in her notebook, circling something in a whirl of blue ink. When Leo smiled, she cast back a cold, irritable gaze.

The professor was taller than he seemed; his corduroy jacket, patched at the elbows, and air of weariness made him a caricature of the rumpled professor. He roamed the stage and described the communities they would study this quarter: migrant laborers in the garlic fields of Gilroy; a Vietnamese enclave in San José; addicts and prostitutes in San Francisco's Tenderloin district; streetgangs in West Oakland. They would visit these communities and talk to people. "Real people," he said, "not headlines, not simulacra. Go alone, go in groups. Take public transportation or your new BMW. I don't care."

At this, the grumbling crested. "Isn't this supposed to be a history class?" someone called out. "This doesn't sound very historical."

"It's dangerous," a girl said. "You can't make us go where we might get hurt!"

"Or catch a disease," another student added, to snickers and shushes.

Leo squeezed her seat and forced herself not to turn around. She could picture the kids in the back: feet propped up, baseball caps turned backward, tank tops and Donald Duck flip-flops and the long, glossy hair of the West Coast girls she'd admired and feared since her arrival. They reminded her of her brother and his teammates, who took over the basement after Saturday games and waited for Maxine to bring them snacks, who got quiet if Leo chanced to enter the room and erupted into laughter when she left.

The professor batted his eyes sardonically. "And why not?"

Again the peremptory voice: "Uh, cause *history* is, like, the past?"

He took off his glasses and rubbed them with a handkerchief. "What I meant was, 'Why can't I make you go somewhere you don't want to go?' Listen, my friend, I don't care how much money your father makes or whether he plays golf with the Attorney General. I'm a tenured professor and this is my class. If you want credit you'll do what I tell you to do." He peered toward the back of the room and his smile spread broad and full. "Are there any other questions?"

The silence was broken only by the slap of seats being vacated, the squeak of sneakers. Leo couldn't look up, her face hot. It was

unseemly, this pleasure, almost erotic—hearing those kids overpowered, crushed. When the door shut behind the last defector, the rush
she felt was dizzying, almost primitive.

"Now we've trimmed the fat," the professor said, to a burst of
relieved laughter. To Leo's right, the Hispanic girl still slashed at
her notebook. "Why is the murder capital of the country two miles
from this bastion of privilege? How did it happen? By the end of
the quarter, I want you to have an answer. It is *not* an accident," he
said. "'No reason' is not acceptable. It's the most popular lie you've
ever been told." He peered at the clock. "Tell me why those people
are over there, and you'll earn a B for the course."

Having spent years among the children of the ruling class, Gabriel
Zamir knew what would come next. He didn't have to wait long.

"How do we get an A?" Leonora said.

"For that," he said, squinting fondly, "you'll need to explain why
you are *here*."

Stanford Out of South Africa. Students for a Free Tibet. East Palo
Alto Community Law Project. The Economic Justice Council. By
the end of the quarter she'd joined them all, racing from table to
table on White Plaza, attending meetings in basement classrooms,
dormitory common areas, a used bookstore on University Avenue
where she sat on a milk crate, choking on the sweet smoke of clove
cigarettes. The expeditions to Gilroy and the Tenderloin were bracing, unsettling—standing under a fierce sun while a fieldworker
answered questions in broken English, or watching an aging hooker
fall asleep in a diner booth, Leo weathered her profound discomfort, the stinging knowledge that she didn't belong there, outside
the bubble. She knew that was the point. She got a B+ for the class.
She knew she deserved it—despite an exhaustively researched paper
on migrant workers, she hadn't answered Zamir's question to his
satisfaction or her own.

The Homelessness Action Coalition. The Lesbian/Gay Alliance.
Chicano Solidarity. So many causes, so little time. She could not
pass a flier without pulling off a tab, or hear a bullhorn without
promising to attend the next meeting. Students for Environmental
Action. Students for a Sweat-free Stanford. Concerned Students

for a Meatless World. The banners hung from the balconies of the Student Union, slogans unfurling, flower-like, in the night: "Just Say No to Defense Contracts!" "Stanford Endowment = Rape and Pillage Fund" "What Part of DIVEST Don't You Understand?"

Not for Leonora the kissing parties on Serra Quad, the Greek Row bacchanalia, day trips to Santa Cruz or bong-stupefied weekends in Lake Tahoe chateaux. Rallies and lectures, amateur slideshows, she sat uncomfortably in molded plastic chairs while speakers invoked Chomsky and Marcuse, Said and Debray, pounded their fists, spat words like "hegemony" and "superstructure" and "communiqué." So what if her GPA suffered? So what if she slept five hours a night? Such concerns were nothing compared to the struggles of East Pali residents, or of Zanzibar, the prostitute she'd interviewed, who called in February and left a shy, incoherent message about the rain, something about a letter from her sister. Leo knew what she wanted. She told herself after mid-terms she'd buy Zanzibar a meal and some clothes. But she never called back.

"Capitalism makes us invisible to each other, and to ourselves," Zamir said in his Winter seminar on labor movements. He sat on the edge of the table while the students plunged chopsticks into takeout boxes. By now Leo had started writing for the *Stanford Daily*, pieces about working conditions for university maintenance crews, admissions and financial aid statistics for minority students.

"And if we can't see the Other, if the Other doesn't exist . . ." he plucked an egg roll from her plate, "then we aren't poisoning his water or stealing his pension or napalming his village. We're maximizing efficiencies. Balancing accounts. It's a disappearing trick: once there were a thousand Guatemalan peasants, but now— *poof!*—there's a profitable banana plantation, with a reliable supply of cheap labor. Too much onion," he said, burping into his fist. The students laughed, all except Leo. "Why is there only one Chinese restaurant in Palo Alto? Where is robust American competition when you need it?"

By spring quarter she was busy with union drives, organizing wage workers at the tony Stanford Park Hotel. She went door-to-door in leafy Atherton and Menlo Park, leaving fliers in the hands of mistrustful nannies. She dreaded the summer, dreaded going home to her parents' smiling ignorance, her brother's mockery, the pale bloated bodies sunbathing at the swim club. She didn't deserve a vacation. What had she accomplished in three frenetic quarters? A handful of squatters granted a reprieve? The administration agreed to "review" its policies on gay and lesbian students? The victories were tiny, cosmetic—you unionized a hundred workers, or fed a dozen kids, but there were thousands more behind them.

"If you can reach just one person, make one life better . . ." her mother said. Leo ground her teeth and looked out the dorm window at the dry hills beyond campus. A massive satellite dish sprang from the horizon, pointing east into the haze. What did one person matter when the world's very machinery was built to grind them into paste? She thought often of the photograph of Steve Biko, wrecked and abandoned on his gurney. She thought of the man in the alley, burning silently and alone. She watched the satellite dish rotating almost imperceptibly, its long sensors tracking signals, processing data. It was the machinery itself you had to reach. You had to learn its codes, speak its language, if you wanted your own message to get through.

"You're not ready. You don't have the background, the research skills," Zamir said in May.

"I'll work harder. I swear. Do you remember my paper on Breton Woods?"

She had her heart set on a Fall graduate seminar, "Radical Underground Movements," which famously drew on Zamir's experiences in SDS. She knew courses could take her only so far, that until she got out of the bubble she'd always be a spectator, gawking at corpses through a car window. But what else could she do?

"These are doctoral candidates, much older than you. They've worked in El Salvador and Chile, interviewed Muslim Brotherhood members in prison—"

"I can hold my own," she said.

Zamir peered over his glasses. She was hardly the first ambitious student he'd found camped outside his office. Since his arrival in 1983 he'd been besieged by idealistic undergraduates with their dog-eared copies of *Bicentennial of Blood*, burning to *make a difference*. Looking at them, you knew their radicalism would survive precisely until the first job recruiters arrived their senior year. But when he saw Leo Gelb in the hallway he'd paused, daunted by her air of controlled urgency. He deflected it with irony, which worked on most students. But it hadn't worked on Leo.

"I'm sorry," he said now. "You don't have the prerequisites, so you can't get credit toward the major. And it won't help with graduate school. The name Zamir is not much in favor at the Kennedy School—"

"Professor Zamir," she said.

He put down the sheaf of T.A. applications he'd been browsing. "Gabriel."

"I don't want to go to grad school. I'm not here for credit, or a letter of reference, and I'm definitely not one of those girls who wait around after class to buy you coffee."

He leaned back and took off his glasses. "Then why are you here?"

This time she was ready: "Because people are hungry and I'm not."

She squeezed her hands in her lap but held his gaze. Zamir took up the papers, relieved to have forced this tactical error.

"'They tell me: eat and drink, but how can I eat and drink when my food is snatched from the hungry? And yet I eat and drink.' That's Brecht," he said. "A little romantic, but there you have it." He expected an eager smile, but saw instead that her patience was strained. It was a good sign: the kids who played along were born sycophants, trained in the manners of the ruling class.

"I'm sorry, but it's not enough. Liberal guilt is boring. And temporary." He turned away from her crestfallen expression. "Come back when you really are hungry."

I remember Gabriel Zamir, but he wouldn't remember me. The morning after the Twin Towers fell I found my way to a "listening session" where students—some in tears, others seething, hands locked behind their necks—spoke of their oppression. They flailed their arms, quoted Susan Sontag or Eldridge Cleaver or the Dalai Lama, talked about people they knew in New York. Everyone knew someone. Everyone had a friend or an uncle who worked in Lower Manhattan. No one in that room knew anyone who'd died, but they *might have*—that was the point, it could have touched any of us. It was all very sad and incoherent. When Zamir, in his wise and thespian way, began to read a poem about life in Gaza, I slipped out into another dazzling California day.

I never took a class from him. I was a writer, on a fellowship, I was hard at work on *The Light Inside*. But even in undergrad I'd stayed away from professors like Zamir: the provocateurs, the public figures whose righteousness seemed to demand more than just keeping up with the material. You had to do something, become someone, *make a difference*. But I didn't want to make a difference. I wanted to write.

For years after Leo's arrest he was regarded with suspicion—denounced by the Gelbs, censured by his colleagues. Were it not for his influence, they said, his contacts . . . But that's just another worn-out story: the one about innocence led astray. How many thousands of students passed through his classroom? How many joined causes, made their voices heard, then went on to lives of benign but meaningless achievement?

How many wound up in El Arca?

Since 9/11 he's been a familiar talking head, a reliable Jeremiah decrying the falsehoods of the War on Terror. I remember watching him on CNN the night of my own pointless foray into what he called "lived history," the night I took to the streets. When, years later, I emailed him about Leonora he responded in the practiced language of a politician. He suggested I read Gustavo Gorriti. He asked how I'd come to live in Peru.

Why are you here?

I never wrote back.

All summer, back in Cannondale, she felt her strangeness like a sheen on the skin. It marked her in the drugstore, the cheese shop, everywhere she didn't belong. She worked long days at a food bank in Newark, waking at five to be there when the first trucks rolled up to the bays. While her high-school friends made photocopies in air-conditioned law firms, or followed the Grateful Dead up and down the East Coast, Leo languished amid stacks of canned goods, crates of wilted lettuce, boxes of bananas so rife with fruitflies they looked blurry. Her co-workers, all Hispanic or black, traded glances of amusement and disdain for the white girl wasting her summer vacation.

"Jesus, Leo," her brother complained when she came home stinking of rotten fruit. "I thought you were *feeding* the bums, not bringing them home with you."

Matt was playing summer league, preparing for his varsity year. He ate and slept with his glove. Her father's beaming pride for his son, her mother's pinched deference, were beyond Leo's comprehension.

"You could come with me," she told her brother. "Mom? Dad? They can always use another set of hands."

"Yeah, right," Matt said. "How's Dad supposed to pay for Stanford if he hangs out with you at the soup kitchen?"

"It's not a soup kitchen. Our clients have jobs, they have families. They can't earn enough—"

"Clients!" he said. "Get a load of Gordon Gecko!"

They all enjoyed their private joke, the one about Leo's bleeding heart. *Saint Leo*, her mother took to calling her. On the phone with his brother, Warren, a Republican Congressman in Virginia, she heard her father say, "Leo's taking care of the family karma." But behind the fond glances she sensed he was afraid. When she tried, one night, to tell him about Gabriel's class, about Zanzibar and Webb Ranch, the kids in East Pali who hadn't been to school in years, he grew silent and wary—as if even now, safely back in the suburbs, his little girl was in danger of contamination.

"What if it were you?" she said, provoked by his discomfort. "What if you'd grown up with nothing?"

"Nobody handed anything to me, Leo," he said. "Those people don't have it any harder than your grandparents did."

"*Those people?* Please, Dad. If you don't know the difference between you and some kid in Oakland—"

"Where do you think my parents grew up? The Lower East Side was just as poor, even poorer—"

"It's not the same," she insisted.

"My father worked seven days a week. His mother supported him and his sisters doing laundry by hand for the whole building.

Sewing their buttons. They didn't have their own toilet until he got them out of the city."

She remembered her grandparents' house in Paterson: the creak of thin floorboards, the drawer full of sugar packets swiped from diners. Her grandmother refused to set the heat above 60 degrees. Leo knew what her father said to be true, she smelled the thrift on her paternal grandparents. It smelled like cheap soap.

"But they got out."

"That's right," he said pointedly.

"At least they had the opportunity to work themselves to death. At least their neighborhoods weren't full of drugs. The cops weren't shooting them for being black." She forced herself to breathe. "I'm saying, they believed in opportunity, in education—"

"Are there people who don't believe in those things?" She could only sputter in reply. Her father pushed back his chair. "What's the score, Matty?"

She ached to get back to Stanford, to things that really mattered. She worked twelve-hour days, came home and locked herself in her room with the reading list for Gabriel's seminar. He wouldn't stop her from auditing, she was sure of it. She avoided her brother and his belching friends, ignored the phone messages from Rachel and Megan. These were not her people, not anymore—but who were?

In August, Matt got a letter from the coach at the University of Connecticut. Would he like to spend a few days on campus, playing exhibition games with other promising high-schoolers? "We're going to need a great third baseman in a year or two," the coach had handwritten at the bottom.

"It's a great opportunity," Leo's father said, staring at his son like a schoolgirl with a crush. Maxine would drive up with him the following Monday. "Try not to miss us too much, Leo," she said.

They were having dinner on the back patio, amid the smell of cut grass, the buzz and crackle of insects frying in the bug-zapper. Grilled steaks, bread and wine in abundance, Phil Rizzuto calling a Yankees game on the radio. It was all she could take.

"What about the car?"

"The car?"

"How am I supposed to get to work?" Leo said. "Did anyone think of that?"

"Chill out," Matt said. "The bums will survive for a few days without your help."

"My *help*?" She looked around the table for support. "It's my job."

"How much are they paying you?" he said. "I thought a job is where they pay you. Your job pays you, Dad. Right?"

"Okay, Matt, cool it," David said.

She felt her control fraying and folded her hands in her lap. Three months of rolled eyes and patronizing smiles, three months being treated like an impostor by people whose privilege was so immense they could not even see it.

"You have no idea," she said quietly. "Instead of swinging a bat at a stupid ball all day, maybe you should try to learn something. Take a look around you—"

"Leo," her father said.

"No, Dad. You all sit here and act like I'm doing something cute, but you have no idea. The people I meet. You don't care about any of it."

"That's enough, Leo," her mother said. "Can we please enjoy a family dinner?"

She fought to keep her voice even. "Yes, we can. That's the whole point. Where do you think this steak came from? Who do you think picked that corn?"

Matt peered at his gnawed cob. "I thought it came from FoodTown."

"How much did you pay for all this furniture? How much were these plates? Don't you get it?" she cried. She dug her nails into her forearms. "Everything in this house has somebody's blood on it. Your whole fucking lifestyle!"

"Now you listen to me, Leonora," Maxine said. "Get off your high horse. It's your lifestyle, too—your clothes, your tuition—"

"*I know that!*"

She flung herself from the table and stamped across the yard. She was furious at herself, at her family, at the desperate people who lined up at the food bank every morning in the ringing heat. They would not stop coming, no matter what Leo did there would be more of them every day. It was pointless, a bad joke—worse, it was a zero-sum game: she and her family had what they had because *those people* didn't.

That's why she was here, she realized, kicking the soil around her mother's roses. The answer was as obvious as it was terrible: She was here because they were there.

The poster read WHAT YOUR $$$ BUYS, and featured a blurry photo of two small children, just ribcages with limbs, lying dead in the street, being eaten by dogs. "Stanford's Endowment Funds 5 of the 10 Worst Corporations in the World," it said, and at the bottom: Stanford Quorum for Investment Responsibility and Transparency

It was all over campus when students returned in September. A memo from Student Activities urged "restraint" in advertising materials, to "keep the discourse elevated and the campus beautiful." A week later, SQuIRT responded with a new poster featuring an Ecuadorian woman with a grapefruit-sized facial tumor superimposed with the Texaco star. An editorial in the *Daily* referred to the group as "extremists"; in the "socially conscious" co-op where Leo now lived, disapproval was taken for granted. SQuIRT was "giving activism a bad name," a senior told Leo. They were "too aggressive for our community," he said, they needed to "focus on ideals and solidarity." One night in the library she saw a piece of paper taped by the elevator: WHAT YOUR $$$ BUYS, it read, over an image of three kneeling students drinking from funnels while a sweaty crowd cheered them on. At the bottom, in the same font SQuIRT used, was the name of a fraternity and the date of a party.

"When the university's greed for corporate profits blinds us to atrocities, we have a responsibility to stand up and say, 'No!' As members of this community, we cannot support genocide, environmental devastation, the desecration of tribal lands."

The speaker was a thin, bearded white man in a brown and gold dashiki. He had a narrow face and a long, sharp nose, and he held a hand overhead, palm out, as he spoke. "Eight million dollars in Texaco. Two million in Unocal. And that's just the endowment. Millions in defense contracts this university takes in each year. Are we going to ratify criminal behavior with our silence?"

"No," said a few voices, with no particular enthusiasm.

"I can't hear you," he said, hand cupped to his ear.

The meeting was in a windowless basement classroom; concrete walls and a metal door made it seem chilly, though it was a warm October night. Leo had expected a horde of rabid activists, but there were barely twenty people in attendance, including an elderly man in the front row who nodded and slapped his knee at inappropriate moments.

"We should call for a boycott!" someone said.

"Boycott Stanford?" someone else said, to low laughter.

A young woman in a black turtleneck stood up. "We need to make our demands clear—a list of unacceptable companies, student oversight of investment decisions—"

"A manifesto!" someone said. "We'll hand it out to incoming students—"

"They don't care what students think. We have to get parents involved!"

It was the same old song. Frustrated, lonely, Leo slumped against the wall and waited for the right moment to slip out. She became aware of a familiar face only a few feet away, a graduate student from Gabriel's seminar. He had a wrestler's build and a flat-top afro, skin the color of raw almonds. He stood by the door and nodded sardonically while the speaker exhorted the small crowd.

"SQuIRT plans to launch an awareness campaign. We can't allow the university to operate in secret anymore." Around the room, chatters of approval, scattered applause. "I propose subcommittees for Outreach, Slogan Development, Fundraising—"

At this the man near Leo smacked his hands together in a meaty, withering ovation. "Outreach! Fuckin'-A, that's what we need. Slogans!"

The speaker hesitated, then went on. "We've contacted reporters from the *Chronicle*, the *Times*, *Mother Jones*, asking them to look into Stanford's complicity—"

"How 'bout more posters? Get some more of that artwork up. Take these motherfuckers out to the woodshed!"

"Sir," said the speaker, "if I could just finish—"

"Don't fuckin' 'sir' me." Everyone in the room turned to look at him—Marlon was his name, or was it Martin? She recalled he was writing his dissertation on liberation groups in El Salvador. He'd spent months interviewing survivors of an army massacre. "I thought you meant to put a stop to this bullshit, not sit here talking about *awareness*. Did Texaco hire you?"

"Listen, brother," said the speaker, who was looking smaller by the second, "hear me out. There's precedent. When Stanford refused to divest from South Africa—"

"You're gonna talk to me about South Africa?"

The speaker winced. "No. Of course not."

"South Africa didn't give a fuck about Stanford's money. The APLA is what they cared about. 'One settler, one bullet.' Thinking someone would burn down their houses, blow up their banks."

The speaker laughed nervously. "I don't think anyone wants to blow up a bank?"

"We're trying to accomplish something positive," added the woman in the turtleneck, "not promote more male-driven violence."

Marvin rubbed his chin. "You're raising awareness," he said.

The woman held her ground. "That's right."

"Gonna give them some *bad PR*, aren't you? Embarrass them. Appeal to their moral sense. I'll tell you something," he said. "If these people had a moral sense they wouldn't be doing this shit in the first place. What you need is some *action*."

"Like what?" Leo said.

Twenty pale faces turned to her. In a breath she understood that Martin recognized her, too, that she'd read her cue correctly. He walked up to the to the man in the dashiki. "Mind if I borrow this chair, *brother?*" He squeezed the back of the folding chair. When he smiled, the hair on Leo's neck tingled. "What if there was someone in this chair you don't like? A child molester, a raper of old ladies. He got no intention of giving up this chair. You gonna stand there and keep asking politely? You gonna tell people what a *bad man* he is?"

Leo felt as if she weren't getting enough air. Marlon picked up the chair and slammed it against the wall. The clanging shock wave spread through the room, driving people from their seats. He swung again, dislodging the plastic seat, which leaped backward and clattered on the floor and then he slammed the metal struts twice against the wall, then the floor, raised a booted foot and stomped until they buckled.

He looked up and grinned. "Nobody gonna sit in that now."

But no one heard him, everyone shrinking toward the far walls, shouting their disapproval, scowling as they headed for the door. When the room was empty he turned to Leo, one eyebrow raised comically. "Good meeting?" he said.

Leo gave him a shaky thumbs-up. "You must be hungry," she said.

Marden Lee, who since 2002 has served as a California state assemblyman for an East Oakland district, remembers Leonora Gelb as "crazy smart, a little confused about things." In his description her ardor and focus were miscast among students who viewed protest as another form of résumé-building and social justice as a competitive arena.

"She was pure East Coast, you could see that," he told me. "She dressed different, talked different. Maybe she had unrealistic expectations about what she was ready for. But this stuff was real to her, I'll give her that."

They saw each other throughout the fall of 1990, though he doesn't characterize the relationship as a serious one. They frequently went out after Zamir's seminar, ending the night in her co-op's kitchen, where they'd share a bottle of wine while Marden recounted his trip to El Salvador, or talk about his childhood on the south side of Chicago. Leo could hardly mask her admiration: here was someone who saw the bubble from the outside, who knew it for the cruel, racist lie it was. She spent weekends at the house in Berkeley where he lived with six activists and community organizers, all black, all several years older. They greeted her with nods and polite smiles, referred to her as "Marden's groupie" or "the white girl." She knew she deserved their suspicion. Why should they accept her when she'd done nothing to earn their respect?

Marden took her to lectures and gatherings in Oakland, angry meetings in mold-stained venues that bore little resemblance to a Stanford classroom. Political discussion alternated with tutorials on the rights of citizens arrested during civil disobedience, self-defense demonstrations, lessons on how to withstand the effects of tear gas, what to say in an interrogation. She knew she was getting closer, becoming someone Cannondale wouldn't recognize. She relished the thought of her mother seeing her there, of meeting her brother across a barricade. She relished their fear.

In November, she and Marden joined a protest outside the office of Stanford's president to demand the hiring of more minority faculty. When Marden and a handful of others forced their way into the building, he told Leo to stay outside. They were arrested an hour later, dragged onto a bus while reporters trotted alongside. She watched from a bench as they pumped their fists out the bus windows and flashed victory signs.

"I should have been inside," she said that night, after bailing him out of jail. "I shouldn't have listened to you."

Marden lay on the bed, hands clasped behind his head. "Wasn't the place for you. How's it gonna look if you're on that bus?"

He was still glowing with the day's success. Through the floor she could hear music, his housemates joking in quick, easy voices. She crossed her arms and said, "It would look like solidarity. Who cares what it looks like?"

"Like white guilt," Marden said. The phrase stung. All quarter, sitting to the side while Zamir's grad students clustered at the seminar table, she'd struggled with it, the same embarrassed feeling she'd had when she saw the photos of Steve Biko—as if she were simultaneously naked and invisible. What was she doing, out here, pretending to care what happened inside that frame? What was the point?

"Listen," he said. He sat up, his voice gentle. Too gentle—Leo felt a stab of alarm. "I know you want to help. But it's not your fight. What do you got on the line?"

She felt heat rising in her face. She would not say, "My self-respect," or, much the same thing, "My desire to live in a better world." *Me, me, me*, she thought—however you spun it there was something grimy and selfish about her, something that undermined every ideal she espoused. Even Marden, she thought, flushing with self-hatred: wasn't part of the attraction what being with him said about *her*?

"Why does it matter?" she said, clutching at something that was

217

rapidly receding. "If I'm willing to fight for your liberation, why do my reasons matter?"

His sad smile was a blow to the gut. "'Cause you think it's *my* liberation."

She returned from winter break to a campus galvanized by the prospect of war. There was a line in the sand, boots on the ground, American flags and "Support Our Troops" signs on the lawns of Palo Alto, as they were in Cannondale. You could not pass a television without glimpsing the cruel, mustachioed Saddam, always in uniform, surveying his weapons with a Stalinesque frown—so unlike the kindly George Bush, who wore shirtsleeves and leaned out of a jeep to shake hands with a young soldier, who addressed the nation in the sorrowful voice of a strict father unbuckling his belt for the child's own good.

"This is our Vietnam!" cried the campus demonstrators. "Read My Lips: No Blood for Oil!" chanted students outside the Hoover Institute. As the deadline for Iraq's withdrawal from Kuwait approached there were honk-ins and walkouts, impromptu concerts on Serra Quad. Gabriel taught class in a superhero costume of red, white, and blue, a Stetson perched ludicrously on his head. "The sword of justice is raised!" he cried, firing off a pair of cap guns. "Freedom must not be trammeled upon!"

It all sounded the same to Leo: the angry speeches, the jingoistic grunting of pundits, blithe pronouncements of generals and senators who insisted war was the last resort. Nothing would stop it, anyone could see that. To its advocates and opponents alike the idea of war had an almost sexual power, uniting them in a strange, ritualistic seduction—though no one could doubt who, in the end, would get fucked.

On the night Bush's ultimatum expired, she drifted at the edge of a candlelight vigil, under skies that seeped orange rain. "SAVE THE IRAQIS!" read the homemade signs. "WAR IS HARMFUL TO CHILDREN!" The students sang songs written before they were born. They hugged each other and cried real tears and as midnight approached they looked mournfully to the sky as if expecting to see fighter jets in formation, slashing the darkness like a cat's claws.

"These poor, poor people," a familiar voice said into her ear. "Where's your candle, Leo? What if Ol' George is looking down, saying, 'If that redhead chick's got a candle, I'll call off the troops'?"

The air smelled of patchouli oil and early jasmine, the fog so thick it felt cottony. She hadn't seen him in months, had refused to let herself leave pathetic messages. "Save your sympathy for the Iraqi people," she told Marden, groaning at her own cliché.

"Saddam must be sleeping easier, knowing these rich kids are on his side."

She tried to punch him but didn't have the energy. It was all pointless: the war, the candles, another scripted drama. She had to remind herself that actual people would die. "Let's go back to the co-op and watch CNN. I think I have some beer."

"What about you?" he said. "You on someone's side?"

In San Francisco's Civic Center the next day, she followed him through a crowd of thousands, a surly and liquid mass that swelled and shifted, insinuating itself between buildings, swamping police lines, thumping drums and clanging pots and pans in an endless rattle that set the nerves on edge. The weather had cleared, the sky packed with fist-shaped clouds that wheeled around City Hall's gold dome. Speakers shouted into bullhorns, cursing President Bush and the oil companies. Signs stabbed the air—*Stop the Madness! Fags Against War! An Eye for an Eye ≠ Justice!*—as waves of outrage rolled through the plaza in deep, orgasmic shudders.

She hadn't eaten. Hunger and the buzz of coffee brought a sweat to her hairline. Unshowered under her long-sleeved shirt, she could smell her own slightly horsey scent mixed with his sharp musk. She was supposed to be in the library, working on an art history paper. While the bombs fell, while innocent people were maimed and incinerated, she was supposed to write a paper on *Caravaggio*. Unthinkable. She knew this was how most people lived, by somehow finding ways to write papers on Caravaggio while children in other countries were murdered, but Leonora would not be like most people.

"If you're doing this, you gotta be ready," Marden said at dawn. He told her to wear black, to take off her rings, leave her ID at home. They'd taken the train from Palo Alto, and Leo practiced glaring at well-dressed commuters until they turned away.

As the sun moved behind the stately buildings, the undertow shifted toward Market Street and the financial district. The crowd was still growing, fed by side streets, a cacophony of carhorns met by angry howls. Leo's pulse banged in her head. Cops in riot gear lined the sidewalks; cries of "Pig!" and "Fascist!" followed by the crack of glass bottles against plastic shields, metal thuds as bodies were thrown across the hoods of cars. Marden pulled her through the current and into a courtyard where a dozen men and women clustered nervously. A pink-faced teenager with a shaved head and full-sleeve tattoos handed out ski masks. Leo clutched hers in both hands and looked at Marden.

"You can still go home," he said.

"Vámonos," the tattooed kid said.

As they neared Powell Street, the crowd barely moving, Leo kept her eyes on Marden's back. Into her head came a litany of things she needed to do—the Caravaggio paper, another on Plath and Sexton. It was her turn to clean the co-op kitchen. Her father's birthday was next week and she still had not bought him a gift. Her stomach hardened into a hot nut. Children were going to die for no reason, she reminded herself. What did Renaissance art matter?

A few feet away, a naked woman, painted with blue and orange flames, hurled herself at a policeman. "You fucking murderers! Baby killers!" The cop barely got his shield up in time; three others grabbed the woman's flailing limbs and she growled deep in her throat and spat at one cop's facemask and he pulled a canister from his belt and sprayed her in the eyes. Up and down the mobbed avenue, small groups rushed the lines and darted back; Leo felt herself duck, felt something whiz overhead and then a great shattering as the window of a shoe store evaporated, raining glass on the police. Her mind whirled—this was the real thing, not a lecture or a photograph. On every side windows smashed, alarms squealed, cops dragged writhing bodies to the sidewalk and raised their nightsticks. She looked up at the surrounding office buildings, where tiny faces watched the melee from dozens of windows. She couldn't imagine what they saw.

"Wait," Leo said, snatching at Marden's sleeve. He shrugged her off. The air was suddenly bitter with smoke. "Where are we going?"

But he was already forging ahead. Someone handed her a length of heavy pipe and then they were pushed apart by a riptide of bodies in skin-tight skeleton suits who rushed across the street, leaping onto cars, and barreled full-force into the police line. At the next intersection, the Chevron building soared skyward out of a cloud of white smoke, like the space shuttle on its launchpad. Its gilded revolving doors were guarded by an arc of police cruisers and orange water barrels, beyond which was mayhem: cops and pro-testors colliding, spinning in pairs as if it were a lurid high-school dance. A fire engine edged forward, its sides crawling with people; amid the shrieks of sirens she heard a hot whoosh and then a cruiser was in flames, an ecstatic cheer flickered all around her.

She couldn't find Marden, couldn't breathe through the smell of gasoline. The pipe hung heavy at her side. A surge in the crowd knocked her off balance, and when she righted herself they were sprinting past, a dozen bodies in black masks, smashing into the cops with loud grunts and the clamor of metal on pavement and then she was running after them, struggling to get closer to those golden doors—she could hear herself screaming, could hardly see through greasy tears—she stumbled and went down and a pile of bodies fell on top of her and rolled and quickly scattered. There was another explosion, there were cops on the ground, protecting themselves with riot shields. She rose to her knees uncertain and disoriented. They were counting on her. She could hear the thud of clubs against soft tissue, taste filthy copper on her tongue—*Why are you here?*—as she climbed to her feet a skeleton-suited body fell into her and she shoved him back with an animal cry and shook herself free.

Step by step she pushed forward, dazzled by flames, until she was only a dozen yards from the revolving doors. Her nose ran, a fist of gas stabbed sour into her throat. When the smoke briefly cleared she saw a body on the ground, set upon by five cops, one of whom tore off the attacker's mask while the rest slammed nightsticks at his limbs, drove the butts into his belly, kicked at his ribs. She could not move.

The sirens wailed and the man on the ground curled up and rolled side to side but she could not make herself move forward. When the cop holding the mask took a running step and aimed his boot at Marden's head Leo dropped the pipe she was still holding and ran.

Retching, eyes streaming, she elbowed across the current, stumbled on bottles and bricks and tripped at the curb, tearing the flesh from her palms as she fell. She dodged through a gap in the police line and headed away from Market Street, at each intersection turning from smoke and noise into the eerie stillness of downtown. She could hear herself panting, whimpering; she stopped on a dark corner to pull off the mask and retch hot mucus into a trash can. She clutched her side, leaned against a building, but then a fire engine screamed past and she started to run again. In Union Square there were cops everywhere, lining every sidewalk. She wiped her nose, spat in the gutter, and ducked into the first set of doors to stand blinking and heaving in the crystal white light of Macy's perfume department.

Later that night the war would begin. Baghdad lit up with tracer fire, glowing submarine green on CNN, the silent and unreal world of alien life forms doomed to extinction. There would be Tomcats and Prowlers, Hellfire and SCUDs, bombs that found their targets and bombs that found something else. Human shields, Abrams tanks, retreating Iraqi soldiers slaughtered from the air while oil fires billowed black and greasy against the sky. There would be questions about the war's legitimacy—stories about U.S. arms sold to Saddam, doctored satellite photos, PR firms paid to invent Iraqi atrocities. Through it all you could hear the chatter of Blitzer and Holliman and Shaw, the stern compassion of Brokaw, and the bland assurances of the President, who that first night explained to us, "There are things worth fighting for."

But in this moment there was only the chilly light of the showroom, the tick and buzz of fluorescents, the whispers of other customers when they caught sight of the girl in black with a livid face and bleeding hands.

"Is there something I can help you with?" A skinny Asian saleswoman stood flanked by two co-workers. They closed ranks at the Chanel counter, trying to maintain their staged elegance, like figures in a Nagel sketch that someone is about to burn.

"No, I'm . . ." Leo was shaky-kneed, blood pounding. Police cars wailed past on Stockton Street, blue light fracturing across the mirrored counters. "I'm okay."

"I'm sorry," said the saleswoman, "but you'll have to leave."

Leo forced her breathing to slow. "I'm looking for the Men's Department." The woman folded her arms. Willing her hand not to shake, Leo took her Stanford Visa card from her pocket and summoned a voice learned in the shopping malls of her youth. "I'm here to buy a birthday present for my father. Is there a problem?"

Before they could reply, she spotted the escalator and strode past the women with chin high. She rode up three flights, swallowing ripples of sobs, washed her face in the ladies' room and browsed a good long time—until her eyes dried, her limbs stopped shaking, until she found the perfect gift: a silk tie, an abstract blaze of blue and red, designed, the label said, by Jerry Garcia.

2

In his landmark study, *The Age of Terrorism*, the historian Walter Laqueur stresses that the primary objective of political violence is publicity. "Propaganda by deed": revolutionaries don't set out to blow up buildings, or hijack airliners, or assassinate ministers— they set out to make people pay attention. To genocide, to racial segregation, police brutality, military occupation. You name it. Theft of land, of resources, of dignity; economic policies that condemn millions to poverty . . . What these things have in common is our indifference, the willed forgetting that rises like a veil between us and "those people"—until we see only massed shadows, hear only guttural, vaguely threatening sounds.

To break through that forgetting is the terrorist's real mission. To burn the veil to the ground. "It's confusing when they kill the innocent," Don DeLillo writes in *Mao II*. "But this is precisely the language of being noticed, the only language the West understands."

According to the government, the Pueblo Libre group, taking orders from higher-ups in the C.F., planned to attack Peru's Congress and abduct legislators from the ruling party. It was to be presented as a hostage swap—as many as four hundred Philosophers were still being held in El Arca, Socabaya, and other prisons—but the military court deemed this motive a fig leaf. "The group planned to line the halls of government with corpses," the judges wrote, citing an unnamed informer. "Knowing the President would not meet their demands, the terrorists planned to murder the [legislators] in cold blood to send a message to the country that the war had begun again."

The language of being noticed—that much I can understand. I can understand what brought her to Peru: her anger, her desire to help, to prove her life had meaning, to become someone other than the person she was raised to be. Reinvention—no one understands that better than I.

But violence, weapons, the readiness to kill, maybe to *die?* Could one really offer one's life for faceless, starving others? Could one do that? Where's my imagination when I need it? Where's empathy? Why can't I *see?*

The truth is I've never understood people like Leo, though I'd encountered my share. At the college I went to—an East Coast, brick-and-ivy affair—there were plenty of students who got involved in causes, "joined the Movement," as people still sometimes said, though the phrase already had an air of nostalgia, like jousters at Ye Olde Renaissance Faire. I avoided those people. I stayed away from their sit-ins and marches, their angry chants and earnest folksongs. *No Nukes! Meat is Murder! End Apartheid! Save the Whales!* I couldn't take such sloganeering seriously. Who was listening? To watch Margaret Thatcher or Ronald Reagan, Yasir Arafat or Bishop Tutu, on the nightly news and believe a dozen dreadlocked students in "Free Mumia" T-shirts could affect their decisions, you needed stronger drugs than I was into.

But there was something else, something I would only come to understand about myself years later, during my own fruitless foray into activism, my brief flirtation with giving a shit: it was fear—fear of violence, of risking myself, a fear so ingrained I could not be near the people who would risk themselves. *Those people*: who slept on the quad in mock shanty towns, who disrupted graduation ceremonies, took the train to Washington to march for this or that, who later smashed windows and burned cars in Seattle. People whose commitment was unyielding, whose fury seemed personal, born of mistreatment or deprivation I'd never experienced. People who had nothing to lose. Even when I agreed with them, which I usually did, my sense that I had something to lose held me back. I stayed out of arguments, took another route to class, avoided contamination.

Maybe that's why it was so hard to get started, why I cringed when I watched Leo's press conference, or thought of her wasting away in El Arca. Despite the broken arm and the piss-stained jeans, despite the weapons and the dead bodies, I recognized her. In the flash of her eyes, the tilt of her jaw, I saw familiar suburban streets, new clothes each September. Tennis lessons. Spring Break at the beach. In her voice I heard a confidence born of comfort, of always being told you have something valuable to say. She was a criminal, they said, she stood in the glare battered and howling and utterly foreign. But I took one look at La Leo and I knew exactly who she was: she was someone with something to lose and she'd lost it.

Rabbi Arturo Eisen Villaran remembers the date of his first meeting with Leonora Gelb: April 26, 1998, a Friday.

"It was my wedding anniversary. Thirty years," he says with a proud smile. "We had tickets to the opera. *Rigoletto.* I'd planned a short service, nothing special. We'd lost a congregant that week, a very old woman. Very generous. I wanted to say a few words, her children were all there. But I was also eager to be home. You understand."

He remembers a damp night, warm, clouds over Miraflores, the orange glow above the nearby Parque Central. After the service his congregants milled in the lobby or smoked outside the door, brooded over by the guard in his fortified kiosk. The rabbi made sure to express condolences to each of the deceased woman's three children, her many grandchildren. As he made his way to his office the guard took him aside and said there was a young woman lingering on the street, watching the synagogue.

"A young woman? Does she look dangerous?"

"No, señor."

"Does she want to come in?" he said with some impatience. "What's the problem?"

The guard shrugged. "She looks sad, señor."

At first Rabbi Eisen couldn't see her, the walkway crowded with congregants. He shook hands, moved toward the fence—and then she was there, a small shadow on the sidewalk, half her face pale in the light from the synagogue's windows.

"Buen sábado," he called out. He remembers her reluctance and the way she stood: arms stiff, eyes trained on the building as if to memorize every corner and eaves, every entrance. Her glasses were fogged, her clothes soaked with drizzle. Droplets of rain glimmered in her hair. When she did answer, he could hardly hear her for the crowd.

"Buen sábado," she said.

It's a very different Leo the rabbi describes, this forlorn and solitary figure—nothing at all like the shrieking battle-axe most people remember. If my dates are right it had been just over two weeks since the Radio 2000 incident. Macho dead. Chaski badly hurt, still bedridden. One can imagine her state of mind. One can imagine the vigilance, even paranoia gripping the house, squeezing the inhabitants until they could hardly breathe. The fear things have gotten out of control before they've even begun.

Many times these weeks, biding her time before she's allowed to go back to the house, Leo has passed by here, lingered at this fence without quite knowing why. But in daylight the synagogue looks different, a silent gray fortress, a lifeless monument. All the lights and the careless chatter confuse her now, all the bodies at their ease. And this stout, kindly man with his gray face and imposing brow, his shirt collar pinching at the neck.

"A beautiful night," he says, brushing mist from his shoulders. "Would you like to come inside?"

She hefts her backpack as congregants sneak glances from across the fence. "Are you the rabbi?"

"I am," he says. "Your accent—¿Estados Unidos?" He switches to English. "Where do you come from?"

"California."

"How nice for you!" His son lives in Berkeley, he says, a place he has visited many times. "Don't tell him I said this, but I go for the wine. You may not have noticed, but Peruvian wine . . .not so good." He shrugs, checks his watch. "What's your name?"

Glancing at the guard, she says the first name that comes to mind: "Linda."

"A lovely name. Twice lovely. Well, Linda, the service is over, but people will stay for a while. You won't come inside?"

The synagogue door glows warmly, strains of familiar music carry on the air. She remembers the night she and Julian stood in this spot, what seems like years ago, how she demanded he let her help. She'd been so naïve then, so ignorant. She thinks of her grandfather's funeral, of the sunlight that came in cold sheets through the temple's soaring windows. Of seventh-grade bar mitz-vot—boys in Brooks Brothers suits, girls with perms and their first high heels, running amok in country-club hallways, scheming to acquire mixed drinks from libertine aunts. A line of Jaguars and Mercedes waiting to be parked by black and Puerto Rican valets. Disgusting. She can see Chaski's pale, delirious face. And Macho—she can't even picture his face, and that's worse.

"You wouldn't want me in there," she says. "I don't belong here."

He remembers feeling perplexed by her hesitation, the toughness she tried so hard to convey. "Too hard," he says. "This nice girl, I thought. Why is she out here all alone?"

"I think you belong," he tells her. He leans closer, until she can smell the cigarette smoke, warm and salty, on his breath. "I'm joking. It's shabbos. Everyone is welcome."

The mist has started to thicken. It will be late when she gets back to Pueblo Libre, barely enough time to finish her chores, maybe half an hour to work on the newspaper. Why can't she make herself turn away? Macho is dead. She never laid eyes on him. What pathetic instinct keeps drawing her here?

"Maybe another time," she says.

The rabbi offers a solemn bow. "The door is always open, Linda."

"I'll remember that."

As she turned away he was again struck by how small and alone she was. He considered walking after her but he still had to make some notes for the morning service, and the opera would start in less than an hour. "I thought I might give her my ticket," he recalls, spreading his hands in bafflement. "Can you imagine?"

Four months later he would be startled by the same feeling, when he turned on the TV and saw La Leo snarling at a roomful of reporters, her face bruised, her arm broken, the footage of the burn-ing house looping across a split screen. He may have been the only Peruvian to respond to that spit-flecked tirade with tears of pity.

When days passed and there was no knock on the door, no swarm of police vans, the paralyzing fear slowly drained from the house, replaced by grim resolve and the sense of timelessness one feels in an unfamiliar airport, between flights. Routine gradually reasserted itself, but Leo couldn't shake the memory of Chaski's pale, vomit-streaked face, the feathers of blood on the stairs, the fear in Julian's eyes. For days Julian slept on the floor by Chaski's bed—the only one permitted to see him—and answered Leo's questions in monosyllables, if at all. He left the house only for shifts at the café. The bullet had smashed Chaski's tibia and narrowly missed the artery. The doctor cleaned shards of bone from the wound and stitched it closed; he'd done what he could to set the bone before he wrapped the leg in plaster. He frowned at the cheap bed linens, the dusty bedroom with its water-stained walls. The leg would heal, he told Julian, but without an X-ray only God knew if Chaski would have full use of it.

Since then the house has been too quiet. No more music, no thumping up and down the stairs. Braced with new urgency, Marta spends even more time upstairs with the cumpas, the drone of her voice vague but omnipresent, lingering in the upper reaches of Leo's awareness. She leaves the house earlier in the evenings and comes back later each night. In the stillness, Leo feels newly volatile, liable to tear up or slam a door for no reason. She spends hours on hands and knees in the garden, cool soil etching itself into the lines of her palms. The violets are thriving; the rosebushes have straightened and grown sturdy, but still no buds have appeared. She remembers the Mexican gardener who used to come to the house when she was a girl—what was his name?—how he mowed so methodically, how Maxine's roses flourished under his care. What had he seen when he looked at their family? What would he think of her now?

When the cleaning is done, when she can find no more ways to be useful, she flees into sprawling Lima, carrying a notepad and disposable camera in a woven satchel. It feels good to get out of that cold house, good to stretch her legs, break a sweat. No one has mentioned the newspaper since the night Chaski was shot, but Leo often recalls how the ink smelled, the clean feeling of the new pages in her hand. Privately she's decided on a date for the second issue: May 10, the one-month anniversary of Macho's death. If Marta won't help she's determined to do everything herself.

She takes the bus to the farthest corners of Lurigancho, where partly finished streets give way to dirt lanes and parched ravines, scrub brush punctuated by mud-brick shanties and makeshift tents. In the bustling corners of San Martín de Porres, in Comas, she observes the hustle and jostle of vendors, the desperation of beggars and half-clothed children; in crowded Barrios Altos the sidelong glances of the perpetually surveilled, the cramped irritability of caged rats. On the medians of clogged thoroughfares, she photographs bent backs and clenched jaws, faces marked by infection and shoe-treads bound with twine, the way young men look away when the police in their armored vehicles drive past. Brown faces, all of them, a different nation than the one she sees in Pueblo Libre or Miraflores. She's heard people talk about "two Peru's," but they're both right here, superimposed on each other and on the city's streets and plazas—the blessed and the desperate jockeying in the same precarious space.

Though she covers much of the sprawled city, often walking ten miles a day, she never goes to Los Arenales, held back by a reluctance that soon turns to self-recrimination. What would she say to Nancy? What could she ever do to help? Leo's mother would be appalled at this dereliction, she knows, having trained Leo in the requisite niceties of her class—and this, she decides, is her justification: the impotence of sympathy, the reactionary falsehood of the condolence call. She won't bother Nancy with kind words, gestures that do nothing but absolve the gesturer of responsibility. She won't set foot in Los Arenales until she has something to show for it all.

In late afternoon she often finds herself on the malecón, drawn to the shrieks of gulls, the rumble of machinery. Her legs wobbly with fatigue, her camera full, the odor of broken stone stings in her sinuses. Above the ocean's labored respiration, jackhammers rattle in tooth-shaking tedium, cut off by the clatter of rocks crashing out of a dumptruck. She stands at the fence, shielding her eyes from the glare and the twisting dust, as a crane drags long, steel beams into the sky.

Vía América. She imagines the finished product, the parking lots and promenades swarming with well-to-do shoppers—all well-dressed, fair-skinned, unlike the workers scurrying through the construction site, complexions paled by the grit of concrete and salt. No, none of these men will ever shop here—if they tried they'd be trailed by security guards, ushered to the nearest exit. In this, it would be no different from Fifth Avenue or the Rue de Rivoli, from the boutiques and restaurants she's gone to all her life. She remembers the disgust on Julian's face the night he tried to scare her away. "You're in the wrong place," he told her. But he was wrong, she thinks bitterly. She was exactly where she was expected to be.

Some days small clusters of protestors gather across the street—teenagers from Poder de Juventud, three Abuelitas de la Ausencia, a crazed-looking Indian in buckskins, waving a tambourine. They hoist pickets, shout slogans that tatter in the gusting winds. One or two cops stand watch at the corner, bored by the performance, knowing as well as the demonstrators that nothing will come of it. No one will even know they were there.

What good is protest when only its most anodyne manifestations are permitted? she wrote in *The Eyes of the World*, issue no. 2. She titled the editorial "A Revolutionary Is Someone Who Acts." *Does such street theater not acknowledge the dictator's power, while allowing him to claim tolerance and freedom of speech? Does he not owe such "activists" a debt of gratitude?*

She shuts her notebook, embarrassed. Who is she to write such exhortations? When has she ever acted? Not in Los Arenales, or the Plaza de Armas. Not at Radio 2000. She talks, pounds her fist—*Something has to be done!*—then runs and hides while others die. On the bus back to Pueblo Libre, she avoids the eyes of the other passengers, pressed cheek to shoulder as they squeak and smash along the avenue. The radio spits more nonsense from the U.S.—*Kathleen, Paula, Monica,* names out of a sorority house, or a bad sitcom—and she groans aloud at the unforgivable silliness. When she enters the courtyard and slams the gate she's flooded with relief: to be here, in a place where things matter, where something can still be done. If only she were one of the people doing it.

DINCOTE files made public during the retrial indicate that the first meeting between Leo and the man she knew as Comrade Miguel took place on the evening of May 3. No details about what was discussed, only that Julian left the house "after a session of self-criticism." The report notes "significant and growing tensions" within the group; "the American, Leona Gelb [sic], is not trusted, and has not been included in planning sessions."

It was a name she'd heard many times, always spoken in lowered voices, deferent tones, as one speaks the name of an older kid at school, admired and feared. Something, some overheard remark of Julian's perhaps, made her think Miguel's involvement went back to the war, that he'd been close to the founding council of the Cuarta Filosofía, if not a founder himself. He's clearly their contact with the larger organization, their "handler"—she's tried, from these occasional mentions, to glean something about the layers of authority, the lines of communication, but she knows better than to ask directly. She would have hoped, but not expected, to meet this Miguel one day. Given the mistrust noted in the files, one imagines the meeting was accidental. One imagines she wasn't supposed to be there at all.

She'd left the house before noon. Marta told her not to come back until nightfall. But she's tired, raw from weeks of tedium, from dragging herself through landscapes of misery. Though the date she'd set for the next issue is a week away, she's hardly gotten started—there are photos to be scanned, articles to be written, the unending struggle with a crashy computer. She'll be up late every night until it's finished, dragging herself from bed at dawn to take care of her housemates, their demands no less pressing for their invisibility.

When she opens the gate in the cream light of sunset, she can feel it immediately: the house holding still, listening to itself—

"—everything always hypothetical, always in the future—"

The voice, Julian's, drifts from a cracked second-story window. Leo catches the gate before it can bang shut. She steps silently past the rosebushes, breath held, and stands below.

"—wait until conditions are perfect," he says, an unfamiliar strain in his voice, almost pleading. "We can't control every possibility—"

Now Marta's voice, farther from the window but somehow clearer: "We agreed to act as a group, not at the whims of an infant. We lost a cumpa and a truck, all so one rooster can crow—"

"That's it, Profesora: we agreed to act! If it were up to you—"

An unfamiliar voice interrupts him—male, patient, gently humorous. "My friends, my friends, we're not here to fight like children but to learn from our mistakes."

"*Our* mistakes?" Marta says.

"Sí, compañera," the man says. His voice is sober, reassuring. They are a unit, he reminds them. A family. Whatever internal disagreements, the outward results express the aggregate of that family's desires. That's how the government will see it, in any case, he says. "Action is paramount, Comrade Julian. Still, one must think of their family. You know this as well as anyone. Lenin clearly understood the dangers of spontaneity."

When she hears Julian's voice again, it's closer, stronger, the light from the window blocked by his form. "¿Sabes qué? Fuck Lenin. And fuck your boring newspaper, with its slogans from the Cultural Revolution. I'm tired of sitting at home, talking about political lines—"

"And I am tired of losing," Marta says. "I'm tired of cumpas getting killed."

"You think a slogan would have protected Macho?"

"I think a leader would have protected him."

"Enough," says the stranger, silencing them without raising his voice. "The point of self-criticism is to move forward, not to lay blame. Comrade Julian, it's imperative you admit to your error. Macho was your responsibility. We cannot afford . . . Comrade?"

Shuffling chairs, a flung door, loud footsteps on the stairs. A moment later the front door flies open and Julian emerges, in his freshly ironed work clothes. When he catches sight of Leo he hesitates, scowls as if she were a door-to-door salesperson, then yanks open the gate and stamps out to the street. Leo watches him go. A moment later, Marta appears in the doorway, her lips pursed in satisfaction. Behind her, the visitor descends the stairs, stopping to examine the needlepoint llama that hangs crooked on its nail: *¡Yo Soy Peruana!*

"Compañera," Marta says, "You aren't supposed to be here."

"No hay problema," says the stranger. He steps past Marta and extends his hand. "Soy Miguel. Y tú debes ser la gringa famosa."

She's imagined him as a hardened guerrilla in a bandolier, or a stern older gentleman with goatee and monocle—but the man before her isn't much older than Marta, trim and rumpled, with nerdy eyeglasses and unkempt hair. With a start Leo realizes she's seen him before, she recognizes his canny, presumptuous expression, though she can't say from where.

"La compañera no habla español," Marta says.

"It's an honor to meet you," Leo says, hurrying to take his hand.

"No Spanish? But then you must have a good translator, to write so well in your newspaper," he says, in nearly unaccented English. He slouches against the doorjamb and picks at a fingernail; a gesture that strikes Leo as deliberate, an affectation. "It is you, writing the articles? I enjoyed the one about the labor laws. The comparison to Pinochet's Chile is well argued."

"Everything in the paper is a collaboration," Leo says. "My work is no more important than anyone else's."

Miguel gives a solemn nod of approval. "Still, one deserves to have her work acknowledged."

"The compañera has many things to attend to," Marta says. "The cumpas—"

"The cumpas will wait."

Marta falls silent, her eyes dull with displeasure. Leo knows she'll pay a price for this overstepping, intentional or not—but after weeks of waiting, she isn't going to miss her chance.

"I don't need acknowledgment," she says. "I only want to help." Encouraged by his silence, she goes on. "I've been in this house for months. We all have. People are suffering. I know it's important to be careful and think things through. But I'd like to be part of that discussion. I want to do more."

She stops, puzzled by his raised eyebrow, his wary, amused smile. "But why?"

"Why?"

"Why do you want to help? This isn't your country. Why involve yourself with the troubles of people you don't know?"

The answer takes even Leo by surprise. "Because no one expects it of me."

No one speaks for several seconds. Then a broad, boyish smile spreads across Miguel's face. "I understand this very well." Turning to Marta, he says, "Compañera, I concur with your discretion. It is absolutely correct that the cumpas not see our friend or know anything about her. But let's be sure we aren't overlooking an asset—a revolutionary must use every available tool."

"Como quiere, compañero," Marta says. "As you wish."

"And what do we call her?" he says, rubbing his chin. "'The Gringa' really won't do."

Leo can't help herself. "Linda," she blurts out. "You can call me Linda."

Again he nods gravely, a gesture leavened by the wry gleam in his eye. She's struck once more by his familiarity—the way he tightens his scarf, cocks his head as if remembering something, a kind of pretense or performance. "Well, Linda," he says, stepping into the garden, "it's been a pleasure to meet you."

"And you, comrade."

When the gate clacks shut, she scrubs victory from her face and turns to face Marta. But the door to the house stands empty, the entryway and living room dark and uninviting. She stands a long time, listening to Miguel's footsteps fade, astonished at this unexpected development, wondering what it means. Julian gone, Marta furious with her—what will come of this accidental meeting?

Linda, she thinks, watching the shadows of sparrows peck at fallen limes. She can feel her heart beating. *Comrade Linda*. Why should a name, a false name, give her such pleasure? She can imagine this person, working side by side with the others—her opinion taken seriously, her ideas about strategy, about justice. Finally she'll have the chance to do something. One day soon, she'll be able to say to Nancy: *This* is how we answered Neto's death.

Comrade Linda. She can picture her confident stride, her days full with purpose. Standing alone in the dark courtyard, she almost envies her.

The children were led into the hills by one of the nuns. When night came, they could see the glow of their burning village behind the ridge. They found a cave and waited there, hungry and parentless, for a week, the oldest—two eleven-year-old girls—helping tend to the youngest. Even the roughest boys cried in their sleep. A patrol of ronderos came and the nun spoke to them for a long time, pushing the air with her hands. When the ronderos returned the next morning, she sat with her back to the cave wall and didn't look up as they took the children, shrieking and clutching one another, to their trucks.

They were sheltered at a camp in an old soccer stadium, fed potato soup and beans and given blankets to share when it got dark. The air stung with cold, and rustled with the laments of thousands of the displaced. Soldiers cursed and fought between the flimsy tents. Occasionally, a soldier came for one of the older girls, who slipped back later mute and shaking. Two of the village children were reunited with their parents in a frenzy of tears; others found cousins or neighbors who took them in. The rest stayed at the camp for two months. They wore oversized uniforms or donated clothes peeled from bales crusty with starch. The officers "adopted" certain children, giving them extra food in exchange for chores. Chaski was again chosen as a runner; he took messages from the stadium to the barracks outside, where soldiers played cards or just paced, bored and drunk. He had no friends in the camp—the story of his parents' collaboration had spread among the refugees so he was looked on with pity but never trusted.

Eventually he was sent to distant cousins in Lima. They had four young children and shared a weedy lot and a common stove with two other families, each of whom lived between unfinished concrete walls with tarps for roofs. There was no school. If a child fell sick there was a clinic two kilometers away in Lurigancho where mothers lined up at dawn. Two brothers from Ica sold coffins for the babies who died in line.

Chaski's relatives made him pay for his food by shining shoes outside the government buildings downtown. By the time he was twelve, he was a pickpocket and a thief. At fourteen, they threw him out and he lived with a pack of street kids in a cluster of plywood shanties next to a ravine that stank of human shit and spilled over in the rains. It was here the university students found him. On their weekly visits they brought food and warm clothes. They talked to the kids about fairness and equality. The Indios were here first, they said—why should they be the ones living in filth while the invaders had houses big enough for a whole village, with special rooms for their wine and cigars? Peru was a rich country, with mountains of gold, rivers of oil, they said. There was enough money for everyone—cholo or criollo, male or female, Quechua- or Spanish-speaking. The problem was that some people wanted more, even if that meant others got less, or nothing. Those people had built a system that let them decide for everyone else.

"There aren't so many of them," said the leader, whom the others called Comrade Enrique. "There are more of us. In every part of the country. That's called democracy. If we want a different system, we have a responsibility to change things."

Enrique read them Mariátegui and John Stuart Mill and "The Declaration of the Rights of Man." He taught them about Manco Inca and Tupac Amaru II and Bolívar the Liberator and Fidel, who stood up to a tyrant and won. It was the first school Chaski had had since he was nine. When Enrique spoke, his restlessness quieted and he remembered how he'd felt when the rebels first came to his village and chose him as their messenger: smart and important, with something to offer. He thought of the men whose shoes he shined in the plaza, who left a coin and then drove away in taxis. He had never ridden in a vehicle that wasn't crammed with people and animals. When the revolution came, Chaski decided, everyone would get to ride in taxis.

"No," he says, in answer to Leo's question. He tilts his face to the feeble sun, distant pain tugging at the corners of his mouth. Small birds chitter atop the garden wall. "I didn't meet Marta until later, when Enrique came back from the campo."

By then, Chaski was sixteen and living in the stairwell of the San Marcos dormitory. The war had begun to affect daily life—whole neighborhoods closed down, blackouts almost every night. Chaski took posters and heavy, locked duffels to drop-off points throughout the city. On weekends he and other Red Pioneers were sent to demonstrations and highway blockades where they swarmed the organizers and tore their banners, raising the flag of 14 de Junio.

"I met Marta only one time," he says. "Then, Tarata."

He sits on the stoop, his casted leg extended like a giant white sausage, metal crutches lying at his side. His T-shirt hangs limp from bony shoulders; his once-contagious smile has been wrecked by the long convalescence, rebuilt as watchful sobriety. Helping him down the stairs Leo tried not to think about his sharp ribs, his sour, exhausted smell. Though he was frail, his body against hers felt solid, her face pressed to his flank. When was the last time she had been this close to another person, or felt an arm on her shoulder? When had she been so needed?

"Enrique was the first person who trusted me, or asked what I thought. We used to make jokes about him in Quechua, right next to him, laughing so hard. We called him *llanqa Yanchachiq*, our 'Pink Teacher.' But Enrique knew Quechua. He studied it at Católica. I used to think, why does a person like this care about me? Why does he spend his time talking to these dirty cholos?"

"But why shouldn't he?" Leo says, still absorbing his story, restless with tenderness, the urge to avenge it all: the lost childhood, the wrecked leg. "More people should act like Enrique. That's one of the things in this country that has to change."

Chaski digs in his pocket for a cigarette. "Who will change it? You?"

He smokes and peers at the latest heap of cuttings, arcs of goldenrod waving at the ground. "Enrique was a good teacher. Not just about history. He taught us how to see. But there were things he couldn't see. After a long time, with cumpas getting hurt, or dying, I started to think, 'Who is going out there with the tear gas and the soldiers, and who is giving the orders?' Now he's a hero. A martyr. But how many cholos died and no one says they are heroes?"

"There are no heroes. We're all fighting the same war, Chaski."

He sucks his teeth, as if to keep something sour off his tongue. "Call me Mateo. Chaski is the name they gave me."

"That's my brother's name: Matthew," she says. Maybe that explains it, the familiarity, the protectiveness. She sinks her trowel into the soil and reaches for her own cigarettes. She hasn't spoken to her family since just after Radio 2000. She'd tried to sound as if everything was normal, but Maxine, as always, could sense something was wrong. "Did you even know I have a brother?"

"Enrique, Julian, Miguel . . . even Abimael. What is this war for them? You see what happens on the street, Leo. You see what happens to Macho."

Leo sits on the step next to him. "You have to call me Linda now."

He shifts to peer at her and another spasm of pain twists his features. Instinctively, she presses a hand to his back, edges closer on the step.

"You sound different," he says when the pain passes. "When I met you, you talked about conscience. Now . . ."

"When you met me, Macho was alive. Neto was alive."

"You didn't want people to get hurt. The revolution needs people like that, too."

"People like that end up under bulldozers."

Even Leo is startled by how harsh this sounds, how hardened. Embarrassed, she looks away. From an upstairs window come the rough, indistinct sounds of laughter—she's struck, not for the first time, by the oddity of her situation, alone in a house full of anonymous men. When she turns back Chaski's face is close, his eyes concerned. For an instant she's seized by the thought of kissing him—not desire, just a certainty that it will happen, her body drifting toward his like a leaf in an eddy—but something in his eyes makes her falter, off balance, she leans awkwardly against him, touches her lips sloppily to the corner of his mouth.

"Leo—" he says.

"My name is Linda," she stutters, struggling to sit up, to manage a rush of emotions: surprise, embarrassment, confusion. His face is gentle, almost pitying, his eyes alight not with attraction but wariness, patience, reading her, waiting for her to see.

"Amiga," he says gently, urging her to push farther, look closer—and all at once she sees. All at once a dozen recollections make sense: the standoffishness of the workmen, countless belittling comments from Julian, Marta's scorn. Why Leo's always felt this odd comfort, even before she knew him—never the vigilance, the ugly shield held at the ready. With Chaski it was not necessary. She's always known, always seen. How could she not have understood until now?

For another moment they watch each other, until he sees that she's entered into the secret. It mustn't be spoken—not here, with so much trust on the line; she agrees to this with a small, sad smile. So this is conspiracy, she thinks, squeezing his arm. This is what it feels like on the inside.

A third-floor window opens with a metallic screech and a low voice calls Chaski's name. With difficulty, he pushes himself standing, levers the crutches under his arm. "Linda?" he says, wrinkling his brow at the unfamiliar name.

She shrugs. "Mucho gusto?"

"Okay, now I'll call you Linda," he says, peering down as if he were the one protecting her. "But promise me you don't forget who you really are."

As May wears on, the house grows quieter—like an airplane at cruising altitude, the roar and rattle of engines settling into the subliminal. Leo's anticipation, the feeling of stumbling blind through heavy curtains, recedes to the background noise of her life. The days grow damp, the breeze carrying an autumn chill that settles in bones and in plaster. Chaski often keeps her company in the garden, crutching himself in circles or doing pushups on the flagstones to keep his other limbs from weakening. He tells her stories about his childhood, what he can remember before the war erased it all. When he asks about her family she just rolls her eyes, preferring to listen, relieved to focus, for once, entirely on someone else. They never discuss their moment of awkward intimacy, the abortive kiss that grows ever more slapstick in Leo's memory. But the new sense of alliance, this shared and unshakable calm, is a constant reminder of that afternoon, and of the secret she keeps nestled like a jewelry box at the back of a drawer.

Julian hasn't come back since the night of Miguel's visit. Without his brash pronouncements, his sarcasm and sudden storms, the house feels unfocussed, the silence punctuated and enlarged by the noise upstairs: the rhythmic thud of calisthenics, call and response, hours-long meetings underlined by Marta's voice. Late in the afternoon, when she's finished with the cumpas, Marta gathers her camera and a small backpack, reels off instructions, shopping lists, and then makes for the front door. Gone is the sense Leo once had of a roommate, a sister locked arm in arm; the longer Julian stays away, the more distant Marta becomes, almost invisible, the house containing the idea of her like a treasured painting in a museum, hidden in a gallery Leo is forbidden to enter.

"I want to talk to you," she says, stopping Marta in the courtyard. "I want to know about the plans."

"You don't need to know these things."

"But I can help you. You don't have to do everything."

"Stop trying to do more," Marta says. "It's like you want something in return."

Leo, stung, refuses to back down. She'd spent the afternoon polishing floors, scouring the stove until her hands burned. "Miguel said I should be included—"

"Miguel is not here. Julian is not here." Then, rethinking this harshness, she leans close to Leo and lowers her voice. "Be patient, Linda. Everything will be explained at the correct time."

With so many hours to fill Leo throws herself into *The Eyes of the World*, taking refuge in the glare of the computer screen and the feeling of ownership. Julian was right about one thing: the first issue *was* boring. Pages of recycled news items, statistics, crude pie charts—even her article on the labor laws was dry, academic. The paper had no real punch or urgency, it lacked the fierce heat of *now*. To peruse the next few issues is to see her trying on new ideas and new styles, reworking the template column inch by column inch, right down to the fonts and margins. Where the first issue was dour and exhortatory—an excerpt from the Havana

Declaration, a full-page analysis of a W.H.O. report—those that followed deployed a knowing humor, a hip and intellectual seduction. The goal now was not to educate but to arouse, to inflame—next to a Greenpeace report on contaminated aquifers, an ad for bottled water; beneath an O.A.S. statement on human rights in Peru, an altered photo of the President with a powdered wig and a speech bubble that says, *Aprés moi, le deluge!;* above a photo of Bill and Monica, a steamy passage from Nicholson Baker's phone-sex novel, *Vox.* The front page of Issue 2 was dominated by a photo from the Protesta de Tetas: riot cops, topless women, the headline in a gigantic tabloid font: *The Beginning of Armed Struggle!* The centerfold of Issue 3 was a collage of photos, both hers and Marta's, dominated by a shot of the blasted cliffs of Miraflores, the giant tumor taking shape as a shopping mall, above a simple caption: *¿El Futuro?*

What most intrigued me was the column she called "The Scorecard": a list of recent actions against the state and its institutions, an accumulation of exploits that, taken together, give the impression of a wave gathering strength, that one day will crest and smash everything in its path. A bodega robbed in El Augustino, a protest at San Marcos against rising student fees, a fire in a police outpost on the southern highway—all framed as triumphs in an ongoing campaign: *We congratulate our revolutionary brothers and sisters!* Fliers confiscated at a high school in Los Arenales, commemorating Ernesto Castillo Rojas, Lilia Flores Naupa, and Juan Vargas Quispe, "who fell in defense of the residents of Los Muertos." *We shall never forget our proud martyrs!*

Starting with the third issue, she always included at least a dozen such entries. I was able to confirm a handful of the incidents in the archives of *El Comercio* and other mainstream papers—but the reports didn't connect them to the Cuarta Filosofía or suggest any greater political significance. Others I couldn't find at all. When I showed the list to Damien, he whistled in sly admiration.

"Do you remember what Che Guevara said, Andres?" Of course I didn't. "'One aspect of revolutionary propaganda must always be the truth.'"

I went back to these "Scorecards" again and again, trying to sort them out, to map for myself their relationship to that truth. I admit I felt an uneasy envy. Propaganda by deed—but in this case the deeds were someone else's, or never happened at all. I thought of Colin Powell with his diagrams and maps, explaining Saddam's nuclear stockpiles to the U.N. Security Council. I thought of Condi Rice's mushroom cloud.

"We create our own reality," someone in the White House had recently told reporters. Who gives a damn about history when there's a good story to tell?

"Come," Marta says, nudging Leo with the toe of her shoe. "Get up, let's go."

Leo groans and rolls over, clutches for her glasses. "What's wrong?"

Marta's face is hidden in shadow. "No questions. Bring nothing. We leave now."

On the bus, Leo sets her jaw and watches the passing city—neighborhoods she recognizes, others where she's never set foot, heading east until the traffic-clogged avenues give way to narrow streets, the sky constricting and darkening as the buildings close in on either side. Men congregate on plastic chairs before unlit storefronts; empty lots echo with the scratch and holler of kids playing soccer in the dark. As they labor up into the hills, the city lays itself out in patterned light, appearing and disappearing behind dark humps of land, flickering through stands of eucalyptus trees. It's not yet midnight—but Leo, lightheaded with curiosity, forces herself to keep her mouth shut.

After almost an hour, they enter a quiet neighborhood of pastel bungalows and dusty lots. They alight in front of what looks like an auto-repair shop—derelict car bodies up on blocks, heaps of tires stacked six feet high like the walls of a hedge maze. Leo follows Marta across the street into a stretch of dense wood; she can make out a broad clearing—a large estate of some kind, or a park—on the other side, a distant squat building lit up like a dollhouse. They crouch low as they move toward the lights, an unsettling sense of familiarity creeping up on Leo. At the edge of the clearing Marta stops and reaches into her bag.

"Put these on." Leo looks down to find a black sweater, a ski mask. She blinks at Marta, opens her mouth. "You say you want to do more?" Marta says. "Show me."

LIMA, MAY 30—The Conquistador's Club in Monterrico was the target of an act of vandalism. Two women intruded upon an evening program featuring the Bogotá String Quartet. Without provocation, they assaulted club personnel and defaced private property with obscene graffiti. The suspects are believed to be associated with the subversive elements that have shown renewed activity in recent months.

[*El Comercio*, 6/2/98—my translation]

The clubhouse sits at the edge of the woods, a modest Greek temple surrounded by a broad terrace that looks out on the eighteenth green. Through tall, brightly lit windows they can see people sitting in rows, the backs of their heads held still; strains of violin float across the fairway like an enchantment. It's an oasis, a dream floating above the infernal city; the sky feels closer, riddled with starpoints, the air sweet with the tang of eucalyptus. As they squat by the side of the timer's shack, sweating in the itchy masks, Leo can't help but think of those grade-school bar mitzvot, of the places her father played golf, the club in Armonk where they'd held Grandpa Carol's memorial: old, warty men sipping scotch and gobbling hors d'oeuvres, winking at waitresses a quarter of their age. It's all too familiar—right down to the smell of cut grass and new money. How does she keep finding herself in these places?

Did Miguel send them? Had he ordered Marta to take Leo along? "Make her feel useful," he might have said, knowing the risks of a comrade who feels separate from the others. Or maybe it was Marta's initiative: to test Leo, to call her bluff and find out what she was capable of.

Impossible to know. Impossible even to be sure it was them. But the scene has an appealing logic, a satisfying symmetry, simultaneously indulging her desire to go deeper, to do more, and reminding her yet again of who she really was. I think I'll keep it.

"Go quickly," Marta says, pressing something smooth and cold into Leo's hand.

"There are people inside," Leo whispers, staring at the spray-paint can, blood throbbing in her ears. As if on cue, the last mournful cello notes saw their way across the terrace, followed by applause. "What if someone sees me?"

Marta squeezes harder. Her gaze behind the mask is flat with scorn. "What are you waiting for, compañera?"

When the three sets of French doors swing open, spilling light and garbled conversation onto the terrace. Marta shoves her forward: "Go now, Linda."

Leo watches the elegant men and women stepping outside, the servers holding silver trays. Fifty yards, maybe less—all she has do is run, deliver the message, vanish into the dark. But her feet are held by invisible shackles, breath locked tight in her throat.

"Just as I thought," Marta says.

The whole thing takes maybe thirty seconds. Snatching the can, Marta bounds from the shadows, growing taller and more fearsome as she races into the light. Her dark form barrels into the exiting patrons, who lurch to either side, gasping. She tips over one cocktail table, then another—smashing glass, cries of confusion—until she's alone in a wide circle, floodlights throwing shadows across the terrace like the spokes of a wheel.

"We claim this place in the name of the real Peru!" she cries, brandishing her weapon at the shrinking bodies. "¡Viva la revolución!" The crowd presses back toward the doors, faces twisted in disgust. Leo watches, awestruck, as Marta moves from one side of the terrace to the other, letters emerging in bright red on the flagstones:

VIENE EL—

Before she can write the last word a man in a dark suit rushes onto the patio, catches Marta from behind and lifts her, legs flailing, into the air. The spray paint can clangs to the terrace. A strange silence: everyone on the terrace held immobile, only Marta, struggling like a roped calf—and without thinking Leo springs from her hiding place, sprints into the dazzle of lights, the strangely vivid faces, all a blur. She rushes up the stairs, aims herself like a missile, a growl taking root in her belly, breaking out of her as a scream when she plants one foot and slams the other into the guard's crotch with the sound of a baseball hitting a sandbag.

Then they're running for the shadows, vaulting the low stone wall and dropping to the cut grass, an alarm bell ringing behind them but somehow she knows no one is giving chase. Not yet. Across the springy green, the fairway and paved cart path and into the woods—the crunch of dead leaves and dry bark, Leo's heart slamming, following always Marta's deft and fluid shape as if they were tethered to each other, mirroring each other's movements, until they come out on the road and plunge into the sad-lit labyrinth of old tires.

Panting, wet-faced, they quickly strip off their masks and sweaters, shove them under a pile of rubber. There are lights flashing at the edges of Leo's vision, sounds escaping her throat: an animal's whimper, a mad, high laughter wanting to come out.

"¿Estás bien?" Marta says. "Amiga, are you hurt? Linda?"

She isn't hurt. She feels enormous, fierce, as if she could wrestle a tiger. Her chest is full of delicious air, her vision impossibly sharp— somewhere voices are calling but they can't touch her, here amid the smells of dirt and rubber, the sweet sting of cold. Let the fear come tomorrow, the memory of angry faces, how it felt to land that kick, to really hurt someone. For now she stands gripped in blood sparkle, eyes streaming, clinging to this exultation, this feeling of having come alive.

The first shipment of dynamite arrived sometime in the first week of June: two hundred eighty-eight sticks of dynamite, stolen from a copper mine in the faraway town of San Juan de Lucanas and delivered, according to an affidavit submitted by Lieutenant Jaime Lang Ovieda, commander of DINCOTE's elite Grupo 14, "while the innocent women and children of Pueblo Libre slept."

Neither the affidavit nor Lang's internal report indicate who arranged and paid for this operation and the military judges didn't ask. Nor did they question the precision of the number—two hundred eighty-eight, out of an eventual eight hundred twenty, enough to demolish a building twice the size of Congress. Lang's affidavit was not introduced at the civilian retrial, having somehow disappeared in the intervening years. Leo's lawyer objected to the prosecutor's frequent references to such missing documents. Those objections were overruled.

On June 5, just before the morning shift change, a temporary support in the Vía América parking garage collapsed, and a sixty-foot slab of cantilevered concrete smashed to the tier below. Seven workers were killed. For two days the accident dominated the media, including photos of giant concrete chunks that slid down the cliffs and broke up on the coastal road. Somehow no cars were hit.

"Thank God the damage was not worse," Lima's mayor told TV reporters. *El Comercio*'s headline read ¡MILAGRO!

When Leo returns a few days later, the cleanup is well underway. Trucks line up along the malecón to cart out the rubble, and a squadron of policemen herd reporters and gawkers across the street. The few remaining protestors are confined to a section of the median barely visible from the construction site: the tireless abuelas, the crazy Indian in his loincloth, chanting and shaking his tambourine. She stands damp-cheeked in the chill, the hot reek of fresh asphalt, watching landscapers install a series of undulating metal canopies and a black marble pedestal in the park-like area atop the cliff. Escalators descend from a grassy promenade into the guts of Mammon—perhaps in the exact spot where, months ago, Julian tried to scare her away.

Since the night at the Conquistador's Club she's been jumpy and unstrung, unable to sleep. The power she'd felt racing toward the guard, the exultation as he fell—she'd been, for one dizzy instant, outside of time, observing herself without fear or doubt, a body set in motion by the necessary act, chosen by it. They'd taken separate buses back to Pueblo Libre. She hasn't seen Marta since that night.

"Señorita?"

A tug at her elbow and Leo turns to find a girl standing behind her. Fifteen or sixteen, maybe five feet tall, her face is round and dusky, her cheeks abraded with rash. In one arm, she cradles a baby in a thick blanket. Her other hand holds out a battered box of Chiclets.

"Por favor, señorita," she says. "Cómprame."

The blurt of a siren drives the crowd back several steps. "How old is your baby?" Leo asks. The girl shakes the box and gazes at the infant, who stretches a tiny hand toward the sound. Something in the gesture reminds Leo of Nancy, her furious determination in the days after Ernesto disappeared. She points to the construction site and says, "Do you know what they're building here?"

"No sé," the girl says. "Cómprame."

"It's a shopping mall. For rich people. They're doing all this for the ricos."

The girl's face is blank. When Leo hands her a coin she lowers her eyes. "You have a good heart, señorita. Jesus Christ loves you."

When she's gone, Leo lights a cigarette and watches the workers cart rubble from the wrecked garage. The tambourine jingles faintly in the sunset glare. In that morning's paper, an unnamed official wondered if the construction accident had been an act of sabotage. "Obviously there are people who don't want progress," he said, referring to the incident at Los Muertos. "Nobodies," he called them. "Psychopaths." He'd dismissed reports of a long list of safety violations at the site.

Leo had been disgusted when she first read the comments. But now, watching a line of workers descending into the maw, Leo recalls the article with nervous fascination. "An insult to the new Peru," the official had said. The logic isn't hard to follow: Who could see such ugliness without wanting to tear it down or blow it up?

By the next weekend, a date for the grand opening had been set: August 23, 1998, "a day for all Peruvians to celebrate the country's progress," the mayor proclaimed. A proposal to honor the dead workers with a small statue was voted down. Instead, the government offered twenty thousand soles—about six thousand dollars—to each worker's family. A city alderman was heard to remark that, for those families, "this is the best thing that ever happened to them."

4

She remembers Victor Beale. On the coldest nights in El Arca, when the air threatens to crack and shatter, Leo pictures his battered face, his swollen hands, the sores that covered his neck and torso. She sees him shivering in his underground cell, made crazy by darkness, by the scurries and crawlings of invisible creatures. For two months he languished in that cell, howled there, pissed and shit there. How he must have longed for a glimpse of his captors, for even the roughest word—though he feared them, hated them, hated himself for this weakness. Over time even that hatred ebbed, leaving only the primal, babbling need: to be seen, touched, gathered together. To know he was still alive.

She never laid eyes on him. And yet she can imagine the reek of his terror, feel the dehumanizing agony of his solitude. How easy it is, in the end, to empathize. Too easy, she knows: What can her empathy do for him now?

In articles about her arrest and trial, in Gorriti's history of the Cuarta Filosofía, Beale's name is always mentioned. At her retrial, the prosecutor described the appalling conditions in which he was held. "El Arca is a resort hotel compared to what Victor Beale endured," he said. But the link between Leo and Beale has never been clear. His story is evoked not as evidence but as atmosphere, a bit of gruesome mood music. There's no way I can leave it out of the story. But it's up to me to make the connection.

The scion of a wealthy Arequipa family, Victor Beale Ocampo was a deputy director of the InterAmerican Development Bank, which in the 1990s provided Peru with nearly $4 billion in loans. The IDB was a key driver of the so-called Washington Consensus, under which countries throughout the developing world were forced to privatize major industries, weaken labor unions, eliminate subsidies and tariffs. In Peru as elsewhere, foreign investment soared, GDP rose, hyperinflation was brought under control; but the gains benefited few outside the elite: by 1998, wages were less than half what they'd been a decade earlier, and the poverty rate remained well above 50 percent.

In May, 1998, the IDB and the Ministry of Economy and Finance announced a $350 million initiative to build new hydroelectric stations in the south of the country. An exposé in *Caretas* revealed that one of the plants was to be built on land belonging to the Beale family, for which they would be compensated twenty million soles, or nearly seven million dollars. Such a cozy arrangement would have elicited hardly a shrug—Peruvians of every class had long since accepted corruption as part of the national genome—had not Victor Beale disappeared soon after the article was published.

On June 10, the night desk editor of *El Comercio* received a phone call from someone identifying himself as "a professor of philosophy." The caller dictated a message, which ran in the next day's paper. "For the crime of theft, a hand must be amputated," it said. "A cancer must be cut out with the sharpest of knives." It demanded that the sale of the Beale family's land be cancelled, the parcel redistributed to tenant farmers, the twenty million soles given as ransom. The President refused to negotiate. He vowed to pursue Beale's captors "to the end of time."

They hadn't told her. When she saw Beale's picture on the TV in the bodega—young and handsome, with a prominent brow and an expensive suit—that was the first thing that came to mind. He reminded her of her brother and his groomsmen, all confidence and oblivious charm, the world ever bending itself to their expectations. But her comrades hadn't told her—just as they hadn't told her about Radio 2000, or the cumpas' arrival, or anything about their plans. From the first she's been cut out of the discussion, consulted only regarding the most menial tasks. Only Miguel seemed to recognize her value: an asset, he'd called her. But where is Miguel now?

"Why didn't you tell me?" she asks Marta that night. She stands at the front door, blocking Marta's way out. "Didn't you think I should know about this?"

"Let me pass, compañera."

"The whole country is looking for him, Marta. I had a right to know."

"Again you talk of rights?"

Above and around them, the house is listening. Without looking up, Leo can sense Chaski at the top of the stairs. It's the first time since the night at the golf club that she's exchanged more than two words with Marta. If Leo had believed that her heroism would be rewarded with trust, that she'd at last be admitted to the inner circle, she was wrong. Nothing has changed—only the intensity of her anticipation, the frustration of endless, uneventful days, not knowing what was happening, even in other parts of her own house.

"I need to leave, Linda," Marta says, trying to step around her. "Let me pass."

"I want to know where you're going."

She's answered by the same unblinking expression—too familiar. In a rage Leo flings the newspaper at Marta's feet. "I'm sick of being left out of everything. I'm sick of being told you don't need me. You needed me at the Conquistador's Club, didn't you?"

Marta bends to gather up the newspaper, holds it out until Leo, abashed, takes it back. "I already told you. If you want to leave, leave," Marta says. She pulls Leo aside and steps past. "Why are you so angry, compañera? Finally something is happening. Isn't that what you wanted?"

Something is happening. Though she'd known nothing about it someone has done *something*—and it dawns on her now that she never really believed anyone would. The months of secrecy, the fiction of the art school, the tedious rote of the cumpas' training—at times she'd half-believed it was all an act, a game they'd all indulged in together. Like the incidents in "The Scorecard"—a bodega robbery, a military garrison vandalized, a hold-up on the Cuzco bus. She's written of such things with revolutionary braggadocio, described them as great victories, precursors to war.

And what if they were?

For the next few days the thought plagues her, scratching at her awareness like a specter: What if all along the war were being revived, blows being struck, while she's spent months on errands, housework, oblivious to it all? It disorients her, this opening of possibility, of another story running parallel to her own; it tilts the ground she walks on. She remembers the vision she'd once had—of a city dotted with houses like this one, people like her and Marta, preparing to change the world. How fanciful she'd been then, driven by grief and wishful thinking, by the romance of resistance. How sober and disquieting that vision seems, now that it's real.

Needing to steady herself, to focus, she throws herself back into the newspaper, scribbling notes and queries in the middle of the night. The clack of her fingertips on the keyboard, the concreteness of images returns her, for a few hours, to the world of presence. She rides buses all morning in search of photos, alights on random corners, talks to vendors in a reeking fish market in Callao, tourists in Miraflores jewelry boutiques, surfers at the Playa Redondo. But the specter never quite leaves her; on the street she moves with new vigilance, a heightened attention to her words and gestures. Out of body—in every part of Lima she feels watched, evaluated, but she knows the observer is herself.

For the first time since February, she goes back to the Hostal Macondo and interviews Ricky, who tells her about growing up in Pucallpa during the war, about his uncle, Carlos "The Eagle" Poma, a notorious rondero who went on to become vice governor of the Ucayali region. Later, she climbs to the roof and peers into the dim closet where she'd once lived, long since reclaimed by mops and old blankets. She leans on the slate wall and takes in the city's torpid sprawl. Six months, she thinks—half a year since Neto died. She remembers the signal—the burning number 4 that lit up the night—and how she'd told herself, without entirely believing, that it was meant for her eyes. Someone had seen it, she thinks. But who?

That night she types up what she remembers of Chaski's story: Sendero's arrival in his village, the army's rampage, his experiences in the camp and on the streets of Lurigancho. Where he gave no description she adds vivid detail—the stray dogs who ate his parents' tongues, the face of a village girl who was raped by a soldier. Where something reads as counterrevolutionary—the rondero's wife who bought clothes and toys for the orphans; the business class Chaski enrolled in after Tarata—she leaves it out. She brings herself nearly to tears thinking of the innocent boy he once was, the wounded man he's become—and of the secret he's kept from everyone in the house but her. After an hour of tinkering she lays out this narrative of injustice and noble suffering—the tale of a promising life abused and discarded by the social order—on page three, under the headline ¿Por qué Lucho? or Why Do I Fight?

With one last column to fill she pens her masterpiece: "The Banker: A Fable." It's the story of "Vincente Bell," a mid-level bureaucrat in the "Bank of Washington" who concocts a scheme with his cronies to get rich by selling worthless land for an unnecessary construction project. "Everyone wins!" Bell declares, to which one crony adds, "Everyone who matters." One morning, walking from his mansion to a waiting limousine, Bell is seized by a group of "brave fighters" and taken to the campo, where he spends years planting potatoes and digging wells, learning firsthand "the superiority of this life [. . .] the cruelty we have heaped upon such undeserving victims" before returning to Lima to fight for justice for the people he once exploited.

It's no *Moby-Dick*, but it will do. She's especially pleased with her research, having used details of Victor Beale's actual house in Barranco, and the building in San Isidro where the IDB has its offices. It has the ring of authenticity, the logic of the real— rereading the story, Leo has to remind herself it's not true. The descriptions and dialogue have lodged in her mind, images of things that never happened, whole scenes easily mistaken for memories.

But they could have happened—that's what matters. They *feel* true. No one reads *The Eyes of the World* for a factual account of history. You don't motivate people with facts, you motivate them with stories: people's experiences, their tragedies, their pain. What matters is that logic, that authenticity. Who even knows what the facts are? Had Neto's killers worried about facts? Was *El Comercio* objective when it described Beale's captors as "criminals and traitors"? It's exhilarating, this new approach, a liberation. Let others waste their time chasing what "really happened"—*The Eyes of the*

World will offer a better story, a more coherent reality. It will tell a greater truth.

"You need to arrange a new drop," Josea says. "Tell Marta. Álvaro doesn't want the packages coming to his store anymore."

"Did something happen?" Leo says.

Josea shrugs, watching her over the rims of his eyeglasses. Behind him, the café mutters and clinks with mid-day traffic; well-dressed women squawk over cappuccinos. As always at these brief rendezvous, she feels herself relaxing into his easy humor, his air of wantonness. Her sense of urgency softens and for a moment she's just a twenty-six-year-old woman having coffee with an older man. A *single* woman—when was the last time she went on a real date? How long has it been since she's taken a man to bed? Before she can stop herself, she pictures Josea and Marta as young lovers, younger than she is now, and shifts in her seat. Conspiracy, it turns out, is an aphrodisiac. Since the night at the Conquistador's Club, she's wanted to fuck every man she sees.

"Álvaro is superstitious," he says, half-turning to watch the pedestrians outside. "He has a store to protect, customers, merchandise. He's a businessman. Without a doubt he's the smart one."

"Chaski told me he survived a massacre. During the war."

Wincing, he removes his glasses and cleans them with a paper napkin. "Everyone survived something. If they didn't die, they found a new way to live. We had no choice. Even an animal stops fighting when he knows he can't win."

"No one stops fighting. Not if it's for their lives."

Josea laughs at this. "You, too, amiga? Whose life are you fighting for?"

She puts down her cup, bristling at the old accusation. "That's the wrong question and you know it. That's how we lose. The point is to keep fighting. La lucha es lo importante."

"Lower your voice, mija," he says, leaning toward her—close enough for her to smell the sweet leather of his cologne. "Listen to me. Álvaro has a point. This thing with the IDB asshole, Beale, this kidnapping. I don't want to know anything about it. It doesn't matter who did what—you've got their attention now. And if they decide . . ." He trails off, some old anguish fleeting through his gaze.

"Mira, Leo. It's different now. Things are more open. The government feels more secure, so they allow demonstrations, things like this, up to a point. A newspaper is one thing—"

"We aren't demonstrators."

"Then who are you? What are you doing?"

Leo bites her lip, furious at this condescension. "When you need to know, you'll be told, compañero. Until then, you just need to follow instructions."

It's a deliberate provocation, but Josea only smiles and sips his beer. "Tell me, who's giving these instructions? Has the great Comrade Julian returned?"

"Comrade Marta is in charge now."

"Comrade Marta," he repeats. He drums his fingers on the table. "Listen, Leo, I've known Marta a long time. I know her . . . determination. But loyalty, trustworthiness, these are not her best qualities."

"She's loyal to the people she respects."

At last her words have the desired effect: Josea sucks his teeth and turns back to watch the street. Of course he'd malign Marta—in this country of machistas no one expects a woman to be capable of leadership. Who needs Julian? Who cares where he's slunk off to lick his wounds? She and Marta will show them how capable two women can be. In fact, Leo thinks, this is the perfect topic for her next editorial. A title comes to her immediately: "The Sheath Is Mightier Than the Sword."

"We're up to twelve pages," she says brightly, sliding a copy of *Don Quixote* across the table, the SyQuest cartridge nestled inside. "Some great images. Spot color on the covers and centerfold. Let us know if we owe you."

Wordlessly, Josea puts the book in his satchel and returns her copy of *Moby-Dick*.

"I hope you enjoyed it," she says.

"Who wouldn't enjoy all that struggle? And in the end, everyone is destroyed by a dream." When she lays a coin on the table and stands, Josea reaches for her wrist. "Leo. Hija. I hope you're keeping your eyes open."

"Call me Linda," she says, measuring out her condescension. Then, pitching her voice so the women at the next table can hear,

"We're having fun, tío. Don't worry! The art school opens next month. Come by and we'll paint your portrait. No charge."

What else? What am I missing?

It's late June in Lima, the dismal months of winter taking hold. The August arrest, the press conference, El Arca—it's all looming on the horizon, though I can't quite make it out. Like a pointillist painting: the closer I get the fuzzier it becomes.

Of this last, critical period there's little record, less verifiable fact. Like the dunes of Los Muertos the weeks spread bare and treacherous, only scraps of thatch and trash, bent shards of metal, to indicate anyone ever lived there. Government documents, heavily redacted. Faded issues of *The Eyes of the World*. Leo never discussed how she and her comrades passed these anxious, in-between days. As far as I know, no one ever asked.

There are three items left in the Leo File. Three disintegrating scraps between me and a bright void. The first is a note from DINCOTE's report, referring to a second meeting between Leo and Comrade Miguel. It took place in Lince, not far from the café where she delivered the fifth issue to Josea Torres. It's unclear whether the meeting was planned, but I suspect not. I suspect Miguel was following her—the report describes Leo as "confused and agitated" when he approached her on the street. They ducked into a bar— the Taberna Los Perros—where they spent only half an hour. It's unclear what was talked about. It's unclear what any of it means.

I've gone back to that corner, not far from Damien's apartment. I've walked that stretch of the Avenida Canevaro—bank branches and drab hotels, a profusion of optometrists—hoping to find some lingering trace. When I peered into Los Perros I thought I could still see them, side by side at the bar, he in khaki pants and a tailored shirt, she in too-large jeans, a wool sweater moth-eaten at the wrists—

Compañero, has anything happened? Have I done something wrong?

No, Linda. You've done excellent work. The house, the newspaper, it's all very helpful.

I look forward to doing more.

—but it's as if the film were degrading, the soundtrack lost. They clink glasses. He touches a fingertip to her wrist. It makes me uncomfortable to watch them, undetected. What right do I have to spy on them this way?

I withdrew, sucking at the outside air like a swimmer after a dive. Lima rushed past me, oblivious. I had the urge to grab someone and shout, "It matters! Look what's happening—it matters, don't you see?"

I'm running out of time. In less than two months she'll be taken off that bus in a hail of gunfire. The house in Pueblo Libre will burn. All the way back to Damien's I fought a sense of displacement, of walking outside the real story in my mind. My reflection in car windows was thin and indistinct. I thought at any moment I might run into them—Leo, Miguel, Julian, any of the characters I'd been living with. But each time I turned the corner, there was only an empty street.

. . .

LIMA, JUNE 28 —The National Police have arrested two suspects for the outrageous attack on the Conquistador's Club last month. The women, identified only as residents of San Juan de Lurigancho, are known sympathizers with terrorist groups. In a statement . . .

[*El Comercio*, 7/1/98—my translation]

For a long time she stares at the page, long enough for the lines to blur, for the dueño of the bodega to ask if she's alright. As she had after Victor Beale's disappearance, she feels dislocated, doubled. A headache springs up between her eyes.

There's tension in the house, raised voices drifting from the third floor. Ignoring them, Leo mounts the stairs two at a time, banging on the metal door until the voices quiet. A moment later, Marta comes down the stairs.

"Who are they?" Leo demands, shoving the newspaper at her. "Tell me the truth."

Marta bats the paper away. Leo follows her down to the kitchen, shaking with anger. "They didn't do anything, Marta. They weren't even there. They'll be tortured—"

"Keep your voice down."

"We have to do something. We have to help them."

"We are helping them," Marta says. "Still you don't understand?"

Still trembling, sick to her stomach, Leo lowers herself into a chair. How had it never occurred to her someone else would be blamed? It means they're in danger, all of them, the stories are all getting confused: those innocent women, Victor Beale, Álvaro, anything could happen now, that's the only truth that matters.

When Chaski enters the kitchen, Marta won't look at him.

"Compañera," he says. "Come back upstairs. We need to resolve the question."

"I told you the discussion is over."

The contempt in Marta's voice takes Leo aback, beyond the usual dislike with which Marta talks to Chaski, or about him. Josea's warning is fresh in her mind; with the news about Victor Beale, about the women's arrest, such disunity feels newly threatening, potentially fatal.

"Marta," Chaski says, then with a glance at Leo switches to Quechua, a long and patient monologue to which Marta hardly seems to be listening. He enumerates his concerns by counting on his fingers, emphasizes a point with a gentle rap on the table.

"I've heard this all before," Marta says in Spanish. "Such reformist garbage is what led to the problem in Los Muertos. Your analysis is incorrect, and a strategy based on incorrect—"

"Incorrect according to you."

"I am in charge here," Marta says.

"No one came to this house for you, Marta. No one swore loyalty to you."

"They swore loyalty to the goals. If you don't believe in those goals, you can leave."

Chaski's voice is hard, more forceful than Leo's heard in months. "Some of the cumpas are considering new goals. And new leaders."

Marta smiles at the challenge, raises her chin. "Are those cumpas also homosexuals?"

The silence is sudden and sharp as an ice storm, so total the refrigerator makes Leo jump when it switches on. Chaski's face stamped with concentration, as though Marta kicked him in his bad leg. Leo has to stop herself from leaping out of her chair—it sickens her, this rank bigotry, sickens her to think Marta had known all along, had been waiting for an advantageous moment to fling it in Chaski's face

But she holds her tongue. She can't afford to take sides in this fight, to risk whatever confidence of Marta's she still enjoys. Marta's position is precarious now, mutiny in the air. Any hint of allegiance to Chaski will only discredit Leo. It will only weaken her hand.

So this is revolutionary sacrifice, she thinks.

Honor is to be useful without vanity.

"Where is Victor Beale?" Leo says. Marta and Chaski turn to her and she meets their gazes one at a time. "Where is he? Tell me, one of you, or I'm leaving."

They all watch one another, Chaski anxious and unsteady, Marta's face tight with assessment, calculation. "Is he in this house?" Leo says. When there's no response she goes to the front hall, shouts up the stairs, "Are you up there, Victor Beale?"

Marta hurries after her. "Lower your voice . . ."

She rushes up the stairs, Marta right behind her, and yanks on the metal door until it rattles and bangs in its casings. But she knows he's not there, even as she's shouting into a dark stairwell she knows they'd never keep him so close. Before she knows where she's going, she brushes past Marta and flings open the front door, hurrying past the spindly rosebushes and along the side of the house, into the forbidden backyard, until she comes to the old metal shed.

"Stop, Linda!" Marta hisses, following close behind.

"Is he in here?" Leo smacks the shed and the sound sets the neighbor's dog howling. "I'll leave tonight, Marta. I swear it." Above the rooftops of Pueblo Libre, a clammy orange dusk is descending. Leo takes out a cigarette, lights it with a shaking hand. "If you don't trust me I can't stay."

In the late mist Marta looks suddenly smaller, more solitary. She stares at Leo, her eyes busy with calculation. "He's not here," she says. "I don't know where he is."

"Then where is he."

"I don't know. No one here knows." She crosses her arms, twists her lips into a bitter smile. "So you see, Linda? We are not trusted either."

Leo sucks at the cigarette, her thoughts caroming from relief to disgust: another false alarm, another event she'll never touch.

"Four months," she says. "We've been here four months, Marta."

"No," Marta says. "We've been here for years."

Slowly, Leo's heart stops pounding. The air is cool, expectant. She can sense Chaski watching from the kitchen window. What does he see when he looks at her? What do any of them see?

That's when she remembers the beggar girl, standing at the site of Vía América while the drills shrieked and jackhammers chewed up the cliffs. She thinks of the wrecked garage, the massive hunks of concrete spilling down the cliffs to the ocean.

You have a good heart, señorita, the girl had said—as if the heart could possibly matter, as if, against the world's grinding machinery, a heart were anything more than a small, throbbing lump of meat.

"Come inside," she tells Marta, not knowing if the steel in her voice is real or just another bid for respect. In the end, she thinks, it will hardly matter. "Let me tell you my idea."

Two days later, Comrade Chaski left. Accompanying him were Alonso Pantoja Sánchez and Osmán Arce Borja—a.k.a. Comrades Tadeo and El Blondi. They walked out of the house at 8:06 a.m., turned south, and proceeded to Lorenzo Garza's bodega, where Tadeo bought a liter of milk, before disappearing from the pages of DINCOTE's report. There's no speculation as to why they left or where they went—and in fact the number of fighters who remained would be a matter of dispute in the days after the raid. In his affidavit, DINCOTE's Lieutenant Jaime Lang Ovieda admitted to frustration at this sudden departure. The government's priority was to keep the Pueblo Libre group together, he insisted, so as to make their eventual capture easier: "A single, definitive operation, it was felt, would minimize the risk to the public."

That night, Leo sits against the bedroom wall while Marta gathers her belongings. One by one she peels the photos from the wall, piling them unceremoniously in one of the camera cases, which she latches shut and slides into the hall. Things will be better now, more honest, Marta says. The group is stronger without Chaski and his "clique." The cumpas who stayed are dependable, ready to act.

"They're men," she says. "They aren't afraid to fight."

"But how long will they stay?" Leo says. "First Julian, now Chaski. Soon it will be just you and me."

"Or maybe you will also leave."

A week ago, Leo would have shuddered at the accusation. But Marta's right: things really are clearer now. "You need me," she says. "If you're going to carry out the plan, you need me here."

The plan. It's all she's thought about since it sprang, fully formed, from her mouth the other night. She and Marta had sat up for hours while Leo described her vision: the demolition of Vía América, its utter destruction, the vulgar behemoth sliding like a calved glacier into the sea.

It could be done. Over and over she'd insisted it could be done, convincing herself as much as her comrade. Even after the accident, the construction site was not well guarded, she said. Marta knew how to use explosives. Surely some of the other cumpas did, too. Surely they knew where to get them? She closed her eyes, shuddered as if in the throes of a righteous orgasm: it was perfect, a direct strike at capitalism, at exploitation, the decadence of the elites. The message would be clear and unignorable, delivered in spectacular fashion.

Best of all, if they acted soon and were careful in their preparations, nobody had to get hurt.

"When will we tell the others?" Leo says now. Her stomach aches from too much nicotine. She had not spoken to Chaski after the scene in the kitchen. His pale face in the window had withdrawn when she and Marta headed back inside. Now it's too late. Leo hates herself for failing to stand up for him, for choosing Marta and the revolution over someone who'd been kind to her, who'd trusted her. But there's no time now for regret. Chaski may feel disappointed, even betrayed—but one day he'll understand.

"The opening is in less than two months," she says. "We need everyone's input. We'll make a list, assign each person a task. Once we break it down—"

Marta says quietly, "Linda."

Leo, nodding—"Right, okay."

"You understand, there can't be a 'we.'"

She understands. She'd worked out the logic herself: the gringa's hands have to stay clean. But to hear it spoken aloud fills her with an unexpected dread. In El Arca she would have years to remember this conversation, to recall how the word—*we*—grew large until it dwarfed her, how she stayed up nights considering the question: *Who is "we"?*

It doesn't matter. After months of talk there's finally a plan—it's perfect, glorious, and *hers*. If the cost of this parentage is that she be removed from the plan, that she watch it grow and take wing independent of her ministrations, at least she'll know it belongs to her, could not have been conceived without her. It stings, this removal, throbs like an abscess. But it is not too high a price.

"In the campo, we learned to trust our leaders," Marta says. She takes out a cigarette, but her feigned nonchalance can't mask the note of unease. "We learned to listen to them. If the group isn't united, it's vulnerable. Anything can happen."

One day, she says, someone came, a commander, very respected. He said two men from a nearby village had been arrested, accused of being with Sendero. The villagers feared that the army would soon arrive. The commander was going to defend the village, he said. He was looking for fighters to accompany him.

"Did you go?"

Marta shakes her head. "Casi wouldn't allow it. We argued. Some of the others disobeyed but I stayed. He was our leader." She takes a long drag, blowing the smoke into a dark corner. "Everyone who went to that village was killed. They found three cumpas on the Cuzco road with plastic bags tied over their heads."

Leo stares at her hands. She reaches for her cigarettes but finds the pack empty. Something in Marta's story is nagging at her. "14 de Junio. The group you were in. It was part of the Shining Path, wasn't it?" When there's no answer, she says, "That's why the army didn't let Casi go. He was in Sendero."

"A lot of people called themselves a lot of things. All that matters is what they did."

Leo nods, reaches for Marta's cigarettes. All around them the room holds its breath, the sharp, still point on which the night turns.

"Why did you tell me this story, compañera?" she says.

"Because it's the truth."

"To scare me?"

"You are already scared."

With that Marta hoists her bedroll and lifts her camera case from the floor. Her footsteps recede down the hall and up the stairs, to Chaski's old room. Leo listens to the creaking of Chaski's bedsprings overhead. The rest of the house is as silent as the day she moved in.

"But I'm still here."

What happened the next day, or the day after that, can never be known. DINCOTE's report ends with Chaski's departure, what came after having been destroyed or withheld, if it was ever written. I have no more telling newspaper items, no more curious details from Gorriti's article or Rabbi Eisens with their serendipitous meetings. I have only questions that can't be answered, truths lost to the black hole of time. It was inevitable, I suppose, this boundary. I've come to the end of my story, the line beyond which I can't see.

Or maybe I've come to the beginning.

It was the Fourth of July.

5

"It's a sad day to be an American, Leo, I'll tell you that much. Can you believe this crap?"

Leo smokes against the wall of the bodega, white sun slanting across her chest.

"I swear," her brother says, "if I hear one more person defending him . . . I mean, seriously, we're like the laughingstock of the planet. It's a sad day to be an American," he says again. "Maybe you've got the right idea, Sis."

She allows herself a cold smile. Matt only calls her "Sis" when he feels superior, a subtle reminder that she's older and yet, in the family's reckoning, so much less accomplished. Already in the course of a five-minute phone call he's managed to mention his promotion, his new office on the 103rd floor—"with a view out to, like, Bermuda"—and his salary, a truly stomach-turning sum which nevertheless is not quite enough for him to buy the bigger apartment he and Samira have decided they need.

"What is it you do, again?" she asked.

"Arbitrage."

"What does that mean?"

He laughed and played along. "Beats me!"

Now he starts in again, about the scandal, the taped phone calls, the stained blue dress—"No shame, this dumbass! Doesn't he understand he works for *us*?"—caught up like the rest of the world in a kabuki show of no consequence, oblivious to the world's true agonies. For all his sheltered arrogance, she'd thought Matt had more sense.

It hardly matters now, she thinks, peering into the dim bodega, at the old dueño behind the counter. In a few weeks such trifles will be reduced to their true proportions, drowned out by the euphonious rumbles of the plan as it erupts, at long last, into reality.

"Don't blame me," Matt says. "I voted for Jack Kemp. Hey, Leo," he says, "did they ever find that guy?"

"Who?"

"The one you told me about. Your friend from work or something. Remember?"

It takes a second to realize whom he means. Seven months on, it's hard to picture Neto's face—and when she does, it's not the bashful kid in the Pearl Jam T-shirt she sees but the black-and-white image on a thousand picket signs. At one point she'd told herself she was doing all this for Neto. What does it mean that she hardly remembers him?

"Yeah," she says. "They found him."

"Is he okay? I mean, where was he?"

Matt's concern is so unexpected, so out of character, that she almost tells him everything: how it all feels so precarious, how she hasn't slept for weeks. She wants to tell him about the plan, how she's imagined it down to its most minuscule detail, to lay it out for him in all its beauty. But her baby brother—with his co-op apartment and perfect wife and view of Bermuda—would never understand.

"He's fine. It was all a misunderstanding."

Even Matt can hear the lie. "Leo, are you okay? The 'rents are kind of freaking out. Dad says they haven't talked to you in like a month."

"What do they want to talk about?"

"Well . . ." he says, as if talking to a mental patient, "the credit card, for one thing. I guess they want to know where all that money's going. They're worried about you."

"Of course they do. Of course it's all about money. People like Mom and Dad—" She stops herself. Another lecture, another editorial—what did it matter? Inside, the TV on the counter flashes an image of towering palm trees, lush grass, a profusion of rosebushes. The entrance to Vía América, she realizes with a groan. A crane is lowering something onto the black pedestal: a statue of Christopher Columbus, chin raised to the city, arms outstretched. Just then someone tugs at her belt and she looks down to find a beggar boy touching his hand to his mouth in hunger.

"I don't know, Matt," she says. "Maybe it's not going so well."

"So leave," he says, sounding, in his blunt surety, just like their father. "Come home. If something's bothering you. Just quit."

"Quit?"

"You don't owe these people anything, Leo. Your happiness is all that matters."

Stunned, she stares at the phone. The proprietor comes out from behind the counter, brandishing a broom at the beggar boy. *Your happiness—?*

"—coming down there, maybe around Labor Day," Matt is saying. "You can show me around, have a last hurrah. Samira really wants to spend time with you. She hardly knows you. What do you say, Sis? You must be ready for a good meal and a shower."

The voice is so earnest, almost beseeching, she has to remind herself who's on the other end: just another American, looking for someone to save.

Your happiness—?

"I have a shower," she says, then sets the phone in its cradle, savoring how his empty chatter shrinks to nothing.

At the 2002 civilian retrial, Lorenzo Garza Strauss testified that the defendant made frequent calls from the payphone in his bodega, often arguing with whoever was on the line, hanging up agitated. The government claimed to have records, provided by Telefónica, of calls to "known subversives," but refused to produce those records, citing national security. Leo's lawyer challenged the testimony on the grounds that Garza was legally blind, but the presiding judge dismissed this with scorn:

"I think the señor knows who was in his store."

That night she waits on a concrete bench, squinting at *Moby-Dick* in the thin glow of a streetlamp. It's been months since she read even a page of it—she's confused by the interstitial sections, unsure what the crew of the Pequod have been doing all this time. It's a warm, wet night, a quarter moon sailing through tears in the clouds. Across the street, young professionals stand outside the Café Haiti, smoking and perusing the menu, their laughter ringing clear in the night's otherworld lucidity.

For two weeks the plan has occupied her dreams. It comes to her personified, an object of desire, of an almost rabid lust, whose face she never quite sees. In daylight she finds herself in a state of double consciousness, body engaged in some rote task while her mind is picturing the cataclysm, anticipating the exquisite satisfaction when Vía América is swallowed by the sea.

But things are not happening fast enough. With just over a month until the opening, Marta seems unmoved by urgency, content to lock herself away with the remaining cumpas to debate this or that philosophical point, to rehash dogma. "Soon, compañera," she says when Leo confronts her, then ascends the stairs once again with her mug of tea. Waiting was hard enough before the plan— but now this inactivity has come to feel like a kind of indolence, an immorality.

Around nine o'clock, Julian sets his tray on the bar and unties his apron. She waits until he's disappeared down the alley, then shoves *Moby-Dick* in her bag and follows. When she next catches sight of him, he's exiting a shop with a bouquet of flowers clutched under one arm. Her steps quicken in anger and an odd jealousy: all these months of waiting, living on three-day-old stew and bad cheese, while he consorts with the leisure class, wasting money on something as sentimental and bourgeois as *flowers*?

She keeps him in her sights through the silent streets, past the dark synagogue, the stacked condominiums painted with light. After ten minutes he stops at a roundabout and lights a cigarette, standing under a bronze statue of a horseman with sword raised against the pearled sky. The floodlit, dignified homes, each with its wide metal gate; a steep, tiled roof; the pompous statue—all familiar somehow. When he crosses the street to one of the houses, presses buttons on a keypad and opens a door in the gate, Leo crosses after him, stepping into a scene from a luxury magazine: a driveway of cut stone circling a marble fountain, from which streams of water shoot through penumbras of colored light.

"Where are you going, cumpa?"

Julian spins, guiltily clutching the flowers. The house rises behind him, three stories of white stone, brick balconies and oriental roofs, trees trimmed into unnatural forms. "Listen to me," he whispers, taking a step toward her as the iron lanterns flanking the front door flicker on. "Go back to the house. I'll come later—"

"Did you forget about us? We're all there because of you."

As he scans her face, panic shining in his eyes, Leo has the exhilarating sense of their having changed places. She feels larger, stiff with authority—while Julian, her tormentor, has shrunk to a comic figure, entirely at her mercy.

"Augustín," comes a voice. Julian's eyes go still. He flashes Leo a pleading look and turns to face the woman in the doorway.

"Buenas noches, Señora," he says with a mock bow, producing the flowers from behind his back. She's in her sixties, wearing a dark green dress with a high collar, a necklace that gleams in the lantern-light. Fine-featured, with a sharp nose and small ears studded with diamonds, her hair a graying auburn cut fashionably short.

"You're very late."

"I told you. I was working."

The woman's eyes flick over Leonora. "Who is this?"

"This? Oh, she's my new girlfriend. Te presento—"

"Linda," Leo says, linking her arm in Julian's. "Mucho gusto conocerle."

Julian forces a laugh. "Good, Linda. Que bue-no!" he says, enunciating as if to an idiot. "This is Señora Ma-ri-a An-to-nietta E-che-varria de Ze-la-ya de Du-e-ñas." Then, to the woman in the door: "No habla español. Yo soy su profesor."

"I see." The woman's gaze moves between them, her irritation checked by thin-lipped stoicism. When she reaches out her hand, Leo almost takes it. "I'll tell the girl we're four for dinner," the señora says, accepting Julian's flowers, already turning back to the bright foyer. "Now go inside. The general is hungry."

Julian cinches Leo's arm tight to his ribs. "Sí, mamá," he says.

Julian's father, the retired general, is thickset, imposing without being particularly tall. His eyes are close-set with tender pouches, his complexion patched with whiskers the razor missed. He gives the impression of grumbling even when he's made no sound at all. In the library, where an oil painting of Simon Bolívar hangs spotlit between shelves filled with Shakespeare, Hugo, Dante, he sips a glass of whiskey, turning it in the light, while his wife delivers observations in a bright, fricative accent Leo can't place.

"Mamá," Julian says, draining his glass. "You understand English. Why do you make me translate everything Linda says?"

"I also understand when a dog barks," says the señora. She has not looked at Leo since they arrived. "Pero in esta casa, se habla español."

"It's a lovely house," Leo says. "Did . . . Augustín grow up here?"

The señora won't meet her gaze. "Both of my sons did. They had an ideal childhood. Lima was different then. Safer. You weren't bothered in the street, shouted at. They used to ride their bicycles to Barranco without the least danger."

Leo waits for Julian's translation, then feigns vacuousness. "It seems safe now."

"It has been ruined. By people with no respect for history or culture. Criminals." She laments the pestilent shoeshine boys in the plazas, the new buildings that block the ocean view. "When my sons were born, we knew every family in this barrio. We saw their children at festivals and weddings. We didn't worry those children would one day point a gun at us. The invasions changed all that," she says. "Isn't that right, General?"

Julian's father sighs into his glass. "Leave it alone, mi amor."

"There are police everywhere now. And beggars. Young men whistling at women. People banging on pots and pans. They think the city belongs to them. And the government allows it," she says. "It lets the animals do as they please."

She sets her glass next to a framed photograph: a younger version of herself flanked by two teenagers outside the Louvre. The shorter boy, coarse black hair and chipmunk cheeks, is clearly Julian; the other has lighter, curlier hair, a quarterback's shoulders, a finely sculpted face that resembles his mother's. It could be anyone's family, Leo thinks, recalling a similar shot of her own family at Buckingham Palace that hangs on the kitchen wall.

Following her gaze the señora asks, "Augustín told you about his brother?"

"I've heard a lot about him."

"But he didn't tell you that tonight is Casimiro's birthday?"

"Mamá . . ." Julian says.

"No," Leo says, distracted by the photograph, by Casi's beauty, his posture of easy confidence. She feels the señora sizing her up: her frayed jeans and shapeless sweater, the bandanna that can't quite restrain her unwashed hair.

"I didn't think so. I'm sure you would have dressed differently."

In the dining room, they sit at a long table of polished walnut while a plump indigenous woman in a maid's uniform sets plates before them and refills their glasses. "The food is wonderful, señora," Leo says, tucking into a perfectly marbled steak, cold Caesar salad, asparagus thick as her thumb and sizzling with garlic and ají pepper. She forces herself to chew slowly—when has she last eaten this way? She tries not to think of Marta and the cumpas, the boiled potatoes they've had every night this week.

"This is Casimiro's favorite meal," the señora says. She looks down the table at her husband, raising her voice slightly. "You remember that, General?"

"Sí, mi amor," the general says.

While Julian and his mother discuss cousins in Miami, friends he hasn't seen since he left school, Leo concentrates on the rich flavors, the musical clink of silverware, safe in the cocoon of her presumed incomprehension. She struggles to absorb this new idea of Julian, to reconcile oil paintings and Argentinian steaks with the hotheaded radical who'd once thrown her into the street. When she meets his eyes she makes her face soften in fondness, playing along. But the señora hasn't forgotten Leo, has only allowed the meal to lull her, cobra-like, the wine to wear down her vigilance.

"Tell me, Linda, how long have you been in our country?"

After the translation, Leo says, "About nine months."

"And still you don't speak Spanish?"

The wine has made Julian's voice throatier, his gestures sloppy. "She's from the United States, mamá."

The señora ignores him. "And how did you meet Augustín?" This time, Leo really does have to wait for the translation: though she's heard the name several times now—*Augustín*—her brain still won't connect it to the man she knows.

"We met at the café," she chirps. "I ordered an Inca Kola."

"Of course." Then, to Julian, "You must meet many girls at that restaurant."

"I thought he was so charming," Leo says, reaching for his hand with a thrill of dark pride at her ability to play this role—inamorata, well-bred ornament—so convincingly. "You must be proud to have a son who's so smart and hardworking."

"Trabajar en un restaurante no es difícil," she says. The general moans, "Maria, please . . ." but she pays no heed. Preempting translation, she says, "Es una diversión. Algo para adolescentes. ¿Tú me entiendes?" she says, watching Leo's face.

"Mamá, I told you—"

"Augustín was a brilliant law student. Did he tell you that? But my baby doesn't care for responsibility. He has always avoided the difficult things. He doesn't understand that a country is built by hard work and sacrifice. That without these things you have anarchy, like we had for twelve years—children with guns, not willing to be adults, not willing to work, who only want to take what has been earned by others."

The general, who'd spent this recital probing his back teeth with a toothpick, clears his throat. "I can tell you, cariña, those children shot their guns like adults."

"Adults don't shoot guns at innocent people."

Julian leans back in his chair. "The army also killed innocent people, mamá."

"The terrorists killed them," the señora says. She has not taken her eyes off Leo. "No one died who distanced themselves from the animals, or reported them to the authorities. No one who made their loyalties clear."

"Lupe!" the general calls out. "Time for dessert." Leo glares at Julian, whose translation has lagged, until he tells her in reluctant English what his mother just said.

"But what if your loyalties aren't clear?" Leo holds her voice steady as the señora's. "What if it's your friend or your cousin, someone from the same village?"

"Linda," Julian says.

"Eso no importa," his mother says. "Si tu amigo sea terrorista—"

"What if it's someone in your own family? You expect people to turn in—"

"I expect people to denounce terrorists."

Ignoring Julian's alarm, Leo switches to Spanish. "Señora, would you denounce your own children?"

A flicker at the señora's jaw. Leo holds her breath, waiting for the señora to lose her composure, throw wine in her face. But she's played right into the señora's hand.

"If they associated with terrorists, they would no longer be my children."

At this, the general pushes back his chair and brushes crumbs from his shirt. "Your children . . ." he starts to say, but seeing his wife's face he stops himself. "The war is over, my love. Now it's time for coffee."

After he leaves, the room is very still, the warm-lit space too large. The señora refills Leo's glass, sets the bottle firmly in front of her.

"Of course the young are susceptible to all kinds of ideas," she says. "In Argentina it was the same: the communists and the liberation theologists and the Jews. They appealed to the sense of grievance. They seduced many young people, corrupted many families with their fantasies. The army was forced to fight at their level. No había opciones. No se puede pelear contra el fuego sin que la gente se queme."

"Mamá—" Julian says helplessly.

"Tú me entiendes, Linda, ¿no?"

"Sí, señora," Leo says.

For the first time, a genuine smile crosses the señora's face. "What I don't understand," she says, "is what a person like you is doing in this country. Don't you have a family in the United States?"

"I work for an NGO."

"Which one?"

"It's called Oportunidad Para Todos. We work with poor women in the new communities. We teach them how to read, how to open a bank account—"

"Yes, I know of it. Wasn't that group involved in a problem recently?"

"Last Christmas. The government destroyed some homes in Los Arenales. Several demonstrators were killed."

"Were you there?"

"Yes," Leo says. "One of my friends died."

The señora nods thoughtfully, folding her napkin into a perfect square and setting it on the table. "You must have told Augustín about it. I remember he was very upset."

"Señora—" Leo says, but she cuts her off.

"Well, I don't understand how stupid a person must be not to know how to read. You seem intelligent. Why would you choose to work with such people? I myself would be ashamed if a lazy girl from another country had to teach me to read."

"Mamá, this is enough," Julian says. "Linda? It's time to leave."

But Leo won't be moved. *This* is where the revolution is fought, she tells herself: against French wine, the family silver, the jeweled crucifix on the wall. "I'm sure you had the best tutors in Buenos Aires, señora."

Another carnivorous smile—and now she sees the resemblance between Julian and his mother. "Yes, I did. And still I brush my own hair every day."

Now Julian comes around and tries to pull out Leo's chair. "I think I'll take Linda home, mamá. You're very rude."

"Others are not so fortunate," Leo says. "I'm sure you care about them. That's what Jesus teaches, isn't it? 'As you do unto the least—'"

"It's people like you who harm them by giving them such ideas. If those women had stayed in their homes, they wouldn't need to read or open bank accounts. They knew everything they needed to know when they lived in the campo."

"If those women had stayed in their homes they'd be dead."

"Por el Sendero Luminoso."

"Or by someone else. The army didn't ask if you were rich or poor. They didn't distinguish." Leo brings her eyes to meet the señora's. "As you know."

The señora sniffs and answers wearily, disappointed by this direct thrust. "What I know is that my sons are attracted to cheap, impertinent women. But they'll grow out of it. Augustín," she says, turning from Leo as if she were an unpleasant smell, "I found some old photographs I want to show you. Please come upstairs."

Outside, Leo sits on the front step and lets the mist cool her face, realizing how parched the wine has left her, how stifling those paneled walls and chandeliers, the portraits of gluttonous ancestors in absurd uniforms. The neighborhood is quiet: a few notes from a passing car, the hiss and mewl of a cat cornering some nocturnal intruder. She breathes in the night-blooming jasmine, holding onto her fury, controlling it. So this is what Julian is fighting against, she thinks. All these months she's been cowed by what she saw as his authenticity, the purity of his ideals, when in fact she and Julian were just the same. The realization gives her power over him; she hadn't been sure what she wanted when she came looking for him. But she knows now.

A deep voice from the shadows cuts into her thoughts: "'Call me Ishmael.'"

The general stands a few yards away, backlit by the library window. The tip of his cigar pulses bright red.

"A classic," he says in English, pointing to the book in her hand. "When I read it in university I thought, 'Melville is a strange name for a Peruvian.' Because this book describes perfectly the Latino mind."

Leo eyes Julian's father, who seems not to notice the mist darkening his shoulders. She's had enough of polite conversation, enough pretense for one night.

"Thank you for dinner, señor."

He smokes his cigar, regarding the colorful fountain, the broad gate that seals them off from the street. "Always the impossible quest, the fantasy of total victory. A man must fulfill his destiny. He must stop at nothing, even if he tears down the world in his obsession. This is Ahab, no? God's plan has a pattern. It can be read in only one way. I've met many men like this. Prophets. Tyrants. Murderers."

"Animals," Leo says. "That's what your wife calls them."

"Men like this have always controlled Peru. They believe it is a different century, that the palaces of Madrid can rise again." Leo watches his face, not sure if he's saying what she thinks he's saying. Behind them, the front door opens and the señora's voice beckons, low and dangerous.

"Someone must put an end to this fantasy, Linda," the general says. "Someone must save us from imaginary white whales the common person can't see."

From the taxi she watches the neighborhood slide silently by, the cliffs rising before her eyes as the car descends in a long curve toward the ocean. Julian sprawls opposite her, head touching the window, face broken by light and shadow. He looks younger, some-how, newly vulnerable. Leo squeezes her hands in her lap, roused and inflamed by that vulnerability.

"Great party, eh?" he says. "I think she really liked you, you know?"

When he turns to her she lunges, smashes her mouth against his, shocked by the crack of tooth to tooth, slides her tongue over his in an access not of desire but of dominion.

"Soltera, Jesus Christ—"

She kisses him again, inhales the smoke and wine from his hot mouth, giddy with her newfound advantage. They're the same—he can no longer deny it. No more condescension—now he has to treat her as an equal, a point she proves with a gentle slap to his cheek. "No more jokes, *Augustín*. No more bullshit."

Julian turns, slowly working out from under her, until he has the leverage to shove her roughly back in her seat. "Fucking women," he says. "I told Chaski you were a bad idea. But that fool doesn't listen, just like you."

"Basta," she says, smoothing her clothes. "We need a leader, not a child. Would your brother act this way?"

He grabs her chin and squeezes. "You don't know anything about my brother."

"I'll scream," she says. The taxista glances nervously into the rearview. "How would the general feel if his son got arrested for attacking a girl?"

Julian glares another second, then retreats to his window. "He's heard worse."

Under the bright sky the beach looks spent and desolate. Scattered red lights dot the ocean, blinking in a slow, garbled code, falling away as the taxi climbs toward Pueblo Libre. Julian's face in shadow, she thinks of the photo in the general's library: one son confident, brimming with manhood, the other still awkward, standing slightly apart.

"When they came to the house that day—Marta and Josea—she refused to speak to them," he says. "They wanted my father to contact people in the military, in DINCOTE, to use his position to get Casi released. She wouldn't allow it."

"Why?"

He smiles to himself, a smile of pure loss that strikes, in Leo, an unexpected chord of compassion. "Because the military doesn't detain innocent boys from good families. They only detain terrorists."

A few blocks from the house Julian signals the driver to stop and hands him a bill, waving away the change. "Today's his thirty-third birthday," he says as they get out. Leo walks carefully, staying as close to Julian as she dares. "She's still waiting for a ransom note from Abimael. She keeps a bag of American dollars under her bed."

The streets are unusually still, even the neighborhood dogs holding their tongues. They walk in silence—almost companionable, shoulders brushing. Leo struggles to make sense of this new dynamic, these close-held secrets and what they portend.

"Marta and I came up with something," she says. "A plan. I think it could work."

Julian stares at the sky, now a slab of white wool stretched tight over Pueblo Libre. He stops to light a cigarette. "I'll talk to Miguel."

She lifts the cigarette from his fingers and takes a hard drag. "No more talking. The cumpas who took Victor Beale didn't spend their time talking."

Maybe it's her creeping sense of victory that makes her approach the house so heedlessly. Maybe it's because of the wine, the bruised tingle of the kiss on her lips, that she fails to note that every window is dark. Only once her key is in the gate does a quiver of unease rise from the shadows: it's too quiet, not a stray laugh or a murmur of music. As they step into the courtyard, Julian stops and breathes a warning; several thoughts come at once, with icy clarity—*it's not yet midnight—where is Marta—have the others left like Chaski— where will I go*—she notes the blankets over the windows, senses movement on the roof—just as the darkness folds around them, a hand clamps her mouth and barrels her toward the front door, Julian's body pressing behind her, many feet tripping over one another as they're rushed through the entryway, the living room—a shadow in the stairwell, another in the kitchen—as she braces to be struck or thrown to the floor one thought comes to her: *We never did anything.*

In the dark bedroom, the hands lower her to the floor. The room is crowded with bodies. An unfamiliar face looms close, pocked cheeks, a smashed nose—*Tranquila, Linda, tranquila*—as she thrashes toward the corner, shoes slipping and squeaking on the wood floor, clawing at the hand on her mouth. Then Marta crouches before her.

"¿Estás bien, Linda?" Leo shudders, gasps for breath. "¿Estás bien?"

She nods, swallowing the taste of metal, eyes burning. Marta scans her face and reaches for her hand. "Sí. I'm okay."

"Gracias a Dios." Marta exhales, slumps to her knees. "I didn't know where you were. I told César and Elvis to wait outside. Chini is on the roof. We didn't know who would come." The man with the pocked face watches carefully. "We had to be ready."

"Ready for what?" Julian says.

Marta whirls around to stare at him, her jaw working wordlessly. She looks back at Leo, at the men standing by the door.

"César," Julian says, "What the fuck is she talking about?"

Squaring his stance, the man with the pocked face says, "We thought they found Linda, too, compañero."

"Who found her?"

"The militares," he says. "The dogs who killed Josea and Álvaro."

277

The new issue hadn't arrived at the usual distribution sites. When César and Esteban went to the furniture store they found the front gates chained, the office windows blackened. A street vendor told them the store hadn't opened in days. César found a locksmith to open the back entrance. He had to force the door, which exhaled a blast of soot and smoke, kicked up a snowstorm of burned newsprint, black ash swirling, a crazed rat fleeing over their feet. In the middle of the room, tied to a chair and surrounded by charred bundles, they found Álvaro, his body untouched by the fire but his face a livid blue, arms crusted with blood where the ropes shredded his skin.

Julian stares at César. "Nobody else was there?"

"No, compañero."

Leo's hands and feet have started to itch. She feels an intense need to stand, a confusion about how one would do this. "Josea?" she manages.

"He was found a few hours ago under an overpass, not far from his shop," César says. "They shot him in the back. Then they cut off his balls, wrapped them in the front page of *The Eyes of the World*, and shoved them in his mouth."

"Oh, fuck . . ." Leo hears a voice—English, obviously hers—pinched and gasping. She clutches her abdomen, tries to focus on what César is saying but all she can think of is Julian's mother. "Oh, fuck . . . I don't understand—"

"Be quiet," Julian says.

"They didn't do anything," she says, her voice odd, quivering. She remembers her last meeting with Josea—how long ago? *Hija*, he'd called her. He was worried, she sees that now. But she'd been preoccupied with arrangements, payments. She'd ignored the signs. "Alvaro didn't want it anymore. The newspaper. Josea said after this one—"

"Linda," Julian says, his voice low and even, and she falls silent.

He goes to the window, pulls the blanket aside and lets it fall. He stalks out of the room and they all listen to his movements through the first floor. César and the others—Elvis, Esteban, Martillo, when did she learn their names?—exchange glances. They watch Marta, who stands by the door, hands at her neck. When Julian returns Marta clears her throat, still struggling to regain her composure.

"What are you doing here, compañero?" she says.

Julian ignores her. He says something to one of the other cumpas, who nods and pads upstairs. "Listen to me. Nobody leaves this house. Nobody goes anywhere." His voice is braced with urgency, a clarity to his words that pushes the panic back toward the walls. "You did well, Marta. You were smart."

"I asked what you're doing here," Marta says. She turns to Leo. "Compañera? Why did you bring him?"

Startled, Leo tries to say something but Julian holds up a hand. "Later. Right now we have to think carefully. No one leaves until I talk to Miguel."

"That's not possible," Marta says. "Not for me. Julian, you know—"

"It is possible."

"No, I have to see him," she says, her voice rising. César and the others shift in place. Julian takes Marta's arm, holding firm when she tries to pull away.

"Hermana," he says. "You are known. Just like Josea. You both worked with my brother." He watches Marta's face, something passing between them that Leo's never seen—something old and irrefutable, deeper than mistrust. "They're looking for you now."

"And when they come?" Marta whispers.

"They won't. They don't know this house. If they did, you'd already be dead."

They watch each other, listen to each other breathing. Marta starts to cry, tiny inhalations almost inaudible over the sound of Leo's own heartbeat. Again she pictures Josea's face, his wry, fatherly smile. *Everyone survived something*, he'd said.

Then, an awful thought: "Oh my god," she says, "Chaski."

Marta's sniffling abruptly stops. César curses under his breath.

"Claro," Julian says.

"He needs to know. What if they're looking for him?"

An uncomfortable pause, silent glances among the others. Quietly, Julian says, "They're not looking for him."

"How can you be sure?"

"Linda," Marta says. "Think."

At first she can't decipher Marta's meaning. When she does, she tries to stand but her legs have gone numb. "No," she says, pressing herself to the wall. "No, that's impossible. That's impossible!"

"Keep your voice down," Julian says.

"Why would he do that? I don't believe you." César holds her elbow to keep her from falling. "It's impossible. Why would he do that?"

"It was a message," Julian says.

"A message?" Her voice tightening, rising, she yanks her arm from César and lurches toward the door. "What message?"

Then Julian is standing over her, squeezing her shoulders. She knows his scent, his body's distinct presence. "Listen to me," he says. "Compañera, listen."

A year later, on a night of such pitiless cold that the fillings in her molars send steady, metal pain through her jaw, she'll watch the stars through the window of her cell and repeat the word: *message*. Billions of stars, smeared and shivery, vast explosions so far away they can't be understood though we try to read them, to shape them into tales for children—anything to contain that violence, to make it knowable. But the message can't be contained or controlled. It comes out of a clear blue sky and smashes into the tidiness of an ordinary day. You'll never know who sent it. Like those impossible stars: a burst of energy traveling untold distances in search of a recipient. It doesn't matter if you understand. There's nothing to understand. Only the fact of the message itself, proof that someone or something has taken notice of you. A sign that your own message, however tentative and unformed, has been received.

"What's the message?" Leo says. "Julian, what's the fucking message?"

ANDRES

"And what's with Colm?"

"Gone back to Ireland. Last week. I think his father is sick."

"That's too bad. What about your Dutch friend, Lisbeth?"

Jeroen made a sound of contempt. "That one was always too good for this place. She's in Lima now, I think, doing something for KLM."

"Oh? Maybe I'll give her a call. She's a good dancer."

"Ya, too good for you!" he said. "Ah, please accept my apology, Señor el Rey de la Salsa. When do you come back to our humble city, by the way?"

When I talked to Jeroen I felt nostalgic for Babilonia, for icy days that started at noon and ended at dawn, reeling past ancient churches in a sweaty haze. I missed my little room with its garden view, the hummingbirds, the wash of bells in the hills above. Most of all, I missed the sense that nothing I did meant anything, or had consequences for anyone. It was a profound kind of freedom—one I'd begun to suspect was gone for good.

He updated me on the usual suspects: Oswaldo was back from guiding his tour, a plaster cast on one ankle from what he called a "cunt-related accident" in Punta del Este; Flor and Mark had hooked up for a few weeks, until one night at Paddy's she poured a drink over his head, to the general amusement. He asked again when I was coming back. "Or has La Leo recruited you into the revolution? Please don't tell me you've become political, Andres. No one will recognize you."

"Have you seen Lu?"

A half-second pause. "Not much. She's working a lot, I think."

I could glean, from his careful nonchalance, what was happening in my absence: the speculation, the whiff of scandal. Everyone knew what it meant that I'd been gone so long. They'd seen it before: Mark's long hiatus and short-lived marriage, Oswaldo's tours, the comings and goings of countless expats. It was what appealed to us about this life: you could get out whenever it set its hook too deep. It was a dream you could wake from at will—and like a dream, once you'd woken it made no sense to worry about the people inside.

But I would not forget about Lucrecia. I was not one of those people, I told myself, who left a mess for others to clean up. I was someone who lived up to my responsibilities, and eventually I would live up to this one. I owed her that much.

It had been a week since we'd spoken. She'd left several plaintive voicemails, describing her listlessness and cramps, nausea so intense she'd missed shifts at the restaurant. Her ears rang, she'd become sensitive to light. She told her mother she'd started doing yoga, to explain the slow, achy way she walked.

"Winter is almost here, Andres," she said. "Soon is Inti Raymi." Her family had relatives coming for the festival, she said. How would she keep this a secret?

Inti Raymi was the Inca New Year, Babilonia's Mardi Gras: a four-day bacchanalia timed to the winter solstice. The streets and hostels flooded with jubilant partygoers, the clubs stayed packed until breakfast. I'd hoped to be back by then, to turn in the story and go home in time to celebrate. But all I had to show for six weeks of research was a file swollen with illegible notes, a voice recorder on its third set of batteries, a dozen failed attempts at a lead. Each morning I downloaded more case studies, more articles and transcripts; each night I sat up long after everyone had gone to sleep and stared at the words, trying to believe the preposterous things they said. I wanted to tear up the pages, to hide under the bed. Was there any behavior that wouldn't be defended by somebody, somewhere?

There was not. For confirmation of this all I had to do was check the news. The revelations which had been so shocking three years ago had become commonplace: waterboarding, black sites, targeted assassinations, domestic spying, the baldfaced lies with which these were hidden or explained away. The Pentagon was still denying the recent drone strike in Pakistan—despite the photographs of dead children and wailing mothers, despite condemnation by the International Red Cross—while defending the Predator program as "necessary to protect American lives." I clicked from site to site in a kind of delirium, until I lost track of which country I was reading about. The stories overlapped, the repetitions, reflections of the one in the other—a kind of historical plagiarism, as if the same sick, lazy people were writing the lines.

"You're wasting time," Jack said. "Iraq? Guantánamo? People are tired of that shit."

"But it's the same story. The belligerence, the overreach. People need to see . . ."

"It's not the same story. Look, dude," he said, suddenly serious. "I'm starting to worry about this. The primaries are getting all the clicks now. That's what people are sharing—not this torture stuff. It's super-depressing."

"Primaries?"

"I want to run this thing, but we gotta do it soon. Two weeks at the latest. Stop getting distracted, okay? Time to kill your darlings. Forget about all these *ideas*!"

But I wasn't distracted. On the contrary, each day I grew more committed to the story, more certain it needed to be written. I just didn't know how. I'd read Maxine Gelb's book, *The Leo I Know*, consumed it in a long afternoon of cigarettes and coffee, looking for clues; but it gave me the same feeling as all the newspaper stories, the sense of skimming over a glass surface, unable to break through. After seeing the house in Pueblo Libre, I'd written ten pages about life inside: the waiting, the ironies of domesticity, the weeks she must have spent on *The Eyes of the World*. But imagining these things felt like a violation, like breaking and entering. The next morning I deleted it all. I took the photo from the press conference and taped it over my desk. Leo's burning eyes stared right through me, into Damien's guest room, as if she could see the ashtrays and beer bottles, the heaped laundry, the drawn shade.

You? she seemed to ask. I couldn't look away. They sent *you*?

But I had to find a way. With two weeks left I would have to cross the line. I went to Calle Tarata, where a black obelisk marked the site where twenty-five people died. I went to La Cantuta, and then to the hillside where the murdered students were buried; to the ordinary house in Surco where Abimael had been captured; to the Vista de los Incas golf resort, on the spot where Los Muertos once stood. I took photos, scribbled notes—as if such tokens might cohere into a kind of presence. I stood across the avenue from the Chorrillos women's prison, its block-long roof frilled with razor wire. *She's in there,* I told myself, peering at the high walls. *Leonora Gelb is in there right now.* The walls stared back, stubbornly two-dimensional.

One morning I took a bus downtown and stood on a long line of people waiting to visit Congress. The line followed a high, spiked fence, through which I could see flowerbeds, shade trees, an imposing statue of Bolívar on horseback. The ornate white building floated behind it all, majestic and dreamlike. Soldiers patrolled the line. Vendors and beggar children jostled around us and on the opposite corner protestors hoisted photos of Leo's screaming face plastered over with the phrase *¡Muerte a terucos!*

I waited over an hour, fighting a growing sense of unreality, the feeling that I was just another tourist, waiting to be entertained— the soldiers, the protestors, were all part of the show. When a drunk started to put on an incoherent mime act, everyone in line laughed, until a soldier dragged him away, to a smattering of applause.

Eight hundred sticks of dynamite. Five thousand rounds of ammunition. The court said they planned to storm this building, shoot hostages, overthrow a government. It named Leonora Gelb, of Cannondale, NJ, as the architect of this implausible bloodbath. This was the story I was supposed to be writing. But nothing in my experience equipped me to understand such a thing. As the high gates opened to let a file of soldiers in berets and desert camo pass through, it came to me that I didn't even believe it.

I left the line, sat on a bench and stared at my notebook. I didn't believe it, any of it: that she intended to invade this fortress, to blow it up, to kidnap anyone. I'd never believed it. It was all, finally, beyond my ability to imagine. I sat a long time, amazed by this revelation. That's why I couldn't write it, I realized, why all the research in the world had not sufficed. How do you write a story that you don't believe?

. . .

That night I sat in bed staring at my computer, not typing a word. Stephanie lay reading with her back to me. Since the morning in Pueblo Libre she'd been gentler with me, mildly encouraging. She seemed to find my frustration amusing, even cute—as if I were a cocker spaniel trying to turn a doorknob. I must have made some sound of despair, because she turned to me with a look of concern.

"Still stuck?"

"I don't know what to do," I said. She watched me, waiting. "I don't think I can write it. But I have to write it." I'd come that far, I said, spent months thinking of nothing else, but I still didn't understand. "How do you do it? All these stories . . .death, torture, everyone killing everyone. How can anyone . . ." I shook my head at my own childishness. "I just wanted to do something that matters. Like you, what you write really matters."

She peered at me as if she saw something new, still too faint to understand. She used to believe it mattered, she finally said. She used to think risking her life to write stories about the war was an important political act. When she'd first come to Lima, in the last months of the war, she'd sought out student radicals and blacklisted reporters, lawyers for accused terrorists, aid workers who sheltered fighters coming in from the provinces. She'd spent a week at a training camp in the jungle, where fifty cadres studied bombmaking and read Sun Tzu. She recounted all this in a distant, wondering voice, as though it were someone else's life. One day, at a protest in the Plaza San Martín, a woman she knew, a mother of five, was arrested. Soldiers dragged her to the ground and beat her, aiming their clubs between her legs, while Stephanie crouched behind a bench a few yards away.

"What a reporter is supposed to do is take notes, maybe a photograph," she said. "But that's not what a human being is supposed to do."

"What did you do?"

She propped herself on an elbow. In the dim light I could just make out the shape of her brow, her thin nose. The faded bruise had left a ghostly map around her eye. "I wrote the story. Almost nobody picked it up. The *International Herald-Tribune* cut it to ninety words and ran it on page ten."

"Stephanie—" I said.

"What I'm saying is Leonora Gelb isn't a mystery to me. Under the right circumstances, around the right people, that could easily have been me." She poked my arm and I startled. "Who knows, Andres? Maybe it could have been you."

She was joking, but I was surprised at how it stung. I knew it would never have been me—caring about something enough to put my privilege, my safety on the line. Not this me, not Andres. We both knew.

What I wanted to tell Stephanie, what I wanted to convince myself, was that I hadn't always been this way. Once, a long time ago, I'd thought of myself as a good person, an honorable person. I recycled, donated to Oxfam, gave other drivers the right of way. I was part of the solution, as we used to say—though how that worked wasn't entirely clear. It had something to do with writing, with teaching writing, something about how art could help create a better world.

But after seeing the images from Abu Ghraib I could no longer tell myself such lies. I knew I was responsible, that the empathy I extolled was just a front for cowardice. I couldn't bring myself to read my students' stories—anguished tales of teenage cutters, lonely vampires, prom dates gone awry—or to consider my own novel, with its tiny, foolish concerns. A fever of renunciation stole over me, a suffocation I felt each time I saw the photos: bruised men lying atop one another, Lynddie England with her leashed prisoner, the black-hooded scarecrow on his electric torture-box. When the term ended I sold everything I owned—furniture, stereo, a vintage Fender Telecaster, my long-suffering Ford Probe—all the meaningless accumulations that sickened me, that felt like a kind of pollution. Not until my apartment was empty, my footsteps echoing on the hardwood, was I able to breathe again.

In Babilonia, I'd kept my possessions to a minimum: one towel, one set of sheets, just enough clothing to get by. I could have afforded a bigger room, something with a kitchen, but I preferred that small space—as if I were a package that might break if it slid around too much. I took no pride in this austerity; there were no politics behind it, no principles. It was a compulsion, a kind of spiritual anorexia: I needed to be free, and the more things that clung to me the less free I could feel. That's what I didn't tell people about life in Babilonia: it wasn't what I did or felt, it was about who I needed to be.

But I couldn't be that person anymore. Leo's story, everyone's stories, Stephanie's black eye, the murdered children in Pakistan—it was as if a charm had lifted, as if the outside world I'd tried so hard not to think about had started to think about me. What it saw was all too easy to imagine: someone who had given nothing, suffered nothing, who'd told himself a bogus story of reinvention but who, in reality, had changed nothing more than his mailing address. A novelist, a layabout, a teacher, the Salsa King—in times like ours, didn't it all amount to the same thing?

I had two weeks left to atone. The next afternoon, I went back to Pueblo Libre alone. I walked Calle Almagro a dozen times, considered the house from different angles—the Big Wheel still lay wheels-up in the garden, the Toyota sat dormant at the door. As night came on, the dark house receded like a missing tooth. When I heard a neighbor's gate rattle open I hurried off, a stealthy gringo, a fugitive. Back at Damien's I sat in front of Leo's photo, smoking cigarette after cigarette. I didn't know which of us was staring at the other. *It's your last chance*, I kept thinking. I opened the computer and typed a single line. I typed it again, in boldface. I tried a different font. Then I took a red marker from the drawer and scrawled it across the photograph: *WHO AM I?*

Again the court approved her parole, and again the protests flared. A radio station urged listeners to demonstrate outside the homes of the judges and lawyers, and the Justice Ministry was repeatedly defaced with right-wing graffiti. Outside the Chorrillos prison, demonstrators set tires on fire and spilled trash into the avenue. The mayor took to the airwaves, warning the attorney general of "dangerous reactions" throughout the city if Leonora were to be released.

"La Leo is safe where she is," he said. "Outside, who can say what would happen?"

"The poor girl. They will tear her to pieces," Damien said, glancing up from a magazine at the TV, where the old footage ran in silence, captioned by one word: *¿Libre?* Carlito was in the shower, singing at the top of his lungs, getting ready for another night at El Castillo. The tension between them had settled into polite indulgence; when I saw them together they spoke in complete sentences and rarely touched. Carlito's dislike for me had hardened into disdain, expressed occasionally in small gestures but more often in a bland astonishment that I was still there at all, that I hadn't simply dissolved of my own insubstantiality. Damien was never anything less than gracious, but I'd begun to sense a mild anticipation when I talked about my progress, as if he'd heard a rumor I might be leaving soon.

"You won't join us?" he said now. "Yesenia has been asking for you . . ."

"That's the last thing I need," I said. She'd left me a message that day, asking if I would give her another dance lesson. The old Andres would never have turned her down.

"Poor, poor Andres," Damien said. "Life was much simpler in Babilonia, no?"

In the next room, Carlito's hair dryer whined to life. Damien turned to straighten photos on a shelf. When I saw the back of his neck—slightly sunburned, as if he'd just cut his hair— the care with which he lined up their books, I felt a surge of affection and gratitude. He'd put up with me for two months. What had he gotten in return?

"I'm going to finish soon," I said. "Really. A few more days. Some loose ends."

His hands stopped moving but he didn't turn around. "You know you can stay as long as you need."

The next day, as I walked up the Avenida Brasil with its proliferation of fast-food restaurants and its gladiatorial combi traffic, I vowed to live up to my word. I would take care of a few last items, plow ahead, meet my deadline—and to hell with what I believed, what I could or couldn't imagine. *Something* had happened, that much was undeniable; figuring it out, telling the real story, had become an obsession. Leo's world had taken over, expanded to the very edges of my awareness. Nothing else mattered.

The house was the largest on the block, broad and angular in a way that made it look flat against the whitish sky. Its neighbors shrank back as if to hide from its many windows. In the wet weather, the green paint around the windows looked darker and the roses—some withered and losing petals, others open obscenely wide—stood garish against the walls. But something had changed—had that curtain been drawn yesterday? Was the car parked in a different spot? Feeling my blood quicken, as if from a slug of strong coffee, I walked to the gate. Part of me was shocked to find it open.

"¿Sí?" said the woman who came to the door.

I'd expected a skinny criolla, possibly blonde, but this woman had the bronze complexion and wide features of an indigena. She was in her thirties, short and broad-shouldered. She wore a pink sweater and a long skirt, and her bare painted toenails stood out against the white tile of the entryway.

"Me llamo Andres," I said. My heart thudded with disbelief. I could hardly get the words out. "I'm sorry to disturb you."

"¿Sí, señor?"

"Can I come inside? I'd like to see your house."

Her bemused smile slowly turned anxious. She moved to fill the doorway. From what I could see, the inside was nothing like I'd imagined: high ceilings, wall-to-wall carpet, warm light from hidden recesses. It confused me, as if everything had been rearranged since my last visit. Behind her, a tiny raincoat slumped on the floor beside a pair of Dora the Explorer boots, and over a small glass table hung a crude needlepoint of a llama in a bowler hat, the phrase ¡Yo soy peruana! scrawled in jaunty yarn letters.

"Don't be frightened," I said. "I know it's a strange thing to ask . . ."

"¿Que quiere aquí, señor? We don't want to buy anything."

I felt myself smiling crazily. "Of course not. I just want to look, okay?" She watched me steadily. I had the urge to rush past her and I closed my eyes until it went away. I gestured at the house as if maybe she'd never seen it before. "Something happened in this house."

At this the woman raised her chin, recognition smoothing her features. From another room, a man's voice called out but she ignored it. She took a step toward me and pulled the door shut behind her.

"Nothing happened here, señor," she said. She spoke in the voice of a mother scolding a child. "Whatever you are talking about, it was a long time ago. No one wants to remember things like that. Who are you to come here and bother us on a Sunday?"

"I'm a writer," I said. To my ears, it sounded limp and desperate. I sensed the neighbor woman listening on the other side of the wall. "I'm sorry to intrude. But I need to understand what happened. This is history, people's lives. It's important." I held out my hands as if to receive alms. "All I need is five minutes."

When I sputtered to a stop, she waggled a finger in my face. "Don't tell me what is important. This is not your house. It's not a museum. We bought this house. Our children live here. It has nothing to do with you."

I was still smiling like a moron. I almost took her hand. "Just five minutes?"

She crossed her arms. For an instant my heart leapt. "The war is over. We don't want writers, we want peace. Go away now," she said, stepping back inside. "If I see you again across the street, watching like a thief, I am going to call the police."

Another loophole was discovered, paperwork to be processed, protocols followed to the letter. It could be weeks, the news reports said, or not at all. Lucrecia was calling every day. Her father suspected something, she said. If he found out, he would throw her out of the house. Jack had stopped calling entirely.

Desperate to accomplish something, to check even one thing off my list, I went to San Isidro to visit Dr. Rausch in his clinic. We had more to talk about, I told myself—our interview had ended badly, before I'd gotten what I needed. It was a fine, chilly morning, the air tight and clear—football weather, Fitzgerald would have called it. I found the address on a wide lane of fan palms and fruit trees. A guard told me to go around the side, where I was buzzed through a plain steel door into a pleasant waiting area. A rococo settee upholstered in striped satin sat below a framed print of Picasso's "Don Quixote." By the slow blink of the receptionist's eyes, I knew I was not the usual visitor, that the men who usually stood in this room wore suits and gold watches, brusquely making arrangements for daughters or wives who waited in the car.

"It's perfectly natural, of course," said Dr. Rausch. "You must forget the expectations of others, the so-called conventional wisdom. What is wise about allowing lives to be ruined?"

He sat behind a giant mahogany desk, half of which was covered with globes of various sizes—new and antique, some with topographic texture, others lit from within. He had not been surprised to see me—as if he, too, sensed something unfinished.

"Is that how you felt during the war? As a doctor did you think it was your duty to help people, even if those people were . . ." I could not come up with the right word. I did not want to say "terrorists."

He frowned and steepled his gnarled hands. "Those years hardly matter now."

"How can you say that?"

"Have you read your Joyce, my friend? 'History is a nightmare from which I am trying to awake.' But it is the idea of history itself that keeps us asleep, prisoners to an imagined continuity. Once we discard this idea, we wake immediately. We are free.

"Now," he said, "let's talk about why you're really here."

He showed me around the clinic: the procedure room with its gleaming steel fixtures and immaculate sinks; the recovery area, bedecked with vases of silk flowers and photos of tropical beaches. Only the absence of windows distinguished it from any other doctor's office, that and the air of poised watchfulness. There was no margin for error, I understood—if something should go wrong even the power and money of the men who brought their mistresses here could not protect Dr. Rausch. Those same men—judges, politicians, executives—would crush him under the full opprobrium of Peruvian law.

"Most women need only an hour or two to rest. It's quite amazing, how quickly the body heals itself. More than one has told me she feels like a new person entirely." He leaned on his cane with both hands, rheumy eyes sunken in their orbits. I must have looked nervous, searching for something to rest my eyes on. I felt dizzy, disoriented—I'd never imagined myself in a place like that.

"You'll come at night," he said as he led me back to the waiting area. "Your friend shouldn't eat for twelve hours before the procedure. Call that day and let the girl know when you'll arrive."

"Wait," I stammered. I'd only wanted information, I said. "I don't know yet, if this is the best . . . option?"

He fixed me again with those wet, steady eyes. On the wall behind him, Picasso's Quixote was just a jumble of black lines under a burning sun.

"My friend, you are a writer, yes or no?" When I didn't answer, he reached for my shoulder. I hated him then. "A story must move forward. One action followed by the next. Good or bad, wise or foolish—someone must decide.

"I have lived longer than you," he said, "and I can tell you there is nothing noble about suffering. Those who cannot avoid it take no pride in it. Those who can avoid it are fools not to."

I left the office in a state of giddy irritation, blinking in the light as I walked through the center of San Isidro, past high-end boutiques and sober French restaurants, a lingerie shop across from an eighteenth-century chapel. At a streetcorner, I sensed someone approaching—a beggar, an old woman in dusty skirts, but a policeman's quick whistle intervened and she turned aside. How was any of it possible, I thought? Had any of it—the war, Dr. Rausch, Leonora—really happened? I could not reconcile that fastidious clinic with the stories I'd been told, the impossible juxtaposition of gentility and barbarism everywhere I looked. How could such things live side by side?

"I want you to come to Lima," I told Lucrecia. "Can you take a few days off?"

"Lima? Why?" She'd never been to the capital, unlike many of her friends. When people talked about Lima, Lu looked uncertain and vaguely horrified, like a student driver who gets handed the keys to an eighteen-wheeler.

"I miss you, Lulu," I said. And it was true. I missed her small ears and her agreeability, the comfort of her body at night. I missed the feeling of being in a taxi with her at dawn, the old buildings sliding past, the sugary new light. "I want you to go to a better doctor. I want you to feel better," I said, adding, "I'll pay for everything."

"When you come back, I feel better."

"Lu, you have to take care of yourself. I'm worried about you."
I could hear her wavering and I pressed harder. "We could have a
little vacation. I'll take you to a nice restaurant. You can see the
ocean for the first time."

She was quiet a moment. "But Andres, is Inti Raymi soon." Her
family would celebrate the New Year with days of feasts in their
neighborhood, far from the tourist revelry. Her uncle Teófilo was
coming from his village near Andahuaylas, she said. Teo had been a
rondero during the war. He'd helped defend his village. "My father
says you can come to our house to meet him. You can talk with Teo
about the terroristas."

"You told your father about me?" I said.

"Amor," she said.

I stopped on a corner. Across the street, a modern building
soared into the haze, dark glass skin warping the low shapes that
surrounded it. "I've talked to so many people," I said. "I just have
to write it, don't you see? I have to finish the story, so everything
can be like it was before. Te quiero, Lulu," I said. "You know that?"

She was silent a moment. "Sí, Andres," she said.

I could hear cars honking, men's voices arguing. "So you'll
come?"

Another pause. My heart soared. "I have to think," she said, her
voice fading with doubt, as if I were a stranger who'd called with a
ludicrous proposition. I suppose I was.

It was Yesenia who showed me the way, if unwittingly. She called
again, teasing me for avoiding her. "Maybe after so much time in
Babilonia, you are afraid of Lima woman? Don't be afraid, Andres!
Only I want to make a friend of the famous writer."

She invited me to an art gallery in Barranco, where a friend of
hers had a show. Why not? I thought. My days had grown pur-
poseless, clogged with fruitless effort. As Jack's deadline loomed
I veered between despair and a lunatic conviction that inspiration
was around the corner, taking aim at me. Either way, it was out of
my control. Why not have a little fun before the curtain fell?

The gallery was a long, narrow space with wood floors and

exposed girders. A wall of windows looked out on a deep ravine that ran to the ocean, crossed by a quaint footbridge on which tourists bunched up to take pictures. I sipped white wine while Yesenia held my arm and chattered to her friends in Spanish too fast and slangy for me to follow. They laughed en masse, expressed mild interest in me—less in my being a writer than in my living in Babilonia which, like Yesenia, they seemed to regard as both shrewd and faintly lascivious.

While Yesenia and her friends gossiped, I wandered amid the sculptures—narrow, tormented shapes, vaguely human, ripped off from Giacometti except for colorful paper strips that sheltered the figures or wrapped them like shrouds: snatches of advertisements for perfume, cruise ships, luxury cars. It was an obvious, vulgar gesture, and I quickly grew bored. What did any of this matter? In 1991, a car bomb had destroyed a police station a few blocks from this gallery. The next year, DINCOTE captured three Philosophers in a nearby hostel. I looked around at the lousy art, the tourists swarming the bridge below. Was this what anyone had fought for?

Eventually Yesenia came to fetch me, dragging me to the sidewalk where her friends were flagging taxis and checking their phones. "Larcomar! Larcomar!" they shouted to one another. "See you at Larcomar!"

"What's Larcomar?" I said, as our cab zoomed through a long, palm-lined curve.

She rolled her eyes and pulled me closer. She was flushed and gap-toothed, jarringly pretty. "Andres, you are like a primitive!"

Even after months in glittering Lima, I was unprepared for Larcomar, which spread bright and broken across the cliffs of Miraflores. It came in and out of sight as the taxi traced the curving shoreline, a riot of color, crawling like a wasps' next. We waited at the top of long, curved escalators for the others to arrive and sound washed up at us: gusts of conversation, the ocean's roar, shrieking children, trashy pop songs; below was a frantic pit surrounded by window displays, video screens—the churning stomach of an electronic monster. I was mesmerized, incredulous—as if the malls of my childhood, with their crass trinkets and sickening food courts, had been reborn as this strobing, hypertrophic maze, every face smeared with delight.

As we descended to the first of many levels—Banana Republic, Gucci, Dunkin Donuts, screens flashing with new cars, celebrities, local tourist attractions—Yesenia swept an arm, as if to embrace all the noise and commerce, and beyond it the ocean with its ribbon of sunset. Paragliders traversed the marbled pink sky, tiny silhouettes in transit to another world. "You see, Andres? My city is beautiful!"

She marched us to T.G.I. Friday's and waved a pale, bangled arm until a hostess found a table large enough to accommodate our party. I felt empty, somehow terrified. While the others gorged themselves on hamburgers, barbecued ribs, flagons of imported beer, buckets of fries, I watched the room of young professionals in their pressed pants and button-down shirts who chatted on cell phones, clinked glasses, laughed and shouted from table to table and snapped their fingers for service. Above the bar, a TV flashed news from abroad: John McCain, the New York Stock Exchange, South Waziristan, Roger Federer. No one was watching. A friend of Yesenia's got up to talk on his phone, pacing blindly before the kitchen door; when a waiter came through holding an overloaded tray, they nearly collided and he shot the waiter a malevolent glare. I set down my fork.

"You don't like the food?" someone asked.

"I already ate," I said.

Across the room, a wall of tall windows looked out on the chaos. From where we sat you could see part of the two levels above; and beyond, high-rises presided over the malecón, a puzzle of lit windows looking down at us. Somewhere not far from here, the rumor went, Leo's parents had bought a small apartment for her to live in. No one knew exactly where. But as I drained my glass I imagined it was in one of those very buildings, that somehow she could see us even now. When a group of servers swarmed a nearby table to sing "Happy Birthday," in English, I pushed back my chair.

"Where are you going, mi amor?" Yesenia said, blinking sweetly.

"Back to Damien's. I have to start writing."

"Tomorrow!" she said. She reached for my hand, to the amusement of her friends. She was a little tipsy, smiling at her own forwardness. "Why you are always so serious? Look at this. The people, the ocean. Stay with me, Andres. Look at my city. You don't think is beautiful?"

Everyone was watching us. I made a big show of lifting her hand to my lips and she blushed. As I made for the exit I took a last look at the room, the garish scenery, the bloated faces. What I saw wasn't beautiful. It wasn't even Peru.

"No way," Jack said, when I called him two days later. "No freakin' way, dude."

"Just listen—"

"Are you nuts? Did you catch some tropical brain-wasting shit?"

"Listen to me. It makes sense, don't you see? Everything I've been trying to figure out. This is the problem, why I've been so blocked— the house, the guns, everything she said . . . it's the missing piece. Don't you see?"

I was babbling. I closed the computer and turned away so as not to disturb people around me. A light wind was picking up. Seagulls sidled nervously along a brass railing and out over the ocean pelicans fell from the sky as if shot.

"Let me get this straight," Jack said. "I sent you to Lima like two months ago to write about Leonora Gelb—*the real Leonora Gelb*—and this terrorism shit. I flew you first class! I'm sitting here waiting, while you read, like, *philosophy books*. I've got a business to run! And now you call me with this crazy-ass theory. What did you think I was gonna say?"

"It's more like a month and a half."

"You've lost it, dude. I'm going to pretend this conversation never happened—"

"Just listen," I said. "Can you do that?"

At a nearby table, two Japanese women surrounded by shopping bags watched me cautiously. I tried to light a cigarette, but the wind was too strong. After two days at Larcomar I'd become a fixture, moving between Friday's, Starbucks, and a cantina called Sol de Havana where the bartenders had handlebar mustaches and the waitresses wore hats full of plastic fruit. The security guards all recognized me, muttering into their wrists when I changed tables or went to the restroom, but I ignored them, as I ignored the many calls that came in—Yesenia, Lucrecia, two this afternoon from Damien. I subsisted on lattés, croissants, and rubbery enchiladas, buffeted by the tides of shoppers and gawkers and after-work drinkers that surged and ebbed down the escalators. But I was making progress, banging at my laptop for hours without pause, all of it finally coming out, every bit of it: Leonora's story as it had never been told before.

"All this time there was something I didn't get, some piece of it," I said. "What they said she did, or planned—it was too far from my experience. I had no way in . . ." I hunched over and worked the cigarette lighter until it caught. "Hemingway said a story's like an iceberg—nine-tenths of it you can't see—"

"Dude—"

"This is what's under the water, Jack. It's so much more interesting than the facts! Everyone already knows the facts. They can look them up. We're going to tell them what they don't know. *That's* what's interesting here. That's the art."

I sucked hard on the cigarette, watched the wind whip the smoke into nothing. I was keyed up, brimful with the story. For the first time in weeks, or years, I felt a sense of purpose. It was all I could do not to hang up and get back to work.

"I don't give a fuck about Hemingway," Jack said. "I don't give a fuck about art. I hired you to write a story. A *true* story—"

"But that story makes no sense!" I said. "A girl just turns around and decides to invade Congress? To assassinate people? It's not even her country! No way, Jack," I said, sliding the computer into my bag. "It's bullshit. I won't write bullshit." A guard was coming toward me and I walked the other way. The main courtyard was packed with people lined up for the latest *Mission: Impossible* movie. "Give me two more days," I said, shouldering through. "Then you'll see for yourself. I just have to write about the raid, her capture. Then you can decide."

There was a long pause. "Sorry, dude. There's no time. Honestly? I was interested in this for like ten minutes, but it passed a couple months ago."

"Jack, wait—"

"Don't worry, you'll get a kill fee. Send your expenses to HR.

Listen," he said, "thanks for trying. Really. Give me a shout if you want to do a column sometime."

I stepped onto the escalator, clutching the handrail as Larcomar fell away. It was late afternoon, a sunset the color of clouded tea reflected in hundreds of windows above the malecón. I needed to get home, to lock myself in the guest room and finish the story. When Jack saw what I'd made, he'd reconsider, I felt sure. He'd have to admit it was more interesting, more believable—a better story. If not, I'd figure something else out. All my research, all the time I'd asked of strangers, their generosity—I could not repay them with nothing, though nothing was what they now expected of me. The wind dropped, a light spatter of rain began to fall. I'd find a way, I thought, rising into that many-eyed gaze.

When I got back to the apartment, Carlito confronted me in the living room. "Where have you been? Damien was calling you."

"I was working."

"Working," he repeated, not bothering to hide his contempt. Damien stood in the door of the guest bedroom, his back to me. For a second I had the crazy idea they were moving out, that they'd decided the only way to get away from me was to leave. But when he turned, I was shocked to see that he'd been crying. I could just make out Stephanie sitting at the edge of the bed, tightening the straps on her backpack.

"What's going on?" I said. "Steph? Are you alright?"

Her face was blank. "You'll have the bed to yourself again."

I tried to think of something to say. Had she somehow heard something? Had she talked to Jack? I cursed myself for not coming home earlier, for not explaining it to her myself. I owed her that much. I sat next to her and put a tentative hand on her back.

"Listen, I'm sorry I didn't talk to you. It's just, I finally knew how to get started, you know? But I want your feedback. I know you're busy. I know you've got things to deal with back in Babilonia, but . . . well, can it wait? Just a couple of days?

"I haven't told you this, but you've really helped me. To understand things. To see the big picture." The thought of her leaving alarmed me, her half of the bed empty; unweighted by her belongings the room might float off like a soap bubble until it popped. "The truth is I wanted to write something you'd approve of."

She hadn't looked at me this whole time, though little by little her back stiffened to my touch. Now she spoke quietly. "There was a riot. In a prison in Kandahar."

I could hear the tea kettle whistling outside the door, the hush of the others listening. "A riot? What prison?"

She shook her head. "They didn't tell me the name. My brother's team . . ." She let out a breath. "They cut his throat. They killed him."

We sat without speaking, her shoulders rising and falling against my hand. Once, twice, I rubbed her back, but this motion was absurd, offensive in its pointlessness. She endured it only because she didn't have the energy to ask me to stop. I remember staring at her hair, tousled and dull in the dim room, and waiting to feel pain, to overflow with grief, like Damien. But part of me just wanted to get back to my story.

"Andres?"

"Yes?"

"My flight leaves in two hours."

"Okay."

She finally looked up, her eyes dull and beyond patience. "Could you go to the other room and let me change?"

As I pulled the door shut, my eyes fell on the photo taped to the wall, the desperate scrawl: *WHO AM I?*

In the living room, that same face stared back from the TV: the wild hair and raw eyes, the feral mouth, white spit at the corners. I was trapped, beset by her image on all sides. Damien sat hunched on the couch, head in his hands, Carlito next to him with arms flung across the cushions in indignation. As I tried to think of what to say that could explain my unforgivable presence, the picture changed, the words *En Vivo* flashed on the screen. An older woman stood on the steps of the Supreme Court, speaking into a bank of microphones.

"All Peruvians join with me in celebrating justice," she said, reading from a piece of paper. "Peru today is a fair and modern country, where the rule of law protects everyone without bias. David and I want to thank our legal team, and the many people in the government who have given their time and energy . . ."

It was the first time I'd seen Maxine Gelb up close, live, not fossilized in old newsprint. She was small and narrow, with deep frown lines and a thin, sharp nose. High cheekbones and pixie-cut gray hair made her look whittled by exhaustion, polished by her long martyrdom. Only her eyes—bright and accusatory, painfully knowing—resembled her daughter's.

"We are pleased that Peru has decided to look forward, not backward—" she turned briefly to cover a cough and someone started to shout, a man's voice, cracking with fury. The camera turned to look for him in the crowd. When other voices joined in, the lawyer pulled Maxine away from the microphones and back toward the building. There were more shouts—and then a series of fast, loud pops, smoke. The camera swung wildly, knocked askew by fleeing bodies, ducked heads. Finally it steadied, zooming in on a small cloud rising from the pavement: firecrackers.

I found myself standing behind the couch, kneading the cushions. I wasn't getting enough air. Carlito and Damien were looking at me as if I'd had something to do with it. I thought they were probably right.

The picture shrank to a small box in the corner of the screen. A brassy news anchor with golden hair said something about horse breeders in the Urubamba Valley. Behind me, the bedroom door opened. It was six o'clock, a soggy June evening. I was broke, out of a job. And Leo was free.

IV

THE EYES OF THE WORLD

1

Now the signs are everywhere: in the markets and plazas, among the nondescript apartments along Salaverry, the glass and steel towers of San Isidro. Hints of connection, harbingers of what's ahead. On a bus shelter in Breña: *Cut Out the Cancer!* Splashed across a KFC: *Viene el Cuatro*. A rash of windows broken at government offices. A diplomat's tires slashed in Monterrico. A grocery truck gone missing. An abandoned highway checkpoint burned. All pieces of a larger puzzle, evidence of the invisible network of which she knows herself to be a part.

On clear days the scar of the number 4 is still visible where it was burned into the hillside months ago. Leo had received the message, even then. She'd answered its call. So what if she still doesn't know the means of transmission, if she can't map out the wires and wavelengths? Its power derives from its elusiveness, its absence of origin. The signs are everywhere. She herself is one of the signs.

On the appointed night she waits in a small city park, watching a line of cars crawl to the base of the bright tower. The hotel seems to have erupted from the earth, thirty stories of glass and glittering steel, its upper floors sheathed in a reddish nimbus. Passengers step from taxis into golden revolving doors—foreigners blinking nervously, politicos who ignore the gloved bellman's greeting, diamond ladies who enter the lobby without a glance to either side. She had not wanted to come. For days she'd vacillated, torn between duty and disgust. But she'd known all along what she would do.

As she passes, dazed, into the realm of crystal and brass, two men in black suits step into her path. They motion for her to open her coat. This, too, she'd expected. In the weeks since Josea and Álvaro were killed, security has gotten more visible all over Lima; although their deaths were blamed on the ongoing gang war, the government clearly expects reprisals. But the incidents have followed no clear pattern; Marta says the government itself is responsible, stirring up fears to justify a crackdown. Julian paces the kitchen, fuming with inactivity, while the remaining cumpas argue endlessly. Trapped in the house they are all blind and deaf, no way to distinguish the message from the noise.

"Go ahead, señorita," the guard says. Under her coat she wears a prim cotton dress and sandals, a silk scarf of Marta's draped over her hair. After months in jeans and heavy sweaters she feels liberated by the light clothing, energized by disguise. Crossing the lobby, she takes note of exits and stairs, the elevators opening, the bartender who looks up as she walks by. In the high-ceilinged dining room, she scans a sea of tables doubled in tall windows, faces vague as sea creatures. She stands too long in the entry, visible to all, brought back with a jolt by a hand waving in her direction.

"Hi, Daddy. Sorry I'm late."

"Baby!" David jumps up to embrace her, holds her at arm's length. "Oh, Leo, I'm so happy to see you!" He pulls her close again. "You look so thin, I almost didn't recognize you. Are you eating enough?"

"I'm fine," she says.

Another hard squeeze. "Look at you! My lord, Leo, you're like a regular Peruvian. My little girl's gone native."

"Don't say that," she mutters. But he's disarmed her already, and she scolds herself for how easily she navigated this trough of luxury, how quickly she's reverted to an old self: the good daughter, the suburbanite, the crypto-reactionary.

"What do you want to drink?" he says. "Should I order a bottle of wine?"

"Whiskey," she says. "On the rocks."

He cocks an eyebrow, nods his approval. After months of idle jokes, suddenly he'd booked the trip—three days of golf and fancy meals, this jewel-crusted hotel in San Isidro. He'd left messages at the bodega, but by the time she called back his flight was two days away and all her vague reluctance couldn't dissuade him.

"What about Mom?" she'd asked, horrified.

David was evasive. "Sweetheart, when was the last time we did something just the two of us?"

When the drinks come, they touch glasses, and David mangles a Spanish toast. "Salute, sweetheart. Happy birthday." For all his forced cheer, she can feel him scrutinizing her: for signs of damage, of contamination. She sips warily, braced by the burn of whiskey. "It's a nice city," he says. "I had no idea. Very modern, cosmopolitan. And the golf's not bad!" he says. "Have you ever heard of the Conquistador's Club?" The hotel, he says, had arranged a tee-time that morning. Afterward, a driver took him to the Plaza de Armas, the Plaza San Martín, the Museum of Gold, then to Miraflores.

"Leo, your mother would have been in heaven. I had lunch at a sidewalk café, waiters in bowties. It was like Europe! I don't know if I'd want to live here, though. A lot of soldiers everywhere. A lot of guns. What's wrong? You look pale."

"No, nothing." She stares into her glass, refusing the image of her father at the Café Haiti. He's been here only a few hours and already the city has been colonized, transformed. "Those places are for tourists," she says. "They're not the real Lima."

"I know that."

"There are eight million people in this city. Most of them have never even been to the Museo d'Oro. They get kicked out of restaurants like this."

"Leo," he says, as a waiter approaches, "I know."

In the warm light her father looks older than she'd remembered, his hair a bit thinner, reading glasses magnifying his already owlish eyes. She's never been able to stay angry at him for long—all through high school, while she and Maxine fought like raccoons, her father knew how to absorb her anger, to soften the target so Leo would exhaust herself without injury to either of them. Unlike Maxine he's never laid claim to political rectitude, nor seen privilege as anything but a blessing and a reward. Maybe, Leo's sometimes thought, he escaped her wrath because he seemed an unworthy adversary, beyond hope.

"I want to see the rest of it," he says. "I want to see *your* Lima. The places you work, the people. What are you doing tomorrow?"

She looks into her glass. "You want to see how the other half lives, Daddy?"

"I want to see how *you* live. To understand why you're here," he says, reaching for her hand. "Please?"

As the waiter opens the wine, she lets herself imagine it. She'd take him to Los Arenales, to Lurigancho's cramped bazaars, to the wreckage of Los Muertos. *People lived here,* she'll tell him. *They had children who wanted to go to school.* She'll introduce him to Nancy, show him pictures of Ernesto. *People like me,* she'll say. *They were just like me.* Her father's not a bad person, she thinks, watching as he sniffs the cork and smiles to the waiter, sensing the swell of his pride as she tastes the wine, the pleasure he takes in being able to treat his daughter to a five-star meal. He's kind, generous—at least to his own. What if he could be made to see everyone else—to really *see* them? Isn't that the ultimate goal? If he could be made to understand, at last, the true cost of such extravagance, what need would there be for protests? What need for bombs?

"It's settled then," David says. "I'll pick you up around ten. We'll go everywhere, you'll show me whatever you want me to see. What's your address, honey?"

"My address?" she says with a flicker of alarm. David watches her intently, a smile frozen on his lips. "But what about golf?"

He takes her hand again, as the couple at the next table tuck into their meals, elbows working, knives flashing.

"I'm only here to see you, Leo. I just want to make sure my little girl is okay."

. . .

Do you want coffee? Tea? I'll ask the girl to bring something. No? You must be thirsty. Hungry. No? They tell me you have refused the meals. Listen, I think it would be a good idea for you to eat something—

Really, Leonora, you are going to need your strength. A lot of people want to talk to you, and not all of them are so friendly. You'll want—

A lot of people. They want to hear what you have to say. Everyone is waiting to hear your story. Look, this is very important. Your big opportunity, you might say. I'll have her bring you something. Water, maybe? Or you prefer Inca Kola?

It's a joke. Please. I'm not trying to frighten you. You're smart enough to understand that. Nobody is going to hurt you here.

Of course not. Does this look like that kind of place? Would there be a sofa, windows, a view of the park? Please, it's important that you trust me. You've been here two days and nobody has touched you except the doctor. So why don't we talk about—

Nobody has touched Señorita Ramos either. You have my word. If she recovers, well, yes, of course, we want to talk to her. But she is also intelligent. I'm sure we can have a reasonable conversation—

Maybe, maybe not. Unlike the others, she still has something to protect.

Yes, of course I know. She never told you? Well, I understand: one doesn't give too much information, even to one's compañeros. But you must be close friends, no? With so much time together, you either become very intimate or you form rivalries. In a house like that . . . forgive me, but with women most of the time it's arguments over men. Some of my colleagues say all Sendero women are lesbians, but this is far from the truth.

No, of course not. Nobody is Sendero anymore. Just as nobody is a Philosopher.

'What's a Philosopher?' Very good, amiga. You play your role nicely. I forgot that what you were doing in Pueblo Libre was entirely innocent. You came all the way to Peru to open a school. The Eyes of the World Art Academy. That's who those fighters were, shooting from the windows? They were artists?

Well, maybe. Maybe I don't understand modern art. Actually, I knew an artist once. Can I tell you about her? A beautiful girl, a painter I met at university. She wanted to paint me. In the nude. I hope it's not strange to tell you this. We're friends, you and I, aren't we? Do you want a cigarette?

I let her paint me. For three days, many hours every day. I can tell you it isn't easy to sit for so long, when you're nude and a beautiful girl is staring at you. What I thought . . . well, I would have sat for a month! But when she showed me the painting it looked nothing like me. It didn't look like a human being—the features, the colors, everything was distorted and ugly. Broken. I was disappointed. I didn't understand how someone could look at me and see . . . that.

My essence? No, I don't think so. That's a very naïve idea, if you'll pardon me.

Oh, I said something foolish, made a joke about her professors. I was angry. You want to know what she said? 'Art is more real than the world.' I laughed at her. You can imagine how the story ends.

But if you feel that way, you should have opened the school. You could have painted anything, made any artistic statement you like, and nobody would have cared. In this country, nobody worries about art anymore. We worry about car bombs. Why didn't you open your school, Leo? You could have made things that lasted forever, instead of involving yourself with these terrorists who accomplished nothing except to die young—

You don't think so? Well, I wonder what your definition is. I wonder if Victor Beale's widow would agree with you. Or the students of the Colegio Santa Ana. Or the tourists on the bus to Ayacucho. The whole list of incidents right here in your 'score-card': dynamite stolen from a Tuttweiler mine, a radio tower sabotaged . . .

Are you alright? Do you want some aspirin for the arm? I would offer you something stronger but we can't give your embassy any-thing to get upset about. They want this to be simple. So no drugs,

I'm sorry to tell you. The doctor says the break is clean. Once we take care of some things, he'll get you in a plaster cast.

Antibiotics? Are you sick?

I see. Well, I'll ask. Amoxicillin? You should have it later today.

Yes, of course we talked to the embassy. At some point, someone will come to see you. They will want to see that you're being treated well. It's not the Continental Grand Hotel, of course, maybe not what you are used to. But we have nothing to hide.

Once the charges are made, I'm sure they'll send someone. But I don't think they're so eager to get involved. An American terrorist? It won't sound very good on the front page of The Washington Post, *and President Clinton has . . . other problems.*

Well, that's up to you. I wouldn't decide too quickly. You'll want a good lawyer—

No, it's not so simple as that. Señorita Ramos is a Peruvian citizen. The law is going to treat her differently. If you refuse the embassy's assistance, it will be a pointless sacrifice. Another one. You know something? You're very romantic. No wonder you and Augustín Dueñas found each other. Maybe you have some idea you'll die next to your compañera, like Thelma and Louise? Well, like I said, there is art and there is Peru. And we are only here to talk about one of them.

Yes, let's talk about why we're here. I would like to help you, Leonora.

Well, if I were to let you go right now, you wouldn't survive the night. And if you go to prison do you know what will happen? I'm not trying to scare you. Do you know how angry people are? There are people calling for your execution. People who say we should declare war on the United States. It's a bad situation. The

Minister of Defense wanted to present you to the press right away. He told me himself: 'Show her with the blood on her face.' He's a stupid man, an opportunist. But who's going to blame him? You understand? You'll be blamed for everything: the Colegio Santa Ana, Victor Beale, the Cuzco payroll—every incident mentioned in your newspaper. 'The Gringa Mastermind.' This is what they are saying. It's what your friend Marta's lawyer will tell her to say. So you have to understand: I'm the only person who wants to protect you. Everyone else would be happy if you disappeared forever, including the U.S. Embassy.

By talking about what you're going to say. By figuring out how to put the responsibility for all this where it belongs. You and I need to agree on a story. And it has to be a good one. We need to explain what you thought you were doing when your cumpas were kidnapping and burning, preparing to attack the country's institutions—

Yes, I know that. But it doesn't matter if you or the others in the house did these things personally. Don't you understand? Your comrades in Chorrillos, in Los Arenales, in Huacho, Abancay—no one is going to worry about who you knew, or who said what to whom. Viene el Cuatro, ¿no? You believe the same things, speak the same revolutionary shit. Do you think the average person cares about organizational structure?

Justice? No, they don't care about justice. What the country wants, from the President down to the most ignorant campesino, is to put all the Philosophers into a basket and then set it on fire. To get you out of their sight completely and forever. A tribunal will want the same thing. They aren't going to waste time with minutiae, especially not for a foreigner. Trust me, okay?

Maybe you want some coffee now? Beatríz!

I see. Well, can you wait a few minutes? The guard will take you on the way back.

I know that, too. Of course I know. But it's irrelevant. It's right here in The Eyes of the World: *Soldiers taken hostage in Victor Fajardo province? If that had happened, I would certainly know about it. A bomb at a military parade in Cangallo . . . Explain to me, Leonora, because I know you are intelligent—if someone in Lima reads about a bomb at a military parade in Cangallo, if they believe this to be true, why does it matter whether there really was a bomb?*

Every story is a true story. You understand this as well as I do. People are terrified by what they believe the same as by what they see for themselves. Maybe more. And the government's responsibility is to make sure its citizens don't live with terror.

Come in! Gracias, Beatríz. Azúcar para mi. Poquito no más. Leonora, you want sugar or cream? Nada para la señorita. Gracias.

Yes, I suppose that is ironic. Maybe you and she would have been friends. She could have taught at your school! But what I am saying is that art is less real. Of course it is. That's why it's imperative for people to know the difference. Someone has to sort these things out. To keep them apart. Excuse me, Leonora, but this country is so poor. Have you gone to the campo? There are children dying every day with no food or medicine, no schools. There is nothing but work, pulling a few potatoes from the fucking dirt, living like animals. This is not the United States. People can't afford to worry about fantasies like whether the President puts his dick into some girl. If Peru is going to take care of people like this, the line between what's real and what's not real must be clear. The art has to stay in the art school. When it comes into the streets, it's not art anymore.

Are you finished?

You can't be serious. Listen to what you're saying. 'The comfort of the elites'? It's not the elites who are terrified by a bomb in Cangallo! This is the definition of 'elite': you don't have to be terrified. You go to Caracas or Miami. You buy an armored car and hire bodyguards. How many elites died in the war? It's the common people who are vulnerable. They can't build walls around themselves, and so they live with terror. These are the people who most want you dead, Leonora. You yourselves are the elite. You and that little asshole, Augustín Dueñas. Cannondale, New Jersey. Stanford University. Your father, the corporate attorney, last year with an income of . . . let's see . . . three hundred and sixty-two thousand dollars. And your mother receives a large inheritance from her father in 1996—some property, investments . . . Please, Leonora, let's be honest with each other. Don't pretend you're someone you're not. That time is over.

Well. That's between you and your parents. But I have to tell you, it seems kind of sad.

Because they seem like nice people. Honest people. Not the kind of people to deserve this treatment. But you disown them, disrespect them, use their money to finance the terucos. And despite all of this they are here, right now, in Lima, fighting for you.

. . .

The dining room has gotten more crowded, the crush of late diners raising the noise to an incoherent babble. The meal sits like a stone in her gut—red wine, prawns, risotto thick as wet concrete. Sharp tingles between her legs: the bladder infection she's been expecting sending its first signals, quick pangs like a knot of twine yanked tight.

"Did you know there was a bomb outside this hotel?" her father says.

Leo looks up from her crème brûlée. "What?"

"It was years ago. They parked a van in front of the building. Three people died. The concierge told me about it. He said the front of the building was like a dollhouse. You could see people sitting up in bed.

"I guess it was one of these terrorist groups," he goes on. "Eat the rich. That kind of thing. It was pretty bad here for a while, I guess. You probably know all about it."

314

"Why would I know about it?"

David sips gingerly at his port. "Sweetheart, relax. I meant you know about the history. You've studied Peru. This wasn't so long ago. I'm sure some of your friends remember the war. Or the people you work with."

She folds her hands in her lap. "Everyone remembers."

"The irony is that we're not all that rich. It's not like I could buy this hotel. I couldn't afford to come here every day. For lots of people it's out of reach, I get that. But look around. Most of these people are working stiffs, like me."

Leo watches his face and tries to keep her composure. For an hour she's fought growing alarm, told herself it was only natural for her father to want to see where she lives, to know she's safe here, among the savages. But something in his voice, a studied nonchalance, plucks at her attention. She should not have accepted a third glass of wine.

"Do people ever talk to you about it?" he says.

"About what?"

"The war, Leo. The bombs." Another quick and empty smile. "I saw on the news, something about one of the terrorist groups trying to do it again, make some kind of comeback. I couldn't really follow the Spanish—"

"Why are we talking about this?"

"They said it started someplace called Los Arenales. Isn't that where you work?"

"Dad—"

He sets down the glass and considers his next words. "I worry about you, Leo. We haven't seen you in so long, we don't hear from you—all we know is what we see on the credit card bill. And then we hear you work in one of these neighborhoods, around these fanatics . . . *Gracias*," he says, taking the check from the waiter. "You're smart, Leo. You know how to handle yourself. But these people can rope you in before you know what's happening. Like a cult. A guy at the State Department told your mother that in the '80s—"

"She called the State Department?"

David frowns, hands the check back with a grateful smile. Leo's never seen him so controlled, so two-faced. She had not thought him capable of it.

"Try to see it our way, honey. Try to put yourself in our shoes. What's the name of the group you work for? They told us there was a situation a few months ago, something about the Army and protestors. You weren't involved, were you?"

All she can do is stare, hold her roiling abdomen. She tries to remember where the exits are. She wonders whether he might try to follow her home.

"You need to be careful, Leo. You're a foreign national. If you get caught up with something like this . . . you might not know what's happening. Maybe they ask for a donation, or to help with something harmless, handing out leaflets, or—"

"What are you saying, Dad?"

He scans her face a long time. "Oportunidad Para Todos. That's it, right? Leo, your mother was told it's a front for a terrorist group, the same one that kidnapped that guy from the InterAmerican Bank."

She shakes her head against the haze of wine and warm fat. Her tongue is so thick she can hardly get the word out. "Terrorists?"

David leans toward her. "Sweetheart," he says quietly, "I have two plane tickets home." She startles, tries to stand, but his grip on her wrist is firm. "Just listen. You've done what you came to do. You had your adventure, helped the people you wanted to help. But things are dangerous now. Look around. Did they frisk you in the lobby? In the taxi today, we got stopped twice. You don't want to be here if these people start shooting each other again."

"Daddy—"

"I know you would never hurt anyone, but these people don't know you—"

"This is where I *live!*" She tries again to pull away. The room is impossibly large, repeated forever and without exit in the dark windows. With his free hand, David takes an envelope from his breast pocket and sets it before her. "Happy birthday, sweetheart," he says with a meaningful gaze. "It's five thousand dollars. Keep it, give it to your friends, I don't want to know. But that's all, you understand? The credit card won't work anymore. What's done is done. You don't have to tell me anything. But Leo," he says, squeezing until she looks into his eyes. "I want you on that plane with me on Monday."

. . .

Five thousand dollars. Five thousand . . . Her father's voice rings in her ears as she squats by the toilet, willing the silky risotto, the slick mussels, to stay where they are. She'd rushed from the table dizzy and watery-eyed, her father calling after her, tourists and boozy ricos looking up as she passed.

Yet another disguise: the sullen American daughter who can't hold her wine.

The bathroom floor is brownish-red marble, cool beneath her palms. From hidden speakers, Sinatra sings "Mack the Knife," his voice clarifying the perfumed air. That she should find herself here, prostrate in this nest of vulgarity; that she should have come in the first place, like a dog to a whistle . . . Despite all she's seen, the months of preparation, despite Neto and Josea and Álvaro—that she still springs to the sound of her master's voice, sits vacant and docile while he lectures her about the fucking *war* . . .

She knows now why he came alone. She would not have left with her mother, would not even have stayed at the table as long as she had. That was their gambit, the only card they could play: that in his innocent love he could convince her—and so it was not love, it was a ploy to get what they wanted, what they couldn't accomplish through fair play or force. Typical, she thinks, gathering breath, typical American behavior: when you can't have what you want, when you can't control it, you reach for your wallet. Doubtless he would have doubled the offer.

So why can she so easily see herself on that plane? A window seat high above the clouds, a glass of wine—why is the image so peaceful, fringed with sunlight? She could give Julian the money, sneak away without a word, then watch from a distance as the plan is carried out. Like her father said, she would have made her contribution—but with no risk of getting caught. Wouldn't any of her comrades do the same?

At the sound of the bathroom door opening, Leo holds her breath. She searches for a weapon—a box of tissues, her own shoe—would her father have gone to the authorities? Would he turn in his own daughter?

But it's only a housekeeper, humming to herself as she wheels a cart across the floor, singing a few words in Quechua while her cloth squeaks over the mirror. Leo hauls herself standing and straightens her dress before leaving the stall. The housekeeper is setting out an array of rolled hand towels, bars of fancy soap. When Leo catches her eyes in the mirror, she returns an insincere smile.

"¿Todo bien, señorita?"

She's young, Indian, in a starched blue uniform and white collar. Seventeen, at most. A child, already cleaning other people's shit. Five thousand dollars is more than this girl will see in her lifetime— the owners of this hotel, its well-heeled guests, have made sure of that. Their very lives depend on it. And Leo's father wants her to be safe.

"Todo bien, compañera," Leo says.

The girl blushes in confusion, checks to see if anyone else has heard before flashing another false smile and wheeling her cart to the door.

No, Leo won't leave. Not for money or parental love, not to make anyone feel better. She won't be who they want her to be, who they'd raised her to be: an investment, they'd no doubt call it, one that's now in jeopardy. Just getting up from that table had been a small victory. Escaping this sickening hotel will be another. She'll walk out without a word, stop for no one. She won't return her father's desperate calls. She'll follow through, for once in her life, match words with deeds. One victory leads to another. She has the taste of it in her mouth now. She means to keep winning.

When the door swings shut, she takes up a bar of soap—beet red and speckled with pumice. Leaning over the wide basin, she makes three slashing marks across the mirror: the number four. She can feel it behind her as she walks away, a crude and garish sign superimposed on her reflection. No one could miss it, or mistake its message:

You are not safe.

2

The raid began at the height of the morning rush hour. Thursday, August 6, 1998. According to government records more than forty members of DINCOTE's special forces took part in the operation, including a dozen from the elite Grupo 14. They converged on a house in the Jacaranda neighborhood, less than a mile from the sprawling Defense Ministry compound known as the Pentagonita, with orders, according to those same records, to "minimize casualties."

The house—two stories of slapdash construction set off from the street by a high, rusting fence—was empty. Instead of armed subversives they found a kitchen full of unwashed pots, floors strewn with blankets and cigarette butts, copies of the day's tabloids, as if the people who'd been living there had left on a few minutes' notice. In the overgrown backyard, under a rotten pallet, agents found a hinged concrete slab with a length of rope for a handle. Opening it, they stared down into what one reporter described as "a scene from the Dark Ages": a stone well, two meters by three meters and reeking of excrement, at the bottom of which lay the body of Victor Beale.

His death was determined to have been caused by diabetic shock due to starvation. His bloated body had wounds to the head and abdomen, but rather than torture these turned out to have been made by rats. In a corner of the filthy well lay a crumpled copy of *The Eyes of the World*.

"So they have the newspaper, so what?" Julian says. He stands at the stove, waiting for coffee, while on the radio the President fulminates against the traitors. "You find it in lots of places. Schoolchildren are reading it."

"Schoolchildren don't kill people," Marta says, "or make demands of the government."

The kitchen is dim, voices dampened by the blankets over the windows. Leo is half-listening, poring over *El Comercio*. The light is sallow, smoke-filled; it feels as though they haven't left this room, this very table, for weeks.

"You don't like killing, Profesora? Maybe you should go back to teaching." He sets three mugs on the table. "¿Quién sabe? Maybe they gave it to him to wipe his ass. Eh, Linda? You see how useful your newspaper can be?"

"It's *our* newspaper," Leo says without looking up. *Cangallo. A gathering of veterans was interrupted by protests over military pensions,* reads a story on p. A-18. She sets her cigarette on the edge of the heavy glass ashtray.

"As usual you are not thinking," Marta says. "Until now, only a few hundred people know about our paper. Now the President is talking about it on the radio. Who are these cumpas? Why do they kill an innocent person? What is the strategy?"

Julian waves this off. "Strategy isn't our problem."

"Dying is our problem," Marta says. "Torture, this is our problem. El Arca."

Leo hardly hears these arguments anymore, the dog-like snapping of jaws as Marta and Julian jockey for control. They've all spent too much time in one another's company, confined to airless rooms that smell of pasta and wet towels, only the chatter of the radio to distract them. Since the night Josea and Álvaro were killed, no one has left the house—only Leo, and only for groceries and the dinner with her father. Most of the day, Julian and Marta are locked away with the cumpas—working out the plan, they tell her, choreographing its many aspects. The garden is Leo's refuge, but after an hour the damp chill settles into her joints and she retreats to the mute computer but the bladder infection makes it hard to sit for long. She thinks sometimes of Señora Zavallos and her father, a house lit up with jazz, aswirl in chatter. In El Arca she'll remembers these weeks as one stage in the inexorable contraction of her world: from city to barrio, barrio to house, to a stone cell not shown on any map. She'll huddle knees-up in a corner and pray to grow smaller still.

"We have to say something about this," Leo tells them now.

Marta and Julian lock eyes. "Comandante?" he says, with exaggerated courtesy.

"We say nothing," Marta says.

"We can't just pretend it didn't happen. The whole country is talking about it." Leo reaches for a pen. "We could say this is what happens when the government is unresponsive to the people: things get out of control, violence is inevitable . . ."

Marta's voice is flat and dangerous. "You will say nothing."

Leo lowers her eyes to hide her indignation. Since Julian's return, they've hardly spoken—glimpses in the morning, Marta pale, raw-eyed, as though she'd been pleading with someone all night long. *I have to see him*, she'd said, on the night Josea and Álvaro were killed; Leo hasn't had the courage to ask whom she'd meant. Late one night she found Marta at the kitchen table, smoking and writing on a legal pad. *Mi vida, te extraño tanto*, Leo read, before Marta snatched up the pad and walked out.

"We have to make it clear we weren't involved," Leo says, keeping her voice even. "We have to remind people that our goal is to help—"

"Nobody cares who killed Victor Beale," Marta says. "Who knows if a person named Victor Beale ever existed? This is not the point."

"What is the point, Comandante?" Julian says.

"The newspaper," she says. "Maybe somebody died reading *Los Ojos del Mundo*. But how did he have that issue when all the copies were burned in Álvaro's office?"

He stops with the unlit cigarette halfway to his mouth. In the silence the image forces its way across Leo's consciousness: the bloated body, twisted by cold, the lightless eternity, the rats. Nausea gathers in her throat but she bites it back. Impossible: to die like that. Impossible to inflict it on someone, a stranger. But what if there was no body? What if it were all just someone's fantasy, no more real than "The Banker," Leo's own creation? She glances again at the article on the table: *A gathering of military veterans . . . The protestors carried brass musical instruments which they played loudly as the veterans spoke.* Could the government have made up the story? Could they be so brazen as to have invented Victor Beale?

"Let's say you're right," Julian says. "What do you want to do about it? Run away, forget everything?"

"No," Marta says. "I want to move faster."

At this a slow smile emerges on Julian's face. Leo looks helplessly from one to the other, as if watching through a pane of glass. How easily she finds herself on the outside, even now. She uncaps her pen, crosses out the first line of the article. *A military parade,* she writes. It sounds more official, more pompous. A better target. And "musical instruments"? It sounds like a high-school marching band, some half-serious skirmish involving pom-poms and poodle skirts.

No, she thinks. Victor Beale can't go unanswered. The government can't take control of the truth in this way. It can't be permitted to determine what's real.

A bomb, she writes. *The military parade was interrupted by a bomb.*

Of all the things she'll wonder about in El Arca, all the unanswerable questions that keep her company through years of ice and stone, none will confound her, or bring as much secret amusement, as the question of Julian. How, after months of rancor and suspicion, they'd ended up sharing a bedroom, a bedroll, smacking their bodies together every night like rutting pigs until they rolled apart and slept, legs tangled, yanking one blanket back and forth until dawn.

It was not loneliness or desperation, not the clinging together of terrified souls. Certainly nothing as foolish as love. She'll consider and reject each of these clichés, coloring at the thought of the garbage the lawyers had wanted her to spew: that he'd seduced her, that she was drawn to his strutting masculinity, rendered helpless and quivering by the allure of revolution personified. She'd laughed in their faces, but in private she wept furiously: that they'd see her as such a pathetic dupe, such a *girl,* her life's most urgent effort reduced to the silly tropes of romance.

On the night they'd learned about Josea and Álvaro, Julian stayed awake long after the others had gone upstairs. Leo woke to find him standing at the window, head bowed. The taste of him still in her mouth from the kiss in the taxi. She pulled him down to her bedroll and undressed, put his hands where she wanted them, moving against him until his body's own ferocity took over. Sex, for Leo, had never been about romance—romance was a waste of time, superfluous to the act itself, to pleasure. But that night was about more than pleasure: it was an opening, a secret compact. She'd seen his fear, his vulnerability; taking it into herself she'd helped him to master it, but only by making him acknowledge it, by asserting her right to share it, a right he could never revoke.

They'd renewed the compact almost every night since. During the day she hardly thought about it—until the inevitable bladder infection. It wasn't romance, it was fucking: a shot of pure, liberated present. From time to time she thinks of the afternoon when he'd hit her, and for a day or two she refrains, mulling her motives, reassuring herself. But their sex is a separate matter, a correction. What use in depriving herself when it pleases her, the hard press of him, the pressure and release and brief floating out of time. *Why* doesn't matter. Why does there need to be a *why*?

But tonight she finds him strangely passive, distracted. There's little heat, not enough force, his broad hips hardly move as she rides him. After half an hour of fruitless lurching she rolls off of him, gently twists his nipple. "What's wrong with you?"

With a grunt, he sits up and yanks his boxers on. His cigarette lighter casts bronze light on his meaty shoulders, the ever-present scruff at his jaw.

"Have you thought about what I asked?" he says.

She sighs, deflated, staving off dread. "I can't. Please don't ask me."

His exhalation spreads silver smoke in the light from the window. "Then everything is wasted. All this time for nothing."

"I've done everything I was told. Rented the house, bought the food . . ."

"It's your plan. You want to let it die?"

After months of delays and legal battles, Vía América has entered the final phase of its monstrous birth. The grand opening two weeks away: a gala event with movie stars and soccer heroes, foreign ambassadors, a performance by Ricky Martín. The windows and video screens have been fitted, parking spaces painted; trucks deliver merchandise night and day, lined up along the malecón, where Christopher Columbus beckons, the colonialist patriarch reimagined as grinning ringmaster of a circus of consumption.

August 23. When limeños wake up to find their party cancelled, their billion-dollar bauble in sea-thrashed ruins, there will be no doubt what it means. Never again will her comrades ask what she's doing here.

"You said you had everything you needed," she says.

"That was before Victor Beale."

"I don't see what difference that makes."

Footsteps overhead, a door closing: Marta coming down the stairs, putting a pot on the stove. *I have to see him*, Marta said, one more secret she's kept from Leo. For a second Leo hopes she'll come into the bedroom, that she'll see her and Julian like this.

"You remember what happened at Los Muertos, right?" he says.

"Of course I do."

"You remember Ernesto?"

"Compañero—"

"Listen. Ernesto was known to us. He and the others—Juancito, Nalda. Chaski met them at the business school. They went to some meetings together, listened to old cumpas talk about the war. It was theory to those kids. It was cool. When the government decided to tear down Los Muertos, Chaski convinced them they had to do something."

"And they got killed for it. I was there."

"They were making a film about the protest. They were on the *roof*." He fixes her with a stare. "What about the others? The ones who burned the cars?"

"What about them?" she whispers, gripped by premonition.

"We don't know who they were."

Again the feeling of being split, doubled, of another story sliding beneath her own. She struggles to her feet, moves abruptly between the window and the door. "I don't believe it," she says. She walks the room's edges, digs a fingernail into the plaster. "You never liked Chaski. Any of you. Because he's gay, that's why you blame him."

"That's Marta's problem," Julian says, stubbing out the cigarette. "Marta didn't like him because he followed my brother around like a kitten. He brought Chaski home once, you know? I think he wanted to upset my mother—a dirty cholo in her beautiful house. But they liked each other right away. They sat talking until midnight, like a couple of old gossips. I don't care that he's gay. I care that he's a traitor."

"He's not," she says, but her voice isn't convincing, even to her. Had it all been Chaski's doing: Josea, Álvaro, Neto? Had he been the invisible hand all along? But he'd protected her, soothed her. He'd introduced her to the others. A sudden dizziness strikes and she touches a hand to the wall. Was she, too, part of his plan?

Now Julian is standing next to her. "I don't know, and neither do you. Marta's right. There's more going on than we know. We have to be able to defend ourselves. We need the guns."

"I already told you. There's no more money. My father cancelled the credit card."

"He didn't cancel his own."

She pulls back, examines his face, his hands. She hadn't told them about the money, the thick envelope she'd flung onto the table, her father's grieving eyes. It had been so clear then what she needed to do. But that was before Victor Beale, back when it was still clear what everyone needed.

David's flight leaves in the morning. If she takes an early bus she'll just catch him. She has no doubt he'll give her the money. He won't even argue. All it will take is one more performance: as the sweet, helpless daughter needing to be rescued, the innocent expat ready to come home.

. . .

Actually, that's an interesting story. ¿Te cuento en español?

But I've heard you speaking Spanish, Leonora. You don't remember? It was only a few months ago, at a protest in the Plaza de Armas. You were about to do something rather stupid . . .

¡Sí! Exactly. So you do remember.

Of course I knew who you were. Even before that. The minute you set foot in Los Arenales. There are a lot of things we don't do very well in Peru, God knows. But it's not quite the "banana repub-lic" your mother says it is. We know how to keep track of terrorists. We've had a lot of experience with that. Unlike the Americans, who are required to act as if someone is not a terrorist and give them a chance to do what they're going to do before you can arrest them or even watch them. As if it's a kind of game, each side gets a fair chance. That country doesn't make a lot of sense to me.

Yes, of course, we are all Americans. ¿Sabes qué? My father's from Baltimore. I lived there until I was nine. My brother went back to the U.S., during the war. He teaches Spanish in a high school. He says he'll never come back to Peru. It breaks my mother's heart.

Your mother said many things. I don't blame her. If it was my daughter . . . Well, she also has to play a game. This is the situation you've created for her.

Yes, your father was also there. But only your mother and the woman from the embassy spoke.

How did he look? He looked like somebody had died.

Sure, you can go back to your cell. But I thought you wanted to hear about Rosa.

The painter. That was her name. She was from an old family in Trujillo. Not a rich family. They had lost most of their land, but were still members of certain social clubs, et cetera. This is how she grew up. When she came to Lima and met children from the true ruling class, I think it was a shock to her. Always, she spoke and moved as if she was enduring mistreatment—but in a noble way, to set an example. What can I say? I found her very appealing, and also impossible. She was beautiful, too, but in an older way, very simple. I knew that she had political activities, friends writing for leftist magazines or involved with 'cultural education.' I didn't pay attention to that. I told myself that her involvement was minimal, that because she was an artist she couldn't participate in anything

so . . . mundane. I was in love, so I was ready to believe anything if it maintained the image of my beloved. Very dangerous, of course, not to see clearly . . .

No, never. I wasn't interested. All I wanted was to spend time with Rosa, even though she laughed at me. I was like her pet. I didn't want other people around. Well, of course this couldn't last. One time, she left for a month. Some friends told her about a doctor who was going to the Emergency Zone to work with orphans. She wanted to paint them. When she came back, this was when she asked me to model for her. I think she enjoyed it that I didn't like the painting. She wanted me to be offended. She said it was her new style, she could no longer paint in the oppressor's vernacular. This was her phrase: 'the oppressor's vernacular.' She showed me something, a document, like a diploma. It said she would give her life for justice, that she'd proven her dedication to the country and its people. A lot of nonsense about love and hate, the future is the mother of the past, or whatever. The document was signed with a name I had never heard. 'Who is Mira?' I said. She told me it was her new name. From now on, I have to call her Mira. She also said this group didn't believe in monogamy, that she had slept with other men and other women, that it was important to be loyal to everyone, not just one person. We argued. She said she couldn't love someone who accepted reactionary bourgeois fantasies. I didn't understand any of this. It seemed like a performance, like she was saying these things only so someone else could hear. I thought she had lost her mind.

I left. I was very angry. Occasionally I would see her at demonstrations, standing on a platform screaming something. She became well known as an artist. Many groups used her work in their propaganda. But we never spoke again after that night.

Actually, I do know what happened to her. You know the MRTA, the terrorist group? You remember two years ago they took over the Japanese embassy with everyone inside? There are films taken after the army went in. It was shown on the news. In one, you can see the President walking through the house, going up the stairs and stepping over the bodies of terrorists. On the last step before the second floor. That one is Rosa.

Yes, terrible. But I'll tell you something strange. Only when I saw this I understood something about what she wanted, and what her group was trying to achieve. Because when I look at this footage, of these people whose bodies are destroyed by bullets or bombs, for the first time I see a world that looks like her paintings.

Reality? I don't know. Maybe she was only trying to make the world as ugly as what she already imagined, to make people accept her vision. This kind of art, it's not more real than the world, just more arrogant.

Actually, I haven't thought about her in a long time. Even when I saw the film, I don't think I felt anything so terrible. It had been almost a decade. At one time . . . at the beginning, when my heart was broken, I had an idea that this is why she changed her name: to protect me, so I wouldn't see the person I loved saying and doing these things. For a time, I told myself this, and it was a consolation. But I don't believe it anymore. That would have been an act of love. And although terrorists always say they love the people, I find they are not capable of loving an actual person.

Cowardice? A sense of shame? Otherwise, why not use your true names? If you believe all of this bullshit, the manifestos and propaganda. If the Philosophers are so proud of what they're doing why don't they admit who they are? When we find you you should stand up and say 'Yes, I am a fucking revolutionary.' If you're so sure the people are with you. Why won't you say who you really are?

On the contrary, we had nothing to do with what happened to Josea Torres.

You can believe it or not believe it. The man is working with terucos, helping to recruit more criminals. If we caught him, wouldn't we tell the whole country about it?

A message? You think the government sends messages like this? What's the message, that a man should eat his own balls? What does this mean?

I really don't know. Maybe it was ronderos. Or someone in your own organization. You have to understand this as the consequence of what you started. You and Julian. You think you can control it, that you make the rules of the game, but there are others who don't acknowledge those rules, or who are playing a different game entirely. You're not the only group to operate outside the system. Of course there are others who have different aims, who maybe see themselves as part of the system, although the system itself doesn't acknowledge them. These groups can't be controlled or predicted, the things they do can't be interpreted in the normal way.

Yes, that's what I'm saying. I told you already: every story is a true story, or becomes one. That's why we need to talk about what you'll say tomorrow—

Because things must be called by their proper names. Because there is a natural division between what's real and what's not real, and when that division is confused society can't function. Maybe in the U.S. it's different. There you're so used to fantasies no one cares anymore what the fantasies mean or what they refer to. Peru can't afford such confusion. A country can't survive when it doesn't know the difference between truth and lies.

Tomorrow? Tomorrow we'll introduce you to the country. The minister insists. It seems your embassy has begun to feel some urgency about the matter. Maybe they don't like seeing your mother on television, even if she is very entertaining. Or maybe they want it resolved before the human rights people get involved. But everyone agrees this problem can be fixed quickly. Everyone wants the same thing.

For you to go home, of course. Nobody wants to see you in El Arca. The minister will have his presentation, the press has a few days shouting about the 'terrorista gringa,' and then you go back to the U.S. and after a year or two you'll be free and you can return to Stanford University and give speeches with Gabriel Zamir about oppression and injustice and the brave martyrs of the Cuarta Filosofía. Nobody will care.

It's simple. You say, 'I'm sorry, I made a mistake, met the wrong people, fell in love with the wrong guy, etc. etc.' As a favor to our friends in the United States, the President agrees to let you return to your country and serve a light sentence of some kind, giving money to an illegal group, or I don't know. Madeleine Albright gets something to brag about, Bill Clinton can stop talking about his cock . . . It's called 'bilateral transfer.' Like if someone's child went to the neighbor's house and broke their window, but the neighbor lets the child's parents decide the punishment—

Don't be foolish. Señorita Ramos is Peruvian. You have to think about yourself now, Leonora. You have to think about your family. Think of it as a moment of total freedom, an opportunity to tell a new story about yourself.

Of course you can think about it. The guard will take you back. I almost forgot—here is the amoxicillin you asked for. And ibuprofen. I hope you feel better.

Well, in that case you would go to prison for a long time. Five years, maybe ten. But let's forget about that, okay? Who would benefit from such a sacrifice?

Yes. That's right. This is what was discussed.

No. You misunderstand. I don't want you to lie. I want you to tell the truth. By tomorrow at noon, you have to decide what that is.

. . .

The first time she sees him, she doesn't know what she's seen. Walking quickly through the jostling market, eyes down, sensitive to every inquisitive gaze, she ignores the jolt of unease, the uptick of her vigilance. Everywhere now this feeling follows her—from parked cars and high windows, combi drivers, park benches. Even in crowds she feels scrutinized, picked over by anonymous eyes. But this feeling is smaller, intensely specific. Not until she's back on Almagro does she know what she felt was recognition.

The next day, on the Plaza de la Bandera, she feels it again: a watching eye, patient, unthreatening. She says nothing to Julian or Marta. On Sunday afternoon, as she walks the busy avenue outside Católica, she knows she's being followed. She steadies her pace, turns onto a quieter street and heads west—she can feel him behind her but she won't let him get any nearer, not yet. After ten minutes, she finds herself at the edge of an empty parking lot. The faded sign reads *Zoológico Nacional.* With a dry laugh—when did she turn into a character from a bad spy novel?—she digs in her pocket for a coin.

The zoo is unkempt, plastic bags and paper scraps gliding across parched enclosures, turtle ponds clogged with old leaves and floating tufts of scum. Only a few visitors stroll the shady paths—elderly men with granddaughters or nurses, middle-aged women with haunted eyes. As she passes the monkey cages half a dozen stark, wrinkled faces turn to watch; a single giraffe stands warily by a half-built wall. She stops on a shaded footbridge and lights a cigarette, watches the alligator napping in the mud below. Even the dragonflies that perch on its rough hide don't wake it, the splashing of fish in the brackish water.

"Do you think it's alive?" says a voice behind her.

Chaski is standing a few feet away. With a glance she takes in his newly short hair, his clean shirt and ironed pants, the single aluminum crutch. The small gold cross hangs, as ever, at his neck. It's the same person, the same contagious smile. But that's precisely where the danger is, she tells herself. Julian, her father—whatever their resemblance, no one is who they say they are anymore.

"Leave me alone," she says. "I don't know you."

"Yes, you know me, Leo."

"Don't call me that. Why are you following me?"

"You're my friend."

"If I were your friend you wouldn't have left. You wouldn't have left any of us."

"Those other people aren't my friends," he says. "They're not yours, either."

They wait as a group of schoolchildren approach, jabbering and shouting, their teacher nowhere in sight. The children throw sticks and bits of trash over the side, calling to the alligator, who takes no notice. Flustered, Leo turns from Chaski and follows them across the bridge, into a dense eucalyptus grove, trying to compose herself, to quell her apprehension. Whether Chaski was an informant or not he'd left her, hadn't he? He'd betrayed her. Now he calls her "friend"?

They emerge at the edge of a meadow and she lingers by the split-log fence. In the near distance, two vicuñas stand drinking from a stone fountain; three others dot the meadow's farther side. Too many thoughts fill her head—suspicions, questions, half-made theories of why he's sought her out. Soon enough, she hears him approaching, but this time she doesn't wait for him to speak.

"You're a coward," she says.

"Leo—"

"You brought me to that house. You brought all of us. You said you needed my help, you were going to do something. Then you left."

"I was shot," he says.

She fixes him in a stare. "That's not why."

Chaski's mouth opens and closes. He turns to watch the vicuñas poking their noses into the wind. "No, that's not why."

She's never seen vicuñas up close before—like a cross between a deer and an ostrich, with scrawny legs and long, fragile necks. There's something foolish and dainty about their woolly middles, too vulnerable. One raises its head to look at them, then prances madly to the other side of the fountain. When she looks again at Chaski, she knows absolutely that what her comrades have said about him is false.

"I left because I don't want to lie anymore. About anything," he says. "The lying is like a sickness. It will kill all of us.

"I've been doing this since I was fifteen, Leo. Where has it gotten me? The glorious revolution. Where has it gotten any of us? Nacho, Casi, Neto and Nalda. So many people I knew hurt or dead. Some of them are dead because of me. Always we say we want to fight, that everyone will be happy after the war. But you can't be happy if you're dead."

"It's not about happiness," Leo says, trying to believe it. "It's not about you or me . . ."

"I know people who can help you," he says. He reaches for her hand. "There's a place you can stay. You need to leave that house."

She bats his hand away. "Are you crazy?"

"You don't understand what's happening. Things are not what you think."

"How do you know what I think?"

"I know what they think. I know how they talk about you. You're in danger, Leo."

"My name is Linda," she says.

"No, it's not."

She fumbles for a cigarette, realizes with a pang of misery that she left them on the bridge. "Did you tell them about Josea?"

Chaski looks up sharply. It's the first time she's seen him genuinely angry and it shocks her. "Álvaro was from the same village as me. Our grandmothers were cousins—"

"Did you tell them?"

"Do you think I could do that?"

"I don't know. I don't know what anyone can do."

A distant gabbling on the path behind them, and then the school-children come racing past, shrieking and shoving, their harried teacher chasing after them with a torn map. That morning Leo had woken alone. She'd gone looking for Julian in the kitchen, on the second floor, but when she heard his voice behind Marta's closed door she tiptoed back downstairs and out into the garden.

"What's going to happen?" she says. "If you're really my friend, tell me what I don't know."

He can only hold her gaze for a second. When he reaches up to touch the cross at his neck she understands: he doesn't know any more than she does. They'd never trusted him, either.

"You see? You are a coward," she spits, suddenly overcome with fury—at her own ignorance, everyone's ignorance, their unforgivable blindness. "You can't help me. You can't help anyone." She can hear the ugliness in her voice but part of her is strangely excited. "Stay away from me. You're not a Philosopher. We don't need people like you."

When he speaks again the resignation in his voice fills her with contrition. She wants to take it all back, to cling to his legs and beg forgiveness.

"Anyone can be a Philosopher, Leo. Any angry kid in Los Arenales or Lurigancho or La Ensenada del Chillón. Out in the campo everyone's a Philosopher. All they have to do is say it." He offers a last, sad smile. "Isn't that what you did?"

She watches him retreat down the path, limping toward a sky streaked with pink cream, until the shade swallows him. From the other direction the schoolchildren's shrill voices float over the meadow, past the ludicrous vicuñas, who stand at the fence in naïve curiosity. Following the sound, she finds the children clustered before a high glass enclosure, jostling one another, chanting a ragged song and smacking their palms against the glass.

"*Ti-gre! Ti-gre!*"

Their teacher is still absent. A few boys toss garbage and small rocks over the top of the wall; the girls scream, shrinking back in fear and delight when a low-slung, muscled puma emerges from behind a boulder and stalks fluidly past. Leo catches her breath. Sand-colored, graceful as a slow-beating heart, the puma scans its shabby prison, only the twitch of an ear betraying its awareness of the taunting children. Unperturbed, it moves back into shadow and vanishes, reappears on the far side of a heavy tree bough, flanks rippling, impossibly long strides carrying it from one end to the other in a determined, dreamlike glide.

"*Ti-gre! Ti-gre!*"

She stands among the children, the outline of her face mingling with their reflections in the glass. As they scream and bang, the puma makes another pass, moving with purposeful steps to the far end of the enclosure where it lifts its nose to sniff regally at the air.

Fifty yards away, the vicuñas gambol blithely on the meadow. Watching them, the great cat lowers itself to its haunches. How easy it is to imagine: the lunge and flash of muscle, the cloud of dust. How quickly the vicuña's shrieks would go silent. How could they put them here, side by side, she thinks? Her hands shake with terror and loneliness. She wants to slap the children's nasty little faces. She wants to run all the way home, hide under a mound of blankets. What cruelty or sick humor doomed these animals to such torment?

"Ti-gre! Ti-gre!"

The puma glides solemnly past, turns to look at Leo and then, uninterested, away.

3

The weapons were delivered on the morning of August 12—guns, ammunition, and grenades acquired from a Panamanian dealer based in Guayaquil, Ecuador, paid for in American cash. Alfi Nuñez, who drove the van, testified that he arrived in Pueblo Libre at 1:15 a.m. and waited as instructed on the Avenida Venezuela until two men got in, blindfolded him, and drove through side streets. They stopped on a quiet block across from a three-story house. There were no lights on, but as they unloaded the crates Nuñez said he looked up and saw "a white girl wearing a red bandanna" watching from a third-story window. He remembers thinking this strange— he'd heard stories of gringos who fought in Colombia or Argentina, but never Peru. Peruvians, he thought, had more pride.

When Nuñez testified, Leo's attorney was forbidden to raise his status as an "arrepentido": he'd spent three years in El Arca before being paroled in return for cooperation. There were hundreds of such penitents, during and after the war—they were often shown in televised purification ceremonies, wearing white hoods and gloves, kissing the Peruvian flag. Thus sanctified, their stories became unimpeachable and led to the arrest or disappearance of thousands.

"This woman you saw," Leo's attorney said, "did anyone speak to her?"

"No, señor."

"Nobody gave her instructions?"

"Nobody."

"Are you sure she was involved? Maybe she was an innocent spectator."

Nuñez emphatically disagreed. The gringa was a part of everything, he said. In fact, he was certain she was in charge of the operation. The cumpas who'd met him were just muscle, following orders. In fact, he said, as he was leaving the courtyard the woman might have made a sign in the window for him to see. With her finger, she might have traced the number four.

So now there are guns.

Later that weekend, thieves broke into a warehouse in the Industrial Zone belonging to the Contreras Garment Company, which manufactured uniforms for the security detail of Peru's Congress. A company official would later confirm that the uniforms recovered from Calle Almagro were the stolen garments.

As for the much-reported "blueprints of Congress," they were not submitted as evidence and have never been shown to the public. In his affidavit, Lieutenant Lang referred not to blueprints but to "a detailed map showing the exact location of every legislator." This likely refers to a seating chart customarily made available to the press, enabling reporters to call specific lawmakers during important votes—a distinction rarely made in the media, though it would have been known to anyone reporting on Leo's case.

Guns, dynamite, uniforms, blueprints . . . It's all coming together.

After Josea Torres' death, arrangements were made to print *The Eyes of the World* at a shop in Los Arenales owned by Eladio Huatay, a cousin of Comrade César. On the afternoon of August 18—five days before the Grand Opening of Vía América—Leo brought the files for the eighth issue to Huatay, with unusual instructions: he was to prepare everything but hold the print run until she returned later that week. There would be one last file, she said, a photo image for the back page. Once she'd delivered it, the issue—"el último," he recalls her saying—would be complete.

It's growing dark by the time she leaves Huatay's shop, a still and silent dusk that seems to start beneath her feet, rising like bathwater. She takes a winding route through Las Brisas, not admitting to herself where she's going until she's standing across from the boarded-up offices of Oportunidad Para Todos. Ten months, she thinks. Almost a year in Peru. She remembers the optimism she'd felt at first, the exhilaration, speaking to a room full of Quechua women, mapping simple English sentences: *Can you help me? How much does this cost?*

But they didn't need English, she thinks. In that, Julian's mother was certainly right. They didn't need bank accounts or bookkeeping skills. They needed justice.

In four days, they'll have it, she thinks, wondering suddenly if she'll ever see this place again, if she'll ever come back to Los Arenales. Julian says there are arrangements, that after Vía América they'll go somewhere safe, just for a while. "Trust me," he says, "You'll have nothing to worry about." Wistful, she looks at the pavement, bends to pick up a dirt-crusted bottlecap—a souvenir, she thinks, pressing it into her palm until it leaves a deep impression. Then she goes to see Nancy.

For a moment she can't recognize the woman who comes to the door. She's lost at least twenty pounds, her hair is limp, gray at the roots, the skin of her neck gone papery.

"Leo. What are you doing here?" Nancy says.

"I wanted to see you," Leo says. She stands tall, tries to project confidence, reassurance. She's the bearer of good news, after all. "I wanted to see how you are."

"How we are? We're the same. What did you think?" Nancy scans the street before stepping back from the door. "Okay, Leo, come in. My god, how skinny you are."

The living room has also changed—the couch moved to make room for a console TV, the table replaced by a bigger one. Ernesto's face stares back from every wall and windowsill—generic, smiling images like the ones that come inside store-bought frames.

"We didn't know what happened to you," Nancy says. "Were you traveling?"

"I'm sorry I never came. I didn't want to make things worse."

Nancy's hands shake as she takes her cigarettes from the coffee table. "How could you make it worse?" From upstairs comes a low thud, a shuffling noise, as if someone were dragging something in circles. But Leo can't take her eyes from the photos. When she looks up, Nancy has fixed her in a hard stare.

"Have you seen your friend Chaski?"

"Not for a long time," Leo says. And it's true: the man she saw at the zoo was not her friend. He had a different name, a different face. "Have you?"

"Oh, yes. The son of a bitch was here. He came just a few days after they found Neto. To express his sadness. To tell us all the *cumpas*"—she spits out the word—"felt our loss. She sweeps an arm at the new television and table. "You see their compensation. Payment for a fallen soldier. I hope you stay away from that maricón," she says, just as another thud sounds over their head. "They were looking for him only a few days ago."

"Who was looking?"

Someone calls for Nancy in a weak, frightened voice. "Wait here," she says. "I was making dinner. We'll eat together and you'll tell me your adventures."

While she's gone, Leo examines the photos one by one: Ernesto as a boy of ten in shorts and a blue jersey, one foot on a soccer ball; as a teenager perched on a stone wall with half a dozen other kids; an infant propped up between his older brothers. His broad, credulous face is unfamiliar, not the face on all the placards.

They hadn't been close, Leo thinks with a pang of guilt. Not really. She'd called him a friend but in truth she'd known little about him. After he died he became a convenient rallying cry, a sign of her virtue and righteousness. It was a kind of cruelty, she thinks, flushing with self-loathing, a theft. What gave her the right?

"You were in Lima all this time?" Nancy says, standing over the stove and smoking. "This ugly city? Why not see Chile, Argentina? These are civilized places."

"I got involved with something," she says. "Another organization." Nancy's hands move slowly, her back straight, while Leo talks in generalities: the art school, the classes they'll offer, the frustrations of bureaucracy. The grand opening is this weekend, she says, though there are some last-minute details to work out.

"We're going to have a real impact. Something people won't forget. I promise."

Nancy's hands fall still. "And what about your family? Don't they want you to come home?"

She shakes off the memory of her father in the hotel driveway, golf bag at his side, emptying his wallet as if she were a mugger. How sad he'd looked, how beaten. "They know this is more important. They raised me to think about other people, to do something for them. Like you raised Neto."

"Strangers," Nancy says. "People you don't know or understand."

"Those are the people we have to learn to understand. Isn't that what we did at Oportunidad? If we only help the people we know we perpetuate inequality and hatred. The class system—"

She breaks off, seeing Nancy's wariness harden into impatience. Without a word, Nancy sets her cigarette on the edge of the stove and leaves the room, returning a moment later with a folded sweatshirt which she thrusts at Leo.

"Take this. It belonged to Ernesto. But you should have it."

Tentatively, Leo holds up the bulky sweatshirt—baby blue with gold block letters: UC BERKELEY. "He always talked about it," Nancy says. "It was his dream, where all the great American revolutionaries came from. He thought it was so cool, the students with their marches, fighting the police. Isn't that where those students were shot?"

"I think that was in Ohio."

"Four students. *Four.*" She sets two plates on the table and scoops spaghetti from the pot. "Nothing like it was here. At San Marcos, La Cantuta—"

"I know."

"Hundreds of them," she says. "Babies. Following these psychotics in Sendero, these butchers who didn't care about them. I told Neto, 'Don't get mixed up with them. These people don't care about you.' They talk about helping people, but what kind of help brings the army into our neighborhood? Taking our money for their taxes, then blowing up the schools and banks we built with our own hands.

"After Los Muertos, where was Chaski?" she says, brandishing a fork. "Where were you, Leo? Who helped those people when their homes were destroyed? My family came here with nothing, you understand? Nothing was here. But we built a community. We didn't do it for ourselves—we did it for our children! Why should we build it if our children are going to die before they can make something for their own children?

"I hope you understand me," she says. For an instant, the old Nancy is visible—her proud chin, her formidable gaze. "El pueblo no lo necesita. They say they are fighting for el pueblo, but el pueblo no lo quiere."

Throughout this speech, Leo holds the sweatshirt in front of her like a shield. Now she folds it carefully, her face burning. "I know how you must feel."

"Hija, you know nothing. You are as stupid as the day I met you."

At the front door, Nancy takes her elbow. "Do you know what he said? That son of a bitch, when he came to buy us a television? He said Neto was a hero. His death was a call to arms! Is that why you came? To tell me this nonsense, that my son was a hero?"

Leo's voice is barely audible. "No. He wasn't a hero."

"Then why? What was he?"

From every side she feels Ernesto watching, his face trapped forever behind cheap glass. She makes herself look into Nancy's eyes. "He was useful," she says.

As the Grand Opening approaches, silence tightens its grip on the house. In the halls, the stairwells, Leo and the others exchange nods and move quickly past. At night she and Julian hold their breath, gnaw on their knuckles to keep gasps and grunts from leaking out.

"Don't worry," he whispers afterward. "It's all taken care of."

"The cumpas know the plan? They understand what they have to do?" She shakes an empty cigarette pack, tosses it in the corner. "How do they know where to put the dynamite? How will you get it all over there?"

"Linda, stop asking," he says. "We agreed: no details. You just gotta trust me."

With Marta, too, she resists the urge to plead for information—a need made easier by Marta's air of distraction, a visible disquiet that intensifies each day they're confined to the house. On Friday morning she comes to Leo in the garden. "You can send these for me," she says, squatting next to her, flapping a stack of envelopes. "Please."

Leo glances at the address but there's no name, only a street she's never heard of. "I don't know, compañera. Did you ask Julian?"

"Linda. Amiga." Marta shoves the envelopes at her. "I am asking for help."

"Like you did at the Conquistador's Club?"

She hadn't known she'd say it, had pushed her resentment away to a place where she no longer thought about it. She'd rescued Marta, when the guard got the better of her it was Leo who came to her aid, who set her free. But instead of gratitude she's endured growing scorn—as if it were Marta who felt wronged, as if it were Leo's unforgivable transgression to have seen her fail. Was that it? Was Marta's ego so fragile she couldn't acknowledge her debt to another cumpa, another woman?

"It was supposed to be you, painting the slogan," Marta says, withdrawing the letters, her eyes dark with disappointment, as if it were she who'd offered to do Leo a favor and been rebuffed. Before she goes inside, she hands Leo that day's *El Comercio*, open to a digest of news from the provinces.

CANGALLO. Alejandra Valentín Naupa, age 14, died yesterday in the Sacred Heart Hospital. Valentín, a student at the Colegio Santa Ana, was among six children injured by the bomb that was detonated at the military parade on August 2. Three of the victims have been released from the hospital, while two others remain in critical condition. The resurgent terrorist group Cuarta Filosofía has claimed responsibility for the vicious act.

Leo reads the capsule twice. She looks up at Marta. "I don't understand. There was no bomb. How can there be victims when there was no bomb?"

"It's in your newspaper. It's in *The Eyes of the World*." Marta looks down at Leo as if she were a common pest, or a weed not worth the energy to pull. "You think nobody is as smart as you?

They can't tell the same lies? I only hope you are more careful in your bedroom, *compañera*."

When she leaves, Leo reads the article twice more. Somewhere in the house, a door slams. Somewhere the radio is playing a pop song, one she's heard dozens of times. All lies, she thinks. Everywhere: her newspaper, the government's newspaper, every word out of anyone's mouth—even Marta's photos, the last of which still hangs on the wall: three young boys crouched by a heap of trash, the light perfect, the grainy blacks and whites, everything composed for maximum effect. It's too much, too painful—there's no story worth believing anymore. Hadn't she come here for the truth? Hadn't she done everything so the truth might at last be heard?

．　．　．

Please, calm down.

Leonora, please sit down. You can't—okay, listen, there's nothing I can tell you while you're shouting and throwing things around my—

Don't touch that. Leonora, if I bring the guards in they will put you on the floor. Is this what you want? You want to come to your presentation looking like this? Crying and screaming like an infant? They will think you are a crazy person.

I'll tell you when you sit down.

Good. Alright? Now I will tell you. Señorita Ramos has been taken to a hospital.

I don't know. Listen, her injuries were very serious and the doctor—

No. I am telling you the truth: she's alive. You have my word.

Yes, I know. The guards also heard her. That's why we called for the doctor. Trust me, she'll have the best care—

Do you believe this, Leonora? Maybe you've seen too many movies. The guards are human. I am human. You really think we can listen to someone in pain—our compatriot—and take pleasure? Listen to yourself. It's unreasonable, when we've done—

No. I'll tell you what's reasonable. What's reasonable is when you're taken from a bus by soldiers, you do what they tell you to do. You don't run, and you don't take out a gun. It's a lucky thing, Leonora, that you weren't also shot.

This matters? The number of bullets? Explain this. Three would have been more acceptable? Five, a little worse? I'm trying to understand, but you make it so difficult. Your people are stockpiling weapons, dynamite, planning to attack the government, to take hostages. On any provocation you take out your guns. Yet when we shoot back, you call us murderers and fascists. Isn't this childish? I expect this from Philosophers, from the brother of Comrade Enrique. But I had a different opinion of you.

Maybe I thought because you're not Peruvian you couldn't possibly believe the ridiculous things the terucos say. Yes, you were playing the role very well, speaking the lines—but in the end I thought you would recognize the poor quality of the script and decide, reasonably, to play yourself again. Did I make a mistake about this?

But I've already told you: There's nothing you can tell me that I don't know. It's what you tell the world that matters. The details are insignificant, just as in your newspaper. But what you and I both believe is that the truth must be presented in such a way that the greatest number of people can understand. Isn't that what truth is?

Yes, of course I know about Comrade Enrique. In fact, I met him once.

No, a few years before that. At the university. Rosa introduced us.

Quite possibly. As I've said, she wasn't interested in monogamy. Maybe she painted him, too. But to me he was another person shouting slogans, one more Guevarista without the slightest idea about the country or the people he said he loved. After Rosa, I forgot his existence. I was surprised, last year, when I heard his name again. Only when I looked into the file did I remember—

From his brother, of course. Comrade Julian was very clear about his intentions to avenge Enrique, the Great Revolutionary. Of course he had only one version of the story. What's in the files is very different.

Leonora, does that story make sense to you? Of course not. Yes, Casimiro was arrested during a demonstration. He attacked a soldier with a knife. He was held for a few days, but when they realized he was the son of General Dueñas . . . as you can imagine he was treated very carefully. They expected the General to appear at any moment, but he never came. Eventually, Comrade Enrique was released and he disappeared—

Let me finish. He was known to be in Bolivia for at least two years. The next time we heard of him was in 1996. He was in the jungle in Madre de Dios, at a training camp, with others who couldn't accept that the war had ended. At a certain point, the Army had to intervene, and several of the subversives were killed during a gunfight.

Yes, I'm sure it was him.

But why does this upset you? You didn't know him—

Please, no more stupid questions. We had no choice. Should we wait until the cadre is operational? Should we wait until they come to Lima, with car bombs, assassinations? We knew who they were and what they wanted, Leonora. There's no point in fighting a war with half measures. If you believe in something, you defend it entirely. You do what is necessary. Isn't that right?

Of course they were told. The head of DINCOTE spoke to General Dueñas personally.

Please sit down. You can't talk to her right now. What would you say? How could you possibly help her? No, right now we have to make sure to help you. We have less than half an hour to decide what you'll say—

Leonora, if we didn't want to help you, why would we have arrested you? Why not leave you in the house, to die with the others? Haven't you asked yourself this?

No, I'm sorry. There's no time. You can use the bathroom when we go downstairs. Now sit down and explain to me, like you are going to explain to the reporters, like you are going to explain to the Peruvian people: How does it happen that someone like you is renting a house with terrorists? If you yourself are not a terrorist, if you know nothing about guns and dynamite and plans to attack Congress. You need to explain this very clearly. You need people to see your side.

Yes, that's what I said.

But . . . Leonora, there were uniforms, maps with escape routes marked, seating charts. It's very clear what was being planned—

Vía América? The shopping center? Why would anyone bother—

Well, I don't . . . I'm sorry, explain this again?

Enough. This makes no sense. For three days the country has heard about a plan to kidnap congresistas. This is what you'll be held responsible for. It's time to decide how you will present yourself. The country is very upset. People are demanding something be done. And something will be done. I'm trying to make sure it isn't done to you.

No. I told you, we don't have time. We are expected in only—

I see. Yes, I suppose that would look bad. Fine. But please hurry. Beatríz! The señorita needs to be taken to the bathroom. Go ahead. The guard is outside.

Yes, what is it?

No. I never told Comrade Julian. If he knew his brother was dead, what would he have to fight for? Without Enrique, he would have been no use to us.

You're right, of course. But it's one thing to tell people the truth if someone is lying to them. It's much more difficult when they're lying to themselves.

. . .

The woman who came to the Sociedad de Imanuel on the night of August 21 was frightened, exhausted, her clothes so large she seemed to be hiding in them—nothing like the hardened zealot who would appear on TV a few days later. Rabbi Eisen didn't ask why she'd come, or what she wanted. He wasn't surprised to see her lingering just beyond the fence, as she'd done months earlier—ever since that night, he realized, he'd been expecting to see her again.

"Come in, come in, Linda! Are you alright?" He holds the door for her, puts a hand in the small of her back. "You'll have to forgive me, it's a little busy here . . ."

The lobby bustles with congregants, hugging in greeting, filing through a set of high wooden doors. Some turn to stare at Leo, alarmed by this nervous gringa in the shapeless Berkeley sweatshirt.

"I didn't know there was a service," she says. "I'm sorry. I shouldn't be here."

"Not at all, not at all," he says, steering her through the doors, into the swell of the cantor's song. "Please, join us."

"I don't want to disturb anyone."

The rabbi's laugh startles her. "We're here to celebrate shabbos, to be together, to praise God. Why would you disturb anyone?"

It might as well be the same temple, she thinks as she takes a seat in the last row, remembering the low-backed chairs and dark carpet, the well-dressed families milling in the aisles at her grandfather's funeral. She fidgets with the prayerbook as the rabbi mounts the bimah, waving to someone in the front row. He whispers to the aged cantor, who nods and keeps singing. Children scamper through the aisles, but no one moves to quiet them, even as the rabbi clears his throat.

Sanctuary, she thinks. They call this room the sanctuary. She shouldn't be here.

"Señores, amigos, se damos la bienvenida en esta noche de paz."

His Spanish disorients her, as in a dream where the usual things are said by the wrong people. How stupid, she thinks, to have expected English. "We honor God with our togetherness," he says, nodding to the last straggling arrivals. She watches his hands holding the lectern, the crooked smile he shows the congregation. "We love God by loving one another. On the Sabbath we put aside our daily tasks and open our hearts."

The organ breathes through the room and all rise for the Sh'ma, which the rabbi and cantor deliver walking through the aisles, arms open in joy. Leo's acutely aware of her shabby clothes, her unbrushed hair, the empty seats next to her that no one will fill. She'd sat alone at Grandpa Carol's service, too, watching old friends greet one another, men and women in their eighties offering condolences to her mother while Matt stood by Maxine's side, hands clasped, a portrait of respect and grief.

She shouldn't be here, she knows that. But what's outside this building, the endless city, feels untraversable, full of hidden dangers. The house is no refuge, not anymore. All day the others have been locked away on the third floor, as if they'd forgotten her completely. It hardly matters—no one would speak to her anyway, no one would answer her questions. She wouldn't trust their answers if they did. On the bus, the sidewalks, everyone is watching her; even at a coffee shop, the look the cashier gave her was so odd, so knowing, that she'd fled without paying. Why hadn't she asked Nancy about the men who came looking for Chaski? Were they arenaleño? Were they military? Nancy had wanted her to ask, Leo can see that now. But she'd missed her cue.

She tries to steady herself with thoughts of Vía América, to run through the next day's tasks—but as the congregation sits what comes into her mind is a night at Nancy's, almost a year ago now, a welcome party for the new volunteers. She remembers the German girls—what were their names?—who'd invited her to go surfing the next day. She remembers Neto's smile when she admitted to liking Pearl Jam. He'd loaned her a CD, she suddenly remembers, a concert bootleg, but she'd never returned it.

"We remember those who are not here tonight," the rabbi says. As he reads the list of names, congregants bow their heads. A young couple in the next row put their arms around each other's waists. At Carol's funeral, her mother and aunts had wept lavishly, but Grandma Bess was dry-eyed. Some of her grandfather's friends were Holocaust survivors. Others had left Europe before the war, arrived terrified and destitute to scrape out their livings in sweatshops and construction sites until they could buy their way out—or until their children bought them out. Like her grandmother, most didn't weep. Their faces were sad but proud. It bothered Leo, this impropriety, as did the stories they told later at her grandparents' house, the off-color jokes. Their laughter flooded her with anguish. On the flight back to San Francisco she was still indignant, angry at them for having survived and prospered, for living long enough to look back with fondness on their suffering.

Yitgadal veyitkadash sh'mei rabah. *Amen.* As the rabbi says Kaddish, Leo catches herself mouthing along, words she hadn't known she remembered: b'alma div'ra kirutei, veyamlikh malkhutei. The hushed voices cast her mind in slowness, as if she were returning from a long journey to a place she hadn't expected to see again. How infuriating, that of all things *this* is what she remembers: these alien syllables, no more intelligible to her than Chinese or ancient Greek. How strange that despite this unknowing, this unbelieving, the words still bring a chill to her spine.

Yitbarakh veyishtabbah veyitpa'ar veyitromam veyitnasay

veyithaddar veyit'alleh. She fixes her gaze on the lamp flickering above the ark. *Those who are not here:* Neto, Josea, Álvaro. She tries to picture each of them, to honor their memories, but it's her grandfather's face she sees, winking his approval at her college graduation. Her lips move unconsciously—Oseh shalom bimromav, hu ya'aseh shalom—when she looks around the room she sees a hundred mouths moving in unison.

None of them knows what they're saying. It comes to her like a surprise gift, a relief: They don't understand the Hebrew words any more than she does. They're all faking it, playing their part. The realization brings an unexpected surge of fellow-feeling. This performance is what binds her to these people, she thinks. Incomprehension is what makes her one of them.

Aleinu v'al kol yisra'el, v'imru: *Amen.*

Later, in the rabbi's office, she can't hide her unease. She jumps at noises in the hall, repeatedly goes to the window, though only reflections stare back. It will be a different kind of school, Leo explains, a different kind of art. Not just landscapes and still lifes, sunny trifles for children to show their parents.

"I want them to think about other people, to imagine their lives," she says, rising to peer out at the dark street. The rabbi notes her abrupt gestures, how she talks too quickly, fills in silences. "Otherwise, what's the point? Why only paint what you see every day?"

The rabbi says he'll be happy to tell his congregants about the school. Many have young children who might be interested. Leo turns back with impatience.

"But they won't be interested. That's the problem. They won't approve." She's adamant on this point, as if trying to convince herself. The kind of art she wants to make—it would upset people. That's what it's *meant* to do.

"But you underestimate us," he smiles. "There are many here who appreciate—"

"They can't. If they did—" He notes her shaking hands, the control it takes for her to lower herself into the chair. She's up again a second later, back to the window. "I'm sorry," she says. "I shouldn't have come here. Is there a back door?"

The rabbi leans forward to examine her face. "Are you hiding from someone?"

She starts to answer, but stops, open-mouthed, as if struck by some terrible, forgotten errand. Shaking her head, she drops back into the chair and draws her legs up—like a little girl, the rabbi remembers thinking. He thought he should call someone, that this poor girl was in crisis, maybe having some kind of breakdown. And in a country where she had no people, where she might not know anyone at all.

"Who are you hiding from, Linda?"

"It could be anyone," she says, touching her forehead to her knees. Everywhere she goes, she says. Why won't people stop staring at her? "Maybe it's God," she says, looking up with miserable eyes. "Isn't that who's supposed to be watching, Rabbi?"

"Watching?" he says cautiously. "I don't know. Yes, of course God is—"

"But wouldn't he approve? Why should I feel like I'm doing something wrong? It's His work, right? It's what He's supposed to do. I don't even believe in Him! But somebody has to. If He's distracted, or too lazy. Somebody has to do *something*."

Soon enough the rabbi would understand what she was trying to tell him. He would see her bruised, livid face and blame himself for not having heard. Or had he heard? The congregation mingling downstairs, the building alive with community, had he understood too well what her words might mean?

He leans forward, offers a soothing smile. "Do you really believe this, Linda?"

"You're a rabbi," she says. "Isn't God supposed to help people? To feed them?"

"What I mean," he says, "is do you think you can take His place?"

As he walks her downstairs, one hand on her shoulder, he tries to ignore the feeling of accompanying a prisoner to the gallows. They pass quickly through the crowded lobby and at the door he invites her to come back once the art school has opened. He assures her she'll find eager students among the congregation.

"Don't worry, Linda," he says. "No one can have a problem with art. With education. Where would our children be without these things?"

Leo smiles weakly. For a moment he thinks she might ask to stay. Someone calls to him from across the room, a woman he's known for decades, whose sons moved to New York long ago and never visited or sent for her. When he turns back, Leo's already moving past the guard into the dim orange light of the street. He watches for another few seconds—how small she is against that darkness—then closes the temple door.

4

"Because it doesn't make sense. It doesn't add up."

"Nothing makes sense, Andres. This is Peru."

"But why would she say those things, make that sacrifice? She had to know what would happen. What was the point?"

Damien filled my glass and leaned back on the couch. Carlito was working late, and with Stephanie still in Canada the apartment felt large and sterile, carefully staged.

"She'd been in custody for three days," he said. "Pissing on herself—"

"No, she's too controlled, too aware of what she's doing. Have you watched closely? There's something else."

"That's journalism," he said. "There are always holes. The truth is very messy. It's the story that has everything accounted for, every thread tied, that you can't trust."

"That's not good enough," I said, provoking another Gallic shrug. "It was *over*. There was nothing to gain or take responsibility for. Why not just go home?"

"Shame? Pride?" He was almost laughing now. "Andres, this is not the most stable person. Six months with the Philosophers. She has to justify it, to prove it to herself. If she takes the government's offer she breaks this vow. She tells the world she is not the person she claimed to be."

I rolled my glass between my palms. The dark wine glimmered. "That's what her mother says in her book: She had these principles, she felt she had to stand up for them."

"You see?"

"But I don't buy it."

I was so close. I'd worked out everything else: the motivations and misunderstandings, the logic that brought her to that threshold. I'd written more than a hundred pages, working in a fever, moving myself often to astonishment. I'd been studying the footage of the presentation for days, caught by some cadence in her tirade, some canny glint in the eye. She was trying to tell me something.

Who am I?

"Look at this," I said, opening a folder of news clippings. "*El Comercio*, August 23: 'Seven Philosophers lost their lives in the assault on Calle Almagro.' *La República:* 'Between seven and nine militants died.' The radio, TV news—you hear the same thing: seven people. Seven or eight. Then, August 26, *El Comercio* says there were six people killed. Every paper after that," I said, laying one sheet after another on the table. "'Six terrorists.' 'Six people.' Now it's the official body count."

Damien glanced at each article and set it aside. "I don't understand."

"What happened to the seventh person?"

Slowly, he put down his glass. He looked at me as if considering for the first time that I might not be just incompetent but also deranged. "So there was confusion. It always takes a few days—"

"Sure," I conceded. "Maybe. But what if they got it wrong? Or they didn't even have to get it wrong, but what if she *thought* they got it wrong? If she thought someone survived. You see? If she's just a stupid foreigner caught up in something she didn't understand, then there's still a problem, there are more Philosophers out there. By the logic of its own story the government has to hunt them down. But if she knew what she was doing, if she's La Leo, the revolutionary—"

"The Gringa Terrorist—"

"If the real terrorist has been caught, you can't ramp up the war again. The public won't support it. What if she thought it was the best chance for him to get away?"

"Who, Andres?"

But I had no answer, not yet. Damien tapped his fingertips, shook his head as if to clear a vivid dream. "You give her too much credit," he said. "You make it sound as if she really were the mastermind they tried to portray."

"Isn't that what she would have wanted to believe? Wouldn't you?"

August 22, a dry and mild Saturday afternoon. The skies over Pueblo Libre brushed with gauze, a gentle wind lifting the scent of jasmine from neighboring gardens. At the appointed time, Leo waits in the courtyard, face to the sun. She squints up at the silent house, the sparrows lit on the bare lime tree, and remembers the day she met Señora Zavallos, the picture she'd painted of a school rampant with children. It had never been anything but an alibi, a lie. But she'd told it so often, imagined it in such detail, she feels a twinge of regret to think it never came true.

One more task. One last bit of preparation and everything will be in place. The others spent the night rehearsing, visualizing, running through contingencies—though Leo stayed awake listening to their heavy movements, Julian didn't come downstairs, and at last she stumbled into dreams of wild surf, anguished whispers; she was missing someone—a terrible absence, akin to dread—but she didn't know who. At dawn she'd woken to the feel of him next to her, his hand resting cool and gentle on her thigh. They fucked in silence, slowly, each distracted but working to pull the other into the secret circle. When it was over, he propped himself on an elbow and stared at her.

"What?" she said. She pulled the sheet over herself, surprised at her self-consciousness.

There wasn't a trace of mockery in his expression, none of the old contempt. Affection, perhaps, and maybe something sadder. He seemed unable to look away. It wasn't love—she wasn't foolish enough to think it was love. But it might have been something better: respect.

"Don't worry," she said, reaching for his chin, pulling at the wiry hairs. "We'll be careful. Marta will only be gone an hour, and I'll be back after I see the printer."

He nodded, his mouth slightly open. For an astonished heartbeat she thought he might burst into tears. But then he said something even more shocking:

"I trust you."

She shook her head mutely, moved by something she couldn't yet grasp. Deep down, she must have understood.

"Remember that, okay?" he said. "Compañera? Leonora?"

He rolled away, pulled on his clothes, lit a cigarette. She said nothing—or she said something pointless and instantly forgotten, unlike the hundreds of things she's said to him since, words of true understanding that crystallize in the frozen night of El Arca.

"Sí, mi compañero," is what she said, but by then he was at the door.

When Marta emerges from the house, in the floppy hat and cheap sunglasses Leo bought for her, Leo has to stifle a laugh. She looks like a housewife, a trendy urbanite on a beach outing. She looks, Leo realizes, strikingly beautiful—a beauty Leo had forgotten, or learned to see past, over the months of routine and rivalry. She'd stopped looking at Marta—at all of them, even Julian—except through the veil of the plan. But as she and Marta stare at each other what comes into Leo's thoughts are those first days in the house—before the cumpas and Radio 2000, before Josea and Álvaro, before exigency turned them into strangers—the two of them together, barely speaking a common language but not quite needing to. It had felt to Leo like having an older sister, her wisdom and protection cloaked in unfathomable experience.

What comes next? she wants to ask. But she won't, not now, here on the verge. She won't give into the old needs, or deface the plan by losing her nerve.

"Vámonos," Marta says.

"Are you sure about this?" Leo says. "Maybe you should stay."

"It's four o'clock. We need to go."

"Stay here," Leo says. "I can do it, I swear. Just give me your camera."

"Linda—"

"Why take the risk? Really, you can count on me."

The courtyard fills with the rustle of sparrows. The house seems to lean over them, as though César and the others are listening from the third floor. Marta hesitates, stares at the gate as if, after weeks of seclusion, she can't recognize the outside world.

"No," Marta says. "I have to." With a nervous smile she adds, "I am the photographer."

As they cross the courtyard, Leo steals a glance at the rosebushes: three small buds on the tallest cane, tiny green fists still reluctant to open. She's been watching them for days. All that work, she thinks. When will she have something to show for it?

The entire print run of *The Eyes of the World*, no. 8, was confiscated from Eladio Huatay's shop almost as soon as the presses stopped. Four dry, dour pages, the final number had little of the panache of its predecessors—no poems or repurposed ads, little humor. Notably, there was no "Scorecard" highlighting the noble exploits of hidden revolutionaries. More notable still was the blank space on the back page: a white void, an empty frame that would forever await its image.

The essay arranged around this space was entitled *¿Quiénes Somos?* (*Who Are We?*), and was clearly intended as the centerpiece. Unsigned, the essay glosses the history of modern Peru from Independence through the dirty war and "its so-called end." The theme is clear: a war is not over until its wounds have closed, until "people's hearts have been pacified, and the physical, spiritual, and national body made whole." At the same time, the author—whether Leo, Julian, or a combination of the two—asserts that the Cuarta Filosofía should be seen as a unifying force, their actions as having been designed to bring Peruvians together, to remind them of their common bonds:

"Until we embrace all our brothers and sisters, our body will remain broken . . . Peace is not peace if it demands we leave parts of ourselves behind."

At Leo's civilian trial, the prosecutor read the entire essay aloud, alongside rhetorically similar passages from old Shining Path communiqués. (Once again, the defense's objection was ignored.) He cited its veiled reference to Victor Beale—"one eye closed in return for the thousands you have plucked out"—as proof of coordination between the Pueblo Libre and Jacaranda groups.

But despite its excesses, its militant posture, the essay is no

357

manifesto. To me, it reads not as a threat but a plea: for justice, for recognition, even forgiveness. Knowing what we know now, it's impossible not to see it as a swan song, a final bid for empathy from people who had all but given up on being understood:

"We are the ones you want to forget. But we have not forgotten you."

It's Marta she'll remember, Marta whose face and voice, whose secrets, will come to her every night. She'll remember the long walk to Miraflores, the feeling of ease that crept over her the farther they got from the house. And the light, its thick liquid quality, warm honey of the afternoon sun, neighborhoods alive with strolling families— the weeks of paranoia seem suddenly absurd, a child's fantasy. How absurd to think anyone could find them in a city of eight million. How narcissistic to think they're looking!

Like shreds of a torn photograph: she'll remember the long silences, the glances and irrelevant words. She'll assemble them piece by piece, rearrange them with tweezers and glue, each iteration resulting in a different image.

The thick traffic on the avenues, the wafting stink of gasoline broken by long, cool drafts of ocean air. As they cross onto the malecón they pick up the pace. It's nearly five o'clock, the sun starting its descent into a nest of coral and rose. Leo can feel Marta's growing disquiet; several times she seems about to say something but stops herself. Over the ocean, two paragliders' colorful canopies wink in the late light and Leo stops to watch, savoring what small seconds of leisure remain. The gliders soar upward in the ocean drafts, legs rising at the top of their arcs, then abruptly drop, gliding in long, hawklike curves over the cliffs before swooping back out to sea. How small they are, she thinks, struck by the grandeur. Marta moves next to her and they stand a moment without speaking. Far below, tiny surfers etch white lines into green metal.

They don't see the barricade until they've rounded the last curve, the jeeps parked grill-to-grill across the intersection, men in fatigues smoking or leaning on their rifles.

"Puta madre," Marta says, drawing back into the entryway of an apartment building. "A checkpoint. We have to go back."

"Why is the military guarding a shopping mall?"

"You should have thought of this, Linda," Marta says. "You should have known."

Beyond the roadblock, the lush promenade flows to the edge of the land—bright new flowers, rustling palms, Christopher Columbus backlit by a perfect sunset. Vía América finished at last, awaiting only the masses that will crawl over its glossy surface like maggots on meat. When Leo peeks out, the soldiers are staring in their direction. She feels her breath quickening—she wants that photograph, they *need* it. Ducking back, she starts to ask Marta something but Marta is clutching her arm, pulling her close.

"Leo, go now," she says.

"I'm not going back without that picture."

"Not back: leave. Take a bus somewhere. Anywhere. Call your father and go home."

Unnerved, Leo takes a step back. "What are you talking about?"

"Nobody will stop you. Nobody will look for you. I swear it. Listen to me," she says. "The newspaper is finished. One photograph—it's not important. You did what you wanted, what you promised. So go now. Please. Before it's too late."

Leo stares into the opaque shine of Marta's sunglasses but can't see what's in her comrade's eyes: fear, calculation, or some other inscrutable motive. She fishes a bent cigarette from her pack, flicks her lighter with trembling fingers. Even now, she thinks, pulling the smoke deep into her lungs. Even now, they don't believe. Once, she knows, she was tempted. She jumped into the car and sped away while the people behind her burned. But she's not that person anymore. She takes another long drag and drops the cigarette, crushes it with her toe. Before Marta can stop her, she steps into the street.

"Hola! Hola!" she shouts, hurrying toward the checkpoint with an imbecilic smile, a fatuous bounce in her step. "Hola, amigos! Me llamo Linda. ¿Como está usted?"

The soldiers gather around her, blocking her path, competing to display the most malevolent glare. Leo speaks haltingly, mangling words, misplacing accents. "Shop-ping? I go shop-ping?" She points to the statue behind them, fumbles in her pocket for the slab of plastic. "Expresso Americano, amigos. ¿Comprendo?"

One soldier examines the card while the others frankly assess her breasts. They're all younger, some still teenagers; from their embarrassed expressions it's clear they've never talked to a gringa, maybe never seen one up close. An older man, their captain, strides up from behind the jeeps. Short and swarthy, his face is round as a pie, adorned with a mustache that looks pencil-drawn. A fat black holster slaps against his hip. The other soldiers straighten and pull back when he addresses them.

"Está cerrado," he tells Leo. He points back up the street. "No se puede entrar."

Leo mimics bewilderment. "Shopping?" she says, waggling the card. "¿Qué hora?"

"Está cerrado," he coughs. "Hay que volver mañana. Andale, señorita."

"My guidebook," she says, standing on tiptoes and letting a note of entitlement creep into her voice. "*Lonely Planet*? It says I go *Ví-a A-mé-ri-ca*. No comprendo?" The captain shakes his head, tries futilely to interrupt. When he reaches for her shoulder she jerks away, hands on her hips. "Hey, you can't treat me like this! I'm an American citizen! Yo soy Americano—"

—and then Marta is between them, as Leo knew she would be. She stands close to the captain, speaks in Quechua, leads him back to the jeep. She shows him her camera, cocks her hips while he handles it. Her voice is higher, with the teasing, nasal quality Leo's heard from street vendors and pop singers from the provinces—it's startling, this side of Marta, but Leo knows it's no act or transformation, just one of her friend's many selves. The other soldiers laugh at something Marta says and the captain blushes, his irritation giving way to amusement as they all look at Leo, who stands with arms crossed, shaking with staged anger.

"*Fie minute*," the captain coughs, turning with exaggerated chivalry to let them pass. Marta claps her hands and kisses his cheek, to the delight of his subordinates, but Leo's already crossing the street, heading toward the high metal fence that marks the edge of the cliffs.

"That was foolish, compañera," Marta says when she catches up. "Why do you take this risk?"

"So you could rescue me," Leo says. "Now we're even."

The mall is too wide to shoot directly from above, so Leo backs along the fenceline, squinting into the roar of the ocean wind, searching for an angle. The image has to be perfect, complete—Peruvians needed to see the whole ugly tumor to appreciate what had been cut out. From one vantage point, the entire structure is visible but not the towering statue with its sleazy gaze; hurrying to another, they can capture only part of the mall, the rest obstructed by the jut of the parking garage. Marta stands on her toes, hooks her fingers in the fence and holds the camera overhead, but all she can get is a slice of the upper level: Sol Alpaca, Godiva, something called Sam's Fifth Avenue.

"It's good," she says, glancing back at the soldiers.

"Not good enough," Leo says.

At a gap in the fence she plunges into the shrubbery, thorns and branches catching her clothing, scratching her arms. With effort she frees herself, picks her way down a gully of dirt and scree. How long now since Julian brought her here, how many lifetimes? The path falls steeply toward the highway, a crevasse of jutting rocks scattered with food wrappers, chunks of sod and broken concrete, a New York Yankees cap crushed and half-buried in the soil. The wind fists into her mouth as she edges downward. It was a test, she thinks, looking back up, guessing at the spot where he'd pushed her to her knees—the first of many. Everything has changed since that night. But it's still a long way down.

"More stupidity," Marta says, descending carefully behind Leo, her sliding steps sending showers of pebbles into space.

And suddenly it's there, spread out before them: Vía América in all its philistine glory. Sunlight knifes off plate glass and unlit neon, reflects in giant LCD screens and brass railings and steel café tables. The corners and angles distort their perspective, giving the many-tiered tableau a dreamy depthlessness. Devoid of people, the mall and winding cliffs look like an artist's rendering—nature superimposed by glorious modernity, overwritten by it, liquidated.

At the far end, cantilevered above the ocean, the crown jewel sits dazzling and impregnable. Its cavernous entrance flanked by giant red guitars, the Hard Rock Café beams an empty smile into the sunset, like a warrior with one foot propped on a carcass. She can't help but admire the nerve of the builders, their determination to erase everything—history, language, culture, geography, blasted and hammered and ultimately consumed by this gleaming shell. They almost succeeded.

The clouds shift, sunlight casting a scarlet glow over the facade, where giant red letters proclaim their message:

SAVE THE PLANET

"That's the shot," Leo says, giddy with satisfaction. "Take the photo and let's go."

The captain and his men are waiting up above, calling angrily through the fence, gesturing with their rifles as Leo and Marta scramble back to the road. After hurried apologies, they put the checkpoint and the towering Columbus behind them, moving swiftly up Avenida Larco where the city's horns and pedestrians start to reassert themselves. The noise comes as a relief after the unreal calm of Vía América. Leo walks in long strides, propelled by triumph. A tourist! She'd gotten what she wanted by acting like a tourist, like exactly the kind of foolish parasite they'd built it for in the first place. A block later the thought comes to her with searing, delightful irony: She was Vía América's first customer.

At the bus stop, she turns to Marta, pulling her into an embrace. "I'll be back soon," she says, squeezing too hard. "Tell Julian we did it. Tell him everything's ready."

Gently, Marta extracts herself. "Yes, I will tell him."

Something in her voice, a somber note, makes Leo pull back. For the first time since Leo's known her, Marta won't look at her.

"You'll be there? Tonight, when I get back," Leo says. "Won't you?"

Slowly, Marta takes off her sunglasses, and the shape of her mouth steals Leo's breath. In an instant the breadth of her error comes to her. Of course Marta won't be there. Nobody will. When she gets back from Los Arenales the house will be empty, down to the third-floor crawlspace, her computer, the shed in the backyard. In a flash she sees the immaculate kitchen, the neatly made beds, easels standing in rows—the rest will be gone, all of it, anything that could identify them or reveal anything about their plans. He'll leave her the radio and her clothes, her passport, maybe the stupid llama hanging by the door. But she'll never see Julian again.

I trust you. In a flash that leaves her lightheaded she sees what he'd wanted: a clean break. From here on in she can only be a liability. The logic is as sound as it is merciless. Only a child would ask for more.

As a bus looms up the avenue, headlights soft in the dusk, she tries to hold off the wave of grief that's cresting above her, larger than any she's ever known.

"Come with me to the printer," she manages. "One hour. Marta? Please."

"I can't. I'm sorry. There's something I have to do."

"Then let me come with you. I'll get to the printer a little later. It won't matter. Or I can meet you somewhere. I won't ask anything. I promise, I won't make trouble." In one miserable rush, the tears come. "Sorry, sorry," she says, furious with herself. "I know it's right. I understand. But"—in one hiccup the wave crashes down, burying her under her own wretchedness—"*I'll miss you.*"

Marta's voice is strained, scratchy. "Compañera, control yourself."

"One hour," she says, blinking away her tears. "I've earned this one thing."

The bus pulls to the sidewalk, a kid of fourteen or fifteen hanging from the door. *¡Vamos, vamos chicas! ¡Ya sale, vámonos!* Marta stands awkwardly, her face softening from resolution to reluctance and, at last, compassion.

"I'll ride with you as far as the highway," she says. "No more. I'm already late."

"For what?" Leo says, burning with humiliation. "Where are you going?"

Marta hands the kid two coins and pulls Leo onto the crowded bus. "San Martín de Porres," she says. Then, deciding something: "I have to see my son."

. . .

Not for many months, until that first New Year's Eve in El Arca, will she remember the first thought that went through her mind. Standing at the window of her cell, watching the dark and frozen landscape, she'll hear the quick, distant sizzles of an inmate's home-made firecrackers and it will crash through her memory: the lurch of the bus, the smash of glass and banging on metal, the appearance, amid screams and flailing arms, of men in black masks, guns drawn, pouring in from both ends of the aisle.

Terrorists, is what she thought. The bus had just passed Calle Tarata. *It's a terrorist attack.*

She'll draw her knees up on the narrow mattress and let herself remember Marta as the soldiers took her from the bus: limp and expressionless, dangerously coiled. Shivering violently, Leo will use her tin cup to gouge a thick splinter from the pallet and whittle it to a point, working methodically with no concern for time or discovery. When her instrument is smooth and sharp, she'll choose a spot above her head where the layers of paint are soft and make her mark:

1

"How old is he? Your son."

"Almost six. His birthday comes in October."

Will you be there? Leo almost asks. Squeezed into the narrow seat, she takes Marta's hand and holds it in her lap. She keeps her eyes on the road ahead, the windshield smeared with soot, taillights crawling through new mist.

"What's his name?"

Steadily, as though trying not to break something, Marta says, "His name is Casimiro."

Leo nods, as if to endorse the choice. The gears of the bus grind and stick. Two teenage girls watch the distraught gringa and whisper to each other. As the bus edges up the avenue, Marta winds the film from her camera, flips open the back and hands the roll to Leo.

They've gone only a dozen blocks when some of the passengers turn to look out the back window, murmurs of confusion and alarm quickly spreading row to row.

"And yours?" Leo says weakly.

"I can't—"

Leo looks up in anguish. "Please. Tell me your name."

Marta closes her eyes. "Angélica."

Angélica. She turns the name over in her mind. *Angélica.* She doesn't trust herself to speak without crying. "Tell me more."

Marta shakes her head. A hush has fallen over the passengers, a restless dark outside the windows where four SUVs have pulled even with the bus, flanking it. "There's too much."

"Tell me," she says, feeling space open around her, the twilight isolating her in weightless ether. For a moment she's back on the rooftop of Ricky's hostel, all of Lima silent and insubstantial, one light blazing in the distance. "Tell me everything."

When the bus jolts to a stop, Marta sits up straighter. She scans the other passengers. There's a moment of silence, almost elegiac, and then voices rushing through the street, surrounding the bus, hands slapping on the walls, the roof. With each blow Marta grows more still, withdrawing to that place Leo has never been able to enter. A shimmer rises in the windows, blue and red, now dark with rushing shadows, now blindingly alive.

"When I see you again. That's when I will tell you."

Leo watches the side of her face, as fascinated by its lovely severity as she's always been. Flashlight beams pierce the windows, darting over the rows of passengers, ghostly faces coming in and out of existence. When the doors fly open, soldiers' boots hammering on the steps, Leo squeezes Marta's hand once more, then lets it go.

"By then I'll already know. Won't I?"

Marta's thrusts her hand deep into the camera bag. She's trained her sights on the first soldier. She's already rising.

"Sí, mi hermana," she says. "Then you'll know."

5

One would hardly call it a mirror, this thick sheet of aluminum bolted to the wall, warped and dented over time. No amount of polish could bring light to its depths—the image it offers is dim and elusive, a shade from some Greek tragedy, or one possible future glimpsed in a faulty crystal ball. When she leans over the sink her face looms from the murk pale and ghastly, the scraped forehead and yellowing bruise along her cheekbone, the cracked lips and fever-bright eyes.

Good, she thinks, adjusting the canvas sling on her arm, squeezing and opening the numb hand. *Let them see me like this. Let them see exactly who I am.*

"Señorita," says the guard outside, knocking once, recalling her to the small, locked washroom with its faded green tile and blazing fluorescence, its sickening smell of bleach covering something sour and bodily. She'd slept little, kept awake by Marta's sobs from the next cell. *¿Dónde estás? ¿Mi vida, dónde estás?* she cried for hours, gasps of pain escalating to wails. But no one came.

"Aquí, aquí," Leo answered. She knelt on the cold floor and pressed her face to the bottom of the door. "I'm here."

Near dawn there was a sudden commotion, voices in the corridor, the squeak of a wheeled gurney. Leo hunched by the door, too exhausted to cry out. An hour later they brought her breakfast—a bowl of cold oatmeal and a juice box. She gagged and spat, dizzy with hunger, but wouldn't eat. The heat in her bladder had spread through her abdomen, her joints swollen and creaking. She grit her teeth, eased herself into her stiff clothes. When she caught herself combing her hair with her fingers, she laughed aloud—her friends are dead and dying, but like a good girl from Cannondale she still tries to look her best.

"Señorita," says the guard. He unlocks the door to find her leaning over the basin, a worm of pinkish spit dangling from her lip. "¿Terminaste?" he says, hesitant as all the others who've been told to treat this tiny, wrecked person like a live grenade.

"I couldn't go. It hurt too much." When she swallows, pain bristles along her scalp. The guard eyes her, uncomprehending. "Never mind," she says. "Vámonos."

The hallway hums with ambient noise, a subliminal grumbling rhythmic and ambiguous as speech. When they'd brought her here, stunned and hyperventilating—was it two nights ago or three?—there was a sack over her head, one small hole for air. She could still hear the gunshots and the rotors, still smell the fuel. They'd taken the sack off only for a moment, to give her a glimpse from the back of the car: the smashed-in gate, snipers on ladders, everything floodlit like a Hollywood production.

"Is this your house?" the men in the car shouted. She shook her head, blind with shock. She could not clear the image from her mind—Marta on the sidewalk, twisting in agony, terrified faces looking out from the windows of the bus. It couldn't have happened. A nightmare, she was desperate to wake up. It couldn't have happened.

"Is it your house?" the men demanded. There were flames in a second-floor window, flashes from the rooftop. A radiant vision, isolated and unreal. All she could manage was *I don't know.*

As they sped across the city the car radio crackled and spat: *Se acabó.* It's over. She thought she would vomit, or suffocate. They shoved her through long corridors, righting her when she stumbled, yanked the hood off in time for her to see the cot flying up at her. No one spoke to her until the morning, and that was the lieutenant.

The lieutenant. It still sounds ridiculous, as if he'd chosen this new role as a joke but now refused to go back to the old one.

The guard knocks on the lieutenant's door, cracks it open, closes it. "Espérate," he tells Leo, pointing to a chair. She ignores him. If she sits the hall will start to spin, the sickly lights and gummy, white-washed walls press her toward unconsciousness. There's a tremor in her knees, soreness in her jaw. Her head swims with all she's been told: Julian, Álvaro and Josea, Casi, her own parents. Can it all be true? In this building, with its garbled echoes, the question seems beside the point. *¿Dónde estás?* The anguish in Marta's voice, her despair—these were real. The rest of it has become unstable, vague as her reflection in the metal mirror: Marta stepping off the bus, the soldiers drawing back, spatters of soundless white light against the dusk. The body on the sidewalk, one hand flexing slowly. They'd dragged Leo away before she could get to her friend, thrust her into the car before she could tell Marta she was there, she would not leave her. Two men sat on Leo's back, a hard metal muzzle pressed to her neck as they hurtled and squealed toward Pueblo Libre.

Had she seen these things, or are they mere phantasms, products of a fevered mind? Even this "presentation"—who's to say there will be real journalists, that their articles will ever be read? Who's to say her conversations with the lieutenant aren't themselves scenes in some larger drama whose arc she can't make out?

From somewhere above comes a series of distant thumps, the muted rattle of something dragging—as though she were underwater, as though this cold hall were at the bottom of the ocean. She saw a movie once in which the hero found himself in an immaculate hotel room but there was nothing outside, nothing. The same inscrutable hum at the edges of existence. She wonders if the sound is inside her head.

Then she's back in the office, in the uncomfortable swivel chair. The lieutenant—the man she'd once called Comrade Miguel—watches her with troubled eyes. She already knows what he's going to say.

"Are you feeling better?" he asks vaguely, putting off unpleasantness. She has a memory of seeing him hang up the telephone, though whether this took place days or seconds ago she couldn't say.

"I don't believe you," she mumbles, lowering her head to the desk.

"Leonora—"

"You're full of shit. I don't believe any of it."

"I have to tell you something."

"You can have your little presentation. I don't care. Why don't you do it for me?" She gives a dull laugh, anything to stop him from saying it. "Tell them whatever you want. None of it matters."

"Angélica Ramos has died."

Cheek resting on her forearm, Leo considers the statement, parses its odd verb tense. Why not *is dead*? Why not just *died*?

"Did you hear me?"

"Your friend the artist," she says, her breath wet on the crook of her elbow, "Mira—that was bullshit, too, wasn't it? A cautionary tale." With profound effort, she hauls her head off the desk. "Now Marta. Okay, cumpa," she says, reaching for his cigarettes, her fingers too clumsy to spark the lighter. "Message received."

Lieutenant Lang gently takes the lighter and lights her cigarette. He shakes his own from the pack and taps the filter on the desk without lighting it.

"I'm sorry," he says. "Please, believe me."

Leo sucks on the cigarette, hard enough to shock herself awake. *This is no place for you.* The first words he'd said to her, a hundred years ago, in the Plaza de Armas. *Stupid gringa.* Trying to tell her something, even then.

"It doesn't matter what I believe. Isn't that what you said?" She ignores his look of pity, pushes herself out of the chair. If this really is an act, if they're watching everything she does, why not make it a star turn? "I didn't believe in you, either. You're not very convincing, you know that? I never believed you. Get a better disguise."

As if for the first time, she looks around the office: the heavy black file cabinet, the map of Lima divided into color-coded zones, a framed photo of Miguel shaking hands with the President, another at the base of the Statue of Liberty, his arm around an attractive black woman. A suit jacket hangs from a hook on the back of the door. For some reason this offends her more than anything he's said: that he wears a suit to work, that this murdering toad plays the part of a man who wears a suit.

"Show me," she says. "Show me her body."

"Amiga," he presses an eyebrow with two fingers. "Of course that's not possible."

Another spasm in her belly doubles her over. "If she's really dead," she says, grimacing, "show me. If any of this is true. Otherwise, you can go fuck yourself, *amigo*. You can tell your stories to someone else."

The lieutenant shakes his head, taps his cigarette again but still doesn't light it. He nods at the sling and asks, "How is your arm?"

"It's broken."

"You treat me like your enemy, Leonora, but actually I've been trying to help you. I wish you could understand." He slides his cigarette back into the pack. "We have only a few minutes. Remember what I told you. There are going to be a lot of people, cameras. A lot of questions. You need to speak quickly. This is your only opportunity—"

"If you want to help me, show me her body," she says, lifting her chin defiantly.

"It's important you say the right things. It's important that you remove yourself from this situation. It's going to get worse. You don't want a trial, you don't want to be in El Arca, or one of these places. So tell them: it was a misunderstanding. You're very sorry. You just want to go home."

With great effort, she brings a smile to her lips. "This is my home."

Deflated, he lets a hand fall to the desk. Someone knocks on the door and he barks *Not now!*, then stands and swipes a brown folder from the pile. Coming around the desk, he drops it in her lap. She's careful not to let her smile fade. The garish color and glossy overexposure of the photograph momentarily confuses her. She closes her eyes, opens them, waits for the shapes to cohere.

"You don't belong here, Leonora. Let's agree on this. This is not your story. Now it's time to write yourself out of it. You weren't really part of it, except as a kind of historical accident, a remainder. And now it's ending," he says. His tone is not unkind. "The book is closing. Do you want to be inside or outside?"

She can feel him standing over her but she's transfixed by the photograph: the body sprawled improbably, topless, face crusted with blood; the floor littered with discarded bandages, a wadded-up T-shirt, everything squalid in the camera flash, shiny as a wax museum. The woman's hands pressed to her belly can't cover the black, wet wound. Whoever holds the camera is present only as a faint smudge, the tip of a finger at the edge of the image. Otherwise, the woman is alone.

"She was a mother," Leo whispers. A shoeprint, its tread obscenely vivid, is stamped in the filth by Marta's head. Leo hears her voice catch, feels another sharp squirm in her bladder. She *had* believed him—that's the worst part. She'd been so eager to please him, to impress a higher-up. In that way she'd betrayed them all.

"She was a mother, you shit. *Hijo de puta*. And you killed her."

"No, you did," he says. Leo looks up sharply, expecting cruelty but seeing only regret. "You were supposed to be alone on that bus."

It's too much. She lets the photo fall to her lap. *Come with me. Please*? It's too much, one too many stories. A sob leaks from her throat before she can strangle it. It makes her furious, this weakness, as if she's betrayed them all over again. To hide her tears she lunges up at Miguel, brandishing the lit cigarette, feeling as she rises the stab and squeeze in her bladder, a warm spurt into her underpants. He catches her wrist and they rock against the file cabinet, which totters and spills a stack of folders, a dozen more bright, gruesome photos scattering across the floor. With a muttered curse, he plucks the cigarette from her fingers. Squeezing her broken arm until she cries out and relents, he maneuvers her awkwardly back into the chair.

"Do you believe me now?" he says. "Your being here has changed things, and not only for yourself. It is a kind of corruption. Do you understand?"

She hides her face, sickened by the sound of her sobs. He slides the photo back into its folder, stoops to gather the scattered files, then stands over her and stares disgusted at the dark stain growing in the crotch of her jeans.

"Get up now," he says. "It's time."

Her arm throbs, her thighs prickle with hot urine. Her body stinks of infection—pungent, like rotting citrus. The wet denim sucks at her skin.

"If I have to carry you in there crying like an infant it will be worse."

"You're the murderer," she says. "*You* are. Not me. When this is over, you'll be remembered for what you did. Your name will be written on the wrong page of history."

He nods at the cliché, reaches for his jacket. "Maybe. Maybe not."

"It doesn't matter what happens to me. That's what you don't understand. It doesn't matter how many mothers you kill." She pushes herself out of the chair, grasping for words to distract him. "It's not a story, it's a war. A revolution. And we're going to win. We've already won. All we had to do is start."

He waves off this speech and reaches for the door. "Who knows?"

"Compañero," she says, stepping meekly toward him, "you know."

Something in her voice, some sweetness or surrender, disarms him. He leans forward as if to let her kiss his cheek, recognizing her triumphant smile an instant too late. By then she's sliding her hand out of her pants and pressing it to his face, smearing her wet palm across his cheek, his nose, over his lips, before he can shove her back. She laughs as she stumbles against the desk, as the ashtray falls to the floor with a ring of heavy glass—her broken arm banded by fire, her head knocking against the chair when she sits in the ashes—laughs as the door opens and the guard scans the room in alarm. She's still laughing as he helps her to her feet and fumbles with the hood, laughing at Comrade Miguel, his cheap suit and iron back preceding them out the door.

It takes several minutes to get to the presentation room. The guard leads her down hallways that double back on themselves, up stairways and through open spaces where sound expands, down once more, the sharp ring of the lieutenant's shoes always just ahead—disorienting her, as they've done each time they brought her to the office. *Who do you think you've got here?* she wants to ask. *Who do you think I am?*

When the hood comes off she's standing at an unmarked door, in another featureless hallway. Fluorescent light makes the air feel cold, almost lunar; from everywhere comes the sourceless muttering, the drone and whirr of machinery. As she blinks in the glare she starts to hear sounds on the other side of the door: chairs scraping, a phone ringing, voices calling out greetings, a density of human sound unfamiliar after days in the cell. She shivers, tries to rub life back into her broken arm. There are a lot of people inside, more than she expected. For the first time since they brought her here, she feels afraid.

"Remember what I told you." The lieutenant stands behind her, staring over her shoulder in square-jawed formality. Next to him, a skinny young soldier watches her, his eyes rimmed with hatred. "You'll have one or two minutes. Don't waste time."

Behind him a row of tall windows looks out on a city street, the trunks of palm trees and a sliver of a grassy median. An old man offers newspapers to passing cars. The morning is gray and clean and fills her with longing. There was someone else there, on Calle Almagro that night. For three days she's hoarded the memory, held it next to her body like precious contraband. As the car pulled away from the burning house, before the hood came over her eyes—in that instant she'd seen him: a flash, then darkness. For days she's tried to remember, to make the fleeting image clear. But it was barely a glimpse—of frightened eyes, dark hair, hidden among the handful of terrified neighbors. She can't be sure her brain hasn't filled in the other details—a certain twist to his mouth, a crutch under one arm—to reassure her, to write the ending she wants to believe, the one in which he came back for her.

"It's not over," she tells Lieutenant Lang. "You think it's over, but it's not."

His gaze doesn't leave the door. "I'm sorry. It's over."

"There will always be someone else. History always has remainders." She stares at the soldier—no older than eighteen, with dark, mottled skin and a widow's peak—until he turns away in fury. "Anyone can be a Philosopher."

The guard reaches for the door, but the lieutenant, frowning, stops him.

"Why do Americans always talk about history?" he says. "Something you know nothing about. Something you've never understood. It's an abstraction to you, something that happened before the last commercial break. So you come here, or to Chile, or Nicaragua, to perform another thirty-minute episode. If it goes badly, or you get tired of it, you change the channel. You turn it off.

"You think the people aren't real people, that they disappear when you stop watching," he says. He gives a thin smile. "I wonder, what will happen to your country when you find out that you, also, are characters in a story? And you don't even know who's telling it."

He nods to the guard, who punches a code into the keypad. "Goodbye, Leonora. I'm sorry your stay in Peru wasn't more enjoyable. But then, I really don't know what you came here to accomplish."

There's a beep and a click, the guard yanks open the door and a storm of sound rushes out at them.

"At least I came," she says.

The lieutenant pats her on the shoulder. "Is that all?"

Then he turns her toward the frenzy of flashing lights, the blast of voices, a hundred pairs of eyes that stare hungrily, bodies surging forward to see what will emerge.

"Say whatever you want to say, compañera," he tells her. "But here's my advice to you: Say it loud."

V

DARKNESS AT NOON

They were two years apart, and somewhere in the dim, disintegrate reaches of memory she sees her parents bringing Matthew home from the hospital, sitting close together on the sofa while she clambered for a glimpse of what was in the bundle.

"Now we've got two of them," she hears her father saying, his hand warm and comforting on Leo's head. "Look, Maxi. They're exactly the same."

Her mother, face drawn and drowsy, looked up and said, "Don't be ridiculous. They don't look anything alike."

They were never close. To Leonora's quiet compliance, her love of books, of reading at the kitchen table while her mother cooked, following the words with a fingertip, Matthew brought a storm of sound and movement, endless clamor and, soon, questions, the inborn assertiveness and arrogations of the baby. She can't remember a time when he wasn't a nuisance, or when she wasn't rankled by the pleasure her father took in his confident physicality, his shrugging, uncomplicated speech. *Because they're both boys*— she understood this almost immediately. As a child she resented it, not because her brother had taken something that belonged to her but because he knew it had always belonged to him. Later, she remembers pitying her parents, otherwise intelligent people who'd somehow been gulled. They knew better than to prefer this brute with the baseball glove and comb-damp hair, this hale fellow from whom they'd recoil if they met on the street. It was unfair of her, and she knew it—Matthew was their son, it was only natural they love him—but she couldn't help but think less of them for it.

The week before his garish wedding, Matt jokingly introduced Leo to her soon-to-be sister-in-law as "my former babysitter." Samira looked apologetic. She was lovely, tall and dignified, the daughter of an Argentine financier who'd fled the junta. They'd met in business school. As the best man—also a stranger to Leo—told it in his toast, Matthew stood out on Division Street and stopped traffic until Samira agreed to go out with him. Apparently, she was engaged to someone else at the time.

"I admire this guy so much," the best man said. He was another clean-shaven athlete, a ruling-class trainee. "I kind of want to be him. He won't take no for an answer." The bride and groom had arrived at the reception in a horse-drawn carriage driven by a black man in top hat and tails. Leo asked her mother if they'd specifically requested a black man. Maxine didn't speak to her for the rest of the night.

But he was her brother, and for a time—before adolescence and cliques and girlfriends and SATs, before Stanford and Rutgers, half a decade in which they saw each other once a year and spoke by phone on birthdays, if at all—they'd been friends, building forts in the basement, conspiring to hide David's ties. Once, when their parents went to Europe for a month, they stayed at Grandpa Carol's; four-year-old Matt, afraid of the big, echoey house, begged her to sleep in his room and she complied. Once, when a fifth-grader called her a forgotten name, Matt bloodied his nose. She could pick him out of a crowd with an ease that surprised her—his face, his gait, imprinted on the circuits of her brain. When he did call, she knew who it was before he spoke. The one time he visited her at Stanford, he wound up in bed with one of her suitemates; when they emerged from her room, grinning, at noon, Leo hated the girl irrevocably—this desire to protect Matt, to tend to imagined injuries, confused her. How can you love someone you wouldn't choose? How can distaste coexist with the certainty he'll belong to you forever?

Years ago, she'd found a photograph of David as a young man and for the first time was struck by how Matt had come to resemble him. This was shortly before the wedding, the move to Peru already planned but still secret, and the photo seemed deeply meaningful, a validation of her decision to take responsibility, to give the world as much of herself as she could manage. They were adults now, destined to become their parents in one way or another. A day would come when they would have to ask what their lives had meant. She wanted to have a better answer.

It's this photograph, a black-and-white portrait taken while David was in law school, that comes into her mind on the September morning when she gets the news. Sleepless, shivering, she sits on the edge of a straight-backed chair and squints at the comandante of El Arca—a former Army colonel who treated his assignment as a kind of grim sociological experiment—as he forces his face into an expression of concern.

"What do you want from me?" she says, shaking her head to clear it. After three years of frozen mornings, the cobwebs hang moist and sticky until midday.

"This is a terrible thing," he says. He comes to stand by her chair but is reluctant to touch her. She'll be forgiven her kitchen shift for the day, of course. If the phones are working, he'll permit a brief call. Her father's face persists—the posed smile, the confident eyes—however many times the comandante says her brother's name.

"I don't understand," she repeats. She inspects her forearms, scratches at scaly gray scabs of psoriasis. Her eyes are getting worse, damaged by the cold, by the knife-dazzle of the Andean sun. "Was he on one of the planes? What are you saying? Why would he do something like that?"

The comandante chews back impatience. "Cantor Fitzgerald. This is the name of his company?"

"I don't know. I don't know where he works. What does that have to do with anything?"

The comandante sits on the edge of the desk. When he offers a cigarette she tears off the filter before lighting it.

"It is my understanding," he says, "that they were on the highest floor."

As a child, Matthew was obsessed with *Star Trek*. He wanted to be James T. Kirk, and often affected the clipped speech and brash swagger of the starship captain. He was fascinated by the transporter room—when they drove somewhere he closed his eyes and cried, "Energize!" and didn't open them until they arrived. He pretended they'd all been teleported there, their molecules scrambled and beamed to the destination. He'd look around at their new surroundings, then nod curtly to their father: "Let's go."

He insisted Leo play the game with him, pestered her insufferably if she refused. "How do you even know you made it?" she'd ask, relishing his irritation.

"Look, Stupid: We're here."

"*I'm* here. But how do you know you are? How do you know you're the same person who left the house?"

"Up yours, Leo," he said, for years his favorite expression. But the question seemed valid to her: If they took all your atoms apart, broke your joints and synapses and scattered and then reassembled them, could it be said you were still you? You might look the same, act the same, for all outward purposes you would be identical to the person who'd disappeared in a fizzle of light. But what if it was only a trick? What if the original you, dissolved into energy, was gone?

Arriving at National Penal Establishment No. 15–18, Yuyantambo District, had felt like that: as if everything that made up Leonora had disintegrated and been reconstituted. She'd closed her eyes in a bare courtroom where hooded judges made incomprehensible sounds, and when she opened them she was someone else: her body the same, her thoughts the same, but in some essential way she was different, wiped clean, an alien to herself. Riding in the jouncy pickup truck, wrists bound and chained to a ring on the floor, she recalled the arid, blatantly fake landscapes in which Kirk and Spock materialized: Styrofoam rocks, hulking humanoids snarling from caves. The prison, too, looked fake—her first glimpse of it, far across the altiplano, brought to mind a lonely farmstead, too perfectly staged to convey isolation and otherworldliness. The truck seemed to approach for hours—what she'd taken for a silo resolved into four brick guardtowers, the farmhouse into a sprawled compound of three-story buildings encircled by a minefield.

"Is that why they call it the Ark?" she asked the soldier next to her. After the first hour, she'd stopped looking at the gun in his lap.

Her head rang from lack of oxygen, swam with the smell of gasoline. "Because it's stranded on top of a mountain?"

The soldier looked straight ahead as they approached the first guardpost. "Because it's full of animals."

She'd never seen blue before—not like the blue of the altiplano. A uniform, otherworldly blue, different in the morning than in the afternoon, the change undetectable from minute to minute until the flat milk-hue has everywhere darkened to violet. At midday the blue is a rich and unblemished liquid, like paint, so thick she can almost taste it. She spends hours dreaming up names: *cornflower, royale, ciruela, heartsickness, night.* When it's all over, she thinks, when the last light leaves her eyes, it will be like sinking into this eternal blue, soaking through with it until you dissolve forever.

Nirvana, Picasso, espacio, azul. In ten years she'll never settle on the right name for it, nor feel she's captured its truth.

It's the dark blue of emptiness, the color of aching cold. Each morning her first year she's allowed into a small yard attached to El Arca's north pavilion, the visits timed to avoid contact with other prisoners. When the door clangs shut, she's alone in a ten-meter-by-ten-meter space, one corner dug up and dusty from someone's attempt at a potato patch, the only sounds the moan of wind sluicing off nearby glaciers and the footsteps of the guard up on the walk, his coughs strangely close in the thin air. Shivering, lost in a coarse wool overcoat many sizes too large, she finds the spot where a trapezoid of sunlight sneaks between the towers and tilts her face to study the pure, heavy blue. It's irrefutable, beyond understanding—it simply *is*, and this quality of detached consistency, of being only and entirely itself, terrifies her. Transfixed, she stands at the lip of an abyss—until the door bangs open and guards wordlessly take her back to the cell.

How to describe this first year in El Arca? The malign cold, how it invaded her bones like a cancer, icicles stabbing the meat of her joints, a band of iron fire around her left arm where the break never healed right? How to convey the marrow-shiver and the thinning hair, the split skin of her fingertips that stung as if filled with crushed glass?

Start with the cold, the dull, endless cold, the morning skin of ice in her water cup. Add stone-echoes, faceless and indecipherable, the thick-dirt taste of potato-and-flour soup, hard rolls that smell like bleach. Add the bare bulb hanging in its cage, the shock of the metal toilet seat, the ubiquitous reek of lemon disinfectant. Add the burn of recurrent pleurisy, the constant jaw-ache from grinding her teeth, giardia cramps that leave her writhing and feverish, soiling the sheets in her sleep. The dry rashes that climb her neck and cheeks, a hot tingling that cracks and suppurates and finally infects. Add the useless pain of shrinking breasts; the unexpected, throat-tearing shrieks that tail into laughter; the knocking of a shoe on the bedpost—sometimes for hours, to the rhythm of every song she's ever known. The failed attempts to literally climb the walls.

Add the certainty that she's going crazy, that whatever substance—she imagines it as a clear, viscous glue—holds consciousness together is draining off week by unmarked week. The swift invalidation of any sense her life had meaning. The waning of memory—had any of it happened?—the past crowded out by brown walls, scuffed linoleum, the blank faces of nameless guards who mostly speak in gestures. The daily searches, made to squat naked while they scour her cell for contraband, to hold her arms over her head and frog jump across the floor. Weeks without hearing a human word. Faces she finds staring in the wall. The babbling, senseless stories she tells herself for hours until a guard cracks a stick against the door.

Add the unbearable truth that no one is watching. No one. She's been forgotten by the world, if she ever existed at all.

Her back aches constantly, her spine frozen into the bent position in which she sleeps; she spends hours each day in an approximation of yoga, trying to remember the way Marta moved, how her torso arched, her eyes focused on one distant point. Clad in the overcoat and baggy cotton pants, her improvised stretches generate barely enough heat for her to stand up straight before spasms kick her in the lower back. Sometimes, holding an unsteady Warrior Pose, she can just make out Marta's face, the bowed lips, the arch of her eyebrows, but the image is fading—as if Leo were on that transporter pad, becoming insubstantial, the real world shimmering away.

Energize.

At night she hears distant music—Senderistas marching in the next pavilion, chanting their loyalty to Abimael and the revolution, though Abimael is in another prison and the revolution has been dead for years. She knows why they keep singing: to stitch the past together, to keep a sense of themselves intact. But she has no songs and no one to sing with, nothing to keep her memories from dispersing like dandelion spores. How long had she lived in that house? What had she thought to accomplish? After a few months her presence in that narrative has grown hazy, the events of the previous year confined to images, words on paper, the electronic belch of the judges' verdict, rendered through a voice-distortion machine. Hard to recall what she knew and what she didn't, whom she'd met, what role she'd played. Maybe she really was the "main architect of the terrorist conspiracy," or maybe the "unfortunate pawn of criminals who took advantage of her idealism and romantic disposition." With each passing week it gets harder to choose; both stories are preposterous, equally incoherent, by the time winter brings its brittle stillness to the altiplano, she's no longer certain she was ever there.

How do you know you're the same person?

Because there was no Cuarta Filosofía—not then, not ever. That's what she's decided. The whole idea of it was chimerical, a projection of an archetype that was itself just a well-told tale. There was no Julian, no Chaski—for sure, there were people who went by those names, but they had no more reality than characters in a novel, and like characters they began to evaporate the minute you closed the book. There were no cumpas, no newspaper, no guns—maybe there was not even a house. Maybe it was all just fantasy, an abstraction. Such thinking is not uncommon. In the books I read—recollections of political prisoners, exiles, heretics—the physical agonies are backdrop to the real terror of having one's existence negated: *You accomplished nothing. No one remembers you. You never lived.* Or rather, in such places—the Auschwitzes and Robben Islands, the gulags and black sites, the shitholes beyond description—those agonies are mere precursor, catalyst for the true submission: to let go of one's personhood as a child lets go of a kite, to disown one's story, to disappear.

Disappeared. The word's cruelty makes her shudder. A transitive verb, a deliberate erasure. Casimiro, Ernesto, a burning man without a name. Had any of them existed? She watches the thick blue give way to Andean night, the outlines of mountains and buildings swamped by darkness. In such moments she's briefly recalled to the truth of her old self, like a swimmer surfacing after a long dive. *I'm here*, she thinks, *I'm still here.* A tiny victory. But soon the stars come out, countless billions, excruciatingly clear. Their loneliness is too large to contain in her body. She turns from the window, steadies herself with familiar objects. She pulls the blanket over her shoulders and starts to remember.

"Just another month or so. Maybe three months at the outside. I know it's a long time, baby, but you have to be strong," Maxine says. "A year. God, I can't believe it's been a year. Something's going to change. I know it. So many people are working on this. Stanley's taking meetings every day. Lautenberg's Chief of Staff is on board. Your uncle Warren's talking to people. Right, David? No one's going to forget about you, baby, not as long—"

She stops, her face frozen in open-mouthed surprise. They'd arrived late for this first visit, the bus from Puno having broken down twice. Visiting hours end in twenty minutes and the comandante refuses to make an exception.

"Baby," Maxine says. "Oh, Leo . . ."

"It's alright, Mom." They are separated by a wide table, a partition that rises to chin level, another that reaches to the floor. The walls, painted the color of old toothpaste, smell of ammonia and cheese. Her father stands a few feet back, next to a skinny guard with a prominent red birthmark on his forehead. "I'm fine. I'm okay."

It's been a year since she's spoken English, a year since she's answered anything but commands. Her cheeks are burning. It's too warm in the visitors room. She can hardly muster the words to reassure them, has to contain nervous giggles at her mother's expressions of horror and wretchedness.

"You just look pale. David, isn't she pale?" David's face, his closely held fear, doesn't change. He's disheveled from the long bus ride, his eyes bloodshot from lack of oxygen. He watches Leo secretly, looks away when she meets his gaze. "Do you eat? Is the food . . . We brought you lots of things," Maxine says, gesturing at the floor. But the packages were taken at the main post. "Fruit, and warm sweaters. Chocolate. Oh, God," she says, pressing fingertips to her temples, "David, I can't stand this."

Leo, helpless: "It's okay, Mom. I'm okay." A dull scratching sound, she looks down to find something squeezing into the gap between partition and floor: her mother's big toe, painted in chipped, coral pink. When Leo touches the tip of her own toe to her mother's, Maxine's eyes glaze over in an access of misery.

"Señora," the guard says, taking half a step forward. The toe is withdrawn.

The time lurches and vanishes, like water glugging out of a jug. Her mother talks about her conversations with Governor Whitman, with staffers on the House Foreign Relations Committee, with the Deputy Assistant Secretary of State for Western Hemisphere Affairs. The call she got from Jesse Jackson, whose compassion was an inspiration, who has promised to visit Lima before the end of the year.

"Rabbi Eisen has been so reassuring. He says he'll come next month. Did you know he has a son in Berkeley? Such a small world." In the escalating pitch of her mother's chatter, Leo can sense Maxine tightening her grip, honing herself for the long battle: something evil has taken her child, she's under no illusions about it, something too foul and eternal to be named. To get Leo back will be her life's most grueling, perilous effort. She may, herself, have to die.

"Get this, Leo," David says, wrenching himself out of stupor. "I get a call in my office—an *agent* from ICM. They want to talk about film rights to your story!" His laughter is so forced she digs a fingernail into her forearm. It breaks her heart to see him so helpless, devastated at having learned the truth his whole life was arranged to conceal: that no one is immune to misfortune. "Who do you think should play me? I was thinking maybe James Woods. Or Alan Alda. Maybe Sandy Duncan for your mom. Remember her? Peter Pan?"

Soon enough, the guard says the hour is over. "We'll be here every month," Maxine says. She fixes her eyes on Leo as if to keep her from disappearing. "Sometimes both of us, sometimes just one of us. For as long as it takes. I swear, Leo," she says, and the grimace of terror flashes again, "we will be here, no matter what."

"Señora," the guard says, stepping forward, "por favor—" but before he can touch her Maxine leaps up at him, forcing him back toward the door. *"This is my daughter!"* she cries. *"Mi hija. Don't tell me about time, you little fried-egg fuck!"*

For months they'll laugh about it. "Fried-egg fuck!" David says when their spirits are down, when "another month" has turned into a year, when Reverend Jackson's visit has come and gone and Senator Lautenberg stops returning their calls. It's good for a laugh, for desperate moments when it strikes all of them how fleeting an hour is, how vanishingly small. Over time they'll grow comfortable with the guards. They'll come each month with bags full of candy, DVDs of American movies, cheap fleece jackets, lipstick and tampons for the guards' wives. Maxine brings cartons of vitamins for the many prisoners whose children live with them. This largesse will win them not a single extra minute of visitation, but eventually the guards will allow them privacy, standing outside the room with their backs to the window. When her parents return in November, 2001, after a three-month absence, they'll be ushered into a room with no partitions, permitted this one time to embrace their surviving child—a moment so terrifying that Leo is relieved, the next month, when regular protocols are restored.

"Are you Andres?"

"Who is this?"

"Am I talking to the famous Andres?" The voice was rough, sardonic, like a poke in the chest. He sounded a little drunk. In hindsight, I may have suspected who it was. I may even have been expecting the call.

"What is this about?" I said. I turned to the car window so Carlito couldn't hear. Above the long terminal, airplanes descended through the thick fog one after another—lights first, like knives slashing through potato soup.

"Are you enjoying your vacation?" the voice said. "Hanging around with the rest of the fucking gringos over there? You find some rich cunt in Lima to sit on your face?"

"Look, I don't know what you—"

"You should stay there, with the other faggots, Andres," he said. "It's safer."

Carlito was watching me, and I stepped out into the parking lot, pausing while a plane roared in takeoff and wobbled up into the gray. When the noise faded, I could hear another voice: *Give me the phone*, Lucrecia was saying. *Give me the phone, you asshole.*

"Nobody here wants you, you understand? You and your friends, with your gringo money—you faggots—" He was stumbling now, having made his point without exhausting his contempt. "If you come back to Babilonia—you'll see—" He sputtered a few more insults and then the line went dead.

"Trouble?" Carlito said. I smoothed mist from my hair and watched the sliding doors, the mob of taxi drivers accosting passengers as they came out.

"Just some friends screwing around."

He smiled to himself and pushed in the car lighter. "I wouldn't worry. This is just the way of life for some people. You aren't the first to have trouble with a girl from Babilonia. It's like a sport with them. Americans are the biggest prize—so much money but so naïve, so easy to convince they are loved without other motives."

"Don't talk about her like that," I said. "You don't know anything about her."

"Ah yes. I forgot that I am speaking with a historian, the great analyst of the Peruvian people. Perdóname, Andres."

I was already riled by Ronaldo's call, with its reminder of my long absence, my abdication. I'd talked to Lucrecia only twice since inviting her to Lima, and though I repeated the offer I was secretly relieved she hadn't accepted. Maybe the problem would resolve itself, I found myself thinking. If Ronaldo was back in the picture, maybe it was best for everyone that I quietly slipped away.

I knew such thoughts marked me as a monster. But the alternative was impossible to imagine. When I tried to picture it— Lucrecia and me huddled over a cradle in my unheated room—it seemed more like a sitcom than a potential future. Carlito was right: I didn't know Lucrecia, not really. In the short time we'd been together I hadn't learned the first thing about her. I knew far more about Leonora Gelb—someone I'd never met and couldn't understand at all.

"Andres, permit me, but you don't seem happy," Carlito said, peering into the bright mist, each light with its halo. His concern sounded almost genuine. "You are a burdened man. Why? Because of this girl?"

I tried to laugh it off. He was the last person I would confide in, the one who'd understood me from the first.

"It's nothing," he went on. "It's life. Isn't that why you came to Peru? Why don't you go back to Babilonia?" he said. He waved off my protest. "I'm not insulting you. Listen. You were happy there, no? You have people who miss you. Why stay here?"

I tried to meet his eyes but finally looked away. "I can't," I said.

"Why? Because of this idiot on the phone?"

"Because of my story," I said. "I can't leave until it's finished."

He leaned back and took a deep drag. Smoke poured up from his mouth and into his nose. "Forget about Leonora Gelb, Andres. Forget the Philosophers. Why does this matter to you? No one wants to read stories about terrorists, believe me."

Of course I'd had the same idea many times: walk away, let someone else write it. It had become a favorite fantasy, a sweet liquor for sleepless nights. "Everyone's story is worth reading," I said. It sounded weak, even to me, the kind of cliché I'd been forcing upon students for years. "They weren't just terrorists. They were something else, too."

A fresh crowd of arrivals had begun to pour out of the terminal; cars jockeyed and nosed into the curb. Carlito watched me with something like pity.

"Go back to your people, Andres. Go and be the King of Salsa."

"That's not who I am anymore," I said.

"Do you really believe this?"

He honked the horn, and I squinted into the mass of travelers, faces stunned and hopeful as newborns. Stephanie was making her way across the parking lot, hair pulled back, face pale in the orange mist. A violent embarrassment stung my eyes. I squeezed into the shadows, hoping she wouldn't recognize me. What was I still doing there?

. . .

Inti Raymi had come and gone. Independence Day was just around the corner. Winter had settled on Lima, perceptible mostly as a change in the light—the days still clammy, nights swaddled in mauve, everything flattened by the season, made two-dimensional and transient. True to his word, Jack had wired me a thousand-dollar kill fee, and sent a conciliatory email: *Let's find something else for you to write, k düd? How close are you to Costa Rica?* When I checked *My.World* a few days later, he'd posted Leo's photo, one paragraph about her arrest and parole, and a quote from Gabriel Zamir. He'd made it the homepage story. He called it "The Gringa."

My story had swelled to nearly two hundred pages, chapters bursting with history, with supposition, with reconstructed or wholly imagined scenes. But for all my feverish work, my long nights of manic typing, I wasn't satisfied. The Leonora emerging on the page bore only a passing resemblance to the original. She was still just a character, a golem pieced together from dirt and scraps. Like a golem she lacked the beating heart, the human desire. I slept with her each night, showered and ate and rode the bus with her, but she was still a stranger.

"Andres, you take her too seriously," Damien said, waving away the smoke from Carlito's cigarette. He was tired of me. They all were. Like an eccentric uncle who'd come for the holidays and never left, they humored me, maneuvered around me, occasionally taking the time to correct my outrageous ignorance. "All of them. You overestimate them." There was never a question of the plan being carried out, he said—DINCOTE was watching the house the whole time, had in fact supplied the weapons and uniforms recovered in the raid. "Augustín Dueñas could not have brought this off. The man could not organize a pizza party."

"Just because he was stupid doesn't mean he wasn't a psychopath," Carlito said.

"Desperation and psychosis are not the same thing," Stephanie said.

Carlito raised an eyebrow. "They are not mutually exclusive."

"And it wasn't just them," I said. "They were part of

something bigger: safe houses, training camps, arms shipments. The Philosophers were everywhere. They were ready to restart the war."

There was a long silence. No one would look at me. Finally, Damien spoke.

"Of all people, Andres, you believe this?" His smile was kind and devastating. "Haven't you been through this? The 'Axis of Evil'? Yellowcake uranium, shoe bombs?" He nodded at the TV, where Condoleezza Rice soundlessly lectured a panel of white men. "It is always the same. To mobilize the population, you need a pattern. You connect the dots. The media is always ready to help. But the dots don't actually have to connect. They don't even have to exist."

I slumped into the couch. After all these months, I was still nowhere. With no protagonist, I had no story, however tall the stack of pages on the desk.

"You're asking the right questions," Stephanie said, sensing my despair. We'd barely spoken since she'd returned from Canada. She'd said nothing about her brother's funeral and I was too craven to ask, offering instead sympathetic expressions and unsolicited helpfulness: I made the bed each day, did her laundry with mine, arranged her papers in neat piles. "But only La Leo knows the answers. When will you talk to her?"

I froze, the bottle halfway to my lips. Carlito, amused, turned to watch. My mouth half-open, I forced myself to meet Stephanie's astonished gaze.

"You aren't going to interview her," she said.

"Why would she talk to me?"

"Have you even tried? For god's sake, Andres, what are you thinking?" But the truth was it had never occurred to me to try for an interview with Leo. It could not have occurred to me, I realized, because I'd never quite believed in her, either.

"I thought you said you wanted this story to matter," Stephanie said.

"I did. I do."

"Doesn't Leonora matter? Who is your story really about?"

. . .

You'll want to know about torture.

How could the story be complete without a catalog of atrocities, a loving description of methods used to question the prisoner, to punish her for her misdeeds? Call it "enhanced interrogation" or "detainee abuse," call it national security or a violation of international norms—you'll want specifics, significant details: the instruments used, the questions asked, the frequency and locations of her torment. You'll want sounds and smells, vital signs. *Verisimilitude*: you want to feel as if you were really there.

I could write anything. That she was forced into a dark hole not high enough to stand and left for days. That she was hydrated through a nasogastric tube and not allowed to urinate. Hung by the wrists, beaten with wet towels. It's nothing you haven't heard before. I could describe the feeling of being slapped, wall-slammed, the fear when the chair tips over, the flash of panic when the water hits the cloth. I could tell you she was raped, pissed on, her fingers broken one by one, that they stood her on a milk crate and gave her two wires to hold. And you'd believe it: after Abu Ghraib and Blackwater and Camp X-Ray, torture has entered our vocabulary, just another plot element—like Jack Bauer pressing his gun to someone's teeth, or Saddam falling through the trapdoor. We savor the rush of satisfaction—even as we fret about habeas corpus, proclaim our enduring belief in human dignity. This is how the terrorists changed us: torture is part of the story we all live in now.

In fact, she was not tortured—not during the two weeks at DINCOTE, nor the years in El Arca. She spent the first months steeling herself for it, convinced the waiting was itself a kind of overture. Comrade Miguel (she never stopped thinking of him as Miguel) had said there was nothing she could reveal that they didn't already know, no one left to betray; she scoured her memory for some name or nuance of organization, anything she could withhold, anything worth torturing her for. But there was nothing. Her cumpas had made sure of it. Knowing her captors understood this, that she was beneath even their curiosity, was a humiliation more painful than any they could inflict.

But there was something even worse, that she didn't allow herself to think about until the second year, when she was moved from solitary to the pavilion for non-Sendero women. Her first cellmate, Sonia, was the one to explain it, rolling up her shirt to reveal the scars across her back, the burn marks around her nipples.

"They can't do it to you," Sonia said. She walked with a heaving limp, her pelvis having been broken during her arrest. Once, she'd taught classes in self-defense to women in her village—classes the military said were terrorist training sessions. "If it happened to you, everyone would know."

"That's not true," Leo said, but her eyes throbbed with recognition. What can be done with impunity to others cannot be done to her. Even here, in these desolate altitudes, she has not escaped the bubble of perverse privilege. By the end of the year, she had a new cellmate, Natalia, captured ten years earlier with a column of militants near Jauja. Sonia was one of eighteen hunger strikers who, in October, 2000, were locked to a fence by Special Forces, then beaten with chains. As one of the strike leaders, Sonia was singled out for an example. Her body was not removed for three days from the spot where she was strangled. Maybe you read about it. More likely not.

In her third year, she's allowed to receive letters, of which there are many. They say things like, "Go home, whore," and "Daughter of a Jewish cunt, my husband died in 1989 from one of your bombs." They say, "You are an insult to the Movement and its martyrs" and "I hope El Arca burns to the ground while you scream." Others come from as far away as Paris, Stockholm, Chiapas, Hebron. They say, "You are our sister." They say, "Your sacrifice inspires all who continue the struggle." A Chilean poet writes her an ode, "La Canción de la Filósofa" (*Espíritu de fuego / al campo de sangre viniste de lejos . . .*). The Committee to Free Leo is formed in Northampton, Mass.; they send their greetings, with a copy of the letter sent to President Bush, Secretary Powell, and every member of the U.S. Senate, demanding a suspension of diplomatic ties with Peru until she's released. A law professor at UC Berkeley sends thirty pages of questions from his students. Churches from Orlando to Coeur d'Alene send prayers.

"There is nothing I can tell you that you don't know. The righteous are always persecuted, not least by those who worship the martyr Jesus Christ." She holds Gabriel's letter in trembling hands, reads it dozens of times, to be sure she hasn't missed anything. The one letter she's hoped for, when it finally arrives it takes up less than one typed page, its language so distant she wonders if the department secretary wrote it.

"One can support your ideals without condoning your actions," Zamir wrote, a statement referenced by all parties in his disciplinary hearing the following year.

"You will be remembered," he assured her before signing by hand: *¡Venceremos!*

They would take what was owed to them. She understands it now, the deep symmetry—almost metaphysical—by which the universe maintains its equilibrium. For every action an equal and opposite. Sin and penitence. Everything has a price.

Can the universe be so capitalist? Can it keep such a careful ledger? With all history's bloodshed it could not be the case that the tally came out even, that perpetrators would suffer in their turn. The meek would not inherit even a handful of dirt—wasn't that a given? No, in the end nobody was keeping track, all the stories about judgment, karma, eternal rewards just cruel hoaxes to keep the peasants' mouths shut. What business does a revolutionary have musing on divine retribution, on cosmic quids and quos?

And yet: they took her brother. There is no other way to understand it. They reached out for him, claimed him as payment for a debt he had not incurred. If they can't kill her or torture her they'll get their pound of flesh elsewhere—and who better than Matt, starry-eyed Matt, with his perfect family and his perfect life, his job on top of the world? Through the lengthening days of September, warm winds lashing the altiplano, leaving the prisoners nervous and forlorn, Leo stands at the kitchen window and watches a curl of smoke rise over distant Yuyantambo. She's seen the footage: the monstrous dust cloud, the perfect collapse. Tiny bodies plunging from the highest floors. Matt would not have jumped. He would have waited to the last, refusing to believe good fortune could abandon him. She's tried to imagine his face, as if holding it in her mind could somehow comfort him. But the face she sees is Ernesto's. This failure is the worst of all her many betrayals, clear proof that Matthew's life was taken to spare hers.

"No, no, you can't think this way," says Rabbi Eisen, resting a hand on her wrist. "This thing, this horrible thing—I don't think it's too much to call it evil, as your President does—it is not God's work."

Leo utters a crazed laugh, a cold tear oozing from her weak left eye. She sweeps the rabbi's hand away. A guard stands uncomfortably, scratching himself in the corner. She throws him a malevolent glare: no one in El Arca is allowed to see her cry.

"I told you," she says miserably, "I tried to tell you." After refusing his visits for more than a year, Leo finally agreed to see the rabbi—to make her mother happy, to have an extra visitor not subject to the quota. Once a month she gets ninety minutes in this empty storeroom; the first time, in June, the pavilion captain apologized that there was no crucifix. "How can you just accept it? How can anyone?"

The rabbi opens his large hands. "Linda . . ." He shakes his head. "Leonora, I don't accept it. Of course I don't."

"It's such bullshit. That He'll take care of it. Why would He? Has He taken care of anything else?" She paces the room and the rabbi notes how loose the prison clothes hang on her, how she is becoming child-sized. He notes the sores on her skin, the blue vein crossing her forehead, the milk seeping from her eye. "I'm supposed to believe this is fair, that it's some kind of message? Are you kidding me?"

"No, I don't think—"

"Get a better secretary!" she laughs bitterly. "Like it will change anything!"

"Leonora, there is no message. God doesn't send messages like some criminal in the Mafia. We can't understand this. But we can endure it. We have to."

"Endure it! That's all you people ever say." She shakes her head, momentarily confused by the rabbi's presence. Is he another lawyer? Has he come from New York? "It'll all be made right later, in Heaven. Is that what you're going to tell me?"

"No. I'm not going to say that."

"I won't debate it with you. With someone like you."

"I don't want to debate it—"

"Then why the fuck are you here!"

Frowning, the rabbi lifts himself out of the uncomfortable chair and moves toward her. Leo pushes the air to ward him off, but he puts an arm around her, then another, warning the guard with his eyes not to interfere. She squirms, terrified by the embrace of another body, feels a scream gathering, her knees softening, her own breath damp against her face as she turns her mouth to the rabbi's shirt and wails.

When her tears are exhausted, Rabbi Eisen reaches into his satchel and lays two items on the chair. He gently unfolds the first, drapes the silk tallis over his shoulders and kisses the fringe. He asks the guard for a match and kneels to light the candle, which throws looming yellow shadows across the bare walls.

"Would you like to say Kaddish?" Weak and compliant, she kneels at his side. When he takes her hand she gives no resistance. "Did your brother have a Hebrew name?"

But there has to be a price—hadn't they always said so? Fanon and Said, Gandhi and King. Julian, in his occasional eloquence. Jesus, too. "Someone will pay," was the rough refrain. How could anyone survive this world without subscribing to some version of it? "There are consequences for what we do."

That's what those nineteen men and their masters believed. It's what steadied their hands up to the instant of collision. And doesn't Leo herself believe it, even now? If you poke the beast with a sharp enough stick it must rouse itself with slavering fury, come at you with everything it has. In his own excess will the enemy's weakness be revealed! In the soil of his unrighteousness are planted the seeds of his destruction!

What garbage. What wishful thinking. A ten-year-old couldn't be made to believe it. What will really happen—what has *always* happened—is as obvious to Leo as it is painful to consider: the panic, the murders and abductions, the secret prisons and unmarked graves. Faceless courts and public burnings, machines of death deployed across the sky. The blithe justifications, the endless lies.

"Listen to me, sweetheart," Maxine says. "You've got to make up your mind. Stanley says the deal's still on the table, but it's not going to stay that way. People are getting distracted. The State Department is going to pieces. Please, Leo," she says, "just say the word."

"I already told you."

"We can still get it done. Your uncle Warren can talk to the Armed Services people. Stanley will fix it with the Peruvians. They're as eager as we are to put it all—"

"Mom," Leo whispers. "I can't."

"You can." Maxine's gaze could dissolve glass. "David, you talk to her."

"Leo, honey," he says, but he's unfocused, wrecked by what's happened, suddenly an old man. He holds a handkerchief to his face like an oxygen mask. "We just want you home. We need you."

It's early November, the first time she's seen them since August. The Interior Minister had denied her request to attend Matthew's funeral. Word has gone around the pavilion. Even the women who'd hazed her endlessly, spat on her in the yard, left their shit curled outside her cell, treat her delicately. They leave a wide berth when she passes, as if the message were a plague, and she the doomed carrier.

"She won't do it for us," Maxine says without taking her eyes off Leo. "She won't do it for anyone. She doesn't care what this is doing to us. Do you, Leo? You don't care how hard it is to come here every month, how we have to sleep in that shithole in Puno, ride on that disgusting bus for hours with *chickens*. Do you know how much fucking money we're spending? Do you have any idea how much all this costs?"

"Maxi—"

"She doesn't care about anything or anyone," she says, blazing with the anger that's sustained her since Matt's death. "None of them do."

On the way back to her cell, Leo is uncooperative and loud, calling for the comandante, clinging to bars and knobs. At the entrance to her hall she refuses to move; a second guard is summoned to help drag her the rest of the way. Natalia is on work duty and Leo overturns her mattress, rummages through her clothes until she finds the photograph of Natalia and her four siblings, which she tears into small pieces and flings through the grate, all the while singing at the top of her lungs—*Vengan todos a ver, ¡Ay, vamos a ver!, en la plazuela de Huanta, amarillito, ¡Flor de Retama!*—until the pavilion captain is called and the guards drag her into the hall and throw her to the concrete, kicking at her ribs until she coughs up blood. She's still singing weakly as they drag her to a solitary cell, douse her with water, and shut out the light.

When the doctor visits two days later he trusses her ribs and gives her an injection that fills her head with lava.

"You're a stupid girl," he says, regarding her as if she were a species of rodent. The pavilion is locked down, yard access revoked for three days to punish those who took up Leo's song. She'll be kept in solitary for two weeks, her visitor privileges cancelled for a month. "Why make so many problems? These people have nothing to do with you."

When he leaves, she shudders with relief, lowers herself to her less-painful side and cries. There won't be any deal—not with the Armed Services people, the Peruvians, not with anyone. It's too late for that. Even if she were to do what they ask—plead forgiveness, betray everyone, admit to her own irrelevance—it wouldn't matter. That's what her mother won't see: Leo, too, is part of the price.

Yo soy terrorista. She'd said the words and now everyone knows what they mean.

"Mom," she mumbles in her delirium, the rank, damp darkness miles under the ground. "Mom?" Her mother says she still loves her, nothing can change that. Now she'll have to love her enough for two.

You'll be home for Christmas, sweet baby, her mother croons—a strange melody, something warped and old fashioned like the ancient 78s Grandpa Carol used to play. *My baby's coming back to me . . .*

Though I hardly saw her, Stephanie and I were growing closer. Since returning from Canada, she'd thrown herself into her work. She left early each morning for Los Arenales, where she was reporting on corruption in the neighborhood councils. In bed late at night we spoke quietly, and with a new candor. On occasion I asked her to read a few pages, to tell me what I'd missed or failed to understand. For all her disappointment she seemed resolved to help me—as if, now that we'd both accepted my limitations, we could move forward in a spirit of cooperation, even collegiality.

We never spoke about her brother, though I always knew when she was thinking of him: a stillness came into her eyes and she seemed to shrink into herself, as if space were collapsing around her. I didn't want to intrude on this grief—his death loomed so massive and unfathomable I sometimes felt myself on the verge of tears. But what comfort could I be? I wanted to empathize, to help her feel less alone. But all I could offer was cheap sympathy.

Maybe that's why it felt so important to write a story she'd approve of. If she could see what I was trying to do, I thought, she might be heartened, her faith renewed, even slightly. At worst it could distract her, provide comic relief. One night, I told her about the missing seventh body, laid out my theory that Leo thought someone survived the raid. I showed her a photo that ran in *El Comercio* in 2000: a blurry shot taken in Havana of a man in his thirties walking with a cane.

She watched me with sad eyes, as though I were the one who needed consoling. "What if it really is Chaski?" I said, trying to sell it, to draw her out. "Wouldn't that explain everything? Otherwise she's just crazy, signing her own death warrant. There's no way! Help me, Steph. Let's think about this together . . ."

"Andres," she said. Her face was pink and puffy and a sweet warmth emanated from under the blankets. That morning I'd woken up with my arm around her. "Why did you come here?"

"What? To write this story, you know that—"

"No: Peru. Why did you come to Peru?"

In the dim light the lines of her face were softer, her eyes clear and honest. I was obviously intelligent, she said. I'd had talent, a career, but I'd thrown it away for a life that seemed empty. "I know you said you were angry about the war. But lots of people were angry. There must be something more."

I was quiet a long time. I wanted to give her a good answer, a worthy answer, that might redeem me in her eyes. But she deserved better than that. So I told her the truth.

"There was a protest. The day after the invasion. Seventy, eighty thousand people, right down Market Street." I closed my eyes. I'd never told it to anyone. "Everyone was in shock. We couldn't believe they'd done it. Bush, Cheney . . . after all the marches, all over the world—they didn't care. And they'd done it in our name."

I'd gone with Jack and our other roommate, a poet I knew from Stanford. There was a meetup beforehand, an apartment full of angry people. A woman with a shaved head and steel rings along the rims of her ears paced the kitchen, pounding her fist on the counter. "You're pissed off, right?" people kept asking me. "How angry are you?" As we stomped through the Civic Center other people fell in with us, kids in black sweaters, women in trenchcoats, some carrying signs, others concealing things under their clothes. I tried to feel solidarity, to believe what people were shouting about power and resistance and go with the spirit of the afternoon, wherever it took me. I'd never felt such anger—through me, all around me—it had an odor, a special pitch that made us vibrate like tuning forks, our sense of our bodies, our boundaries, blurring into a fearsome collective. It was thrilling and terrifying, enormous. I thought I could do anything.

As night fell and we encircled the Federal Building, the energy began to gather. The people around me were silent and tense as we shoved toward the barricades. Spittle and rotten fruit sailed out of the dark and splatted against the cops' shields. Sirens squawked, chants and screams carried to us from the periphery. You could feel the ugliness coming on, like a drug swirling into the blood supply. What had seemed a necessary outpouring of civic disapproval was on the verge of exploding. The group I'd come with were all wearing ski masks now. I caught the eye of the woman with the shaved head and she turned away. I understood they were waiting for a signal. When a phalanx of cops moved toward us, billy clubs cocked, they pulled bats and chains from under their coats and, whooping, raised them over their heads.

"I ran," I said. My whole body was tense, remembering. "I ran away. I don't know how I got home. I guess I just kept running."

Stephanie was silent a long time. "It was the smart thing to do," she said.

"No," I said. I turned away and squeezed my fists. Ridiculous tears stung my eyes. Half a million people had died. *Half a million people died.* When I saw those pictures from Abu Ghraib I couldn't contain the shame. I couldn't live with myself.

"It's stupid," I said, my voice shaking, "I just feel like it's my fault."

For a long minute she just watched me. Then she slid closer and put a hand on my chest. It was the kindest thing anyone had ever done for me.

"Oh, Andres," she whispered, "what a monster of ego you are."

It was time. I'd been there too long, leaning on people who had problems of their own. I couldn't abide this feeling of indebtedness. Dr. Rausch was right: every story had to end.

"If you'd asked me a month ago," Damien said, "possibly I could have done something, put you in touch with someone. Before the parole was approved."

"It's okay," I said.

He set down his coffee cup and chose his words carefully. "It's dangerous now. There have been threats. Even an experienced journalist would think twice . . ."

"It's okay, really." In the past week I'd called everyone I could think of—government officials, lawyers, even Raúl Quintana, the former Senderista. No one called back. Leo wasn't giving interviews, her exact whereabouts were unknown, though the media roared with speculation and invective. Secretly, I was relieved that Damien couldn't help. I told myself it was enough to have tried.

That afternoon, I took a bus downtown and waited in line at Aerocontinente. A pretty representative in a powder-blue suit was reluctant to let me buy a ticket in someone else's name. But when I offered to pay in American cash, she brightened immediately.

"I want you to come to Lima," I told Lucrecia. I gave her the flight information, said I'd be waiting when she got off the plane. There was nothing to be afraid of, I said.

"Andres," she said.

I crossed into the Plaza de Armas, drifting in circles among flowerbeds still torn up from Independence Day revelry. "It can't wait any longer," I said. We had to face reality, to do what was necessary. I still cared about her, I said. I didn't want her to go through it alone.

"I am not alone. There is my mother, my sisters. So you don't have to worry." I caught only a trace of accusation, of regret. Finally, she said it: "Also, there is Ronaldo."

I hadn't known if I'd be jealous, or offended, but I felt neither of those things. What I felt instead was a keen disappointment in Lucrecia. She'd insisted so many times she was through with Ronaldo—he was uneducated, thoughtless, she'd said. He'd rather get drunk with his friends than spend time with her. It was a common enough story, but Lucrecia had always claimed to want something more.

"Ronaldo can't help you," I said. "He won't. Lulu, you know that."

She sighed in frustration. "But he is here."

"Is he going to take you to the doctor? Is he going to arrange everything? Please, just come to Lima. It will be so much easier. I'll be with you the whole time." I didn't know if I believed what I was saying, but I didn't want her to stay with Ronaldo. She was too good for him. How could I let her throw her life away? "Afterward, we'll take a little vacation. We'll start over."

I was sitting on a bench across from the Presidential Palace. An old woman sat next to me, her two small grandchildren throwing breadcrumbs to pigeons.

"Andres, what do you think of me?" Lucrecia finally said. "Do you think I would do something like that? To my baby? Do you think I am some kind of brichera? You think I'm a whore?"

The old woman stared at me. I got up and paced, one hand over the phone. "You don't want to help me or start over, only to rid yourself of a problem," she was saying. "You're a liar. You and your gringo friends are the same."

"It's not a lie . . ." I began. But she deserved to hear the truth. "I don't want a baby, Lu. I don't want to be a father."

She made a sound, high and startled, as if something had been snatched out of her arms. I could hear her sobbing, small hiccups that nicked at my heart like a scalpel.

"You are already a father, Andres."

Here it was then: the moment I'd been putting off since the morning in Babilonia when I'd held her and promised everything would work out. Even then I must have known it couldn't work out for both of us.

"No, mi amor. I can't be the baby's father." I stopped myself from apologizing. Let her hate me, I thought, if it helps her get on with her life. "Maybe you're right. If Ronaldo wants to be with you, maybe that's the best thing."

I closed my eyes and waited. The wind picked up, tossing dirt and food wrappers across the plaza. I suddenly wished, with all my heart, I were back at La Luna. Already I suspected I'd never see the place again.

"You will always be this baby's father, Andres," Lucrecia said. "It doesn't matter where you go or even if you forget about him. You made this baby with me. It's a part of you. You should love something that you make. Do you know why?"

My voice sounded strange in my own ears. "Why?"

"Because he will love you. This baby will love you, even if he knows everything about you." She was calm again, poised. She'd been preparing a long time for the worst thing to happen, and now that it had, she'd found she was its equal. "He will look up to you, his American father, and think you are a like a hero, like a superhero so far away. What kind of person doesn't love someone who loves him like that?"

After twenty-five minutes, the judges stood and filed out, leaving stacks of documents on the long table which a clerk quickly collected. Her lawyer sat holding the sides of his folding chair, staring at the empty seats, eyes narrowed as though he were trying to remember something he'd been told years before and could not, at the time, have known was important. The courtroom was the size of a small classroom: cinder-block walls and two rows of chairs set up before the judges' table, no flags or other trappings of officialdom, only rusty brackets spaced along the top of one wall and a thick steel door with an improbably dented gold knob.

"Señores, I was given only one day to review two thousand pages of what the government is calling evidence. Señorita Gelb is not identified anywhere by name. It takes some time simply to know what she has said and what has been said about her."

The lawyer had addressed the judges from his seat—unlike the prosecutor, he was not allowed to approach the table. Leo had met him for the first time an hour before the trial and he spent much of that time berating her for refusing the bilateral transfer. He, too, had been made to wear a hood as they were taken to the courtroom. When he and Leo entered, the prosecutor had already finished his presentation; for reasons of national security, they were not allowed to know what he said.

"Thank you, señor," one of the judges had replied, his voice distorted into a raw, fishlike belch. In their gray coats and shapeless hoods they reminded Leo of chess pieces, the jade bishops on the board in Grandpa Carol's library. She knew they were men only by their hands. Another judge motioned to the back of the room, where two officers in dress uniform stood silently; one officer was given a piece of paper, which he glanced at, nodded, and left the room. They sat in silence, until the door opened again and four guards stood over Leo and the lawyer.

"What's happening?" she said. Her lawyer cracked his knuckles and looked at the ceiling.

"See you tomorrow, Oscar," said the prosecutor on his way out.

A guard pulled Leo to her feet. "What's happening? When does the trial start?"

The lawyer offered his hand. "I'm very sorry," he said. "The trial is over."

The new trial will be nothing like the first, everyone has assured her of that—her mother, the woman from the embassy, her new lawyer, approved by the Interior Ministry a week before opening statements are to begin. One morning, without warning, she's taken from her cell and rushed through the administrative building to the carpool, where three black SUVs wait with engines running. As they bounce down mountain roads to the airstrip she stares at the floor, refusing to look out the window—the villages, the campesinos working their terraced plots, the new shape of the shifting sky, any of these could undo her. All illusions, she tells herself, mirages. Soon enough they'll be replaced by the same brown walls she's stared at for four years.

When a soldier offers a cigarette, she smokes with the window rolled up, terrified to let the sweet air of lower altitudes touch her skin.

"I don't want you to get your hopes up," the woman from the embassy says when she meets Leo at the women's prison in Chorrillos. For four years they've refused calls for a new trial—from the U.S. government, from Amnesty International, from the Interamerican Court. The visits by Congressmen and diplomats are a thing of the past. The Bush administration's priorities have changed since September 11, as Leo knew they would; the human-rights community now has far bigger things to worry about.

And then, a month ago, the Supreme Military Council threw out her conviction and remanded the case to civilian court. "I wish I could say we had something to do with it," the woman from the embassy says. Peru's new government has promised change, a break with the past, a corrective to the brutality of the previous administration. But it can't be seen as caving on such a visible issue. They sit in an office in the prison and Leo can't help but glimpse the pale Lima sky, smell the nearby ocean, she can't block out the sounds of gulls, skateboards, arguments, hawkers, on the avenue outside. After so long on the altiplano, the humidity of Chorrillos slicks her skin like a balm. "It's hard to know if they want you out of their hair, or just to make a show of how reasonable Peru can be."

"Will there be anyone else?" Leo asks.

"Like who?"

In four years, she's heard nothing of her cumpas, no hint of a survivor. She's believed in him, dreamed of him, looked for his messages in cracks of cold stone. She talks to him in her bed at night. *Keep going*, she says. *Don't ever come back.*

"No, nobody."

The woman peers at Leo. "You'll have a chance to make a statement. Keep it short, respectful. *Not* political." She gathers her papers, offers her hand. "Remember, Leonora: Everything has changed. Everything."

The trial is held in a high-ceilinged room in the Lurigancho prison. A hundred or more people sit in the gallery: journalists, government officials, observers from the O.A.S., members of

victims' groups. Their conversations condense overhead into a kind
of weather, brightening and darkening according to what is said by
the witnesses, the rulings of the three judges. When she's brought
in each morning, Leo quickly locates her mother and father, always
in the same place a few rows behind the defense table. The same
young woman sits next to them—light brown hair, ringless ears,
perfect posture. Alone in the back, Rabbi Eisen coughs wetly into
a handkerchief. Once the judges enter she won't permit herself to
look back, but she keeps their positions in her mind, tiny bright dots
amid the dark tide poised over her.

Señora Zavallos, Lorenzo Garza, a teller from American Express.
Alejandra Vega, who'd sold her the computer and scanner. Alfi
Nuñez, who delivered the guns. One by one they tell their stories,
along with many witnesses she's never met: reformed terrorists who
claim to have coordinated with the Pueblo Libre group, to have
taken orders indirectly from "La Gringa"; DINCOTE agents who
followed her all over Lima, even to places she never went; an elderly
couple from San Martín, whose daughter fought and died with the
Cuarta Filosofía in the 1980s, who'd agreed to shelter "a group
of friends from Lima" on their farm the day after the attack on
Congress was to have been carried out.

"Did you know something about these friends? Their names?
Why they were coming?"

The old man speaks so quietly the judges ask him to repeat himself. He can bring himself to look only at his wife. "Well, I heard
maybe there were foreigners with them."

When Nancy Rojas is called, she won't meet Leo's eyes. Her hair
has gone completely white, her skin sallowed by years of heavy
smoking. When asked her marital status, she clears her throat and
says, "Widow."

She knew the defendant, had worked with her for several months,
the prosecutor says. Had she been aware of any subversive activity?

"No, señor."

He reminds her of the demonstration at Los Muertos. Hadn't she
seen Leonora leaving the area with Mateo Peña?

"No, señor."

"No?"

"I was not with her then," Nancy says. "I was looking for my son. Who is now dead."

There are murmurs in the gallery, the scrape of chairs. *Because he was a terrorist!* someone shouts, and is quickly removed. The judges ask for quiet. They remind Nancy that the purpose of the trial is to establish the prisoner's guilt or innocence—"not to express personal grievances from long ago." The prosecutor makes a last attempt, asking if Nancy, a respected leader of her community, believes the charges against the prisoner. The defense lawyer's objection is overruled.

"I don't believe she was a Philosopher, no." For the first time she looks at Leo, with an expression hung between resignation and grief. "I believe she would have liked to be. But she wasn't."

The proceedings continue for two weeks, some days lasting until long after dark, until the mass of reporters and protestors outside lights up like a carnival, with its own generators and vendors and street performers. Riot police have to clear a path for the car to edge through, Leo huddled in the back, dazzled and overwhelmed. Other days, the judges hardly take their seats before some procedural question forces a recess and she's whisked back to Chorrillos, where for the first time in four years she has access to newspapers, magazines, pirated copies of novels passed among the thieves, prostitutes, and drug mules who make up the prison's population. She avoids the yard, takes meals alone in her cell, cowed by the ardor of these women, who crowd her in the corridors to ask if it's true what they've heard about El Arca, if she's seen sisters or husbands who were sent there during the war. Lights-out comes as a mercy; Leo cries herself silently to sleep—not because she might go back to El Arca but because they've made her into someone who wants to.

"Your whole life still ahead of you," Maxine says during the one permitted visit. Leo holds her hands and notes the bony, freckled wrists, how thin and battle-hard her mother has grown. "Please, honey, think: marriage, children—"

"A house in the suburbs?" she says.

"You're only thirty. There's so much time. Say what they want you to say, Leo. Do whatever they want. For once in your life, just be—"

"A good girl?"

Her mother doesn't flinch. "Normal."

Who is Leonora Gelb? That's the question the prosecutor asks the judges. Which of these stories is easier to believe? The sworn testimony of good people, Peruvian people, who paid the price for the terrible choices made by Philosophers and Senderistas—or the incoherent excuses her lawyer has presented, the convenient gaps and romantic clichés? When he replays the footage of the press conference, Leo holds still, heart in her throat, trying to recognize the girl in the dirty sling and piss-dark jeans. So long ago now she's not sure anymore whom she'd thought she was protecting, what purpose she'd thought her gesture could serve. Or had she wanted only to prove something to herself?

"I would sacrifice you without hesitation," Julian told her one night, after sex. "If the revolution demanded it. If I could save myself and keep fighting."

"I would never sacrifice you," she said. "Any of you."

He'd run a fingertip across her bare knee. "You see why nobody trusts you?"

What was true then is true now, she thinks, unable to sleep, her brain speedy with the city's stimulations. She watches lights flow across the ceiling, hugs the lumpy pillow, tries to imagine Marta breathing nearby. But does it still matter?

"The person you've heard described is not someone I know. The woman referred to by the witnesses, the one who signed those receipts, even the one in the video," she tells the judges. "I have never met this woman. She doesn't exist."

She turns to the silent room—the lawyers, her parents, rows of faceless spectators beneath windows made opaque by morning sun. "She was invented by people who wanted to distract the country from terrible injustices. They wanted to tell a different story than the one Peruvians were living every day. I don't recognize her. She is me, but she is also a stranger, una extranjera. And I have tried to understand why."

The statement has come to her in pieces, on the drive across the city each morning, the hours in the court's antechambers flipping through newspapers, watching CNN coverage from Afghanistan and Washington: the wailing mothers, the preening politicians, bodies blackened and left to die. It never stops, she thinks. Nothing changes. It moves from place to place, different faces, different weapons, but it ends the same way.

"I came to this country motivated by love and by concern for the people who suffer. I felt I had a moral obligation to help them. I did not want to be someone who saw suffering and drove right by." What happened next is a matter of interpretation, she says. In one version, she's an activist—feeding the hungry, writing articles about injustice; in another, she's La Leo, plotting violence, shrieking with fury. But in either story she was only a secondary character, never the protagonist. Now, as then, she is only the person others decide she is.

"I love this country, even after everything that's happened to me. I would never do anything to hurt the Peruvian people." She bows her head, takes a breath. When she looks up, it's her mother's face she sees, upturned and pale, made childish by hope. The woman next to her, so dignified and sad—at last her name comes to Leo's mind: Samira.

"I've made mistakes. But I am not a terrorist," she says. "Yo no soy terrorista. I know that's not who I am."

The verdict comes in before the car has arrived at Chorrillos. The driver makes a U-turn on the Panamericana, speeding back to the courthouse flanked by police cruisers. Her parents barely have time to get to their seats. The life sentence is vacated, the lead judge announces. Treason is not an appropriate charge for a foreigner.

The judge holds up a hand to quiet the protests. Twenty years, she says. The possibility of parole after ten. "The charge of terrorism is not proved," she proclaims. Leonora Gelb is convicted of collaborating with the Pueblo Libre group. "But she, herself, was not one of them."

While everything around her erupts into motion, Leo stays in her seat, insensible to the cheers and chants, the awkward congratulations offered by her lawyer, the shouts of soldiers clearing the room. "Baby!" someone is calling, "Baby!" but Leo feels no surprise or anger, only profound emptiness, as though a drain has opened at the bottom of her awareness, her ability to recognize faces, to understand their words, flooding out into the glare. By dusk she'll be back on the altiplano, clattering toward El Arca in a pickup truck much like the one that brought her four years ago, back in a frozen cell engulfed by silence. Only then will it come back to her: the judge's raised chin as she read out the ruling; the woman from the embassy who stood at the door, shouting into a cell phone; the hot crush as they led her to the van, guards circling to protect her from all the bodies, so many bodies, their arms flailing, signs and photos, Peruvian flags waving—or was it to protect her from their voices, the deafening music of all those voices screaming the same name, though bereft as she was she couldn't say whose?

The end of my story, when it came, was both surprising and inevitable, as the end of any good story should be. Late one morning my phone rang with a familiar number.

"I'd like to speak to you," the rabbi said. "Can you come this evening?"

When I arrived, the synagogue was bright and festive. Rabbi Eisen greeted everyone at the door. "I'm glad to see you again!" he said. He seemed to really mean it.

"I should have realized it was shabbos," I said. "Wouldn't tomorrow be better?"

He found this quite funny. "Come inside. Introduce yourself. There will be food and wine afterward."

The service was short and mostly lighthearted. I sat toward the back, mouthing along with distantly remembered prayers, blushing when the rabbi mentioned "our guest tonight, a friend from the United States" and everyone turned to get a look. Later, in his office, I was stunned to find a copy of *The Light Inside* atop a pile of books on his desk.

"I ordered it from Amazon," he said. "I was curious. I don't meet many writers."

"Let me know what you think," I said, though I hoped he wouldn't read it.

"Of course, of course," he said, leaning back with a nod of sabbath contentment. "Andres," he said, "there's someone I think you should meet."

. . .

Of course I'd imagined it many times: me on one side of a table, she on the other, the recorder propped between us to capture every precious word. Prison guards glaring, listening for codes, plans of escape, ready to stop the meeting if it encroached on state secrets. I was the dogged interviewer, charming but firm, leading her time and again from the comfortable shallows to that place where she'd be forced to confront herself. Alternately, we might stroll together in a Lima park on a sunny day, stopping at the seaside for beer and ceviche. Or take in a movie. What all these scenarios had in common was that they could never happen—and I suppose I preferred it that way.

What I hadn't imagined was this ordinary Sunday, the sun just a pale outline behind drifting clouds, this slip of paper in my hand on which the rabbi had written Leonora Gelb's address.

"Destroy it afterward," he'd said as he pressed it into my palm. "Better if you swallow it."

"Seriously?"

He really got a kick out of that. "The look on your face! Andres, come on. Relax."

I'd spent Saturday in a state of nervous near-collapse. I read everything I'd written so far, tore up dozens of pages, scribbled notes and questions which I later compiled, condensed, revised and re-revised. I pored over dates and places, lists, decrees, the infinite verbiage of revolution and reaction. I didn't know how much time I'd have, whether we'd be alone, what topics were off-limits, what the rabbi had told her about me. For all I knew he'd said nothing, thinking only to introduce two expatriates, two failed Jews of his acquaintance. It even occurred to me this might be his crazy idea of a date.

"The main thing is to keep an open mind, to really listen," Damien said. She was just a human being, however large she loomed in my imagination. He usually went into interviews with three prepared questions, broad enough to invite digression, to open unexpected doors. The rest, he said, was just conversation, with all its repetitions and awkward pauses and serendipities, just two people trying to connect.

"Three questions?" I said. "I've got about three hundred."

"You have to decide what's most important."

I looked into the dregs of wine clouding the bottom of my glass. "Who am I to make that decision?"

"You're the writer."

I was awake for another hour, desperately slashing my list, trying to distill everything into a few crucial questions, three keys to unlock the mysteries. Before going to sleep I drafted an email to my former literary agent. It had been a long time, I said, but I hoped she remembered me. I deleted and rewrote the email half a dozen times. A monster of ego, Stephanie had called me—and of course she was right. Though my story was unworthy, woefully incomplete, I couldn't help but want to see it out in the world, to see it live. People needed to read it, I thought. Only in that way could my monstrousness lead to something real and true, something that wasn't, in the end, about me at all.

Though it was after midnight, my agent wrote back almost immediately. She said it was good to hear from me, that she'd wondered where I'd disappeared to. As for the project I'd described, she was "very (!!!) interested." She wanted to see an outline as soon as I could put one together. She saw "tremendous potential" in the story. Creative nonfiction, she said, was all the rage.

It was almost noon when I crossed into Miraflores. The clouds starting to thin, chilly sunlight rinsing storefronts and windshields along the avenues. Even on a Sunday the cranes and backhoes were in full swing, the construction boom still booming, families skirting concrete barriers and police tape as they made their way home from church. The newspapers had described the "beachfront palace" David Gelb bought for his daughter, but in fact her apartment was a mile inland, in a neighborhood of simple two-story cottages that had been partitioned into units. There were small gardens bordered by fan palms and magnolia trees, cats stretched on stoops. It was a quiet and pleasant place, and I couldn't help but think of Pueblo Libre, of the family now living in Leo's house.

We don't want writers. We want peace.

I'd come half an hour early, leaving time for the inevitable failure of nerve. As I walked, I rehearsed our meeting: Should I speak English or Spanish? Should I shake her hand? Part of me didn't believe it was happening, that the person I was going to meet was the same person I'd been reading and writing about for so long—or rather that the person I'd been writing about was someone you actually could meet. As if a figure from a painting were going to leap out of the frame—or, even more fantastical, I was going to jump into that two-dimensional world.

I had only one question: *Was it worth it?* I'd settled on it just before dawn, the apartment silent and still as though time had stopped. There were so many things I wanted to ask, too many for an hour, or a year. But they all boiled down to the same thing. Passing a boxy gray building, I noticed a handwritten sign in an upper window: *No Somos Terroristas, Somos Peruanos*, it said. Two houses later, another sign: *Si no quieres al Perú, ¡VETE!* If you don't love Peru, get lost. For some time I'd been hearing distant voices, the choppy noise of a street gathering, and now I could make out, far down the block, a dozen or so people lingering on the sidewalk, a few men standing in the street. When a car passed, they raised their arms and shouted things I couldn't hear. Drivers honked in response, and the crowd answered with a muddled cheer.

It would come out later that the host of *Ciudad de Reyes*, a right-wing radio show, had disclosed her address that morning, encouraging listeners to "show how this proud country feels about terrorists." But as I retreated to the corner, then took a lap around the block, all I knew was that there was trouble, and trouble was what I'd spent my life trying to avoid.

One street over, the world was quiet. A breeze came up and rustled branches. Squirrels chased each other manically around a tree trunk. I smoked two cigarettes and reminded myself the war was over. It had been over for so long people's memories of it had faded, mutated and crystallized into something with more shine than substance. What was happening in front of Leo's apartment was therefore a kind of reenactment, the people shouting and honking just performers, no more threatening than the men in Babilonia's airport who dressed up as Inca warriors, waving golden axes at delighted tourists.

I stamped out the cigarette and checked my watch. There was no trouble, I told myself. Stories can't hurt anyone. I walked back to her street, buoyed by this realization. I was right on time.

The crowd had grown to maybe thirty people, mostly middle-aged, a few elderly men and women hanging back in the shade of a ficus while others banged on pots and blew into kazoos and poked signs and photographs over the fence. A few faces turned as I walked up, but I made no acknowledgment. They were mere details, peripheral to what was about to happen. The noise was terrific, shrill and nasty; I wondered if the gate was locked but somehow knew it wouldn't be, and as I strode up the path and took a deep whiff of jasmine, I felt a surge of well-being: I was exactly where I was supposed to be.

The crowd fell silent when I knocked on the door. I waited, glanced up at the windows, and knocked again. I could feel them behind me; their presence was like a cloak that wrapped around the scene, isolating the house from everything around it. In another second I knew there was someone on the other side of the door, waiting. I leaned close and spoke clearly:

"It's me."

What happened next could not have taken more than a few seconds, though my memory has slowed it down, distended it into a scene of lavish, cinematic clarity. The door opened and in a glimpse I took in the strange figure: so much smaller than I'd expected, so pale and ordinary my first instinct was that she couldn't be the one. And yet it was her, absolutely: Leonora Gelb, in a long-sleeved dress, a star of David at her collar, head covered by a sheer scarf with a pattern of yellow and brown flowers she was still tying under her chin. I took it all in: the mottled and prematurely lined forehead, cheeks patched with ruined skin, the way she stood square in the doorway as if to project something of herself into the world, to test the waters before going in.

And then her eyes, filmy and impossibly large, swimming behind thick glasses. She was nearly blind—ten years at high altitude had scarred her retinas—and yet I felt captured in an instant, evaluated, digested and filed away for later consideration. It stole my words, every version of a greeting failed me—here she was, the woman I'd invented, Leonora Gelb in her undeniable truth.

"Please—" she said, and stepped onto the porch. Behind me, someone gasped. Just one word—"Please"—and I'll never know

413

whether she meant to invite me inside or whether the word was meant for someone else's ears, someone I had not been aware of, whose presence was suddenly all around us, fixing us like moths in amber. As my hearing exploded into a thin, high whine I could not understand how our places had shifted, I could not follow the choreography—had he come from behind the building or had she pushed me aside?—but then I was slumped on the doorsill, my hands frantically searching my body though my eyes never left her: Leonora, the real Leonora, flat against the wall like a specimen, her eyes open and bright despite the obscene darkness spreading around her heart.

The news accounts would describe a suspect in his thirties, light-skinned, average height. No one had seen him before. No one could say where he came from or where he went. It was speculated he was ex-military, or a former rondero. It was determined that he acted alone. Though asked many times, I've always said I saw no one, and I'll say it again now: It happened too fast. One minute I was standing at her threshold, the next I was sprawled on the step, deaf and hyperventilating, Leo lying a few feet away, one hand clutching her glasses as though to protect them from the fall. How could I remember more than that? Given my position, how could I have seen anything at all?

Sound came back slowly: a dog barking, one car and then another muttered past. Somewhere a neighbor raised a window, a woman started to shout. I couldn't understand a word of it. When I was able to stand I turned toward the fence, hoping to see someone coming, someone who would know what to do. But everyone was gone. I went to the gate and looked both ways but the sidewalk was empty. It was an ordinary street, like you'd find anywhere.

I don't remember leaving her neighborhood, or what route I took to the malecón. At some point, I asked a passerby for the time and he said it was nearly four o'clock. I was out of cigarettes, still shivering, though the day had warmed up nicely, the last of the fog blown out across the city and into the parched foothills. The distant shanty-towns were lost in gray haze, vanished like Brigadoon.

There was blood on my shirt, dried spatters on one leg of my jeans. I sat on a bench and touched the stains again and again.

The moment kept replaying: the darkness in the house behind her, the fatal half-step onto the porch. What shocked me most was that feeling of presence, the nauseous looming from everywhere and nowhere. Each time I recalled it my throat filled and I hunched over, but it was with me now and I would not escape it. When someone touched my shoulder I shouted and leapt to my feet, but it was only a beggar, a round-eyed girl carrying a baby. She stared at me, disheveled and terrified. I pushed every coin I had into her hand.

How had it happened? As the sun began its descent, I tried to understand how I, of all people, had come to that doorstep, what inscrutable force had made me its witness. It was a dirty joke, an historical absurdity—but it had happened, I'd seen it, and even I understood that made it my responsibility. Leonora Gelb was dead. I was the last person she'd spoken to. To my dazed and troubled mind, it was as if I'd killed her myself.

I couldn't go back to Damien's, I couldn't face those people and their questions. By the time I got to Larcomar I was feverish, dizzy with thirst, desperate for the comfort of other, anonymous bodies. I gripped the escalator railing, dazzled by the flashing lights and rich smells, the gusts of conversation. The magnificent coastline scrolled north in a silent, sublime glow of cherry and tin. Below, over the main courtyard, a giant Peruvian flag snapped and billowed in the wind.

"You believe this motherfucker, this son of a cockroach?" said the man on the next barstool, nodding at the row of televisions.

"Incredible," I said. "Do you have a cigarette?"

I smoked and scanned the TV's, dreading the appearance of that ravaged face. But instead I saw something curious: Barack Obama, now the presumptive nominee. He was giving a speech in Berlin. I listened for a while—something about tearing down walls, something about our common humanity—but it was hard to focus. The man next to me, a Peruvian man, kept talking to me, gesturing roughly and shifting his stool.

We are heirs to a struggle for freedom. We are a people of improbable hope. Let us remember this history, and answer our destiny, and remake the world once again.

"This fucking monkey," the man next to me said.

I left coins on the bar and found a seat at the edge of the terrace.

My adrenaline had ebbed and what I felt now was exhaustion, an aching disembodiment. For the first time since that morning, I thought about the story. There would be no finishing it now, no fulfilling the promises I'd made. Without Leo, the story would always be incomplete, a hopeless, arbitrary muddle: the world according to Andres. It was truly my story now—I'd taken it from her. Already I couldn't remember which parts I'd made up and which were true.

Was it worth it? It was a cruel question. I was glad I hadn't had time to ask.

I sat a long time, watching the sun dissolve into the horizon like a liquid pearl. Eventually the dread returned, a shadow of fear sliding over me like a cloudbank. Her face loomed in my memory, wrecked and incomprehensible: *Please*, she'd said. *Please*. There was a rustling sound, a loud flutter that seemed to come from everywhere. My heart slammed. I leapt from the chair, an apology on my lips, and that's when I saw them.

They were floating far above me, far above all of us. Half a dozen paragliders, silhouetted by late sunshine. They rose into the sky, their gliders fanning over them in arcs of orange and gold. I couldn't make out their faces, only arms and legs dangling, swinging lightly, dark bodies twirling in the updraft. Their shadows wheeled and dropped, swooped low over the terrace, eliciting gasps and applause.

I couldn't see the lines attaching them to their gliders. I couldn't tell if anything connected them to the ground. I couldn't breathe. I squinted in the glare and for one vertiginous moment I was up there with them, nothing holding me but the wind's invisible fist. Everything was so small, so far down. A panicked sound escaped my throat, then a torrent—all the pent up fear, the confusion, an inchoate grief that heaved out of me in waves. People turned to look but I couldn't stop sobbing—so hard my throat burned, my nose plugged. When a woman at the next table offered me a napkin, I turned and fled.

In the restroom, I tried to wash the dried blood from my shirt, to scrub the panic out of my face. Soon I'd have to talk to someone, give some account of myself. I thought I should look presentable. A moment later the door flew open and three tanned, tattooed young men came in.

"What are you doing, amigo?" one said. He wore a pink golf shirt and sunglasses atop his head. The other two huddled by the sink, arranging something—I saw a razor blade and a plastic bag, a little pile of powder on the faux-marble counter.

"I said what do you want?" He puffed out his chest and stepped toward me. "¿No hablas español?" I could only shake my head and point to the toilet. He grabbed my arm, laughing as he shoved me toward the door.

"Get out of here, cumpa," he said in English. "This is no place for you."

In the last chapters of my novel, *The Light Inside*, the commune fell apart, a predictable outcome but one that couldn't be avoided— the story simply demanded it. There had been breakdowns, power struggles, infidelities. Eventually a fire, set by one of their own, destroyed most of the camp. In the final scene, my narrator, a failed poet-turned-product manager, stands in the ashes, reflecting on the "beautiful idea" that first brought them there:

> We'd wanted to do something more, to be something more. We wanted to make ourselves believe in something other than ourselves, something larger—but we could only pervert it, only contaminate it, turn it into a funhouse-mirror version of itself and in so doing empty it of all meaning.

The last image is a bird's-eye view of the characters setting out along different roads, "while the smoke of our folly spread heavy on the valley."

It's a well-written scene, I suppose. One reviewer commended its "lyrical grandeur" and "unflinching examination of post-post-modern consciousness," whatever that means. But I can't read it now without thinking: *What bullshit*. I'd believed, at the time, that I was saying something new, something worth saying. I believed empathy had given my characters independent lives. But in truth I'd never really understood them—not their doubt or their fear, not their consuming ambition. I wanted to understand, to know them in myself. But they were just words, just language connected by the logic of stories, a logic that is vast and beautiful but should never be mistaken for truth.

I'd wanted to do better this time. To atone for my cowardice, for my failure to cross the line. Leo was my last chance but she was gone now. Soon I'd have to answer questions, but I had nothing to say, no useful information. Only what I'd written: a patchwork of lies, not worth much of anything anymore.

It was almost midnight when I turned onto Damien's street. All the lights were on, shadows moving behind the curtains. My phone showed twelve messages in the past few hours. I didn't know what I would tell them. I didn't know what I'd do the next day, the next month. Would I go back to Babilonia, or pack up and find another town, another country, somewhere no one knew anything about me? I thought maybe I'd get a job with Oswaldo's tour company, spend a year or two roaming South America before finding somewhere to settle down. Or never stop, just keep running as I'd run from everything. It wasn't so hard, really.

Or maybe I'd finally do something worthwhile, something to be proud of—volunteer in Jeroen's clinic, or take a job with an NGO. Maybe I'd apply to the Peace Corps, or join Doctors Without Borders. Maybe somewhere, someday I'd find the barricade I was prepared to throw myself at, burn my lungs with tear gas, put my body on the line. People did such things, I thought. Real people. Why not me?

What was most likely, I knew, was that I'd go back to the U.S., back to its endless wars and ugly election, to the financial catastrophe that was now unavoidable. I'd find a job, an apartment, buy furniture, hang tasteful art on the walls. I'd meet a nice girl and start thinking about the future: a family, a house, a 401(k). Eventually the years in Peru would come to seem like a dream, something I told at cocktail parties—stories to be wondered at, but not believed.

As I neared the house, a taxi pulled to the curb and stopped. Its hazard lights made a faint ticking in the still night. I watched someone get out, pay the driver, drag a small bag from the backseat. She stared at the house, and at the houses on either side. Then, looking around as though she knew someone was watching, she hurried to the door.

It was Lucrecia. In the light from the window her face was stark and lovely, her features carved like fine marble. Everything was too vivid: her eyelashes against her cheeks, her long fingers as she swept a strand of hair behind one ear. She was so small, so over-whelmed by the vast, alien city. I was wide awake, my heart racing. She shifted her bag and took a breath of determination. When she knocked you could hear it all the way down the street.

I almost cried out, or ran back the way I'd come. But something held me. I couldn't move from that spot. I had the strangest feel-ing of lightness, almost swooning—as if I were watching the whole thing from the outside: the girl on the front step, the man in the shadows. It was impossible to know what either of them would do.

She knocked again, louder this time. The shadows in the window stopped. Time stopped. She looked over her shoulder. And then everything moved in the same direction.

ACKNOWLEDGMENTS

No one could or should write about the history of modern Peru without acknowledging the nearly seventy thousand people, of all ages, backgrounds, and beliefs, who died during the conflict in the 1980s and 1990s. I only hope I have honored their lives and struggles with this work.

This book demanded a thorough education, for which I have the following generous friends to thank: Patricia Bárrig Jó, Luz María Bouroncle, Stephanie Boyd, Guillermo Bronstein, Malu Cabellos, Rafael Cabellos Damián, Marco Cadillo, Lucien Chauvin, José de la Cruz, Jorge Frisancho, Gustavo Gorriti, César Guadalupe, Juan Carlos Guerrero, Oswaldo Jalving, Camilo León Castro, Nancy Mejía, Margarita Mendoza, Lili Medina Mezvinsky, Jaime Rossi, Annie Thériault, and Verónica Villarán.

For reading, encouraging, and sustaining me, thank you to Julie Barer, Michael Barron, Catherine Besteman, Bill Clegg, Laura Cogan, Joshua Furst, Doug and Alyssa Graham, Scott Hutchins, William Merryman, Jeff O'Keefe, Eric Puchner, David Shields, Sarah Shields, Mark Slouka, Mark Sundeen, Vauhini Vara, and Oscar Villalon.

My sincere thanks to the Rockefeller Foundation Bellagio Center, the Ucross Foundation, the Fundación Valparaíso, and Colorado State University, for sheltering and supporting me.

And to the excellent, dedicated folks at Melville House: Dennis and Valerie, Athena Bryan, Andréa Córdova, Stephanie deLuca, Amelia Stymacks, Tim McCall, and everyone else who helped to make this happen.

Finally, eternal gratitude to Tina Pohlman, mi compañera de armas.